TOAST OF TOKYO

Tokyo Whispers – Book Three

Heather Hallman

PRAISE FOR THE TOKYO WHISPERS SERIES

Scandals of Tokyo

"Overall: 5 STARS

Plot/Storyline: 4STARS

Feels: LOTS

Emotional Depth: 3 Broken Hearts

Tension: 4 Thunder Bolts

Romance: 3 Swirling Hearts

Sensuality: 3 Kisses

Humor: Just a touch"

~Becky Vine Voice

Talk of Tokyo

"What happens when you take characters straight out of Victorian England and drop them into Japan? You get an enchanting world with unforgettable characters. I loved the fresh setting, one we don't often see in historical fiction, and Evelyn's determination to be independent and successful was great. Ned was interesting, and their interactions together have me curious as to where the next book will take us. Overall, a great, quick read." ~Lilliyana

"Read this book if you enjoy:
Historical Romance
Enemies to Lovers Trope

Japanese Culture
Historical Detective Story
Strong Female MC
Women's Rights

This book has a little bit of everything; romance, history, social justice, danger and mystery. The writing was excellent, the plot intriguing, the characters well defined, and the pace well set.
Thank you so much @lovebookstours and Heather Hallman for sending me an ebook copy of this wonderful book!" ~ @sarahtalksbooks on IG

"Set in Japan in the Meiji period, this novel tells a clever story about exploitation, politics, cultural integration, feminine independence, and the power of love. Among other things, this book is a very fun way to learn about a period in history and a country with which most Americans have no familiarity. Suki Malveaux's story is told with sharp wit and an eye for intriguing details. Looking forward to reading more in the "Tokyo Whispers" series." ~MaryR

www.BOROUGHSPUBLISHINGGROUP.com

PUBLISHER'S NOTE: This is a work of fiction. Names, characters, places and incidents either are the product of the author's imagination or are used fictitiously. Any resemblance to actual events, locales, business establishments or persons, living or dead, is coincidental. Boroughs Publishing Group does not have any control over and does not assume responsibility for author or third-party websites, blogs or critiques or their content.

ISBN: 978-1-957295-30-5

To Candler for taking care of me and letting me take care of him

ACKNOWLEDGMENTS

I'm very appreciative of the opportunity to work with Boroughs Publishing Group. Thank you, Michelle, for your support of this project. Your enthusiasm inspires me.

Thank you, Jack, for being an outstanding editor. I want to bottle that mix of joy and relief I get from knowing you're editing my words. I'd give it to every writer I know.

TOAST OF TOKYO

CHAPTER ONE

September 1900

Tokyo

Marcelle

Noon bells rang out along Tokyo's Ginza Boulevard followed by cheers from the fashionables lined up outside Koide Department Store. As one of the city's foremost fashionables, Marcelle naturally stood among them.

Cheer, she did not.

She tapped her boot against the brick sidewalk in a jig of impatience. At any moment, Koide's footmen would open Tokyo's first department store to the public, and Marcelle would get a glimpse inside the glass and stone colossus that would one day bankrupt her shop, *La France Boutique*.

The cheering grew louder as liveried footmen stepped aside and pulled open the gilded doors. Men brandishing notebooks and sketchpads rushed to the entrance, cutting off Marcelle's view of the interior.

She turned to her assistant, Yumi-*chan*. "Didn't the newspapermen get their tour days ago?" she asked in their peculiar mix of French and Japanese.

Yumi-*chan* tucked a strand of hair back into her stylishly low chignon. "According to the papers, only a select few were allowed in the store. No drawings or photography were permitted. Monsieur

Koide wanted to whet the newspapermen's appetites, not give them the main dish outright."

"So, our monsieur is a tease." Marcelle added the tidbit to her mental list of things known about the cutthroat capitalist.

From the day construction began on his colossus, gossip about the monsieur had been rife among Ginza Boulevard's proprietors. Marcelle had gathered he was an "overseas Japanese," a man who'd lived in Europe, with the necessary combination of wealth, influence, and ambition to import *le grand magasin* from the avenues of Paris to the streets of Tokyo.

Men like Monsieur Koide weren't satisfied until they'd ravaged the competition. They also had innumerable resources at their disposal. It would cost him so little to lure her customers to his store.

It would cost her everything.

Keeping step with the procession into Koide's, Marcelle and Yumi-*chan* finally arrived at the entranceway. Marcelle closed her square-shaped parasol—a trend she'd pioneered in Tokyo—then marched, head held high, into the beginning of the end of *La France Boutique*.

In the time it took to walk through the gilded doors, Koide Department Store transported her across oceans and continents to the ground floor of Paris's *Le Bon Marché*. The vaulted lobby belonged in a cathedral. Mirrors in gilded frames and glass display cases reflected sunlight streaming through tall windows. Everywhere she turned, an abundance of goods women desired sat on every shelf: gloves, hats, parasols, furs, jewels, perfumes, luggage.

Monsieur Koide had brought a piece of Paris to Tokyo. It was the piece she liked best.

Marcelle led them through the crowd of fashionables, past jewelry displays, and alongside a table of hats topped with lace, flowers, plumes, and ribbons. More than half of the vertiginous creations had already been claimed.

"Monsieur Koide will have nothing left at the end of the day," Marcelle remarked above the atrium's din.

"Newness is the attraction. Before long, everyone will tire of the place," Yumi-*chan* replied in the soothing manner of a mother applying ointment to a child's scraped knee.

Marcelle bristled. Yumi-*chan* meant well, but they both knew she was being more than a tad insincere. Monsieur Koide's department store was an extraordinary accomplishment, unlike anything in Tokyo.

With a small single room for designing, cutting, sewing, fittings, and repairs—albeit with two wax mannequins, a luxury she could only afford because of her benefactor Jiro's generosity—*La France Boutique* couldn't hold a candle to Koide's.

As they neared the staircase to the upper floors, the crush of patrons ceased moving. Marcelle followed their gazes to a man of formidable proportions holding court on the red-carpeted stairs. Tall and robust, he filled his elegant black suit with a commanding presence.

It couldn't be.

Newspaper reporters assembled around him called out questions. "Koide-*san*," one of them shouted over the others.

It most certainly was Koide, in the flesh, and seeming for all the world like a theatre star addressing his admirers.

"What was your inspiration for the department store?" the reporter finished.

Monsieur Koide shifted, giving Marcelle a view of his impressive profile. He had a smooth, regal brow, bold jaw, and the hooked nose of samurai warriors she'd seen in woodblock paintings. His black hair had been cut short and shaped with a light pomade. Rough and refined, he appeared impervious to—and master of—the carnival of glamor surrounding him.

"My father, and grandfather before him, spent a great deal of their careers abroad, learning foreign customs ..."

Marcelle leaned forward to make out the cut of Monsieur Koide's suit. An expert tailor had sewn the jacket to emphasize the length and breadth of the monsieur's torso. Indeed, there was no sign of suspenders. The tapering of his jacket at the waist suggested the presence of a belt beneath. Only a man daring in his haberdashery would employ belt loops on his trousers.

Monsieur Koide knew fashion.

She stretched farther for a better view of his lapels. Round. Another nod to present-day trends.

"*Mon Dieu,*" she cried and grabbed her nape as a searing pain struck the muscle between her neck and shoulder.

Monsieur Koide paused in the middle of whatever he was saying and gazed upon the crowd. Marcelle's heart stopped and she ducked behind Yumi-*chan*, which was no easy feat since Yumi-*chan* only reached the top of her chest. The movement sent pain straight into her fingertips. Biting the inside of her cheek, she suppressed a whimper and gave her muscle a furtive massage.

Yumi-*chan* peered back at her. "Have you hurt yourself?"

"Don't look at me," Marcelle hissed. "Look at Monsieur Koide. Pretend I'm not here."

Yumi-*chan* faced forward. "But he's looking this way."

"I know that. Ignore me." Marcelle drove her fingertips deeper into the muscle, inflicting enough pain to overcome her embarrassment. Nervous excitement tended to result in painful moments of clumsiness. A scar on her right index finger would forever remind her of the Imperial Hotel's delicious champagne *and* its crystal glass.

After what felt like hours, Monsieur Koide finally carried on with a tale about his elite family's life abroad. Marcelle rose steadily. The fashionables behind her responded with grumbles about foreign women being unreasonably tall. That was all the encouragement she needed to lengthen her posture.

"My education culminated at the University of Oxford in the country of England." Monsieur Koide paused for the newspapermen to finish their scribbles. "During those years, I visited the great department stores of London and Paris. In the famed Harrods department store of London, I had the pleasure of ascending to the upper floors on a moving staircase."

Murmurs of disbelief passed through the crowd.

"You may have heard it's a frightening experience. The London women who rode it alongside me needed a spot of brandy when they reached the top. Personally, I found it quite enjoyable."

A reporter raised his arm. "Koide-*san*, will you install a moving staircase at Koide's?" he called out.

"I have every intention of bringing the latest innovations in fashion, art, and music to the city of Tokyo."

As though their lives depended upon hearing every last word of the monsieur's ramblings, the crush of patrons behind Marcelle jostled forward in what she could assure them was a useless attempt to get closer to the stairs. Preferring not to perish in a department store stampede, Marcelle motioned for Yumi-*chan* to follow her to the opposite end of the staircase.

Aside from glares from fashionables whose boots they'd accidentally trampled, they made it to the staircase unharmed, just as Monsieur Koide was dismissing his worshipping horde with instructions to enjoy their visit to his store. In other words: they should turn over their precious coins in exchange for parasols and make him the richest man in Tokyo.

With a resigned sigh, Marcelle climbed the stairs. One day, the monsieur would be the city's wealthiest citizen. His wondrous bazaar was going to be the toast of Tokyo. No *modiste*, no matter her style or vision, could compete.

Less crowded than the first, the second floor brought a modicum of refreshment. Bright notes from a Vivaldi concerto flitted down from the concert hall. Patrons, perhaps exhausted from having made the trek across the atrium, took a leisurely pace down the clothing department aisles.

Yumi-*chan* gravitated toward a display of thick silks with intricate floral designs in gold and silver threading. "I've never seen anything this beautiful up close," she said. "It must've cost thousands of yen."

Her unabashed awe at wealth always took Marcelle by surprise. For all the tenuousness and spiteful injustices that marked Marcelle's childhood, she'd never known the poverty of Yumi-*chan*'s. "We'll take a closer look after we see what Monsieur Koide has to offer."

Keeping pace with the fashionables filing past each department, Marcelle found her chest tightened in anticipation of her finding a display of day dresses and evening gowns in the latest Parisian styles cut from traditional Japanese kimono silks. When a full revolution of the second floor revealed not a single garment that brought together the couture of Europe with the ancient traditions of Japan, she felt as though she'd reached dry land.

"There's only an art gallery and concert hall on the third floor." Her voice sparkled with victory. "Monsieur Koide will have to try harder if he wants to bury the competition."

Yumi-*chan* widened her eyes and quickly waved Marcelle's comment off.

"Yes, he will," Marcelle insisted, confused by Yumi-*chan*'s enthusiastic contradiction. "The cutthroat capitalist had better study his competitors more fully if he wishes to ruin them."

Yumi-*chan* waved more frantically as she shook her head, then her gaze hardened and rested over Marcelle's shoulder.

The fine hairs on Marcelle's neck rose, and she finally got the point.

Koide.

He would have sneaked up behind her, wouldn't he?

Just in time to hear her insult him on the day of his grand opening. Guilt over the rudeness seized her, then eased with the realization that she'd used mostly French to disparage his character. And there was no reason to think he understood French.

"Why would Monsieur Koide want to bury the competition? That's what makes him stronger." His English was perfect. Likely his French, too, seeing as he'd understood her words.

Readying an apology, because she knew better than to insult a store owner on his first day of business, she turned to face him. She was prepared for his impressive broadness, his samurai's nose, and his dandy attire. What she wasn't prepared for was his smirk.

The intended apology stuck in her throat. So, Monsieur Koide was the playful sort. As it happened, so was she. "I take it you're a man of strength?" she replied in equally proficient English.

"I believe it's called power." The *arrogance*. She wanted to pinch his thick upper arm and put him in his place. "History has shown that men of power provide society with the means of advancement."

Marcelle had heard that line before. "Yet so many people struggle through lives of misery while powerful men grow even more so. Where's the social advancement in that?"

Monsieur Koide twitched his lips. Evidently, he found their repartee amusing. "It's only a matter of time before the modern world brings prosperity to all." He leaned toward her as though to divulge a secret. "That's a foremost tenet for us cutthroat capitalists."

She took in his citrusy, woodsy cologne and musky, masculine scent and knew exactly how it would feel to have her cheek pressed against the contours of his well-muscled chest. Heavenly. Then she shifted her parasol between them. No cutthroat capitalist should be this enticing. "I believe you are a committed capitalist, Monsieur Koide. I also believe you understood the words my assistant and I were exchanging earlier. Do you speak French?"

"I understand a bit of the language, more than I can speak. My pronunciation is awful, or so I've been told." He produced a sheepish, rather endearingly boyish wince. "I grew up with several French friends, my *bon amis*, when we lived on the continent. Later, I spent time in Paris while on break from my studies. The department stores, or *les grands magasins*, are quite magnificent. Sometimes I wonder if I ought to escape this country and spend the rest of my days in Paris."

She pictured Monsieur Koide strolling *l'avenue des Champs-Élysées* with a stylish Frenchwoman beside him, her arm looped through his. *Lucky woman*, she mused, which was ridiculous because she had absolutely no desire to be that woman. She was never returning to Paris or anywhere in France.

On the floor above, the audience applauded the final notes of a Beethoven sonata.

"Am I correct that you identified yourself as my competition?" Monsieur Koide asked.

Who had she been kidding? *La France Boutique* could never compete with a store of Koide's magnitude. "Only a Ginza neighbor. I apologize for not properly introducing myself. I'm Marcelle Renaud, *modiste* and owner of *La France Boutique*, and this is my assistant, Yumi Takeda."

Monsieur Koide exchanged greetings with Yumi-*chan* in Japanese, then turned back to Marcelle. "Pleased to make your acquaintance, Madame Renaud," he said in English.

"Actually, it's mademoiselle." Much to her surprise, she drew out the last word as though to direct his attention to her unmarried status. Did she think flirtatious charm would save her store?

"Of course, mademoiselle." Monsieur Koide drew out the word as far as she. That would make him a flirt, too, which really was a fine quality in a man. "I'm Nobuyuki Koide, owner of a new department store that will hopefully remain in business once its novelty has worn off." He stepped back, seeming to compare her and Yumi-*chan*'s attire. "Are the dresses your design?"

She glanced down at the dress she'd cut from a sky-blue kimono silk printed with scarlet-hued hibiscus. The lacy bodice, cinched waist, and slight bustle represented the height of Parisian fashion. Traditional Japanese lacquered hair clips lent an exotic aspect to her thick, dark curls. Gold earbobs completed the outfit. Yumi-*chan* wore a similarly styled day dress cut from an ivory kimono silk with a black geometric pattern. "They are," she replied tentatively.

He murmured something in Japanese that Marcelle recognized as approval. "Last month, a friend's wife wore a dress similar to yours. She said it was from a foreign *modiste* in Ginza. I made a note to investigate the source. Now it seems the source has come to me."

Marcelle shuddered inwardly. Why had the monsieur made a note to investigate the dress's source? So he could steal the source's designs. That was why.

Whichever friend's wife had pointed the monsieur in her direction could have been one of many of Tokyo's modern elites for whom Marcelle designed. She made gowns for diplomats' wives, cabinet ministers' daughters, geishas, actresses, widows, and the occasional foreign divorcée. Most of her patrons merely wished to impress their social circle. For others, a magnificent gown meant the difference between starving on millet and dining in Ginza's finest restaurants. Regardless of their aims and circumstances, her patrons believed in the power of a Marcelle Renaud original.

They'd never fall for a Koide imitation, would they?

A man drew up to Monsieur Koide's side and whispered into his ear. The monsieur looked over at a group of men dressed in Western-style suits standing alongside two women wearing black celebratory kimonos stitched with elaborate golden motifs. The younger of the two women raised her brow. The elder tilted her head ever so slightly toward the men standing beside her.

Monsieur Koide nodded at the pair, then looked at Marcelle. "I apologise for cutting our conversation short. I must greet family friends."

Marcelle sneaked a glance at the two women. There was a definite similarity between the older woman's prominent nose and well-defined jawline and those of Monsieur Koide. She must have been his *okasan*, mother, and the younger woman must be his wife. But a Japanese wife would stand behind her husband's *okasan*, head bowed, hands clasped before her. That would mean the younger woman was his sister, also an overseas Japanese, which would explain the decidedly Western raise of the brow she'd given

Monsieur Koide. In a dress like the one Yumi-*chan* was wearing, the Koide sister would make a perfect model for *La France Boutique.*

"I'd like to speak with you further about doing business in Tokyo," Monsieur Koide continued. "At the store, we're following the European custom of fixed prices, which reduces our ability to serve a range of customers, but we'll have seasonal sales. If only the Japanese celebrated Christmas. Harrods makes heaps of revenue in December."

"The foreign community in Tsukiji will flock to your store for Christmas goods. The Japanese Christians will follow suit. As for other Japanese customers, *La France Boutique* offers special pricing after the New Year holiday. Young women want to make the most of their new year spending money." Marcelle spoke to him as she would to any other Ginza proprietor, and the way he nodded seemed to indicate his… might it be respect for her business acumen?

"We must speak further," Monsieur Koide said. "I'll give you a tour of the store, and you can tell me more about doing business in Ginza."

Marcelle's heart quickened at the prospect of spending an afternoon exploring Koide's array of goods. Or was it the prospect of spending an afternoon looking at those goods alongside their devilishly handsome, design-thief owner? "It'd be my pleasure."

"The pleasure, Mademoiselle Renaud, will be all mine," he replied with a bow then he met her gaze for the briefest moment, but in that moment spared nothing. Her knees weakened. Recognition unfurled in a rush of heat from her center outward to the ends of her limbs, leaving every part between afire. She'd been the object of men's desire enough times in her twenty-seven years to know everything about that flash of a look. Monsieur Koide wanted her.

Fashionables clustered around the monsieur almost as soon as he turned toward his family's friends.

Regaining her balance, Marcelle located Yumi-*chan* by the expensive kimono silks. A proper woman would banish Monsieur

Koide's look from memory. Marcelle rarely found propriety worth the effort.

Monsieur Koide's look was going to haunt her for days to come, and she was going to relish every minute of it.

CHAPTER TWO

Nobu Koide

Nobu had one foot in the front door of his family's home when his *okasan* appeared at the entrance. She fell into the sort of bow reserved for precious sons, then presented him with a smile that rivalled the full moon in all its brilliance. The performance might have been directed at him, but the guests at her annual moon-viewing party were the intended audience.

"Where have you been for the past two hours?" *Okasan* muttered under her breath.

Nobu removed his shoes and stepped onto the foyer's marble flooring, all the while nodding to familiar faces in the drawing room. "Busy at the store, *Okasan*," he grumbled with a gracious smile for the benefit of those watching.

Okasan knelt on the floor and placed slippers at Nobu's feet. "You promised you'd be here before the party started," she hissed.

"I've arrived, so there's no need to complain." The party was *Okasan*'s premier autumn event, really the premier event for all Tokyo's elites. The women of her family had been holding moon-viewing parties since the seventeenth century. *Okasan* could recount every one of the years it'd been cancelled and the calamity responsible: usually earthquakes, fires, floods, bitter shoguns, political scandals, or a death in the family. Nobu had heard all the stories. Many, many times.

She shuffled a few steps to the side, leaving room for him to put on the slippers. From the drawing-room, Prime Minister Ito observed the activity at the entranceway. Nobu met the samurai-turned-politician's incisive gaze and bowed low. His presence meant Nobu's *otosan*, father, was courting the favour of Japan's foremost politician. "Where's *Otosan*?" Nobu asked.

Okasan gestured to the back parlour. "Sipping *sake* with his friends, of course," she said with such false brightness that she had to be seething.

Okasan's preference, as she'd reiterated over breakfast that morning, would be for *Otosan* to mingle with guests positioned to further the family's pursuit of a title. As the third daughter of a marquis, she'd watched her *otosan* marry off her older sisters to members of the peerage and choose a young man from a family of wealthy industrialists for his youngest daughter. A bureaucrat in the Foreign Ministry, the young man demonstrated diplomatic prowess that would surely earn him the rank of baron, at least. *Okasan* accepted the marriage because she had no alternative but to accept her parents' choice of spouse. One day, her *otosan* promised, Koide-*san*'s vigorous service to the nation would restore her to the nobility.

Okasan believed her day of restoration would be hastened by Nobu marrying a young lady from a titled family, preferably the daughter of a marquis or viscount who would wield his considerable influence on the Koide family's behalf. Fortunately for the Koides, *Okasan* had enough cousins and friends among the nobility to ensure Nobu an abundance of aristocratic daughters to choose from.

Unfortunately for Nobu, they'd been wholly uninteresting. When the day came that one of the reserved, meek little misses mustered even a jot of the desire he'd felt for the stunning Mademoiselle Renaud he'd met the week before, he'd propose marriage without a second thought.

"I'll join *Otosan*," he said at the risk of stoking his *okasan*'s ire.

Her smile only brightened. Anger thus transformed could blind a man. "Our guests are expecting your lively conversation. You and

Otosan would be remiss to deprive them." *Okasan* nodded toward a cluster of guests milling about the drawing-room. "Viscount Nagahara brought his daughters, lovely young ladies who'd make a fine addition to any family. You must tell the viscount about the success you're having at the department store."

Okasan's chiding tone carried the presumption he wasn't doing his utmost to fulfil his filial duty and take a wife. In truth, he wanted to get the whole marriage business over with as soon as possible. He wasn't one of those fools who resisted the inevitable. He'd make his parents happy, then, if need be, find a decent mistress for himself. "After I greet *Otosan* and his friends, I'll speak with Viscount Nagahara and his lovely daughters."

Not that he'd *really* be speaking with the viscount's daughters. More than a few words exchanged with young noblewomen was considered overbearing and ungentlemanly. When he'd first returned from London, he'd spoken full sentences to unmarried women and watched their faces turn unghastly shades of grey as they darted behind the nearest parent.

His reputation for vulgar foreign manners took several years to shake. Now he knew to converse with the *otosans*, exchange a word or two with the *okasans*, and prepare to act pleased when the mute, modest daughters granted him shy smiles at his mention of flowers, musicales, tea ceremony, or whatever artistic endeavour they'd claimed as their life's passion. For this task, he needed a cup of *sake*, or several.

The European-style cushioned sofas and heavy wooden tables usually situated in the back parlour had been removed for a low table that ran the length of the room and sitting pillows as befitted a Japanese event. Beyond the open doors to the back garden stood the moon-viewing platform piled high with pounded rice cakes shaped like the full moon and rice fronds laden with grains.

Otosan sat at one end of the table, having ceded his guests the places of honour in the middle, although he outranked most of them. His grey silk kimono hung loosely at his chest, giving the impression of a man lounging about, taking leisure in the company of dear friends and cups of *sake*. But Nobu knew better. Ever the politician, *Otosan* never surrendered control of his faculties to sweet wine, even among so-called dear friends of the Foundation Party.

"*Otosan*." Nobu bowed. "Apologies for my lateness."

"You work too hard," *Otosan* grumbled as though irritated, even though everyone at the table knew it was a compliment for a son in whom he had inordinate pride. He told anyone who would listen about Nobu's European-style store and how it elevated Japan's status as a modern nation. "Go sit at the other end of the table. I'll speak with you later." *Otosan* spoke dismissively, but Nobu caught the affectionate twinkle in his eye.

He took a seat among the Foundation Party's most powerful, and likely drunkest, members in Japan. *Otosan*'s best friend, Watanabe-*san*, filled a square wooden cup to overflowing for Nobu. After raising the cup to *Otosan* and the best of their nation's political minds, Nobu took a much-needed mouthful of wine. A few more sips, and the *sake* loosened his muscles. Obligations to investors, store patrons, employees, and his parents lightened, and he let himself get swept up in the conversation.

"You must get married right away." The Foreign Ministry bureaucrat seated next to Nobu tried with obvious effort to make his speech coherent. "Get the wife pregnant a few times. Make money. Make friends. Then enter politics. That's when you'll be ready to give your best to your country." He pulled Nobu closer with a twist of fingers down to his shirtsleeve. "We need you."

"We'll prevail next term," *Otosan* said consolingly. "They're the new Party."

"They're not new. They're the conservative faction of the Conservative Party," said another of *Otosan*'s friends, as drunk—if not drunker—than the one who'd yet to loosen his grip on Nobu's shirt. "They call themselves new, so the people think they're new, but they're nowhere near modern. They're begging to sacrifice one of their testicles to bring back the shogunate."

Otosan's best friend, Watanabe-*san*, looked pensive as he filled the wooden cup of the man seated opposite him. "They're determined that our nation should rule over the east of Asia. Ordinary citizens like that. They want the government to draw its revenue from the colonies and stop taxing the people."

"Colonialism gives the army something to do," the man clutching Nobu slurred. "The problem for us is votes. As long as we require military service from every young man, the conservatives will get their votes." He pulled harder on Nobu's sleeve. "That is why we need you, Nobu-*san*. You're not military but you've got the look of strength about you. Forget your department store. You must run for office."

Nobu was plenty aware of the expectation that one day, in the not-distant-enough future, he was supposed to abandon his enterprise, join the Foundation Party, and run for a seat in the Diet, none of which he wanted to think about. He was a man of business, not a politician like *Otosan*, and he was doing plenty for the country as such. Koide Department Store was stimulating Japan's trade, manufacturing, and construction as similar department stores were being planned for Osaka and elsewhere in Tokyo. Nobu would point this out to the man hanging on his arm, but he knew better than to argue with bleary-eyed politicos.

Otosan stood and motioned for Nobu to follow. "Please excuse us, gentlemen. My son must greet several families with daughters ripe for marriage, or my wife's efforts this evening will be for naught."

The man next to Nobu released his sleeve and slapped him full on the back. "I was telling your boy it was about time he took a wife."

The other men lifted their cups in appreciation of the sentiment.

Nobu finished the *sake* in his box and followed *Otosan* to the back garden where guests conversed around the moon-viewing platform.

"I'm going to be in a world of trouble with *Okasan* if I don't put you in front of the Nagahara daughters. There are two of them, a regular feast of possibilities." *Otosan* gave a toothy grin.

Nobu would be thrilled if one of the Nagahara daughters offered something to satiate himself upon, and he wasn't referring to what they were hiding under layers of kimono robes, although he'd prefer a wife who enticed him to bed. He was seeking the elusive spark of the modern. A demonstration of boldness and wit would go a long way toward easing the persistent worry he was going to spend his life with a woman who believed it her calling to mindlessly tend to his needs and agree with every word he uttered.

Admittedly, he desired a love match. Ever the optimist, he held out hope there was a modern young noblewoman among all those tittering daughters. But he was also a pragmatist. Most likely, he was going to find himself attached to a woman who left him hard as a rock for French *modistes* in Ginza.

Otosan approached Viscount Nagahara with a warm politician's greeting. Nobu followed suit. He'd inherited *Otosan's* suave manners though lacked his zeal for political manoeuvring. The viscount's bushy moustache rose with his broad grin. Nobu bowed to the viscountess and her two daughters, all of whom were clad in kimonos of the finest silk. Neither daughter was particularly attractive. Nor were they unattractive. As expected, they kept their eyes downward and delivered their greetings with appropriate softness.

Then, if he wasn't mistaken, the younger daughter's lips quirked ever so slightly. Had her older sister made an amusing comment under her breath? Levity might signal a spirited, adventurous young lady.

Conversation moved to their collective good fortune for the cloudless sky allowing an abundance of moonlight. The daughters kept their eyes dutifully averted and contributed the requisite nods and polite murmurs. What a difference from European women, who would've at least taken part in musing on the autumnal moon's grand scale. Because he was bored, and irreverence was a temptation he frequently permitted himself, he informed the viscountess about his plans to put bloomers on the department store mannequins.

Her façade fell, starting with her jaw, giving everyone around the noblewoman a clear view inside her wide-open mouth.

A stifled giggle might have come from the younger sister's direction. Nobu couldn't be certain he'd identified the sound correctly, or if there was any sound at all since there was only silence when he looked over. But she was adjusting an opal pin in her hair, which could've loosened with what might've been mirth. A good enough sign. Perhaps he'd allow *Okasan* to inquire about the Nagahara daughter.

"They were a lovely pair," *Otosan* said after they'd wished the Nagahara family a pleasant remainder of the evening and joined the guests meandering along the back garden's pathways.

"The younger one seemed to find my mention of the scandalous bloomers amusing. Or at least she delighted in her *okasan*'s reaction."

Otosan nudged Nobu with his elbow. "Humour makes for a happy domestic life."

"I might be interested in getting to know her further," Nobu said as they circled back to the display of pounded rice cakes. "But say nothing to *Okasan* yet. We're busy at the store with planning for the year-end holidays."

"Fear not. If I told her a word of it, she'd have every piece of gossip about the girl within an hour and Viscount Nagahara expecting a proposal."

Nobu cringed at how the rumours would fly and how disappointed—or thrilled—the Nagahara daughter would be when he failed to offer a marriage proposal. "We ought to spare the Nagahara family the burden of *Okasan*'s enthusiasm."

"Which seems to have no bounds." *Otosan* narrowed his hawkish eyes at a group of men speaking in the back parlour. "*Okasan* has known the family since she was a child. One of their daughters would make a good choice." As he spoke, he somehow managed to keep one eye on the men who'd raised his suspicions yet give Nobu his full attention. His political tricks always left Nobu impressed.

"Father, my dear brother needs no reminding that he must marry up to secure the Koide family's place in the peerage." Asako, his younger and only sister and undisputed queen of sarcasm, smirked gleefully as she joined them with a bunch of rice fronds in hand. *Okasan* must have sent her out to replenish the ones that had blown off the moon-viewing platform. Hell, Asako probably volunteered. She'd jump at a chance to be free of *Okasan*'s hovering.

Since returning to Japan five years before, the queen of sarcasm had been exercising her royal rights with abandon. Of all the family, Asako had experienced the most difficulty with their return. She'd been six years of age when they'd departed Japan and hadn't become fully accustomed to Japanese ways. For her, home was Europe, really London, where they'd spent their final years abroad. Leaving had forced her apart from treasured friends and traditions, and the language she knew best for a place that was supposed to be home but felt nothing like it. He hated the keen sense of grief that plagued her.

Otosan glared at Asako. "Don't let *Okasan* hear you say such things."

Asako clicked her tongue. "Mother wouldn't understand. Her English isn't good enough."

"You shouldn't be speaking a foreign language in front of people who don't know it. It's rude." *Otosan* positioned himself toward the group of men he'd been eyeing earlier. "I'm going to speak with our guests. You two should do the same."

"We will, *Otosan*," Asako said in deferential Japanese while giving a proper bow to *Otosan*'s back.

Nobu nodded at the fronds in Asako's arms. "Are you planning to toss those in the trash heap?"

"Absolutely not. I'm going to adorn our platform. But let's walk a little. I need to stretch my legs before applying my fine decorating skills to Mother's display."

They headed back down the garden pathway away from the house. "Is *Okasan* pleased with her party?"

Asako moved the fronds to her other arm and shook bits of dried leaves off her kimono sleeve. "She calmed down when you finally arrived. You've been causing your dear mother a panic these days. She's terrified you're bedding that foreign woman you were speaking with at the store opening."

Nobu bristled. Granted, he'd spent the past week imagining what it'd be like to bed Mademoiselle Renaud, but he'd done nothing at the store's opening to give the impression he was in fact bedding her. "*Okasan* would never say such a thing."

Asako delivered a pointed glare at several women leaning toward their conversation. "Mother was appalled at how she flirted with you. Typical foreign woman, according to our worldly and sophisticated *okasan*." Asako rolled her eyes at the word "worldly."

"All that from watching me greet the Frenchwoman at the store opening. She owns a boutique on Ginza Boulevard." Nobu was proud of how nonchalantly his words had come out since he felt anything but nonchalant whenever he recalled the knowing glint in the mademoiselle's Mediterranean blue eyes. It'd been like she was reading every sinful thought in his head without a shred of judgment. Like he could've voiced every one of his filthy desires and she wouldn't have blinked an eye, just moved nearer, so he could... Nobu clenched his jaw. "You can assure *Okasan* I'm not bedding Renaud-*san*."

"I'm staying out of it. You tell her next time you arrive home before midnight. We rarely see you." Her tone was playful, but he heard the hurt.

They rounded back toward the moon-viewing platform. "I apologise. I'm busy at the store."

"You've got plenty of people who can be busy for you." She widened her eyes as though preparing to deliver information of life-or-death importance. It was a perfect imitation of *Okasan*. "You've got aristocratic blood flowing through your veins. You shouldn't be letting the unseemly business of fashion, and the even unseemlier concerns of money and profit, distract from your true purpose. Marrying well." The queen's sarcasm was reaching new heights.

"The last thing you want is for me to marry, because then it'll be your turn."

He didn't have to look over at Asako to know his comment had brought out a scowl. Asako's mouth closed in a firm line whenever aunts and cousins inquired as to the sort of man she preferred for a husband, or when *Okasan* droned on about the charms of a Kawasaki son or the grand home she'd enjoy as the Ishii scion's bride.

Unfortunately for Asako, she was an only daughter. Eventually, she'd have to accept the man of *Okasan*'s choosing, which Nobu had promised was the wisest choice. *Okasan* might be staunch in her determination that he and Asako marry nobility, but she'd never resign them to lives of misery. She'd find Asako a man whose disposition suited.

They reached the moon-viewing platform, and Asako placed the rice fronds between the plates of pounded rice cakes. "I know my fate, dear brother. To pine away for that which I cannot have."

"Resigned to your fate?" Nobu said with exaggerated disbelief. "That's the most Japanese thing about you, dear sister."

She tilted her head back and let out a hearty laugh without attempting to conceal her teeth. Several women who'd been eavesdropping on their conversation frowned in unison. Asako frowned back. "You must tell *Okasan* you've discovered something Japanese about me. She'll be thrilled."

"It'll give her the hope you've been denying her," Nobu said with an equal punch of sarcasm. If there was any justice in the world, Asako would still be among her bluestocking friends in London, discussing the various ways to torment Parliament until women had the right to vote.

But they were in Japan. Within a few years, he and Asako would be married to high-born Japanese, and *Okasan* would have several high-born grandchildren. He'd be making plans to sell Koide

Department Store while preparing to run for office as a member of the Foundation Party.

Nobu bit back a curse at his parents for having raised him abroad. He'd forever be haunted by a vision of the life he could've had in London: owning stores throughout the city, a woman by his side whose beauty intrigued him, whose thoughts gave him pause, who made him ache to run his hands through her dark, silky locks.

Someone like Mademoiselle Renaud.

Might it be possible to have his London life in the city of Tokyo with a French *modiste*? He had every intention of finding out.

CHAPTER THREE

Marcelle

Marcelle gaped at the machine. The French trade papers hadn't done justice to the experience of observing the flawless plate and steel bobbin, of running a hand along the smooth wooden surface and the Singer name etched in gold.

"Would you like a demonstration?" the Singer representative asked Marcelle, giving her day dress cut from a morning glory printed kimono silk yet another side glance. Some women had difficulty deciding if they favored the eclectic style. "Or would you rather try it straight away?"

"I'd rather try it straight away, but prudence tells me I ought to watch the demonstration first."

The women assembled around the magazine office's worktable tittered. Marcelle had a reputation for paying little heed to the virtues.

The representative rolled up her kimono sleeves and threaded the bobbin.

"That's not how I would've done it," Marcelle said in French to her best friend, Suki Spenser, owner and editor of *Tokyo Women's Magazine* and sponsor of the Singer sewing machine demonstration. They both spoke French, English, and Japanese. Quite literally, she could tell Suki anything. "I would've made a small loop at the top."

The Singer representative glared at Marcelle. Whether that was because the representative somehow knew French or was irritated being spoken over was unclear, although Marcelle would put her coins on the latter.

She nodded apologetically and leaned closer to Suki. "You need to stop talking," she hissed in Japanese for the representative's benefit.

Suki coughed to hide her giggle. "I wasn't the one speaking," she whispered in barely audible French without taking her eyes off the demonstration. "You were. And I need quiet. I must remember every detail. My readers want to know everything about this machine."

The representative frowned again. This time Marcelle frowned back. The Singer woman didn't need everyone's rapt attention for her poor threading. "Your reporters are taking notes. They can write it for you."

"They don't know a thing about sewing machines." Suki's staff comprised three well-educated women from elite families and two former prostitutes who'd sought refuge with the charity Suki had founded. Marcelle couldn't imagine any of them having laid a finger on a sewing machine.

"Perhaps you could write the article for me?" Suki asked.

"You'd have to rewrite every word. Have you forgotten what it was like when I was reporting?"

"You were a wonderful reporter." Suki kept an eye on the demonstration and made a detailed sketch of the bobbin's placement in the slot.

Suki was being kind and completely insincere. Marcelle had roundly failed in proving her competence over the two years she'd spent penning articles for *Tokyo Women's Magazine*. Despite extraordinary effort she'd put into the craft, her words had never come together with the same rhythm and polish as Suki's and the other writers'. Marcelle knew plenty of English fashion words thanks to years of serving as a French maid for the American envoy's wife in Tokyo. She could offer sophisticated opinions on baubles, buttons, ruffles, bustles, and jeweled hairpins in English provided she was speaking. When it came to putting her observations to paper, their brilliance fell flat. She'd seen how thoroughly Suki had to edit everything she'd written. Her best friend would never say as much, but Marcelle had been a burden.

The Singer representative pulled a piece of ripped silk from her sewing box and placed it under the needle. A few pumps of the foot pedal and a quick turn of the silk was all it took for the representative to wave a perfectly repaired piece at the assembled. The women gasped as though they'd witnessed a magician's trick. They very nearly had.

"Might I try?" Marcelle asked.

The Singer representative handed her a piece of ripped silk and stepped away. Marcelle ran the piece under the needle. In mere seconds, she had a neat stitch. How easy it would be to fulfill last-minute orders. She'd be able to give patrons a quick mend. Experiments with new seams and collar shapes would take less time to produce than she'd spent conceiving the idea.

"I'll purchase the machine." In fact, she'd like to purchase two Singer sewing machines. If all went according to plan, after the next promenade, she'd be hiring several seamstresses to fulfill the new orders. Two machines would increase their efficiency. But more than one machine would require a loan. For that, she'd have to ask Jiro. At present, she had no idea how inclined her benefactor was toward assisting her. Two machines were out of the question.

The Singer representative gasped as though she'd inhaled hot tea. "I thought I was here to give a demonstration for a magazine article, and I made the easiest sale of my life."

After the ebullient representative departed, the writers and assistants of *Tokyo Women's Magazine* returned to their work as Suki led Marcelle into her private office. A worktable with several chairs dominated the small space crammed with overflowing bookshelves and piles of papers that grew ever more mountainous each time Marcelle visited. How her best friend had a clear thought in all this mess was beyond her.

Along the opposite ·wall, a tall window overlooked Tsukiji's university district. The foreign quarter boasted an institution of higher learning that educated most of Tokyo's young foreign men, a handful of foreign women, and thousands of Japanese students. It was nearing midday, and the scents of boiled rice, stewed vegetables, and grilled fish wafted into Suki's office.

Suki cleared papers from the worktable for the maid to set down a pot of green tea and plate of sweet potato cakes. Almost as soon as they'd seated themselves on the silk chair cushions Marcelle had sewn for the magazine offices years before, Suki popped a cake into her mouth, then quickly devoured another. Marcelle had always admired her friend's appetite, but this was a bit much.

Suki sighed at her midsection. "The street smells make me nauseous."

"You're pregnant," Marcelle observed.

Suki beamed at the cakes. "Which means I get to eat as many cakes as it takes to settle my stomach." She took another golden morsel as though merely proving the point.

Joy swelled Marcelle's throat. Suki and Griff's first child, Henry, was a darling boy who sprinted at Marcelle's arms the moment he caught sight of her.

"I know it's a girl this time," Suki said.

Marcelle blew steam from the hot tea, then sipped. "A boy would give Henry a playmate."

"But I need a girl. You'll make her the most darling dresses."

"I'll spoil her rotten." Marcelle cradled her cup while picturing a young Suki running through the garden in a lace-edged pinafore cut from a kimono silk printed with delicate roses. "When will she be joining us?"

"After the cherry blossoms." Suki smiled beatifically and pushed the remaining cakes at Marcelle. "How is life on Ginza Boulevard? You haven't dined with us in ages."

Marcelle placed her cup on the table. "Busy, which I like, except for missing meals with the Spensers."

"*Okasan* raves about your designs. She thinks you'll be dressing all of Japan's women in Western clothing."

Marcelle flushed with pride. Suki's mother was a legend in the foreign quarter. When Marcelle first arrived in Tsukiji with the American envoy's family, Suki's mother had taken her under her wing, introduced her to the best vendors, and given her an education on the differences between Western and Japanese aesthetics. Marcelle traced the origin of her unconventional designs to conversations with Suki's mother. "How is your mother faring?"

"As busy as you. You ought to visit. I know she misses you." Suki rose from her seat at the table and pulled something off a nearby pile of papers. A mock-up of October's *Tokyo Women's Magazine* landed in front of Marcelle. "I'd love to know what you think of our article on Koide Department Store."

Marcelle took the mock-up in hand. Suki's artist had succeeded in capturing the chrome and glass splendor of the department store's atrium. "*La France Boutique* has no hope of surviving on Ginza Boulevard with Koide's taking all our customers."

Suki sat back down. "I thought you said there wasn't a single dress that resembled yours in the store."

"Not yet. But the way Monsieur Koide eyed my designs… it's only a matter of time."

Suki placed her thumb and forefinger on her chin: her thinking pose. "He's that ruthless?"

Marcelle shrugged. "To build a store like that? He must be."

"I haven't heard as much around town." Although Suki was no longer the gossip columnist for the *Tokyo Daily News*, she was still the first one told when it came to the foreign quarter's affairs, fights, slights, thefts, and other scandals.

Suki nudged the papers resting in Marcelle's grip. "Will you read the article? You've been there. You can tell me if we got it right."

Marcelle turned to the lines of text before her. The article provided ample and accurate description of the swarms of fashionables pressing their way into the store and the variety of goods on display. One paragraph lauded owner Nobuyuki Koide's marriage of the European department store model with the clothing, accessories, and art precious to Japan. In another, the writer expressed admiration for the store's strict set of guidelines that gave retailers equivalent space and exposure to public view. Whoever wrote the article had been impressed by the monsieur. "Did you write it?"

"Yamada-*san* went to the opening. She wrote most of it. I contributed Tsukiji gossip about the event. I wish I'd been there, but the pregnancy left me bedridden."

Marcelle pouted. "You told me Griff was ill."

"He was entertaining Henry, which reduced him to exhaustion." Suki gave Marcelle's forearm a little squeeze. "Perhaps we can go to Koide's later this week if you're not too busy?"

"I'd love it. Monsieur Koide offered me a private tour. You can join us." A light burn came to Marcelle's cheeks with mention of the monsieur and his private tour. She still wanted to gouge his eyes out for building that damn store, but she also wanted him to treat her like the naughty, needy *modiste* she was. He wanted it too. The way he'd called her "mademoiselle" had been outright flirtatious. Then there was the way he'd gazed at her as they were parting. He'd looked at her as though he would, without any reservations, toss her upon one of his magnificent displays and drive into her until they were both reduced to groans of ecstasy, provided he could get away with it.

Damn him.

More than once, that look had been her undoing.

"I wouldn't wish to interfere," Suki murmured. Sipping her tea, she studied Marcelle. "Is there something I should know about you and the monsieur?"

"Absolutely nothing." Marcelle pressed the earthenware cup to her lips and took a long sip while her defiant cheeks grew increasingly warmer. Setting the cup on the table, she met Suki's gaze. "He's a fellow Ginza proprietor."

"Handsome?"

"Not handsome." With his curved nose and solid jaw, Monsieur Koide didn't have the fine facial structure of Suki's undeniably handsome husband, Griff. "He's tall, an effect of a proper European diet, I'm sure, and has dark eyes that are very…ah, stirring."

"I knew it." Suki grinned. "Is he married?"

Marcelle rolled her eyes. "I'm sure Monsieur Koide is married. He must be at least thirty years of age, and everyone in this country marries by the time they're twenty. Besides, he's from a good family. He was probably promised to some poor infant before either of them could put one foot in front of the other."

Suki tapped her fingers on the table, a gesture that presaged one of her journalistic observations. "Actually, there's a good chance he might not be married. According to the article in front of you, he spent his childhood in Europe's capitals and only returned to Tokyo in the past few years. Had he married, it would've made it into the magazine." *Tokyo Women's Magazine* had the most thorough society pages of any publication in the city. "I hope I'm not mistaken because the look on your face tells me you're smitten with the monsieur. This could become serious."

Marcelle snorted softly. "Do you really think I'd even consider getting serious with a man who is probably, at this very moment, having my designs copied?" She had two serious relationships in her life: one with Suki and the other with Yumi-*chan*. The relationship with Jiro could be considered serious insofar as he'd provided her with the funds to open *La France Boutique*, and they'd been lovers, and might still be considered lovers since they hadn't explicitly ended their affair. That was as much seriousness as she could manage. Hopefully, gods East and West understood as much.

Suki returned the article to its place in the mock-up. "I'm sure he's doing nothing of the sort. He's probably dreaming of his private tour with the lovely French *modiste*. Men adore you."

Marcelle waved away the notion. "It's only because I enjoy bedsport." Most men, when they realized the extent of her enjoyment, tended to profess their undying love. Such declarations inevitably coincided with Marcelle starting to find their humor off-putting, their kisses sloppy, and their noisy eating habits unbearable. Her affairs were short and, for the most part, sweet.

"You're brilliant and beautiful. You'd be married already if you wished."

"I know when an affair has run its course." Marcelle looked at the green leaves floating along the bottom of her teacup and wondered when Suki would cease demonstrating her care by persisting in this useless campaign. Marcelle would marry when she was ready.

Suki rested a settling hand atop Marcelle's. "Might you try to stick it out for once?"

Marcelle gave Suki's fingers a squeeze in return, then refilled their teacups. "I stuck it out with Jiro." Their tryst had been lovely. She'd gained *La France Boutique* along with a wealth of advice from an accomplished man of business.

Suki leaned forward, and Marcelle braced for the point her so-called best friend was about to make. "Jiro was older and married, unattainable, which is why you slept with him for as long as you did. You ought to take Monsieur Koide seriously, provided he's unattached. It's time for you to marry. You've even said so."

"I've said I would appreciate marriage with a Japanese man who'd secure my future in Tokyo. You know how much I love it here."

"Marriage to the right man is a delight." Suki gave a wistful smile.

"You've shown me that." Marcelle nodded at the belly she was just now noticing had a distinctive jut.

"You'll love having children."

"Like your mother, one daughter will do for me." A little girl Marcelle would adore to the ends of the earth.

"Perhaps Monsieur Koide feels the same? He sounds like a decent man."

Suki made falling in love and marriage sound like a neat, straightforward proposition when she herself had never intended to marry a foreigner, then ended up wedded to a British man. Marriage, pregnancy, and all that familial joy that went along with it must cause horrible amnesia.

"How about my favorite little man in Tsukiji?" Marcelle turned the subject to Suki's boy. "When can I get one of Henry's hugs?"

Suki yawned. "How about now? You two can play trains while I take a little rest."

CHAPTER FOUR

Nobu

Back in his office after inspecting repairs to the north-facing exterior wall, Nobu sat down on the leather-padded swivel chair he'd personally designed to match the oakwood desk he'd imported from London, leaned back, and closed his eyes. The pianist in the concert hall on the opposite side of the third floor launched into a Chopin nocturnal. The rolling melody quelled thoughts of earthquake safety measures, unsatisfied customers, quarrelling vendors, and broken valves in the tearoom kitchen. Instead, the sights and sound of London crept in: the clop of hooves, the bells and shouts of omnibus conductors, the hustle of newspaper boys, the vendors selling meat pies. He entered Harrods below the giant crystal chandeliers and took in the rich mingling of cologne and tobacco. He rested against the marble counter before the leather coin purses and admired the kid leather and fine stitching.

Nobu gave a contented sigh.

The city had treated him well. In the English countryside, people stared at him as though he had a pair of horns and fangs. They'd never seen an Oriental, they readily told him, as though that was a perfectly good excuse for the disgust written all over their faces. But in London, he was a diplomat's son, educated at Oxford, who spoke like an Etonian, boxed like an aristocrat, and aimed for a place among the elite capitalists of the world. How it suited him.

He opened his eyes to the shelves of leather-bound books lining one wall, to the deep-cushioned sofa and wingback chairs near the fireplace opposite his desk, to the Persian carpets and velvet drapes, then turned to the task at hand, one which he was most eager to undertake. Earlier, his secretary, Ishida-*san*, had presented him with Marcelle Renaud's response to his invitation for a tour. He'd read the brief missive several times, relishing the way a light floral scent rose from the ivory paper when he pulled it from the envelope.

Suki Spenser, owner of *Tokyo Women's Magazine*, wished to accompany Mademoiselle Renaud on the tour. As much as he'd like an afternoon alone with the mademoiselle, Nobu was in no position to decline the request. The department store relied on the press's good graces. While they toured, he'd present his vision for twentieth-century commerce and consumption and explain how Ginza was becoming the most fashionable destination in all of Asia. This usually earned him impressed looks. He wouldn't mind getting such a look from Mademoiselle Renaud.

A knock on the door broke Nobu's reverie. "Come in."

Ishida-*san* entered with a ledger in hand. The fall of his suit was comparable to Nobu's. It should be. The store's most skilled tailor had designed both. Ishida-*san*'s aspirations were much the same as his boss's. Once Nobu finished building the Shinjuku store, he'd put Ishida-*san* in charge of its daily operations. That would be the real test. Could the aspiring young fellow live up to Nobu's example?

"Sit." He nodded to the chair opposite as he finished penning his response to Mademoiselle Renaud. After folding the cream-colored page, he placed it in an envelope and handed it to his secretary. "Have a messenger take this to *La France Boutique*."

"Right away." Ishida-*san* took the envelope. "I consolidated the revenue from the past three days. The purchases look good." He handed Nobu the ledger.

Nobu studied the figures. The store's launch had created a purchasing momentum that continued gaining strength. It was the best he could hope for. He handed the ledger back to Ishida-*san*.

"Have you heard anything about the ownership of *La France Boutique*?"

No foreigner, much less a woman, could own a store without the support of a Japanese citizen, and a male one at that. Although it was possible Mademoiselle Renaud received her support from a well-meaning Japanese Christian who attended one of Tsukiji's churches, Nobu doubted it. He'd met the minx. Whoever was supporting *La France Boutique* was likely Mademoiselle's lover. He'd have to reconsider his intentions if he learned her benefactor-lover occupied a certain position in Japanese society. Seducing the mademoiselle shouldn't earn him enemies. Nor should she have to endure gossip about inciting a lover's quarrel between the department store owner and her benefactor. In commerce, one's reputation could leave one rolling in profits or debt notices.

Ishida-*san* shifted his jaw as he did when he was about to deliver unpleasant news. "I haven't gotten past the name of the agency on record. Calls itself 'Downtown Company.' No agent was listed."

"Impossible." Nobu sat back in his chair. "The agent's name must be somewhere in the registration."

Ishida-*san* tapped his pencil on the ledger. "I never got to the registration. My contact in licensing could only give me the agency name. He didn't have access to the license. Apparently, there are over a dozen businesses calling themselves Downtown Company. We could visit each one, but they wouldn't be obliged to reveal their ownership or which businesses they happen to own. We've reached the end of the line."

Ishida-*san* had come straight into Nobu's employ from the Imperial University of Tokyo and had never failed to meet his boss's expectations. If he was admitting defeat in learning the identity of Mademoiselle Renaud's partner, then it was remarkably well-hidden, which was unacceptable. "We could make this a legal matter...but that would expose our interest."

"For the sake of clarity, Koide-*san*, what *is* our interest?"

Nobu's interest was simple. He wished to bed Mademoiselle Renaud. She was stunning, the sort of woman who appealed to him on sight. By Japanese standards, she'd never qualify as beautiful. Her hair was the colour of British tea and curled wantonly even when pinned atop her head. She had piercing blue eyes like some demonic creature and a confoundingly high nose. Her height made it impossible for any Japanese man to retain a sense of masculine pride by her side. Except him. He had a few inches on her.

As it were, their heights matched in a way that suggested how easy it would be to reach around and undo the pins holding her curls in place. Or reach down and fill his hands with her breasts, then run his thumbs over her silky nipples until they hardened into pebbles, and she moaned in his ear.

None of which he could do until he knew the identity of the man who'd assisted her in setting up *La France Boutique*. "Koide Department Store is going to be the leader for all Ginza proprietors. Allies in the neighbourhood are of utmost importance. *La France Boutique* is a few blocks away. We'd be fools not to garner their support for our vision of twentieth-century Ginza."

"Renaud-*san* has made a reputation for her designs. Wouldn't it be in our interest to give her a department?"

Ishida-*san* had an uncanny ability to read Nobu's mind. He'd wondered if an affair might eventually become a mutually beneficial business arrangement. But at this point, his needs regarding the mademoiselle were far more basic. "A *modiste* of Renaud-*san*'s talent would be a boon for the store. Before we can make such a proposal, we need to find out who we're dealing with."

Ishida-*san* sat up in his chair. "Why don't I go straight to *La France Boutique* and ask? Women find me irresistible."

Nobu resisted the urge to laugh aloud. The waitresses of the pleasure quarters doubtless assured Ishida-*san* of his charms. While he might be young and passably good-looking, he didn't have a gentleman's worldliness and *je ne sais quoi*. "I'll take care of Renaud-*san*. I promised her a tour of Koide's. Perhaps I can get her partner's name then. I, too, have been told women find me irresistible." Nobu couldn't help adding the last part. The young fellow needed to understand his place. Charming the mademoiselle was Nobu's job.

"Press your contact at the licensing bureau a bit further," Nobu ordered. "Offer a bribe, nothing that will draw attention. A gift of some kind for a mistress or mother. Something from the fur department might be nice for the winter months."

***

The sun slipped behind the mountains to Tokyo's west. Bright orange slashed the silvery sky, giving it the colours of a carp's sleek back. Nobu forewent a rickshaw homeward and strolled down Ginza Boulevard toward *La France Boutique*. The air was pleasantly sultry. The mosquitoes were in retreat, and the cicadas were gone, their screeching reduced to a memory by the high-pitched calls of the frogs and crickets that populated the marshlands upon which Tokyo rested.

Before Koide's grand opening, Mademoiselle Renaud's boutique had never caught his eye. Since then, he'd twice gone out of his way to pass by the store, once when he was on his way to a reception for a retiring Kabuki actor, and a second time when he was going to dine with several young men of aristocratic birth who wished to study at Oxford. Both times, he'd kept to the other side of the boulevard and glanced occasionally at the elegant store situated on the first floor of a two-story wooden structure between a seller of ceramic goods and a seller of Japanese-style paper and writing implements.

This evening he did the same. Through the stream of omnibuses, rickshaws, and bicycles, two wax mannequins hid behind the broad glass windows fronting *La France Boutique*. One wore a day dress made from Japanese silk, like the one Mademoiselle Renaud had worn to Koide's opening. The other wore a Western-style ball gown with a low bodice and voluminous silk skirts. For this one, the *modiste* had used a kimono silk dyed at the hem in a deep shade of emerald-green that lightened until the palest chartreuse yielded to the colour of fresh milk.

Although the store was several blocks from the central hub of Ginza Boulevard, a famous theatre stood nearby and many fine restaurants. Thousands of people passed *La France Boutique* every day. The store's location and the presence of not one but *two* wax mannequins suggested a wealthy benefactor who treated Mademoiselle Renaud in the manner she deserved.

Good for her. Even better for the benefactor.

Nobu should give up.

Kabuki patrons emerged en masse through the theatre's ornately carved golden doors flanked by scarlet banners advertising the current show. He hastened down the boulevard to avoid the swarm.

The problem was he couldn't give up. He hadn't been this taken by a woman for as long as he could remember. Not until he knew for certain she had a powerful lover who satisfied her every desire would he push her from his thoughts.

CHAPTER FIVE

Marcelle

Marcelle stared at the mess that had greeted her and Yumi-*chan* when they'd entered the front door of *La France Boutique.*

Yumi-*chan* took a step closer to the pile of glass shards. "It could've been an accident. The wind could've picked up a rock and sent it through the window."

Marcelle shook her head so hard a tendril broke free from its pin and spun around her face. "The winds aren't strong enough. Someone hurled a rock through the store in broad daylight." She indicated the pieces of glass dangling from the front window. "In spite."

Yumi-*chan* leaned over the glass pile and pointed at something. "That must be—"

Marcelle grabbed Yumi-*chan*'s arm. "Don't touch anything. You'll cut yourself."

"But it looks like paper."

Marcelle leaned over. Sure enough, among the menacing fragments a rock sat partially wrapped in paper. Yumi-*chan* brought out the dustpan and broom and swept through the debris until Marcelle could safely pluck what had likely been the window-shattering projectile. The white paper was a letter written in Japanese. She handed it to Yumi-*chan*.

"We won't let you destroy our nation. You cannot seduce our countrymen to do France's bidding. Leave!" Yumi-*chan* translated. "Consider this a threat to your life," she added in a wobbly voice.

Seducing Japan's men to do France's bidding?

Marcelle couldn't think of anything more preposterous. She was a *modiste*, not a spy for France. She felt no loyalty to the nation of her birth. Tokyo was her home.

Exclamations of surprise from outside the store were followed by loud offers of help. Hidekazu, leader of the street gang Marcelle paid to look after the boutique, stood on the sidewalk along with a half-dozen of his associates.

"You'll hurt yourself on that glass," he called through the open window in quick Japanese Marcelle had come to understand after over a year of receiving his gang's protection. "Let my boys clean the mess."

He was a lanky, jovial youth. At first glance, he'd appeared to be somewhere between twelve and twenty years of age. The longer Marcelle had spent with the young man, the more she'd thought otherwise. Several missing teeth, dark circles under his eyes, and weariness etched in lines on his brow spoke to years of abandonment, abuse, and a precariously untethered life. He was probably closer to thirty.

Marcelle invited Hidekazu and his motley crew inside the store to take care of the glass. They brought with them the tang of alcohol and sweat but made quick work of cleaning the mess.

"As soon as I heard about the window, I came right over." Hidekazu bowed low enough to count as an apology.

Marcelle gave him a stern glance. "Where were you this morning when the rock made its way through my front window?"

She and Yumi-*chan* had spent most of the morning on an errand to procure a swath of Belgian lace. Whoever had thrown the rock must have been watching the store and waiting for them to leave. In all fairness to Hidekazu's gang, the perpetrator might have also made sure there were no witnesses to the vandalism.

"It's always quiet on Ginza Boulevard in the morning." An edge of defensiveness laced his comment. "Is anything missing?"

She didn't keep more than a few coins in the store, and she'd already checked the supply closet and her worktable. Her new Singer didn't appear to have been touched. In fact, there was no indication the vandal had even entered the store. "I don't believe anything was taken."

"That's because everyone knows my gang is watching." Hidekazu tapped his nose. "So, if you don't have anything missing, why would someone throw a rock through your window?"

Marcelle shrugged with raised arms, a French gesture of uncertainty that usually earned her perplexed glances. Hidekazu was unfazed. Unlike her well-born patrons, he didn't seem inclined to dwell on her communicative nuances. "Perhaps it was a ruffian like you? Or one of your gang?"

Hidekazu crossed his arms and puffed up his wiry chest. "No one in my gang would throw rocks at your window. But you'd better believe we're going to find the devil who did."

"This cannot happen again," she said in her most authoritative voice. "The cost of replacing the window is going to break me."

"I'll put my lads on the store from sunup to sundown, and throughout the night. When that worthless piece of horseshit returns, we'll make him regret that rock. And I'll get money for your new window." He scissored his legs in what Marcelle presumed was the fighting stance he'd use when facing the rock-thrower.

After sending Hidekazu to find woven matting to cover the gaping hole where the window had been, she checked the time. Her tour of Koide Department Store was in two hours. How could she possibly spend the afternoon ogling his wares and carrying on frivolous conversation?

Damn her devious, matchmaking, so-called best friend for having excused herself from the tour for some plausible reason related to her many obligations. Suki was supposed to have joined them and acted as a barrier between Marcelle and the intriguing Monsieur Koide, with his mouthwatering stares. Then, after Marcelle had charmed a declaration from Monsieur Koide that he'd never infringe on the designs of local *modistes*, Suki would be there to record his words for an article in *Tokyo Women's Magazine*. And, *voilà*, Marcelle would have nothing to fear from the hulking department store at the center of Ginza Boulevard.

Now, Marcelle had to do it alone without any reporter putting him on record, and at the very time she needed to be handling a rock through her front window. What she really needed was for Jiro, her mentor, benefactor, and lover—although she wasn't sure if they could still be considered lovers—to help. Was she supposed to contact the Japanese police? The Tsukiji police? The French embassy? Was the letter a farce? Were its threats real? And how was she supposed to pay for a new window?

At least she had Yumi-*chan*.

"Can you visit the glass blower in Nihonbashi and inquire about the cost of a new window?"

Yumi-*chan* stood from the corner where she'd been checking for glass that had made its way across the room. "I'll go right away."

"Make sure he doesn't think he can charge us double because we're women. We're on a tight budget with the promenade coming up in a few weeks."

Yumi-*chan* puckered her lips. "A new window is going to be expensive."

"It'll be taken care of." She didn't have enough savings to make the replacement herself. Jiro would have to help. Or not.

Thinking about Jiro reminded her of the kimonos stored in the backroom. Although it appeared the rock-wielding vandal hadn't entered the store, she wouldn't have peace until she knew the silks were safe. She marched to the backroom, opened the trunk where she'd stored his precious heirlooms, and found them unharmed. He'd lent them to her for design inspiration, and she'd never forgive herself if his family's treasures had been ruined or stolen.

On several occasions, she'd pestered him to take the priceless silks back, but he'd dismissed her suggestions. So, they'd stayed at the store, much to her benefit. Even as recently as a few months before, when she'd been seeking a draping style to complement a new design, she'd found herself gravitating toward them. They'd served her well. Even so, the next time she saw him, she was going to shove the trunk into his hands and tell him to return them to their rightful place.

Marcelle selected an upturned-brim hat topped with red spider lilies for the tour. Not only did it complement her day dress cut from a turquoise silk printed with folding fans, but its spikey, scarlet petals were a fitting crown for the role of "invulnerable woman." Life had given her many opportunities to perfect the performance. Today, Koide Department Store would be her stage and Monsieur Koide her audience. She'd banish all thoughts of broken glass and regale him with a show worthy of a ten-minute standing ovation.

CHAPTER SIX

Nobu

Nobu let his gaze fall upon the column of Mademoiselle Renaud's neck as she launched into a discussion about receiving first dibs on leather meant for export. Her skin was smooth as pounded rice cakes. From what he'd gathered of their tour thus far, the mademoiselle would taste like...like mulled wine with orange slices dipped in honey.

"I can make an introduction on your behalf, if you'd like," she said.

What he'd like was a few hours with the mademoiselle at an inn about a block away from Koide's.

Back off, brother, he heard his sister Asako say with the edge of disgust she reserved for men who denied women the respect they rightfully deserved. Her lectures rang in his ears. "Nothing," she liked to intone, "undermines a woman's efforts more than a man who regards her solely as an object of sexual desire."

She was right. Mademoiselle Renaud deserved his utmost respect for her thriving business and creative accomplishments.

"Thank you for the recommendation. Our designers would be grateful for an introduction."

A group of middle-aged women walked past them toward a display of lightening creams. Like other customers that afternoon, their gazes lingered on the store owner and the foreign woman before they turned to one another with hushed conversation and backwards glances. He could give a fig about gossipy magpies. It wasn't as if they could take their coin elsewhere. There was only one department store, and it was his. He liked having Mademoiselle here. Fortunately, she didn't seem to notice the gossip at all.

They left the display of satchels that had prompted discussion of leather vendors and joined the customers through the first-floor aisles. Mademoiselle Renaud had been speaking nearly nonstop since they'd begun the tour. He'd started their conversation with a question about advertising to the foreign quarter. This led to an amusing story about a Portuguese woman who brought Mademoiselle Renaud shreds of fabric that had constituted the underside of an ermine cape until her beloved poodle had chewed it to bits. The cape was a gift from the Russian envoy's wife, and the Portuguese woman needed it for an event at the consulate that very evening. Thanks to a piece of white silk and the recent purchase of a sewing machine, Mademoiselle Renaud performed the repairs in little time. In exchange, the Portuguese woman ordered three dresses, greatly compensating for the time and effort required to repair the cape.

Then Mademoiselle Renaud told him about her new sewing machine and contacts in the silk export markets, which he listened to while wondering if the day would ever come when he'd get to see her naked and reclining on a futon, ivory thighs spread wide, hips rolling, her swollen quim glistening with unrestrained desire.

What kind of grown man still thought like a sex-deprived adolescent?

He wouldn't be thinking like a sex-deprived adolescent had his lust been more recently slaked. It'd been almost a year since his brief affair with a thirty-five-year-old widow ended with her deciding to remarry. He hadn't had a lover since, mostly because he was either building a department store or being introduced to aristocrat's daughters, and he didn't like the world of prostitutes and geisha.

Seduction, as a mutual undertaking, suited him. With Mademoiselle Renaud, it'd be mutual. An exchange of sensual control between two ambitious, worldly proprietors.

"I heard you tell the press about a moving staircase in London. I'd love to hear more about it," Mademoiselle Renaud said over the store's din of customers' lilting conversations and the clatter of heels against the checkered marble floor. Brightness lightened her eyes to a sky blue, and she tilted her head to the side as though genuinely curious. She seemed more at ease than when she'd been filling the space between them with a merry-go-round of stories.

He told her about the plated glass sides and steel balustrades lining the wooden conveyor mat and how several Harrods patrons had fainted before they could bring themselves to take even a single step.

Mademoiselle Renaud ran an ungloved hand along the silk cravats as they passed a display table. "What a pity they missed out on such a thrilling experience. Did it feel as though you were being elevated into the air? Like being in a balloon?"

"It was far more banal, although it made me feel lighter."

They arrived at the foot of the main staircase. "When can we expect one at Koide's?" she asked.

Nobu glanced over at the space where he intended to put the moving staircase. "Provided we survive the first few years, I'll consider it then." This was his fixed response. In truth, he planned to start construction on the staircase next spring because the store was generating more revenue than he'd dared to hope possible.

Mademoiselle Renaud gestured at the customers milling about the first floor. "I doubt survival will be a problem. I, on the other hand, might not make it past half a year with the way you're attracting all the fashionables."

Her tone was light but the accusation plain. He was taking her customers. While they were in fact competitors for a certain type of Tokyo woman, there was plenty of room in those women's wardrobes for them both. "Your patrons aren't going to trade your unique designs for what we offer, at least not at this point."

Mademoiselle shot him a look that pinned him to the spot. "Does that mean one day you're planning to offer customers dresses like the ones I design?"

"I'm no thief. Were we to create our own Western-style dresses cut from Japanese materials, they'd look nothing like yours. Ours would be different, even better. Then your dresses would get better. The goal of the free market is progress. It's a win for both of us, and our patrons."

Mademoiselle Renaud ran her fingers along the decorative ivy wound around the newel post. She'd put away her gloves while they were looking at the satchels because she'd needed to feel the stitching. Her fingers were long and shapely with muscles she'd earned from use. The skin tone was uneven, perhaps from little scars where she'd nicked herself sewing. They were fascinating, elegant hands. Just like her.

She faced him. "I could never compete with you. I don't have the capital to hire as many seamstresses or purchase fabrics as opulent. If luring customers away from *La France Boutique* is your goal, you'll succeed."

Nobu opened his mouth to contradict her. She was talented enough to lure a dozen investors and hire all the seamstresses she wanted. Hell, Tsukiji's foreigners were the biggest gamblers in Tokyo. They loved chasing a windfall. Before he got a word out, she raised her hand, silencing him. "I understand how the world works. I'll fight you tooth and nail to keep my customers. But I wasn't born into a powerful Tokyo family. If you want my customers, they're yours for the taking."

He wasn't a ruthless bastard, and he certainly wasn't going to let Mademoiselle Renaud harbour such an impression. "I've no plans to deprive you of customers. I'm more inclined to increase your revenue by purchasing your designs for my seamstresses, or lure you into one of my departments, although I suspect there's little I could offer to tempt you. Your boutique seems quite successful as it stands, which benefits us both. A flourishing Ginza Boulevard ensures our mutual continuing success."

She let go of the ivy. Splotches of red that had crawled up her throat as they'd spoken now lightened. "I'm pleased to hear as much."

For some reason, Mademoiselle Renaud needed ample reassurance. Was her benefactor unable to protect her business? Did he leave her feeling vulnerable?

If this mysterious benefactor wasn't powerful enough to protect Mademoiselle Renaud, he wasn't powerful enough to be in the same social strata as the Koide family, which gave Nobu hope.

He nodded at the staircase. "Shall we continue the tour?"

So tentative was her smile that he sensed her regard had shifted. Rather than the predatory store owner intent on bankrupting any shop he perceived as competition, he was striving for both of their successes.

"I'd like that very much," she replied.

Before they began the ascent, Nobu offered Mademoiselle Renaud his arm in keeping with European custom.

She placed her hand in the crook. "You are truly a gentleman." Her words were tentative, almost sultry, and they made him sizzle.

Customers stared and nodded with whispers to one another at the sight of him escorting her up the staircase. In Japan, women walked behind men. They opened and closed doors for men. They pulled off and put on men's shoes. His customers looked like they might be on the verge of undoing their chignons with all their headshaking at the act of European chivalry.

"I cannot recall taking a Japanese man's arm in public," Mademoiselle Renaud said with an amused grin. "It feels nice."

"Then you have no reservations about breaking the customs of your adopted country?"

She applied light pressure to his arm as though to acknowledge the intended tease. "I'm usually very careful not to offend, but I always let a Japanese companion take the lead. In this case, I fully trust your judgment." Her eyelashes fluttered in an undeniably flirtatious manner.

His gaze caught on her broad, welcoming mouth. Everything about her called to him, from the dark pile of curls pinned in an artful chignon to the flare of her skirts that promised a full, ripe arse he could use to pull her flush against him. But her mouth drew him in the most. How he wanted to caress her lips, nibble them, part them, and feel his way inside her lusciousness.

None of which was possible until he knew for certain about her benefactor-lover. "My judgment is making it imperative that I ask how your lover feels about your taking a man's arm in accordance with European custom."

"*Lover?*" Her voice pitched higher with the question, then continued to rise until it culminated in a yelp. Her free arm flailed as she teetered. Her weight pulled him downward at the same moment he tightened his hold on her arm.

They landed backsides first with Nobu absorbing most of the fall. His lower back slammed against the riser, and the brunt of their body weight fell on his hip. That he'd kept her from careening down his staircase was worth every jab of pain shooting through him.

Gasps from the first-floor shoppers echoed through the atrium.

Mademoiselle Renaud peeled herself off Nobu. "I'm...so...sorry." Her words came out between short bursts of breath. "Are you hurt?"

"I'm fine. What about you?"

She grabbed her boot. "It's my ankle," she said, her voice nearly a whisper.

"Did you twist it?"

Gods East and West, it'd better not be a break.

Were she to leave the store in that kind of pain, she'd likely never return.

"It just gave out." She rubbed the side of her boot. "This is humiliating. I've made a fool of myself in front of all those women watching us walk up the stairs."

"They're blaming me for not escorting you properly," Nobu guessed. He could practically hear them ruminating on how useless it was for a man to provide his arm if he was going to let the woman fall anyway. The logic of cultural superiority always found a way.

Mademoiselle Renaud continued pushing her fingers against the side of her boot. "You saved me from landing in a heap at the bottom of the staircase. I owe you my life."

His stairs weren't steep enough to be the end of her. She would've survived the fall. But he didn't mind the gratitude. "My office is on the third floor. We'll take a closer look at your ankle there."

She squeezed her eyes shut. "Thank you," she uttered through gritted teeth.

They were only halfway up the flight of stairs to the second floor. It'd be much better for her leg if he were to carry her the rest of the way. She couldn't be much heavier than the stones the masons were using the other day to repair. Much to their surprise, he'd assisted one of them when it'd seemed like the fellow was about to drop the unwieldy rock. The mademoiselle would be easy to lift, easy to cradle in his arms. They'd be up in his office and away from the audience of customers in little time. "You shouldn't be walking on that ankle. Would you allow me to carry you the rest of the way?"

Mademoiselle Renaud looked at him as though he'd suggested she dance a jig in her undergarments, an image he found quite appealing and never should've conjured about a woman of business, an injured one at that. "I'll manage just fine." She held out her arm. "Perhaps you could help me stand?"

While Nobu would've preferred to take her in his arms for the rest of the way to his office, he rose, then helped her up. By the time she'd stood, several of his salesclerks were at hand. He told one of them to secure her other side while he wrapped one arm around her waist and held her arm against his chest with his other. The scent of her sweet, spicy perfume filled him. This wasn't how he'd first expected to wrap his arms around Mademoiselle Renaud, nor had he expected there'd be several of his salesclerks joining him when he did. Even so, he savoured the dip of her waist under his palm, and the lightness of the arm he held pressed to his chest.

With a little hop, the mademoiselle joined him on the next stair. "I could hold on to the banister and make it up the steps on my own. The ankle isn't broken, at least I don't think it is."

That was out of the question. She needed support on both sides. "You ought to put as little pressure on the ankle as possible."

"But..." Her gaze drifted down to the customers, whose gaping hadn't ceased.

"Please...you're making me look like a hero." He nudged her upward. The mademoiselle responded with another hop. "This incident will certainly increase our sales. I'm expecting big gains from your injured ankle. I'll have to find a way to pay it back."

Mademoiselle Renaud looked up at him under thick lashes. "My ankle has expensive tastes."

Nobu glanced down at the mademoiselle's kid leather boot. "I can see that. Fortunately for your ankle, so do I."

When they reached the third floor, Mademoiselle took a tentative step on the injured ankle. "It's not as bad as I'd feared. Just a muscle strain. I could probably walk back down the staircase right now. I know a good bonesetter in Tsukiji. He can brace the ankle for me."

If anything was strained, it was the way she uttered those words. "I can't allow that expensive ankle of yours to leave my store in such a state. At least permit me to have someone come here and look at it. It would ease my conscience. After all, those were my stairs you slipped on."

"All this time I was thinking you were going to get rid of the competition by copying my designs, when you were really trying to get me onto your stairs." She gave him a sly grin that begged for an equally sly reply.

"Apparently, I've failed in my efforts. Next time you come for a tour, I'm taking you into the concert hall. It's treacherous in there."

She widened her eyes. "Lions? Snakes?"

"A regular zoo."

"I adore wild beasts. Next time, you must."

Next time. Thank the gods East and West.

Nobu and the salesclerks aided Mademoiselle Renaud down the hallway to the department store offices. When they entered, his secretaries looked up from their work and followed their progress across the room to his private office. He grunted for them to carry on and led the group into his private quarters.

Velvet drapes had been pulled across the windows to keep the room cool. Nobu opened them for better lighting.

"Your view is magnificent." Mademoiselle Renaud nodded toward a window beyond which lay the breadth of eastern Tokyo from Ginza Boulevard to Tokyo Bay.

"My architects found the perfect angle." After he'd directed them to it.

The clerks led her to sit on the sofa. In the bright light, beads of sweat sprinkled her forehead and damp locks framed her face. She looked like a porcelain doll whose cheeks were a shade too red. She needed a doctor.

He ordered one clerk to seek an herbalist and another to find a bonesetter. He was about to task the final clerk with bringing tea when his secretary brought an English tea service into the office. Following Ishida-*san* was another secretary with a blanket and a small stool.

Mademoiselle Renaud let them prop her ankle on the stool and situate the blanket in her lap. Much to Nobu's relief, she took a hearty sip from the cup of tea he handed her. "I feel much better, thank you," she announced to the assembled.

Nobu sent the remaining clerks and secretaries back to their posts, then turned the chair in front of his desk towards the sofa and seated himself across from Mademoiselle Renaud.

She placed her teacup on the service and leaned against the tufted back cushion. "I apologize for making such a fool of myself. I tend to become clumsy when I'm on unfamiliar ground."

"Then you should make yourself more familiar with the store." *And its owner.*

"I'd like that. You have a fine collection of goods."

He loved that she seemed at ease in his office, in his store. With him. It made him want to shut the office door and take the seat beside her on the sofa and place her hand in his. He wanted to feel those slender, firm fingers that accomplished such superior workmanship laced through his, their smooth and rough places grazing his skin. "I'd quite enjoy the pleasure of..." Her nearness befuddled his thoughts. The words wouldn't come. Even so, he couldn't let the phrase hang there, so he spoke the first English that came to mind. "The pleasure of sitting beside you."

"Sitting beside me?" Mademoiselle Renaud echoed with a raised brow.

His face was in flames. Finally, the correct phrasing made it through his addled brain. "What I meant to say was that I would appreciate the pleasure of your company at the store."

"I'd like that." Her gaze softened in a way that struck him as inviting. Did she want him to take the seat beside her? They couldn't sit that closely with his office door open. Several secretaries had already stridden past the door. Nobu had no doubt the rest sought excuses to do the same.

While he was considering how Mademoiselle Renaud would respond to him shutting it, she clenched her jaw and grabbed her ankle.

Nobu recognised those sudden shots of pain from twisting his ankle in the boxing ring. He moved from his chair to squat next to the small stool where her ankle was propped. "We need to take off your boot."

"I can—" Mademoiselle Renaud leaned forward at the very moment he took her booted ankle in hand, and their foreheads collided with a whack that reverberated through Nobu's skull.

"I'm sorry." He rubbed the tender spot.

Mademoiselle Renaud pressed a hand to hers. "I'm sorry. I only wanted to spare you from having to remove my boot. Are you hurt?"

Thus far on the mademoiselle's tour, he'd injured his hip, lower back, and the front of his head. All of which he'd go through again to have her on his sofa. "It's going to take a lot more than that to hurt me."

"I promise I won't subject you to my clumsiness again."

Her clumsiness was endearing, no matter that it posed a danger to herself and others. "I can handle your clumsiness. I'm as hardheaded as they come."

She laughed gently and leaned back again on the sofa.

"Seeing as my strength is unparalleled," he began, keeping his tone light. He didn't want his suggestion to offend. "You should allow me to remove your boot. I also have a great deal of experience with women's footwear. It's one of our most popular departments."

"I believe that." She seemed to sink farther into the sofa. The fall must have exhausted her. "Please, go ahead."

Nobu placed her boot atop his thigh. The laces came apart with ease. Gently, he pulled the boot from her silk-stockinged calf, taking care not to jostle her ankle. With a slight wriggle, he tugged it free. "Does that hurt?"

"Not at all. Your experience with footwear has served you well."

Since Mademoiselle Renaud hadn't cried out in pain or seethed from withholding it, he felt certain the ankle wasn't broken or even badly sprained. Probably a light sprain from having rolled over it. After setting the boot aside, he lowered her stockinged foot to his thigh. With both hands he steadied it.

Mademoiselle Renaud exhaled with a low murmur, almost a hum.

A hum of pleasure? Of pain? He suspected the former, but worried about the latter. "Am I hurting you?"

"Not in the least." A flush worked its way past the upper edge of her dress and onto the ivory column of her neck.

Pleasure it was, then. Elevated, her ankle must have been getting relief. Was it the positioning of his hands around her heel? He could move—

"You were asking about my lover when I attempted a tumble down your stairs." Mademoiselle Renaud interrupted his plan for how best to handle her ankle. "Had I not been such a clumsy fool, I would've told you there is no such man in my life."

No lover. Victory thrummed through him. Whoever her benefactor was, he wasn't a lover.

"And you?" Mademoiselle Renaud inquired pleasantly. "Do you have a lover?"

Nobu swallowed hard. This unexpected and thoroughly welcome turn in their conversation sent blood coursing through his veins. "There's no one like that in my life."

Their gazes met. The electricity that shot through him could've burned down his store. Neither turned away.

Then he felt it on his thigh: the mademoiselle made a slow circle of her heel against his trouser fabric. An invitation? It felt very much like an invitation, an invitation to touch her, to explore what he could of her. What he wanted of her.

Nobu moved his fingertips over the fine silk of her stocking to the inside of her calf.

Mademoiselle Renaud let out a strained breath between moist lips, her gaze never wavering from his.

This was the seduction he'd known would happen between them. Mutual, challenging, adventurous.

Slowly, he made circles with his palm over the swell of her muscle, barely believing he was massaging the inside of her calf before the open door. Her skirts covered his hand. Any of his secretaries looking in would think his boss was tending to an injured ankle, provided said secretary ignored the intensity of the look passing between his boss and the woman on his sofa.

Heat from his palm mingled with heat from her skin. He pressed his fingers into the warm muscle, kneading gently so as not to exacerbate any injury. It softened under his touch, much to his satisfaction. "How does that feel?"

"Lovely," she said softly, roughly, then inclined her knee to the side.

Another invitation. No one looking in would be the wiser. His hand was under her skirt. He could move it higher, past the curve of her knee, up the inside of her thigh to the soft, wet petals of her quim and delve a finger into the sweet, hot core of her—

Pleasurable, tingling sensations pricked the stretched skin of his cock. May the gods help him, he was going to come in his trousers if he didn't cease these thoughts. But his thinking was a mess. If there was any chance he was misreading her, if what was transpiring between them was an illusion borne of wishful, desirous thinking, he needed to know.

He inclined toward her. "Is this what you want?" He kept his voice a soft whisper. "Do you want me to go farther?"

"Yes." The word burned through him.

He let out a light groan. His thoroughly hard cock twitched in anticipation.

After edging his hand even farther up her skirts, he released the scent of silk mixed with salted honey sweetness.

Mademoiselle Renaud let her head fall against the back of the sofa. He took in the shuttering of her eyelids, the flutter of pulse in her neck, and reached around to the sensitive place behind her knee. Sliding his finger along the bend, he felt her tremble. Again, he slid. This time an airy laugh followed in the wake of her trembling. She was ticklish.

Nobu turned toward the open door. No secretaries passed by. None of them could've heard that breathy laugh. This new information, her ticklishness, was something he wanted to explore when they were finally, truly, alone. Might that be soon?

"I'd like to—"

A clerk hurried through, knocking on the open door. Nobu refrained from finishing the thought. An older man in a dark grey herbalist's kimono followed the clerk over.

Nobu used the barest movement to pull his hand from under Mademoiselle Renaud's skirts. He didn't dare stand. He was stuck there with her foot on his thigh, because if he stood and faced the clerk and the herbalist, they wouldn't fail to notice his cockstand.

Mademoiselle Renaud placed a hand over her mouth and gave a cough that sounded to his ears like a suppressed giggle.

"He's also a bonesetter," Nobu's clerk explained while introducing the herbalist.

The herbalist stepped forward, and Nobu stood without disgracing himself.

After stroking and pressing the mademoiselle's slender ankle in a manner that left Nobu a little bristly, the herbalist declared it a strain. While he rubbed ointment into her soft, smooth skin, which also made Nobu bristle, he ordered her to avoid any unnecessary movement over the following days.

Hope that he and the mademoiselle would soon retire to the nearest inn for lovemaking unlike anything he'd ever experienced faded. He wasn't going to exacerbate her injury. She needed to heal first. Then he'd take her somewhere steps above a lover's inn, somewhere as elegant and unforgettable as she, and make love to her like he'd never made love to any other woman.

With the herbalist's support, Nobu overrode her insistence she was capable of descending the staircase on her own. He took one of her arms and his clerk the other, and they escorted the mademoiselle to the first floor. After dismissing the clerk, he walked Mademoiselle Renaud across the atrium. Her gait was smooth, and she didn't appear to be suffering the sprain.

Outside the gilded doors, Nobu turned them toward the rickshaws lined up at the end of the block. "I apologise for not giving you the full tour. You'll have to come back and see more of what we have on offer."

"I'd like that. I'd also like you to call me Marcelle. I feel as though the events of the day have warranted a more friendly address." The glimmer in her eye was unmistakable. Like him, that moment on his sofa was firmly etched in her mind.

"I couldn't agree more. Please call me Nobu, short for Nobuyuki. It's what my foreign friends call me."

"Nobu." The name seemed to cling to her lips like traces of fine wine. "You should come by *La France Boutique*. I can show you some of my new designs now that I know you're not planning to steal them." As she finished speaking, she furrowed her brow.

"I'd very much like to visit the boutique… Is your, er, ankle bothering you?" He wished her no pain, but he'd rather that her ankle was bothering her than she was once again entertaining the idea of him being a design thief.

Marcelle stopped and released his arm. "It's not my ankle." She wove her fingers around the strap of the reticule hanging from her wrist, then returned her gaze to him. "This morning someone threw a rock through the front window of the boutique."

An attack on *La France Boutique*. That was as good as an attack on Marcelle. And an attack on Marcelle was intolerable. "Do you know who did it?" He'd gladly hunt down and punish whatever miscreant destroyed her property.

Marcelle didn't reply until several store patrons had walked past them. "I have no idea. There was a note attached to the rock. The perpetrator isn't fond of foreigners, apparently."

"What exactly did the note say?"

"It said something about foreigners being evil. I don't read Japanese. My assistant read it for me."

"Those people are…" He wanted to say *bloody horseshit*, but he also wanted to spare her the profanity. "Fools, ignorant fools. Have you spoken with the police?"

"I'm considering it." She tilted her head to the side. "I wonder if it was just a juvenile prank on the foreign *modiste* and nothing more will come of it."

Nobu crossed his arms in front of his chest. He didn't want to alarm Marcelle, but anti-foreigner sentiment was rife among Tokyo's less fortunate. They blamed the West for Japan's modernization, particularly the new tax system and property laws that had disadvantaged them. She could very well be in danger. Unfortunately, the police were likely to suppose, as Marcelle had, that the incident was a juvenile prank. They might not be much help. "You should have someone guarding the store."

"The neighbourhood gang looks out for the store. They swear they'll keep a better eye on what's happening." She sighed. "In truth, they're ruffians, most of them children."

Children watching over Marcelle and her store wasn't going to keep either safe. "I have guardsmen who can keep an eye on your store. They'll start this evening."

Marcelle shook her head. "You needn't go through the trouble. I can find someone else to watch over us. I really can't take away people from your store."

"I insist," he said in the same tone of voice that put an end to business discussions. "I'll send one of my men to the boutique right away." He'd put Ryusuke, his foremost guardsman, in charge of protecting Marcelle and her store.

Nobu held out his elbow.

Marcelle placed her hand in the crook. "That's very generous of you to offer. But, really, you needn't go to the trouble."

"It's no trouble at all. Having my guardsmen patrol the neighbourhood will make us all safer. Now, you need to be back at your store where you can rest that ankle. Unless you wish to return home? I take it you live in Tsukiji."

"I do, but I'd prefer to check on the store."

Nobu would've done the same. He helped her into the rickshaw and instructed the runner to *La France Boutique*. "You must let me know if there's anything else you need," he said when Marcelle had settled.

"I'd, eh, thought we might see one another again." Expectation laced her voice. She was the type of woman who knew exactly what she wanted. How he craved that in a lover.

"I was thinking the same. I'd like to make plans for us." He'd devise something spectacular for them once her ankle had healed.

A light flush sprang to Marcelle's cheeks. "I'll be awaiting your plans."

Nobu stepped back from the rickshaw. "In the meantime, please accept my guardsmen's assistance at your store."

"*À bientôt*, Nobu," she said with a wave. The red, vining flowers on her hat quivered as the rickshaw took off down Ginza Boulevard. Nobu did: hoped that she would *see him again soon.*

CHAPTER SEVEN

Marcelle

The rainy evening kept strolling shoppers, bored students, and entertainment-seekers off the streets, which made for a quiet walk back to Ginza from the Shimbashi neighborhood where Marcelle had met with Jiro's agent, Nomura-*san*.

The meeting had gone as well as she'd hoped. Nomura-*san*, a kind, older gentleman who managed legal matters related to *La France Boutique*, had assured her the rock through her front window was likely the work of delinquent youths picking on the only foreign woman proprietor on Ginza Boulevard. Even so, he allowed for the possibility she'd been targeted by a political or religious group. Such incidents weren't unheard of. Suki had been attacked by a such a group a few years prior.

Marcelle was familiar with varieties of social resentment, having been born into an aristocratic family that had been stripped of property and status in the French revolution. She could well imagine either young troublemakers or resentful adults throwing a rock through a foreigner's window. Seeing as over a week had passed since the incident and there hadn't been an inkling of trouble, Nomura-*san* urged her to wait for him to receive word from Jiro before alerting the authorities. That made sense.

She wished she could write to Jiro privately, but according to Nomura-*san*, that wasn't possible because he'd gone into hiding somewhere, for reasons of which she wasn't privy. She hoped he wasn't merely not accepting *her* correspondence because she'd done something to alienate him. He'd never expressed displeasure. If anything, he took more pleasure in her success than she did. When she last saw him, he called her designs "genius" and complimented her account books.

True, they hadn't been lovers for several months prior to their last meeting, but she hadn't been unfaithful during that time. Nor had she taken a lover in the half-year since he'd disappeared. She considered the affair over and suspected he felt similarly. They'd simply never discussed it outright. Probably, neither had wanted to admit their bedsport was simply no longer interesting.

She hadn't been deceiving Nobu when she'd told him she didn't have a lover.

Not that it mattered. Ten days had passed since her tour of Koide Department Store, and she'd yet to receive any kind of word at all about his special plans for them. His guardsman, Ryusuke, made a point each day of sending his employer's regards. But after what had taken place in his office, she thought she'd be getting more than regards through a third party. He'd practically made love to the back of her knee, then...nothing. Did he simply have a perverse fascination with leg joints?

For her, the moment had been singular. Every touch and every hungry look he'd given her had been a revelation. A thousand times she'd gone over those minutes she'd spent on his sofa, each time burning with desire for him to make his way up the inside of her thigh to her soaking, throbbing quim.

She'd already mapped out their affair. They'd start with daily, if not twice daily, love-making sessions. Tending the flames of passion at the initial stages of an affair was a unique pleasure. It was a time of exploration, and she was curious whether it was merely a figment of her imagination that his shoulder was begging for a bite. Then, after several weeks of blissful exploration, they'd settle into a comfortable, satisfying rhythm of meeting when their busy lives permitted. Probably three times a week.

Although she had no reason to suspect he was married, she was yet wary about his status. Since Paris, she'd sworn never to engage in affairs with married men. The role of mistress was not for her. Nor did she like the idea of imposing on another woman's family. Jiro, for many reasons, had been an exception. But the rule still existed, and if it turned out Nobu was married, she had no intention of carrying out an affair.

But an affair hardly seemed to be in the cards since he'd yet to propose plans of any kind for them.

She'd allow that a business crisis or family illness had derailed his plans. But, more likely, he had reservations about her character. She was an unmarried foreign woman of business. As such, she didn't fit into the usual Japanese categories of supposed womanhood—servant, factory girl, wife, mistress, sister, aunt, cousin, mother…prostitute—which made her an unknown, even dangerous, sort of person. Although Nobu had lived in Europe, where *modistes* with businesses of their own were less rare, he might suspect she was an oddity for having ended up an independent woman on the other side of the world.

Admittedly, patience wasn't her forte. But she didn't want to appear desperate. She'd told him she was awaiting his plans. Now, wait she must. If nothing came of their flirtation, which would be a true disappointment, at least she had a Koide Department Store guardsman watching over her boutique.

Ryusuke, the man tasked with protecting her and Yumi-*chan* from rock-throwing, foreigner-hating brutes, had introduced himself an hour after she'd returned from her tour of Koide's. Every time he passed the boutique, he called out a vigorous greeting that caught the attention of purveyors on her block and probably the next one over. Hidekazu and his gang of young men had practically torn out their hair over the department store guardsman meddling on their turf until Marcelle assured them that Ryosuke was only temporary. She had no intention of breaking her promise to pay the gang for their protection.

Neither Hidekazu and his gang nor Ryusuke were in sight when she returned to the boutique. There weren't any cats around either, yet a faint mewing drifted over as she shook raindrops from her umbrella. The mewing soon stopped, which she hoped meant the poor beast had recovered from its distress. Then it began again, even louder. The sound was so plaintive, the creature must have been in pain, probably injured and lying in the gutter.

Marcelle stepped from under the store eaves and looked into the street, but there was no sign of a wounded cat.

The thready noise started again, more like a whimper this time, and if she wasn't mistaken, it was coming from within *La France Boutique*.

Every hair on her body stood on end.

"*Yumi-chan.*" Marcelle flung open the front door.

The whimpers grew louder, and she raced to the backroom and threw open the curtain.

Yumi-*chan* lay on her side, struggling against towels binding her wrists and ankles, a stained dishcloth stuffed in her mouth.

Marcelle eased the cloth free and tossed the wet rag aside. "*Mon Dieu.* Are you hurt?"

Yumi-*chan* shook her head and moved her lips but only strangled sounds came forth. Marcelle grabbed the teakettle and poured its remains into a cup. Holding it to Yumi-*chan*'s lips, Marcelle's panic receded as her assistant took one small sip and then another. When Yumi-*chan* held up her hand as though signaling she'd had enough, Marcelle went to work undoing the towels on her wrists. The purple tint to Yumi-*chan*'s hands faded to scarlet soon after the restraints came off.

"It was a man... Japanese... in Western-style clothing," Yumi-*chan* finally eked out.

Marcelle's stomach churned vile, burning liquid up the back of her throat. This was all her fault. Whoever had attacked the store had come for the foreigner and hurt Yumi-*chan* instead. "Have another sip of tea."

Yumi-*chan* took the teacup firmly in hand and drank more deeply. After several attempts to undo the knotted towels around Yumi-*chan*'s ankles, Marcelle decided a knife would work better. She grabbed a kitchen knife and sliced through the ankle towels.

Yumi-*chan* stretched out the stiffness in her legs. Clothing was wrinkled, not torn, with no blood or bruising on exposed skin.

Marcelle gently rubbed her leg. "Did he hit you? Force himself on you?"

"I'm not hurt." Her voice was nearly normal. "It was uncomfortable. But I've had worse."

She'd survived life in a brothel for almost a year before escaping to the Jinzai nunnery, and there was no doubt in Marcelle's mind that Yumi-*chan* had endured violences far worse than what she'd just experienced in the store. The only stories Yumi-*chan* had shared of the brothel were the sort that gave them both a hearty laugh. She seemed to have buried the violences and humiliation deep inside her, as any woman who wished to retain control of her faculties would. Being highly skilled in control, Marcelle was well-acquainted with the method. "How long were you bound like that?"

Yumi-*chan* rubbed her wrists where towel marks were already fading. "Not long. The man entered the store while I was making adjustments to Anderson-*san*'s dress. She came in earlier today for a fitting."

Marcelle recalled the appointment, but it wasn't important. Not now. "What did he do?"

"He grabbed me by the arm and put his hand over my mouth." Yumi-*chan* spoke too matter-of-factly for Marcelle's liking. "Then he dragged me into the backroom and tied me up with those towels. He demanded I tell my foreigner boss that he knew all about you, that you were a spy for France, and you wanted to make Japan a French colony."

A blinding, bright light of anger flashed before Marcelle's eyes. Never would she forgive herself for Yumi-*chan* having been attacked on her account. She had a vision of herself finding this Japanese man in a Western suit and clawing his eyes out. The filthy piece of shit on the sole of humanity wasn't going to get away with what he'd done to Yumi-*chan*. "This is outrageous."

"I tried to tell him as much. But he kept repeating that you must return to France or he'd destroy you."

Marcelle rested a hand on Yumi-*chan*'s shoulder. "I cannot tell you how sorry I am that you had to endure this attack over my being foreign." Yumi-*chan* nodded. Her shoulder shook lightly beneath Marcelle's hand. "I'm not returning to France, ever, and you'll never be harmed by this man or any man like him, ever again."

Tears pooled in Yumi-*chan*'s eyes. "I knew you wouldn't back down."

"You never have to worry about my backing down." Marcelle stood and paced the small backroom. No, she'd never back down. But what about the men who'd been tasked to protect her and Yumi-*chan*? Where had Ryusuke and Hidekazu been all this evening?

In fact, their patrols were irregular. During the evening hours, they passed by the store about once an hour. At least, Ryusuke did. Hidekazu and the fools in his gang were less consistent in their walk-bys. Marcelle hadn't minded since she'd been mostly convinced the rock-throwing attack had been a childish prank, and there hadn't been any indication of further threats. In fact, with each day that had passed without word from Nobu, she'd been thinking to dismiss Ryusuke altogether.

Whoever had attacked Yumi-*chan* must have been stalking the store and known neither Ryusuke nor Hidekazu were nearby when he'd attacked.

She should've told the police about the rock through her window. Even if they'd only believed the rock had been juvenile vandalism, they might've sent a patrolman around to check on the store. But she hadn't reported the incident because she'd fretted that Jiro would want to deal with the police himself. Nomura-*san* had confirmed as much earlier today. "I'll go back to Nomura-*san* tomorrow. This time I'll insist upon hearing directly from Jiro by letter or through one of those telephone calls or however he communicates with Nomura-*san*. Jiro will take care of us."

Yumi-*chan* ran a hand over her ankle. Marcelle could practically feel pain shooting through her own. "He adores you," Yumi-*chan* pointed out.

"Not like he used to." Marcelle sighed resignedly.

"You don't want him *that* way."

"True. But life was easier when he was in my bed. Life was easier when I knew where in Japan, where in the world, he was hatching his latest plans."

Marcelle helped Yumi-*chan* to the wingback chairs where their patrons usually sat. After placing a kettle on the stove for a fresh pot of tea, she lit a lantern and walked through the store. There'd been no further damage to the windows. The mannequins were untouched. Jiro's heirloom kimonos and the gowns for next week's promenade were likewise unharmed. Next time, they might not be so lucky. Shivers raced down Marcelle's spine. At this point, she had to assume there would be a next time.

A man bellowed out a night greeting from the doorway. Marcelle jumped at the sound even as she knew full well who it belonged to.

"Apologies for surprising you." Ryusuke's gaze moved from Marcelle at the worktable to Yumi-*chan* seated on the wingback chair. "What happened?"

"We've had another incident," Marcelle replied. "This time Yumi-*chan* was attacked."

Ryusuke growled under his breath and rushed to Yumi-*chan*'s side. After determining she wasn't hurt, he questioned them about what had occurred.

While Yumi-*chan* told him about the attack, Marcelle prepared cups of tea. Much of Yumi-*chan*'s rapid, truncated Japanese went beyond Marcelle's understanding, but she didn't seem to withhold any details of what she'd endured or the threats against Marcelle.

Ryusuke listened with gritted teeth. "Koide-*san* is going to be furious," he said when Yumi-*chan* finished. "He'll give you more protection. Someone will be posted outside *La France Boutique* at all times."

"Certainly, Koide-*san* cannot spare any more of his men." Marcelle cringed at the petulance in her voice. How could she have let herself become whiny? Was she really going to allow Nobu to affect her faculties?

"I don't think Koide-*san* will agree. He's very concerned about your safety." Ryusuke's gaze rested on Yumi-*chan*. He appeared to be considering the wisdom of dragging her from the blighted store before another calamity struck. Marcelle wondered whether it was the department store owner or his guardsman who cared about the safety of those in *La France Boutique*. "I must tell him right away," Ryusuke said as he walked toward the front door. "I'll get Hidekazu and his gang to watch over you while I inform Koide-*san*."

Marcelle smarted with embarrassment at having let her irritation over Nobu's indifference make her sound like a disappointed child. Then she pushed those feelings aside and turned her attention to the relief she felt at Yumi-*chan* seeming mostly unharmed from the horrific attack. Also to the gratitude that a clearly enamored Ryusuke would do everything in his power to ensure Yumi-*chan* never endured such an attack again.

***

Marcelle had just poured fresh cups of tea for her and Yumi-*chan* when Nobu pushed through the front door, nearly slamming it open. Hair was plastered to his forehead. His suit was wet with rain, and he had the wild-eyed look of a man who'd just seen a ghost strolling Tokyo's most famous boulevard. "Then it's true?" He barely had breath to get out the words. "You weren't injured?"

Marcelle couldn't fathom he'd been so concerned that he'd raced to the store. Yet he was short of breath, and he'd furrowed his brow with obvious distress. "I'm fine. Only Yumi-*chan* suffered the attack."

"I see." He continued to scrutinize her as though she had a pilfered baguette stuffed under her dress. Then he turned to Yumi-*chan* with questions about her condition, which seemed to be improving apace—perhaps owing to a certain guardsman who hadn't left her side. While Nobu inspected the pink marks on Yumi-*chan*'s wrist, the sleeve of her kimono fell up her arm, revealing the tattoo of a writhing carp ringed by Japanese characters. It was the mark of ownership by a notorious gang.

He let go of her arm and took a step backward. He and Ryusuke bore identical, quizzical looks. "Did you escape from a brothel?" Nobu asked.

Yumi-*chan* yanked her kimono sleeve down and stiffened. The sting of Yumi-*chan*'s disappointment pierced Marcelle's heart. Ryusuke learning of her past would change his affections. "I've been out of the brothel for more than a year. The Jinzai nunnery settled my debt with the gang. I cannot rid myself of their markings, however."

"Then the man who attacked you wasn't from the brothel?" Nobu asked.

"Had he been from the brothel, he would've dragged me back there."

"Maybe he was seeking payment from Ginza's foreign *modiste*? Thought he'd make the attack look like it came from an anti-foreigner group."

"The gang can't claim payment for me because I no longer belong to them." Yumi-*chan*'s voice was as hard as the set of her mouth. Her determination to leave the past behind was one of her many impressive qualities.

Nobu placed his hand on his hips. "Then you did nothing to provoke the attack?"

His interrogation of Yumi-*chan* had gone far enough. Marcelle stepped between Nobu and her assistant and faced him. "Yumi-*chan* did nothing," she said in English, letting her anger show at Nobu for making the attack Yumi-*chan*'s fault. Why must women always be the cause of their own misery?

Nobu backed away. "I apologise. I went too far. Yumi-*chan* has been through a terrible experience tonight and obviously has been through much in her past."

Marcelle glanced back at Yumi-*chan*. Ryusuke was once again by her side. Any shock he'd felt over her admission had been blessedly brief.

Nobu scanned the rain-soaked Ginza Boulevard, then set his gaze on Marcelle. "I'm purely concerned about your safety."

Everything he said and the way he'd taken command of the situation gave the impression of him sincerely caring about her safety. But it was hard to believe he hadn't made any effort to contact her for ten days, then came marching into her store with this much concern. He must have thought that he could play with her. Accepting his guardsman had been a mistake. She should've asked for money from Jiro to hire her own. "We'll be fine. I doubt we're in any immediate danger. The brute has already had his way with us today."

Nobu's hands returned to his hips, clearly his favorite position for a good interrogation. "Was this the same brute who was here before? The one who threw the rock?"

"I imagine it's the same man. He's under the very false impression that I'm a spy from France. He thinks I'm on a mission to turn Japan into one of our colonies."

The vein in Nobu's forehead throbbed. "That's ludicrous. You're a *modiste* with a store on Ginza Boulevard."

"Obviously."

"I have a friend among the Tokyo Police. I'll summon him." Nobu turned to Ryusuke and said something in rapid Japanese that no doubt meant Ryusuke was supposed to go immediately to the

Tokyo police with a request for a squadron of officers to protect *La France Boutique.*

It wouldn't do. She simply couldn't involve the authorities without Jiro's permission. "You needn't go through all that trouble on my behalf," Marcelle interrupted. "This is a matter related to the foreign community. I'd prefer to consult with police in Tsukiji," she lied with as much firmness as she could muster.

Nobu raised his hand. "I doubt they have the authority to act in Ginza."

"They can act on behalf of foreigners throughout Tokyo." This might be true, she wasn't sure.

"Will they watch over the boutique?" Nobu asked uncertainly.

"I'll request as much."

Nobu paced the front of the shop. "Until you've convinced the Tsukiji police to protect you, I'm going to give you more guardsmen."

Marcelle rested her gaze on Yumi-*chan*. She looked as though she was about to fall asleep on the chair. She needed protection. They both needed protection to continue making beautiful dresses and gowns. Accepting Nobu's guardsmen didn't mean she was going to allow herself to be drawn into his games of ignoring her one minute and rushing to her aid the next. That, she wouldn't do. But she could use his help. "I agree. We need more men like Ryusuke looking out for us," she said in Japanese.

Ryusuke puffed up his chest.

Nobu walked over to the mats where the front window had been and inspected the strings holding the woven coverings in place. "I'll post guardsmen outside the boutique night and day. You won't be harmed again."

This would put her in his debt. Even so, she could use a few more men like large, tough Ryusuke who appeared ready to lay down his life to save Yumi-*chan*. Hopefully, next week's promenade would garner enough orders that she could pay Nobu back and hire guardsmen of her own. "I'll feel better having your guardsmen here," she replied to Nobu, then turned to Ryusuke. "Yumi-*chan* needs to rest. Might you escort her home?"

He looked to Nobu, who nodded. "No harm will come to Yumi-*chan*." Ryusuke spoke with exaggerated gruffness that suggested he was compensating for giddiness at the prospect of escorting Yumi-*chan*. "But first I must make sure that delinquent Hidekazu and his gang will stay outside until the new guards arrive."

While Ryusuke spoke with Hidekazu over who'd been keeping watch outside, Nobu took down the location of Yumi-*chan*'s boardinghouse and told her he'd send his doctor to check on her tomorrow. Marcelle suspected Yumi-*chan* was also going to receive a fine assortment of packaged goods from Koide Department Store's contrite owner.

The rickshaw runner with Ryusuke and Yumi-*chan* onboard pulled away, leaving Marcelle and Nobu under the boutique's eaves. Rain covered Ginza Boulevard, making it even quieter than when she'd arrived back from her visit with Jiro's agent. That seemed like ages ago.

"Shall I escort you back to Tsukiji?" Nobu asked.

Had this been the previous week, she'd be on his arm, letting him escort her home or to whichever lover's inn he favored. Tonight, she was uninclined. His generous care of Yumi-*chan* was commendable. But this was after ten days of ignoring her after giving her the impression he was as eager as she to explore the undeniable attraction between them. He'd made her wait.

Had she taken the initiative to show up at his store, demanding an evening with the monsieur, she would've seemed too eager, too desperate, and she was determined to never present herself as either.

Ceding control of their next meeting to him had been a mistake.

She'd spent nearly all her life dealing with the consequences of decisions others made on her behalf. The past few years had been different. She'd been making decisions on her own. True, she'd been able to make these decisions thanks to Jiro's support. But he'd always made her understand she was an investment, and a good one at that. Businesses had investors and sometimes those investors were lovers. What mattered was that investors let the proprietor make her own decisions.

She needed to forget about the blistering attraction she felt for Nobu and keep their relations to those of neighborly Ginza proprietors. But how did one forget blistering attraction? Distance and work.

After checking the door's lock once more, she presented him with the calm, elegant expression of a woman too poised to buckle under the fray. "Thank you for coming so quickly to the boutique and for all your help. I don't wish to trouble you any further. I can take a rickshaw by myself back to Tsukiji."

Nobu grunted an objection. "I don't want you going anywhere alone, especially tonight. A rickshaw runner isn't going to protect you from an unhinged miscreant."

Marcelle let out a short, amused laugh. It wasn't as though Nobu would do any better than a rickshaw runner. He was too refined, his sturdy, muscular frame notwithstanding. "I suppose you could offer protection?"

Nobu moved his shoulders back as though it took all his strength to lift the muscle-laden arms. "I boxed at Oxford. No one will get anywhere near you."

Safety in numbers was a truism. Perhaps an aristocratic pugilist and a rickshaw runner could get her home. "Then I ought to accept your escort."

Nobu sent one of Hidekazu's ruffians to fetch a rickshaw. While they waited for the runner, Nobu asked how her ankle was healing, although he seemed well-appraised on the subject since he'd been getting daily reports on her ankle from Ryusuke.

"I suppose next time you come to Koide's, I'll have to put you on my arm from the moment you arrive." His suggestive smile riled her, although she didn't show it. She merely fumed inwardly over these downright obnoxious games of his. Smiling at her, massaging her leg, stoking her hope, and then ignoring her wasn't something she'd stand for.

She returned the look with an imperious raise of the brow. "If you recall, I was on your arm when I twisted my ankle."

"Thank goodness you were. I saved you from falling down the stairs."

"You might as well have been the one to push me with your nosy questions about lovers." She sounded flirty, bringing up lovers. Even so, she'd brought up *lovers*. Why do such a thing?

"I promise not to ask any more nosy questions."

Their rickshaw runner they'd requested pulled up beside *La France Boutique*. Nobu held out his hand for her to get in. She gave his offer a long stare, then accepted it because, in fact, her ankle was getting sorer by the minute.

The rain formed lacy webs in front of the gas lamps lining Ginza Boulevard. Marcelle kept as much space between her and Nobu as possible on the short rickshaw bench, which meant they brushed up against one another with each sway and turn. He smelled like his store, of freshly cut wood, leather, and cologne, an intoxicating mixture that made her feel safe and desirous.

For what?

Nobu hadn't made plans for them, which might be because a dire situation had arisen that had demanded his attention. If that was the case, she had to know. Because if it *was* the case...

"I thought I would've heard from you before today." She kept her voice even and her gaze on the red brick buildings at Ginza's hub. "Perhaps with an invitation for us to meet?"

Nobu shifted nearer on the bench until the length of him pressed against her. She could sense the weight of him, the strength he was capable of unleashing, and it made her body loosen. "I've been planning that very thing. I had to make several calls by telephone to the inn and the city office to make sure we wouldn't miss the leaves. They change earlier in the mountains."

Leaves? At an inn in the mountains? That would be... eh, romantic: for the sort of woman who needed an elaborate seduction. Marcelle was not such a woman. She was perfectly content to spend an evening at a lover's inn in Tokyo. There were plenty of inns with views of the mountains, as well as views of the sea, for that matter. "Where exactly were you thinking of us going?"

"I want to take you to Karuizawa in the mountains of Nagano. I have fond memories of time spent there as a child and thought you'd enjoy the town. It has a strong European influence."

Marcelle had heard of Karuizawa. It was a popular resort area for Tokyo foreigners seeking an escape from the summer heat. But she'd never had any desire to go. The slow summer months gave her an opportunity to catch up on her designs. "I've never been there. When were you thinking of going?"

"Next week. I was thinking Yumi-*chan* could see to your business. You needn't worry about her safety. Ryusuke won't let her out of his sights. He's clearly taken a fancy to your assistant."

Marcelle exhaled in relief. "I'm afraid next week won't be possible. I have a promenade in Ueno Park on Friday."

"Excellent," Nobu said with a beaming smile. "I'll be there. I'd love to see your new designs."

Having the owner of the popular Koide Department Store at the promenade would create a very favorable buzz. Suki was going to put a several-page spread in *Tokyo Women's Magazine* about the promenade, which would include mention of who'd been in attendance. Other newspapers might do the same. She'd contacted several with a request for their attendance but hadn't received any confirmation they'd be there. Patrons and friends had promised to attend. They'd be plenty surprised to find the toast of Tokyo, Nobuyuki Koide, among them.

She'd have to share that she'd become friends with Nobu. Or he'd have to explain their relationship, because she was going to be busy with preparations and modeling. Naturally, she was walking the promenade, too. What would he say? That he was interested in taking her to the mountains for an excessively long and unnecessarily romantic tryst?

What if it turned out he *was* married?

Just because Suki hadn't learned of a society wedding didn't mean one hadn't taken place. Aristocratic Japanese could be secretive about their private lives, especially concerning wives, and especially when those wives were multiple, which wasn't uncommon for the nobility. Short of multiple wives, Japanese men of his social standing took mistresses. Would people assume she was his mistress? She'd never be his mistress. That was a point she might have to make clear to her friends and patrons were they to assume the worst.

In the meantime, having him and the buzz surrounding him at the event would be a boon. "It'd be wonderful having you at the promenade."

"Then you'd be free to go to Karuizawa the following week?"

Marcelle flinched. They passed the French patisserie with the *brasillé* pastries she loved. If only it were open, she'd have an excuse to escape the rickshaw. "I'm not altogether certain…"

She needed to put an end to this outlandish plan. Taking off for the mountains when they barely knew one another and had yet to become lovers chafed against her sensibilities. How could he be so confident they'd enjoy one another's company? Their attraction was undeniable, which meant they'd likely satisfy one another in bed, but what about the remainder of their time together? She didn't know if he had sloppy manners—although that was highly unlikely from such a refined individual—or a habit of rudeness to those in service—doubtful after the way he'd treated Yumi-*chan* even after learning she'd been a prostitute. Still, she simply wasn't comfortable with leaving Tokyo, and she wasn't comfortable with him.

"I'm not certain I can leave Yumi-*chan* after the promenade. We usually receive many new orders, and I can't expect her to work on them alone, especially after what happened tonight. That would be too much of a burden," Marcelle said delicately.

They passed through the gates into Tsukiji and the business district where men in European-style suits and university students were carousing in the pubs.

Nobu's jacket sleeve worked against her cape as he turned to her. "I understand your concern about Yumi-*chan*. She's like family to you, isn't she?"

Family. The word never failed to bring a sour taste to her mouth. She didn't have family and had long ago given up searching for it. "I've given Yumi-*chan* shelter, wages, sustenance, and friendship, which she gives in return. To me, she's more than family."

"I take it your family is in France."

"I have relations in France. My parents died when I was an infant. I grew up with poor aunts and uncles who wanted a share of the allowance left by my father. As far as I've ever known, family gives you a bed, chores, and a schoolbag that may or may not be filled with books until the day they ship you off to live with another cousin."

When her parents had begun showing signs of the lung disease that would kill them, her spinster aunt had taken her into her home. For the next three years, she lived with the aunt who treated her with the affection she'd have given her own daughter had she birthed children of her own. One of Marcelle's earlier memories was of the tears in her aunt's eyes when she hugged Marcelle goodbye before her new husband took Marcelle to an uncle's home several hours away by carriage for what she was told would be a short holiday.

It wasn't. Her aunt's new husband was a widower with three children of his own. Marcelle was one too many for his new wife.

"You're living with us now." Her cousin told her a few days later. He was a potato-faced older boy who hid behind doors to frighten her when she passed. Once, she surprised him back with a knitting needle in the thigh.

Once had been enough to take care of that problem.

"It's a miracle you survived such an upbringing."

He sounded understanding, but people with families that take them abroad and attend their department store openings had no idea of what it was like to sob oneself to sleep for want of a reassuring squeeze, a steadying touch, a gentle kiss on the forehead. Anything that would shatter the sheer, unrelenting isolation of a child without a parent's love.

Marcelle didn't resent him for it. Who in her right mind would want to dwell on such things? Besides, her childhood could've been far worse. Women like Yumi-*chan* who ended up at Suki's charity knew horrors beyond her imagination. "There are innumerable ways to wound a child, and I experienced some, though thankfully not all."

At a young age, she'd discovered a talent for avoiding being alone with any male over the age of twelve. It'd served her well.

Nobu gazed at her with surprise. "How did a woman of your education and bearing end up in Japan?"

Marcelle inhaled Tsukiji inlet's loamy scent, heavy on the damp night. She'd perfected the narrative of her arrival in Japan and was happy to share it. "I was working as a *modiste*'s apprentice in Paris. The American envoy to Japan was passing through the city with his family on their way to their Tokyo posting. I ended up mending dresses for the envoy's wife and her daughters. They liked my work and offered me the position of lady's maid. We left for Japan the following week."

"That was fast."

"I admired Japanese designs. They were all the rage in Paris." She'd also needed to escape her lover, Antoine.

"I take it your relations had no objections to your leaving?"

"No one cared enough to stop me." That wasn't exactly true. There was a dear cousin and friends who'd urged her to stay in Paris, become a *modiste*, and marry a man of the middle classes. That might have been a fine life, but as long as Antoine was there, she couldn't.

Nobu growled something in Japanese. "Family should take care of their own. They should've taken better care of you. You deserved a real home, a refuge from the turmoil of everyday life, a place where you could laugh and joke and speak freely."

"Spoken like a man with a loving wife and several adoring children," she snapped back. She shouldn't have let her thoughts get ahead of her, but it'd needed to be said.

Nobu furrowed his brow. "I'm not married, nor do I have adoring children." He looked at her askance. "One doesn't make plans to whisk a beautiful Frenchwoman away to the mountains when one has a family awaiting his return."

Nobu calling her a beautiful Frenchwoman in that deep, melodious voice of his made the whole of her go limp. "I apologize for the presumption. Men with your family background are usually in a political marriage by the time they reach the age of twenty."

"True, but some of us spend our twentieth birthdays abroad and avoid such matches. The benefits of foreign residence are numerous." He gave her a knowing grin.

"I'm in complete agreement." Not only was Tokyo far from France, but the foreign city had allowed her to create a life of her design. She had a store of her own, patrons who adored her, friends she cherished, and lovers who'd succeeded in bringing her satisfaction. If anything was missing at present, it was a new lover.

Nobu would make an excellent lover. As it happened, he *was* unmarried, and she could forgive his ignoring her for ten whole days since he'd been making highly considerate, if misguided, plans for a rendezvous in the mountains.

Marcelle called for the rickshaw runner to stop before the large brick home that had served as the British Legation when the foreign community had first received Tsukiji. This put them a block away from the boardinghouse. Arriving in front of the boardinghouse in a rickshaw with Nobu would garner more notice than she'd like. Far better to sneak up to the door.

Nobu asked the runner to wait for him. Marcelle entwined her arm through his and they walked at a leisurely pace toward the missionary home that had been turned into a boardinghouse for women. His sturdiness as they stepped to avoid a rut in the road stirred a wanton excitement for something more from him, for his touch on her bare skin, for his kiss, which she felt certain would be deep and sensual. Dampness bloomed between her thighs. Perhaps next time they met, there'd be a kiss. His lips seemed a powerful force she'd—

"I'm sorry you won't be able to go to Karuizawa," Nobu said, interrupting her quite pleasant thoughts for the topic she least wished to consider. "I'd thought it'd be the perfect way for us to become familiar with one another."

"It isn't the best time for *La France Boutique*," she replied evenly, managing to keep an exasperated edge from her voice.

"Does your reluctance to go to Karuizawa have anything to do with a man?"

Hadn't they already been over this? She had a sore ankle to prove it. Marcelle came to a halt. The boardinghouse was only a few residences away and she needed to settle this once and for all, or the attraction between them could go no further. She let her shoulders fall with a light exhale. Composure intact, she met his gaze. "I told you I don't have a lover."

"What about the man who is funding your store, your partner in *La France Boutique*?"

Jiro. Yes, her reluctance to take off for the mountains had something to do with *that* man. Until she'd received his advice on informing the authorities about the attack on Yumi-*chan*, she couldn't leave Tokyo. Not that Nobu needed to know these details. "You're referring to Hamada-*san*?"

"Hamada-*san*." He seemed to ruminate on the name. "I'd been curious about your partner. From what I understand, no foreign woman could own her boutique outright. I assumed Hamada-*san* was your lover, but I guess that's not the case?" The question's sharpness made it sound more like an accusation.

"Hamada-*san* invested in my boutique as a matter of business. We shared a bed for a time, but that ended last winter. It's been almost a year since he was my lover. I haven't had a lover since then, and I certainly don't have one now, which I already told you."

"I apologise for doubting your word." To his credit, Nobu sounded apologetic. "I just thought we'd have a fantastic trip to Karuizawa. I can't understand your reluctance."

"My assistant was attacked because she works for a foreigner. I cannot leave her alone." That was as much as Nobu needed to know, and it was sufficient reason for her to balk at a holiday.

"Perfectly understood," he replied, his displeasure abundant in the coldness of his words. "Let's get you to your boardinghouse for the evening. You must need to rest."

"You're too kind."

The perfunctory response was the last word they exchanged until they bid one another good night at the boardinghouse's front gate.

CHAPTER EIGHT

Nobu

Nobu held the bulky box in front of him on his way down Ginza Boulevard to *La France Boutique*. So far, he'd exchanged evening greetings with at least a dozen shopkeepers, each one granting his parcel the odd glance. He should've turned the task over to a messenger or had one of his clerks accompany him with the box in hand. The sight of Koide Department Store's owner hauling goods risked blemishing his authority as the district's foremost purveyor. But this was penance for having bungled the invitation to Karuizawa.

He never should have invited Marcelle on a lover's holiday right after the attack on Yumi-*chan*. At the time, he'd thought the prospect of a sojourn into the mountains would appeal after all she'd been through. He'd been mistaken.

He'd also been in possession of the perfect holiday itinerary. The week before, he'd corresponded with Karuizawa's municipal government about this autumn's weather trends and the course of the leaves' changing. The bureaucrat assured him the leaves would be well into their colours during the dates Nobu had in mind for the trip, giving him and Marcelle gorgeous views. This was fantastic news. Then he secured rooms for them at the inn where the Crown Prince stayed during his summer retreats. Everything was in order. Then, she balked at the idea.

Of course, she balked at the idea. But he'd sold himself on their holiday to such an extent that not even an anti-foreigner attack could sway his resolve. What better way to know for certain if they'd make a good pair than an extended liaison away from the obligations of daily life?

When her rejection smarted, he accused her of not being forthwith about having a lover. Another mistake.

Hopefully, the gift would adequately signify his regret and remind her of that moment in his office when their gazes had met, and he'd known without a shred of doubt they wanted the same thing. His hand even higher up her leg. He'd thought about that moment countless times. The possible ways it might have otherwise concluded lingered at the edges of his mind, beckoning him to indulge in daydreams of how they might have forced him to part with a ruined sofa.

His final mistake, as far as he knew—he'd probably made several more errors, but he wasn't schooled in women well enough to know—was failing to spend the past week wooing Marcelle in Tokyo. Had Nobu known she'd be upset about him not treating her to fine dinners and concerts, he would've forgotten about the trip. But he'd had his sights set on Karuizawa. Any man could take his lover to a restaurant or the theatre. Nobu was not any man. He wanted Marcelle to know that. The trip to Karuizawa would have shown her what he was capable of, giving her the perfect escape from everyday life. That was the kind of lover he'd be for her, one who'd make her forget her troubles and give her the pleasure she deserved.

But the trip was not to be.

"Good evening, Koide-*san*," Ryusuke called out as Nobu approached *La France Boutique*. "At first, I thought you were a troublemaker heading toward the store." Ryusuke contorted his face into the menacing snarl he'd presumably give the troublemaker, then broke into a grin. "Lo and behold, the troublemaker was you." He eyed the box. "Can I take that for you?"

Nobu shook his head. "I'll deliver it personally." He observed the usual theatre patrons, pub patrons, delivery boys, and European-suited workers who passed by the boutique at that time of the evening. "Anything awry on Ginza Boulevard, besides an overzealous guardsman doing double duty to protect a certain store assistant?"

Ryusuke flushed from forehead to chin. "Nothing around here. That gangster Hidekazu will keep watch from the top of the hour. Afterwards, another guardsman from the department store will come by." He scratched the side of his head. "That's when I'll escort Yumi-*chan* home."

"Has Renaud-*san* mentioned when she'll be leaving this evening?"

Before Ryusuke answered, Yumi-*chan* opened the front door of *La France Boutique* and stepped out. A rumble of admiration emerged from his guardsman.

Nobu nodded at the pert young woman who appeared in good spirits despite having been tied up by a criminal two days prior.

"Good evening, Koide-*san*." Yumi-*chan* came over and bowed. "Ryusuke." She added another bow, not as low, and rose with a light stain on her cheeks.

"How are you faring?" Nobu asked.

"I'm doing very well, thanks to your care. The doctor you sent, Ueda-*sensei*, said I was unharmed."

"That's good to hear. And Renaud-*san*?"

Yumi-*chan* nodded to the store's interior. "Busy preparing for the promenade. I offered to stay, but she insisted I rest." She gazed at Ryusuke with devotion that would make the gods weep with jealousy. "We're grateful to have Ryusuke and the other guardsmen keeping watch."

Nobu couldn't stand another minute of the lovey-dovey performance. "How about you escort Yumi-*chan* home, and I'll watch over the store until Hidekazu arrives?"

"I can't allow it. You're a busy man, Koide-*san*," Ryusuke said without tearing his eyes from Yumi-*chan*'s.

"You must make certain our Yumi-*chan* arrives home safely."

Ryusuke's smile could have kept every gas lamp in Ginza running for a week straight.

Nobu bid them good evening and entered *La France Boutique.*

Marcelle sat on a tall stool in front of her worktable. She held a needle in her graceful hand, elongating a shimmering line of thread, then pushing it back through diaphanous coral tulle.

"You shouldn't have left the door unlocked." Nobu placed the box on the table by the entrance.

"I have guardsmen stationed outside my store at all times. What's the use of a lock?" she said without looking up from her work. After lifting a seed pearl, she turned it in her hand. Her sapphire gaze must have found it acceptable because she proceeded to thread it into the fabric. She repeated the process with another seed pearl. Nobu sat on one of the wingback chairs and watched her go through the motions of attaching pearls. Contentment seeped into his bones. He could do this all night.

After a few minutes, she set the fabric aside and turned her gaze to him. The calm she'd induced with her sewing evaporated. In its place, a sizzling sensation penetrated every inch of him.

Colour sprang to the skin of Marcelle's neck. She felt it too. Thank the gods East and West he hadn't alienated her with that ill-proposed trip.

"Good evening, Nobu." Her voice was full of warmth. Already, he felt forgiven, and he hadn't even started apologising.

"Good evening, Marcelle."

Neither moved. He was mesmerised by the curve of her cheekbones and angle of her jaw in the soft glow of the lantern. Light and shadows, artistry and business, gentle curves and a core of steel, a Frenchwoman in Tokyo, Marcelle was a mosaic of contrasts. He was going to learn them all.

Shifting in the chair, Nobu recalled what he'd meant to say upon entering the boutique. "I apologise for my rudeness during our conversation the other night. I should've been more understanding about your needing to take care of the boutique and Yumi-*chan*. I apologise as well for not contacting you sooner. I was determined to whisk you away from town. Then I proposed we leave after the attack when the last thing you should've been thinking about was leaving town with a desperate suitor."

Marcelle placed the needle in a leather case. "Thank you for understanding. I'm inclined to accept apologies from desperate suitors." She gave him a shy grin. "Perhaps we could consider leaving town sometime in the future."

He hadn't realised he'd been clenching the armrest until she said the word "future." He loosened his grip. "Nothing would please me more." He rose from the chair and walked over to the table by the entrance. "I've brought something for your ankle."

"My ankle is fine. There's no need for any more ointments."

Nobu placed the sky-blue box with Koide Department Store written in gold script on the worktable.

With a knowing "ahh," Marcelle straightened up. "Would this be something for an ankle with expensive tastes?"

"You'll have to let me know if it meets the ankle's standards."

She opened the box and stripped away a bundle of white silk. His heart danced when her lips turned upward.

"They're exquisite," she said.

She took off her slippers and placed her feet into the most expensive leather boots in Japan. He'd given the shop owner in Yokohama the dimensions of Marcelle's foot based upon his recall of that day in his office. They were a perfect fit.

She strutted around the shop floor and glanced down at the fine leather. "My ankle has never had such magnificent boots. She wants to show them off. Would you care to join us for a bite? I'm famished."

Triumph filled him. A late dinner was more than he'd dared hope for this evening. He offered his arm. "It'd be my pleasure.

Marcelle took it with a smile.

She led them onto a narrow street off Ginza Boulevard, where he'd never thought to venture. They entered a small restaurant comprising a traditional Japanese-style room with a grill at its centre. A middle-aged couple greeted Marcelle like a beloved niece. She returned the greeting in familiar Japanese.

The wife encouraged them to take seats around the grill. Three men who had shops on Ginza Boulevard and a husband and wife who were the proprietor's cousins were already seated. Everyone addressed Marcelle with the affectionate nickname Maru-*chan* and expressed concern about the missing front window at *La France Boutique*. Marcelle gave them a story about an errant youngster throwing a rock through the window. The vandal was probably being apprehended by Hidekazu and his gang at this very moment, she assured them.

Nobu had to keep from staring incredulously at her flow of Japanese. Several times she produced rather coarse expressions he'd never heard uttered by a woman. Most of the women he conversed with either flattered or gave one-word answers, save his sister, Asako. But she cursed in English.

Marcelle introduced Nobu as her friend and the owner of Koide Department Store. He spent the next few hours telling the group how he came up with the idea for a European-style department store, about the construction process, and how he saw the future of Ginza. Their curiosity had no bounds. Over pieces of grilled fowl, he calculated the number of stones used in the store's west-facing facade. While pouring cups of *sake* for Marcelle and the owner's cousin, he described how they'd used electrical lighting to show off goods in the display cases.

He would've gladly stayed there all night with Marcelle beside him, her eyes flickering with amusement when he joked, her lips parting in admiration when he talked about how he'd convinced

Harrods' architects to visit Tokyo the previous year and advise on the department store interior. Their shoulders and elbows touched often, incidentally, it seemed. Yet, each time, rather than pull away, they seemed to move closer, as though correcting the error of permitting space between them.

"Your Japanese is better than mine," he remarked after they'd said their final good-byes to the owners and began walking down the side streets towards Ginza Boulevard. The contrast between the warmth of the restaurant and the cool night air sent a shiver through him. He pulled Marcelle even closer to his side.

She gave his arm a squeeze. "That's entirely false. You must know every level of polite speech. I converse with friends and store patrons. I always wonder whether I'm being overly polite or terribly rude."

"I doubt they care. They're thrilled to converse with a foreign *modiste* in Japanese."

"Not everyone in Tokyo is thrilled with the foreign *modiste*," she said darkly.

For the first time that night, Nobu recalled the attack on Yumi-*chan*. Marcelle must have thought about it all the time. "Has anyone bothered you these past few days? In Tsukiji? At the boardinghouse?"

"No one. We haven't been threatened." Hesitancy laced her voice.

Just because she hadn't been threatened didn't mean she didn't *feel* threatened. "Have you spoken with the police or the French Legation?"

They reached the crossing between Ginza Boulevard and the Tsukiji gates. Several foreign men speaking what sounded like Italian passed by.

Marcelle stiffened on his arm. "I'm still considering who to contact."

Her tone made him feel as though he was prying. But who was she relying upon for advice? Who was spurring her to action for the sake of her safety, her store? "You ought to contact someone soon. If not the Tsukiji police, then the Tokyo police. I have a friend in the bureau. He's a detective. He'll investigate the incident."

As they passed beneath the gas lamps in front of Tsukiji's gates, he noted the downward cast of her eyes and the stern set of her mouth.

"Yumi-*chan* has an aversion to police. She doesn't trust them. Besides, thanks to you, I'm guarded night and day."

It wasn't enough for Nobu. She was too vulnerable for his liking. "Shall I place a guardsman at your boardinghouse?"

Marcelle let out a small laugh. "The matron would have a fit. Believe me, I'm safe in Tsukiji."

They passed the university district still abuzz with late-night revellers and walked down a broad, tree-lined, and eerily quiet street. Despite the silence and shadows, the foreign quarter imparted a sense of security. Their gates, their policemen, their exotic languages and customs, and their attitude of superiority *vis-à-vis* the rest of Tokyo made them seem impenetrable. If anyone was going to attack Marcelle, it likely wouldn't occur here.

Yet she seemed upset about something.

Marcelle let out a sharp sigh. "I didn't tell you the entire truth about the window breaking."

The confession's preface brought an array of possibilities to mind: Marcelle or Yumi-*chan* had been assaulted. The store had lost money, or an irreplaceable sewing machine, or an important document with the full name of this Hamada-*san* whose identity still chafed like a pebble caught in his sandal.

Nobu had racked his brain thinking of which of the many Hamadas he knew could be assisting Marcelle. But they were all too old, too ugly, too greedy, too boring, or—he was willing to guess— too impotent. Likewise, Ishida-*san* had turned up nothing on a man of business called Hamada with ties to the textile industry or women's fashions. The man was elusive.

And, as far as Nobu could tell, he'd been of no assistance when a rock had been thrown through Marcelle's boutique window. Some benefactor.

He placed his hand over hers as they headed down the road toward Tsukiji's inlet. "You can tell me anything."

"The rock that broke the front window was attached to a message accusing me of seducing Japanese men to further France's interests."

Then it must have to do with that devil, Hamada. Someone believed Marcelle had seduced him into helping her open *La France Boutique* as a cover, or means, for passing information along to France. It sounded fanciful even to his own ears. But people still believed in aliens, demons, and dragons, so who was to say what counted as fanciful in the modern world?

Marcelle could be in danger as long as she continued to be partnered with the man. But what could he say to her? The mention of Hamada had bothered Marcelle the other night. He wasn't going to do that again.

"Such an accusation would be laughable had it been delivered in a less threatening manner," he said.

Marcelle huffed. "It's as absurd as pigs taking flight. But since you're stepping out in public with me, you ought to be careful. This deranged individual might conclude I was manipulating you. He might even come after you."

"I'm not concerned for myself. I may have been raised abroad, which my *otosan* believes has left me incapable of surviving any kind of physical altercation, but I can handle myself if this man approaches."

"Oh yes. You're a pugilist…right?"

The question made him want to corner some poor lout and give her a demonstration. Someone who absolutely deserved a beating. Why did everyone think him incapable of defending himself? He was a beast in the ring. Just because he used more of his brains than his brawn didn't mean he was lacking. "You should see my fists in action. That said, I hope you never have to."

They were nearing Marcelle's boardinghouse. He didn't want to part with her still upset. "Is there anything I can do for you or the boutique?"

"You've done plenty." She brought them to a stop before a line of maple trees heavy with leaves. "Are you planning to attend the promenade?"

He'd been planning to attend the promenade since the moment she'd asked. "Yes, and my sister, Asako, is going to accompany me. She prefers Western fashion."

Marcelle beamed. "Do you think she'd be open to clothing that combines Japanese and Western styles?"

"She was impressed by what you wore at the store opening. You may have seen her. She was the young lady sulking in the kimono because she was wearing a kimono."

"I understand her pain," Marcelle replied with a roll of her eyes. "I'm pleased you'll both be there." Then she met his gaze with an earnestness that made him feel as though he belonged exactly where he was standing.

"I'm glad we spent the evening together: glad you forgave me for being an oaf about the Karuizawa trip." He stopped himself from going on like a lovestruck fool, from saying how glad he was that someone so witty and sensual, so talented and creative, had even given him the time of day. How glad he was that she had the strength to survive a childhood void of love and the audacity to travel with a virtually unknown employer to a completely unknown place on the other side of the world, because in doing so, he'd been able to meet her.

She stepped toward him and laced her fingers through his. Her gaze travelled to his lips.

"Marcelle." He sighed her name at the same moment her mouth reached his. The lightness of her kiss, its tentativeness, its appearance without a word of warning stoked every nerve in his body.

He let go of her hands and reached to the back of her head, weaving his fingers into her silky locks. They kissed softly, purposefully, entering the dance slowly so as not to miss the first nibble, the opening lick, the first determined press.

Marcelle drifted a touch up to his shoulders, bringing them even closer. He loved how their bodies met. They were almost chest to chest, hip to hip.

He moaned raw desire into her mouth. She moaned back a pitch higher: surprise, pleasure, discovery, as though she'd come upon a hidden harbour of white sands and clear blue seas. Their lips seemed to part at the same moment and tongues meet in long swirling strokes that tasted like *sake* and the essence of desire.

She was unfettered lust and female prowess, a wicked, powerful combination that was like manna for his soul.

Nobu eased away to see her. Moonlight through the maple leaves illuminated her delicate nostrils flared with breath. Her half-lidded eyes were almost the colour of the night sky.

"One more?" he asked.

Marcelle responded with a light whimper and tilt of her head. They met in a rough, nearly blistering kiss, as though to mark one another with a promise for next time.

Then they both eased away, the kiss yet reverberating through the whole of him in a blaze of aching need.

Nobu mustered the composure to gently loop Marcelle's arm through his and assert a respectable distance between them as they walked through the boardinghouse front gate. "I'm glad the matron doesn't mind your returning late."

"She'll hold a grudge until I bring her a box of sweet bean cakes."

"We have several good brands at the department store. I'll send some on your behalf."

Marcelle let go of him and walked up the stone stairs to the front door. "Then all the boarders are going to think you're my lover." The observation sounded more like a question and his mind filled with answers of "yes" and "how."

Nobu liked having plans, perfectly made ones. Surrendering to Marcelle's preferences on the matter of how they'd become lovers would leave him delightfully anxious and half-aroused, which might be exactly what she wanted. "I have every intention of becoming your lover." A laugh nearly escaped him at the obviousness of the statement. "As you wish."

In the faint boardinghouse light filtering through the door, her face brightened. "I do, Nobu. I really do."

They bade one another a good night. The last thing he saw before she closed the door was a glimpse of leather boot. Worth every yen he'd spent. Hell, he'd have paid ten times as much if he'd known how the night would end.

CHAPTER NINE

Nobu

Nobu attempted to turn to his side, but his legs were tangled in the bedsheets, and he lacked the will to fight for their release. Stuck on his back, he drew a hand over his eyes. It provided a modicum of relief from the pounding in his head. He'd take it. He'd spent the previous night with his secretaries, drinking their way through what he faintly recalled as some of the best and the worst of Ginza's pubs. So thrilled were the bunch of miscreants to have their boss joining them for a night of carousing, they undertook to fill him with more *sake* than he'd consumed in the previous month.

The pain between his eyes intensified with Asako shouting something about *Okasan* violating her privacy. They'd awakened him with the blasted argument half an hour before and there were no signs of it abating. Nobu covered his ears with two pillows, then used one to cover his face. It cooled his swollen eyes. Then his thirst became unbearable.

After untangling his legs from the bedsheets, he rose and went over to the sink in the corner of the room. A dozen cold-water face dousings later, he was able to throw on a shawl-collared robe and leave his quarters for the dining room. As he'd expected from the late morning hour, it was blessedly empty. He slumped into his usual seat. The sunlight's violent reflection off the table's smooth wooden surface went straight to the tender matter vibrating within his skull.

To avoid a lifetime of blindness, he shifted his chair and waited for the maid to bring something that would slake his thirst.

At least the house had gone quiet. For some reason, *Okasan* and Asako had the decency to end whatever trifling mess had set them at odds on the Christian day of rest. For God's sake.

"Here you are, Koide-*san*." The maid placed a piping hot cup of roasted green tea on the table before him.

"Exactly what I wanted," he mumbled through cracked lips that swelled in the earthy brew's steam.

"Rice topped with fermented beans and raw egg is being prepared. Is there anything else you'd like?"

Seeing as the maid knew exactly what he wanted after a night of excessive drinking, then she also knew there was nothing else he wanted. As much as he wished he didn't have to say another word to anyone, he had to respond or be rude. "That will be all."

The first sip of tea left the back of his throat raw, which matched the feeling in his lungs from having spent most of the night with a tobacco pipe in hand. At least it was Sunday. The Japanese didn't have a sabbath day, or any leisure days for that matter. Having enjoyed the European sabbath days without any religious obligations to distract him from his hobbies and interests, Nobu thought everyone ought to have at least one day of rest every seven days or so. For that reason, he offered leisure days to his employees. To his dismay, they rarely took them.

So on Sundays, to demonstrate how leisure might be done, he meandered into the store after the midday meal. This gave him a chance to play chess with Asako or wander around one of Tokyo's many fascinating neighbourhoods, then deal with any incidents or customers demanding his attention.

Today, he was going to spend the morning hours recovering from the feeling that his head was going to explode. He also wanted to approach *Otosan* for advice.

For reasons he couldn't quite grasp—Yumi-*chan*'s aversion to the police, Marcelle's confusion over whether to use the French legation police or the Tsukiji police, fear they'd do nothing—Marcelle was reluctant to inform any authorities about the attacks at *La France Boutique*. Yet she was obviously in danger.

Nobu wanted to know how much danger and from where this danger might be coming. In his position at the Foreign Ministry, *Otosan* might have heard something about foreigners being accused of spying and might even have an idea about which group of foreigner-hating numbskulls was behind the accusations. Even if he hadn't heard anything, *Otosan* would give Nobu an opinion on how worried he ought to be about Marcelle.

Thankfully, it only took a few spoonfuls of beany-eggy rice with a dousing of soy sauce to settle his stomach. At least he'd had the wherewithal to empty its contents before stepping into the rickshaw on the way home.

Okasan clearing her throat coincided with his swallowing the final spoonful of breakfast porridge. He rested his spoon on the edge of the bowl, took a long sip of tea, then turned his gaze to where she stood at the threshold. "Good morning, *Okasan*."

"Have you recovered from last night's escapade?" Her voice lacked motherly warmth, which he found disappointing considering she'd been the one to rudely awaken him, or at least one of the two who'd rudely awakened him.

"I've had better days. Are you planning on telling me what you and Asako were yelling about on what should have been a peaceful Sunday morning?"

Okasan settled into the high-back chair across from him. The maid immediately placed an earthenware teacup before her. When she'd retreated, *Okasan* let out a sigh. "Your sister has exceeded the bounds of reason. You must speak to her. She'll listen to you."

"She never listens to a word I say. It's a point of pride that she refuses counsel from anyone who isn't trying to burn down Parliament." Actually, he and Asako took a lot of counsel from one another. Having grown up with few peers who understood the joys and disappointments of encountering new cities, cultures, and languages every few years, they'd become one another's closest playmates and confidants. During the family's last few years in London when he was in university, and she became involved with her suffrage friends, they'd spent less time together. In Tokyo, they'd seen even less of one another despite living under the same roof. Still, no one knew him as well as Asako. He was certain she felt the same.

Okasan was equally aware of their closeness.

"Those Parliament burners are the problem. Asako wrote to one of them in London. It was…scandalous." Red splotches appeared on *Okasan*'s rarely blemished cheeks.

"You read Asako's personal correspondence?"

Okasan shifted in her chair. "She left it on the desk in her room. I went in there to ascertain whether she planned to wear a kimono or Western dress to the Gakushuin sports festival. You know she doesn't share her wardrobe choices with me. But this event is extremely important. The emperor's nephew will be doing the relay with his classmates, which means the emperor and empress may very well be in attendance. Recently, on such outings, the imperial couple and their relations have been wearing Western dress. But the courtiers accompanying them are always in kimono. *Otosan*'s invitation to the grandstand is the surest sign we're close to receiving a title, and we cannot squander an opportunity to make a favourable impression with the imperial family. I'll be in kimono, and I was frankly hoping Asako would dress similarly even though we all know she prefers Western dress. But nothing had been pulled from her wardrobe. She knows how important this afternoon is to our family, yet she spent the morning penning a letter to one of those women."

"I assume the letter was in English."

"I can read English."

Nobu doubted it. *Okasan* could read French and a smattering of German. London was their final home abroad. By the time they arrived, *Okasan* had grown weary of devoting herself to foreign tongues. She was a passable speaker, but he was fairly certain she couldn't read. "What did the letter say?" he challenged.

The splotches of crimson on *Okasan*'s cheeks doubled in size. "It was a love letter."

"How do you know?"

"I saw the words 'love' and 'kiss,' and she wasn't talking about loving or kissing a man in Tokyo. The only conclusion I could reach was that Asako had kissed the woman to whom the letter was addressed."

Realization rang through his hazy brain—Asako had been romantically involved with one of her suffrage friends.

It made perfect sense. It answered questions Nobu had often pondered about his sister's lack of enthusiasm for the opposite sex. The more he thought about it, Asako's letter was less of a surprise than her carelessness in leaving it on her desk.

Unless she'd wanted *Okasan* to find the letter. He wouldn't put an act of passive rebellion past his sister. "What was Asako's response?"

Okasan lifted the teacup and murmured something he couldn't make out into the earthy brew. Then she took a small sip and placed it back on the table. "She said the letter was private and I shouldn't be reading her correspondence. She didn't deny its contents. Frankly, I don't hold an opinion on whatever childhood fancy your sister entertained while in London. Women grow out of these phases. Asako needs to forget about her so-called friends and find herself a husband. Sending love letters abroad will only interfere with the happiness she needs to find in her home country."

While he agreed in principle Asako would be better off forgetting about her friends in London and working toward finding an acceptable match in Japan, he'd recently gotten a better understanding of the heart's longings. He'd never forget kissing Marcelle outside her boardinghouse the other night. "These sorts of attachments take time to resolve."

"It's been almost five years since we returned to Tokyo. Time is running out for her to find a husband. No man wants a bride past the age of twenty-five."

"Asako knows all this," Nobu pointed out despite the obviousness of such a statement.

"Please tell her to be done with this unnecessary friendship. It'll only hurt her."

"I assume you told her this already."

Okasan examined her rounded nails. "I've only realised upon reflection what I ought to have said. I was angry at the time." She placed her hands on the table and let out a deep breath. "I slapped Asako and forbid her any future correspondence with anyone in London."

Nobu curled his fist around the teacup. Had he been there, he would've caught *Okasan*'s hand before she landed that slap. "Did she hit you back?"

"She knows better."

He would've guessed as much. Asako knew her place in the filial family. She wouldn't strike back.

Okasan gave him a pleading look. "Only you can talk sense into her. We leave for the sports festival in a few hours. I want her to join us."

***

As Asako entered the library an hour later, dressed in elegant, rose-hued silk, Nobu put down a book of Basho's breezy haiku poems, which had succeeded in taking the final edges off his *sake* hangover. "So, you're attending sports day?"

Asako gave him the same scowl she always wore whenever she was in kimono and collapsed into the wingback chair beside him without a measure of care about how she was wrinkling the luxurious garment. "It's important to *Okasan*. It's the least I can do after destroying her innocence."

"She's sorry."

Asako tapped the armrest. "I know. She's said so several times."

Asako met his gaze, then turned away. Avoidance wasn't like her. She was made of steel. Nothing bothered her. Except for mosquitoes. And honeybees. She was skittish around small animals like squirrels and hedgehogs.

He wasn't one of those animals.

The shame and frustrated longing she must have been feeling had landed their jabs, and those bastards were downright tough. He glanced down at the book of poems on the table beside him. "*Okasan* will make her peace with the letter. Nothing you wrote will change anything, really." He suspected he was talking about their relationship. But they didn't talk about their relationship. So, it was hard to tell.

Asako lifted the voluminous sleeves of her kimono as though seeing how far she could raise her arms with the silk still touching the armrests. "I realise as much."

Good. Then she realised things between them were the same as always.

Except he knew her better. Or just recognised something he'd known all along. When he was thinking clearer, he was going to revisit their time in London—the disagreements over nothing, the purposeful distance, the repeated falsehoods—that had stuck in his mind. He suspected they were going to show that years before, she was telling him, all of them, her secret.

Women fell in love with one another. Asako was one of those women. While he was convinced she'd meant for her secret to be revealed, that she'd come to find *Okasan*'s hovering, her interfering, and her god-awful matchmaking unbearable, the act of setting a secret free unleashed forces beyond one's will. It turned an isolated hillside cave into an appealing abode.

Knowing things were the same between them ought to make a dark hole in the middle of nowhere less appealing.

Asako met his gaze. "*Okasan* thinks I'm making myself miserable with my attachments abroad, and she's right. I am miserable. I want to be back with my friends in London." Tears shone in her eyes. "My heart wants what it cannot have."

Her unhappiness sank into his gut like a lead weight. "Then these feelings for your friend in London aren't a childhood fancy?"

Asako shook her head.

"*Okasan* thinks you'll grow out of it."

"That's not possible," Asako said with another dismal shake of the head.

She was miserable, and there was no obvious solution to her misery, only two incontrovertible facts. The Koide family wasn't returning to Europe, and Japanese women of her status, especially only daughters, were obliged to marry and have children. That was her filial destiny. She couldn't simply choose to be a *modiste* like Marcelle—not that Asako had any artistic talent—or a teacher or physician, which frankly seemed a better fit. Women of high status occasionally did such things, but this was only after fulfilling their duty to marry and bear children. After marriage, she might have some freedoms, but marriage was an inevitability.

"We both have a duty to marry. As much as we may hope otherwise, these will probably not be love marriages."

Asako gave a short laugh. "There's no chance of that happening."

"Then find a man, bear with him, have a few children. Then you can have the life you want. You'll find friends in Tokyo who want to destroy all society holds dear for women to get the vote."

Asako finally gave in to laughter, as he'd hoped, but it was too brief. "I'm not convinced I can bear the burden of attending to a husband."

Any man who wished Asako to submit contentedly to wifely duties would find himself royally disappointed. She could, however, give the appearance of wifely obedience, which a certain type of man might appreciate. "What if your husband was a good man, the sort who was kind and gentle, and fond of children, and whose preferences were similar to yours?"

Asako ran her fingers along the swirling brocade flowers on the armrest. "You mean a man who has friends with whom he shares the same sort of feelings as I do with my friends?"

"Exactly."

Asako let out a mulling sound. "I'd need your help in finding that kind of man."

"I can do that," he replied, then shrugged indifferently because if Asako felt like she had him wrapped around her little finger, who knows what she'd ask for next. "That way *Okasan* will be too busy with preparations for your wedding to bother me about my nuptials."

Asako pointed a finger straight at his face. "She wants you married first. Besides, it might be a while before you can find the right man for me." Asako gleamed with delight like she did when they practiced archery and she was the first to hit the bull's-eye.

"Is that a challenge, dear sister?"

Asako scowled. "No need to rush, dear brother. You're so busy at the store, after all."

The return to pleasant bickering made the world feel right. Judging by the brightness that had returned to Asako's face, she felt the same. He'd find her a husband with preferences like her own, although he'd have to be exceedingly discreet, which meant the task would take time.

"While you're looking on my behalf, you ought to keep your hands off foreign women with broken ankles."

How the bloody hell did she know?

He'd never mentioned the incident to Asako, and Marcelle's ankle hadn't been broken. "Who told you that?"

"Your secretary is Ishida-*san*, right? He told his *otosan*, who told our *otosan*, who naturally informed *Okasan* you were fawning over a foreign woman's feet."

"I take it *Okasan* wasn't amused."

"Not even the slightest hint of a smile."

"I wonder how she'll feel when I announce we're engaged to marry," he said with utmost seriousness because Asako's reaction was going to be one for the ages.

She swayed and hugged her sides as she gave in to the hysterics. It was exactly what he'd wanted. She needed that kind of laugh.

Yet, it irritated him. Marcelle was an accomplished, educated woman, and alluringly beautiful. Any man would be fortunate to marry her.

Asako gasped and bolted upright. "You're serious."

"What if I was?"

"*Okasan* would more readily accept my spinsterhood than your marrying a foreigner. That's why we had to leave London. Foreign spouses were off the table." *Okasan* had insisted on their return to Tokyo after he'd finished his studies at Oxford for the express purpose of him taking a Japanese bride.

"I'm joking, and you know it." For some reason, his tone contained a hint of disappointment.

"Dear brother, you have a *tendre*." Once again, she rudely pointed a finger at his face. "Look at you. You share the same misery as me, and like me, you must perish the thought."

Asako was right, but she'd forced him to the offensive. "We're obliged to marry. There's nothing in our filial obligations that says we cannot marry a foreigner. Christian Japanese are doing it all the time. I could very well marry Mademoiselle Renaud."

"*Okasan* would never allow it."

"*Okasan* would bend if I insisted."

Asako gave an exaggerated shudder. "*Okasan* would make your life, and your bride's life, a living nightmare. You may be her favourite, but she'll never accept foreign blood in the family. Pursue the Nagahara girl. She'll make an obedient daughter-in-law. *Okasan* will be content with a viscount's progeny, and she won't mind when my husband and I fail to give her grandchildren."

The thought of going through the ritual of wooing the Nagahara girl drained him of the precious little energy he had that morning. "She doesn't appeal."

"In that case, I'll find a bride for you while you are seeking a husband on my behalf."

"Perish the thought, dear sister. *Okasan* would no sooner have a member of the Pantaloon Society as daughter-in-law than scale Mt. Fuji."

Asako laughed heartily. "I'd never go to the Pantaloon Society for your wife. You're more of a Bloomer Academy kind of suitor."

Nobu gave her an unamused glare. "I told Renaud-*san* you'd attend her fashion promenade this Friday. Are you still able?"

"Usually, I'm not particular about fashion, but for my *future sister-in-law*, I suppose I could do it."

Nobu ignored Asako's descriptor and considered his list of promenade attendees. Friends' wives had said they'd attend. Several of the department store clerks would be there to note trends for the upcoming design cycle. The newspapermen he'd encouraged to report on the event promised they'd be there, too. The day was going to be perfect. "Excellent," he replied. "What will you tell *Okasan*?"

"I'll tell her I'm going to spy on her behalf, and report all the scandalous things foreigners do at their unorthodox events."

"You may have to do a bit of invention."

"I shall use my imagination to its fullest on the gracefully clad beauties. After all, I must please *Okasan*," she said with a twinkle in her eye.

Several hours later, as he passed through the gilded doors of Koide's, he suddenly realised what Asako had meant by "using her imagination." When he did, he inwardly complimented her on an exceptional double entendre.

***

Satisfied his employees could finish the day's business without him, Nobu returned home earlier than usual with a mind to speak with *Otosan*. The family had already dined, and the sky was clear as a bell, so Nobu climbed the flight of stairs to the rooftop terrace where he found *Otosan* with a telescope close by.

Since returning to Japan, space art had become his passion. During their years in Europe, *Otosan* would gather his paints and brushes and venture into the forest to capture a rare species of tree, flower, bird, or woodland creature. The demands of his Tokyo life made that sort of escape less convenient, so he'd turned his attention to the heavenly bodies. On clear nights, he retreated to the rooftop terrace, fixed his telescope on an astronomical spectacle, and recorded scenes on his sketchpad that he later brought to life on the easel in his study.

"What is it tonight?" Nobu approached the telescope tied to the terrace railing.

Otosan nodded at the telescope. "Take a look."

Nobu peered through the eyepiece and the familiar brown and yellow striations of Jupiter filtered through. "That's quite an angle."

"No photograph could capture the contours. Not to mention the dimensions of that magnificent red spot. Only the human eye can do it justice." *Otosan* had strong opinions about using photography on the night sky.

"Will you begin drawing this evening?" When *Otosan* had an unusually good view, he'd stay up all night sketching and painting.

"Not tonight. I'm going to enjoy a good night's rest now that *Okasan* and Asako have made peace." Otosan rolled his eyes despairingly at the heavens. "I thought that fight would never end, but your sister was on her best behaviour at the sports festival, and your *okasan* is going to forget that her daughter has been sending love letters abroad."

"To a woman," Nobu said because he wanted to see *Otosan*'s reaction.

"These things pass. It's a phase. Your sister will outgrow it."

Nobu doubted that, but he held on to his words. This was a debate that time would resolve for all of them. "How are dealings at the Ministry?"

Otosan put down his sketchbook and picked up his pipe. During a long exhale of smoke, he looked out at the flickering lights dotting the city. Judging by the vigour in his step since returning to the maelstrom of Tokyo politics, Nobu guessed *Otosan* was less disappointed to have left Europe than pleased to be in the thick of the Foreign Ministry's plans for their nation.

"It's a seething ocean of discontent. The Ministry has been tasked with rallying allies for a future clash with Russia. Our little islands are going to take on a Western power. We're on the brink of pan-Asian rule, a dream our ancestors couldn't even begin to imagine. One day our emperor could rule over China. But first we must defeat the great Russian bears. How we go about this task is the cause of much debate, not all of it friendly."

"The wages of war are high." Nobu had studied enough history to prefer wars waged between foreign markets over those waged between armies of young men.

"So are the profits," *Otosan* said with a penetrating stare at the city lights as though he could make them flicker at will. Nobu pitied the unfortunate soul who attempted to outmanoeuvre men such as *Otosan* who seemed to know exactly how the chips would fall before the cards had even been dealt.

He turned to Nobu. "Did you come up tonight for the thunder god's planet or to hear me opine about foreign affairs?"

"Neither. I came to ask what you thought of a situation that has befallen an acquaintance of mine, a foreign woman."

"The one with the broken ankle?" *Otosan* raised a brow.

"I heard you've been talking to Ishida-*san*'s *otosan*. Fortunately, the ankle is not broken. But one of our foreigner-hating citizens took it upon himself to throw a rock through the front window of her store. Then a few days ago, her assistant was attacked, probably by the same criminal."

Otosan hit his tobacco pipe against the terrace railing, sending a clump of ash to the floorboards. He stamped out the embers, then walked over to his table and filled the pipe again. "Did she survive?"

"She's fine. She's also Japanese, which I suppose could've made a difference to the lunatic. It seems the attack was meant to deliver a message to my acquaintance, the Frenchwoman, Renaud-*san*."

Otosan gave the tobacco a light press. "Let me guess, he told her to leave Japan?"

"He accused her of being a spy for France."

"What else did the man say?"

"Something about her seducing Japanese men. Renaud-*san* worries this man might come after me for my association with a French agent."

Otosan lit the tobacco and gave it a few puffs. "Every day there are rumours of another assassination plot against one of our ministers for destroying the Japanese way of life. For our worship of the West. It's utter foolishness to wish for a return to an era of isolation and swordsmanship, especially when we're poised to rule over vast swaths of our dear planet."

"Then you think Renaud-*san* and I are in danger?"

Otosan took a drag from his pipe and exhaled a cloud of smoke into the cool night air. "Doubt it at your peril. I'd hate to see anyone approach you with a weapon. You'd succumb in an instant." *Otosan*'s chief complaint about his children's education abroad was their lack of training in the martial arts. Nobu protested that he'd emerged victorious from plenty of schoolyard scuffles and had done his fair share of boxing at Oxford.

Otosan wouldn't acknowledge either.

"The brute is welcome to come after me," Nobu said with confidence that earned him a raised brow from *Otosan*. "I've entrusted Ryusuke with keeping watch over Renaud-*san*'s store. But I'm still concerned. She's reluctant to go to the police."

"The Japanese police won't do anything, and the foreign authorities can't do much. Do *you* have any reason to suspect Renaud-*san* of being an agent for France?"

Nobu bristled at the question, even though he'd known *Otosan* would ask. "She doesn't profess any allegiance to France, nor does she aim to keep a low profile. She lives a very public life. Her store is on Ginza Boulevard."

"Giving her access to elite members of society. Sometimes the best hiding place is in plain sight."

"True." Still, Marcelle was putting on a promenade this week. Spies might hide in plain sight, but they didn't draw unnecessary attention to themselves. Her mysterious benefactor and former lover, Hamada, however, plainly wanted to hide. "Do you happen to know of a Hamada-*san*, a man of business who makes investments in women's boutiques?"

"I know several Hamada-*sans*. None of whom are investing in anything save their *sake* and their mistresses." *Otosan* let out a snicker.

Marcelle had been a mistress, but that wasn't something Nobu was going to bring up with *Otosan*. "Renaud-*san*'s benefactor is a Hamada-*san*."

"Is it possible he's in cahoots with her? And with France by extension? European nations find it inconceivable that a small island nation on the outskirts of Asia could become a world power. They're scrambling to learn as much as they can about us. A beautiful woman often does the trick."

Nobu tapped his arm against the terrace railing. He didn't like hearing *Otosan* indulge these accusations even though he'd known that was exactly what *Otosan* would do. "Marc—I mean, Renaud-*san*, isn't trying to lure anyone into giving information to France."

"Don't fret too much." *Otosan* waved a hand dismissively. "Most likely she's become the target of a misguided fool."

Hopefully not a dangerous one.

Otosan dumped his tobacco and gave the smouldering mass a definitive thwack with the underside of his wooden slipper. Then he turned to Nobu with a sly raise of brow. "I take it you're attracted to European women?"

Nobu smiled sheepishly. "I won't deny it."

"I had a mistress in Berlin and another in London. Neither relationship lasted more than a few months. They were young women, eager to experience the world beyond their borders with a man from the Orient." *Otosan* laughed. "It was good fun while it lasted."

"I knew about Lady Higgins in London. Do you recall the time I saw you at the opera?"

Otosan chuckled. "I can still see your face. You looked as though you'd spent all day picking weeds in the sun. Does your Frenchwoman bare nearly half her chest when dressed for a night on the town?"

Nobu twinged with lust at the image of Marcelle's breasts brimming over her dress. "Sadly, she's fond of the kimono neckline."

Otosan laughed heartily. "We all must bear our burdens. Yours, my son, are the envy of most men."

"I don't doubt that. I also don't doubt that you'd appreciate my leaving you alone with the thunder god. I'm going downstairs for an evening meal."

"*Bon appétit.* That is what the French say, isn't it?"

"I believe so. Good night, *Otosan*."

On the way downstairs, Nobu luxuriated in the feeling of a burden having been lifted. Marcelle wasn't in serious danger from foreigner-hating lunatics. The Hamada fellow was another story entirely. He'd failed to keep her safe, and she wouldn't be safe as long as he was her benefactor. She needed to end their association. She could accept other investors. He'd be happy to arrange meetings between Marcelle and Koide's investors. He doubted she'd accept investment from him, at least not yet.

For now, she'd accepted Italian leather boots and his invitation to Karuizawa sometime "in the future." He wasn't going to push his luck.

CHAPTER TEN

Marcelle

Autumn gusts across Ueno Park sent Yumi-*chan*'s hat askance.

"Don't move or you'll muss your hair." Marcelle reached into her satchel for the bag of pins. Fortunately, they were on top. Yet another thing going unexpectedly right. She had a good feeling about today.

The cloudy skies yet permitted sunshine to peek through. The winds were picking up, but the models' clothes and hats would remain in place with the proper application of pins. She added another to Yumi-*chan*'s hat and declared, "*Voilà.*"

The promenade should begin at noon as scheduled. Yumi-*chan*, three women from Suki's magazine, and Marcelle would walk in her latest designs along a winding stone pathway under boughs laden with autumn-hued leaves. Inspiration for the new designs had come from the Paris magazines wherein models wore dresses with long, fluted sleeves and small bustles to enhance the waist. Nothing being sold in Tokyo was nearly as fashionable.

Marcelle had ushered the models to a cluster of cherry trees about an hour prior to make certain their dresses, hats, stockings, and shoes were impeccable. She lifted the front of the long cape shielding her dress from prying eyes. It was cut from an oxblood red kimono silk with a pattern of golden fans. A perfect garment for the New Year celebrations. Every fold was crisp, every lace overlay taut against the silk.

"Time?" she called out to Yumi-*chan*.

"Eight minutes until noon," Yumi-*chan* called back from her adjustments to a model's hem.

Marcelle grimaced at a loose thread along the edge of her sash, then tucked it under the fabric. The promenade was promising to be a success beyond what she'd dared hope, mostly thanks to Nobu, the man with the most passionate kisses in Tokyo and, as it turned out, *La France Boutique*'s most ardent supporter.

He and his darling sister had arrived half an hour before. She wore a dark blue dress under a jacket of the same color with silver stripes down the front, giving her the appearance of a jaunty lieutenant. They'd waved at Marcelle and her models, then greeted numerous people who arrived thereafter, presumably his friends or department store patrons, and newspapermen from Tokyo's major English and Japanese papers. He must have invited at least a dozen attendees.

Suki and Griff had arrived at around the same time with the members of her magazine staff who weren't modeling in the promenade. Then Suki's mother came with Professor and Mrs. Garrick, the American couple who'd opened their home to Suki and her mother after Suki's father had abandoned them for France. A half-dozen young foreign women from Marcelle's boardinghouse and several young Japanese women from Yumi-*chan*'s were also present, along with quite a few *La France Boutique* patrons.

Marcelle itched to impress every one of them with her designs.

"Time," she called to Yumi-*chan*.

"Noon," Yumi-*chan* called back.

"*Allons-y*," Marcelle replied. Yumi-*chan* took her place at the head of the models' procession and led them to the starting area where the crowd had gathered. Throwing off her cape, she gave her ensemble a twirl. A smattering of applause hung in the air as she sauntered down the pathway.

Marcelle had told the models to compose themselves as though their incomparable beauty had the city of Tokyo on its knees. Each one of them followed her orders to the letter. Then it was Marcelle's turn. Summoning the haughty demeanor of a daringly stylish Parisian mademoiselle, she flung off her cape, placed a hand on her hip, and followed her fellow models.

Nobu stood at the pathway's edge, his stature blocking the view of those behind him. She winked as she passed. He responded with an encouraging nod. Then she continued onward, pleased to see how many of Tokyo's citizens happened to be enjoying an afternoon in the urban park and, coincidentally, her promenade. They paused their strolls and whispered to one another while pointing and nodding at the dresses. Around one bend, she overheard a young woman comment on the promenade's "unique and breathtaking designs." Marcelle nearly broke stride to throw her arms around the mademoiselle.

The models in front of Marcelle reached the turnaround ahead. She considered urging them to walk farther, then decided against a sudden change of plans as it might ruin the serene, elegant ambiance they'd succeeded in creating.

Just as she was about to take the turnaround herself, a man rose from a park bench and walked toward her with determined strides. He wore baggy blue pants tapered at the ankle and a tunic with rolled-up sleeves like any other day laborer. But under his wide-brimmed hat, his eyes were calm and intelligent. He curled his lips into an adoring smile.

She would've recognized him anywhere.

"Jiro," she said and stopped. The lines on his face had deepened. His cheekbones had sharpened. Her dear benefactor, esteemed mentor, and former lover looked as though he'd aged a decade.

Two years ago, when she'd met Jiro Hamada, she'd been writing fashion reports—terribly written pieces of drivel—for *Tokyo Women's Magazine*. That day, she'd gone to Yokohama for a promenade in the hilly district. Upon arriving back at Tokyo's

Shimbashi station, rain was coming down in sheets. She almost reached the hooded cover of a rickshaw outside the station when a man several decades her senior stepped in front of her. The runner suggested a game of rock-scissors-paper to settle the matter of who got the rickshaw. Before Marcelle could insist she deserved the rickshaw by virtue of her membership in the fairer sex—a card she played when necessary—the man asked where she was going. When she replied Tsukiji, he suggested they share the rickshaw as he was also heading to the foreign quarter.

Months later, he admitted to lying that day in Shimbashi. He'd been on the same train from Yokohama and had followed her out of the station, determined to make her acquaintance. As a lover, he was impeccable. To a fault. Outside of bed, he taught her about Japan's history and culture, the everyday customs, the ways of thinking and feeling that she'd observed but hadn't made sense of. He kept lists of every gift and favor he received to reciprocate in kind, no less and no more. Any less would make him seem ungrateful, any more would create a debt. She learned that the love of his *okasan* was the greatest he'd known. Fear of his *otosan* had turned to hatred but had made a better *otosan* of Jiro.

Most significantly, he pointed out things about herself that she'd always known but hadn't been wise enough to see. She was an incomparably talented *modiste*. She needed the pace of a thriving global city, Tokyo in particular, to stimulate her designs. Matters of money and business came naturally to her. She'd make *La France Boutique* a grand success.

He gave her the funds and practical support to open *La France Boutique*. After she returned his initial investment, she shouldered all the store's expenses and paid him a small sum each month for maintaining the licenses and permits. She became a woman of independent means, because Jiro had wanted the satisfaction of showing Tokyo elites that with the right guidance and investment, a woman—a foreigner no less—was capable of business success.

For Jiro, she broke her vow of never becoming a man's mistress, and she had no regrets. She wouldn't punish herself for being a pragmatist.

"Are you well?" she asked.

"I am," he said in that calm, authoritative way that put her at ease. Then he stepped forward in the direction she was headed. Likewise, she resumed her stroll along the pathway. "You look beautiful, Maru-*chan*," he said, using the affectionate nickname he'd given her. "The dresses are a testament to your talent."

His words made her swell with pride. Without altering her poised presentation, she spoke only loud enough for him to hear. "Why have you come, dressed like you should be building bridges and railways?"

"Didn't Nomura-*san* tell you to expect me?"

"He told me to await your response. I thought he'd send along your message to the boutique."

Jiro let out a deep breath. "I've made several attempts to meet with you at the boutique, but your many guardsmen make it impossible to do so discreetly. I feel terribly about what happened to Yumi-*chan*. I was incredibly relieved to hear that she was mostly unharmed. I'm afraid my enemies have made *La France Boutique* a target."

Marcelle slowed her pace to prolong their time together. Soon they'd leave the tree-lined area, and she couldn't be seen conversing with a laborer. "Your enemies? Why would they make us a target?"

"They want to draw me out of hiding."

"Well, they certainly go to incredible lengths for you, don't they? Tying up Yumi-*chan* like that." Anger threatened to unravel her composure. She was angry at Jiro for being absent when she needed him. Even more so, she was angry that Yumi-*chan* had been attacked *because* of him. "They accused me of being a spy. Why would they do such things to draw you out of hiding?"

"That's too long a story for this leg of your promenade."

"Are you in danger?"

"This isn't the place to discuss it." Sadness and resignation played in his voice. It made her stop in her tracks. And it made her sad.

"Where's your model's pose, Maru-*chan*? You look like you're about to burst into tears. I don't want you fretting on my behalf. I came here to assure you that Nomura-*san* will always be available to provide any help you need. But there's something else you need to know. It's about Tokyo's department store tycoon, Koide." Jiro's jaw tightened.

Had he seen Nobu at the start of the promenade? Had he caught the way Nobu was looking at her? In all their time together, Jiro had never elicited a promise of fidelity, and they hadn't been lovers in nearly a year. She'd thought for certain their intimacies were over. "Koide-*san* and I have been seeing one another in a way. I wouldn't do anything to hurt you. We hadn't been lovers in ages, and I was thinking—"

Jiro's laugh made her pause.

"That's not what I meant, Maru-*chan*. Our affair ended long before I left. This has nothing to do with us. I saw you and Koide together this week. It looked like you were stealing away. Perhaps for a night of passion? Trust me, you cannot continue this affair. End it before he hurts you. He's using you for reasons having to do with his family and politics. Be assured of this. The attack on Yumi-*chan* and the rock through the front window were the work of his family. They're trying to draw me out of hiding. And it's working. Here I am, because of the trouble they caused you. I'm telling you to stay away from the man. For your safety."

Marcelle could barely take in breath. What Jiro said made no sense. Nobu was trying to prevent the attacks on *La France Boutique*. He was more concerned about her safety than she was. "Koide-*san* assisted me after the attack. The guardsmen at the boutique are from his department store." As the words came from her mouth, she realized how damning they sounded. Was Ryusuke really keeping watch at *La France Boutique* or was he waiting for

Jiro to arrive? What of Ryusuke's feelings for Yumi-*chan*? He seemed to be in love with her. Was it merely a ruse?

"Of course, those are his guardsmen," Jiro said gently. "They're studying you for the best time to attack, the best way to provoke my presence. They're only going to get more violent the longer I stay away."

But why would Nobu go to such lengths to draw Jiro out of hiding? He could have simply befriended her with a dinner at the Imperial Hotel's French restaurant like most suitors, bought her a stylish brooch, and even bedded her at a lover's inn, if he was inclined. But Nobu had pursued her with the most expensive boots in Japan and invited her—practically begged her—to go on a trip to the mountains. He'd brought newspapermen to her promenade. And his sister. Was Jiro suggesting she was in on the scheme? "Can you at least tell me why you're at odds with the Koide family?"

Jiro let out a deep breath. "It'd benefit the Koide family to rid the Foundation Party of my influence."

Marcelle might have heard of a Foundation Party in Japan's national Diet, but Nobu had never mentioned it. "Koide-*san* is a man of business, not a politician. I don't think he even knows who you are." Nobu hadn't known Jiro's name when she'd mentioned it. He could've been pretending not to know, but his response hadn't struck her as disingenuous.

Jiro grumbled under his breath. "He knows exactly who I am. You must trust me in this. He's going to hurt you. I hope that hurt is done only to your heart and not to your person."

She trusted Jiro as much as anyone. He'd never betrayed her. He'd kept his promises. But he was suggesting that not only had Nobu lied to her in denying knowledge of Jiro, but also that he was capable of causing harm to her store, to her assistant, to herself. None of that rang true, not one iota. Nobu was a man of business who took care of dozens of employees and had taken care of her when she'd been in need. His motives were pure, of that she had no doubt.

She wanted to tell Jiro all of this, but there was a promenade to finish, friends to greet, and a man waiting who cared about her and might start worrying that she'd gotten lost in the woods. "I have to keep going. The promenade is coming to an end."

"I'm sorry to have upset you during your promenade. If only I'd been in Tokyo these past few months, then I would have been able to keep him away. I only want to protect you." Affection filled his voice.

"I know you want the best for me."

"I've told Nomura-*san* to provide a new window for the boutique and to give you money for that sewing machine you bought. He said it allows you to complete orders in half the time." Marcelle opened her mouth to protest that she could afford the Singer, but he silenced her with a raise of his hand. "If you need anything else, let him know."

"Will I see you again?"

"I'm leaving Tokyo. Tell Nomura-*san* if you have any more trouble of any kind. If you even suspect it." He inched in the opposite direction.

"Take care of yourself," Marcelle called softly to his retreating figure.

Jiro raised a hand but didn't look back.

Marcelle's heart raced. She was utterly baffled. While she couldn't believe Nobu was using her, she felt certain something was amiss with Jiro. She had to push him from her mind, focus on the promenade. Finally, her heartbeat slowed, and her trembling hands calmed. Setting her mouth into a smile as graceful as autumn leaves drifting to the ground, she headed toward the promenade's start.

Cheers of congratulations from the assembled greeted her. Suki's photographer already had the models lined up. Marcelle joined them in posing for the camera, then answered reporters' questions about the style of her designs and the work she did at the boutique. Patrons and friends told her how lovely the models had been and about the enthusiastic response from passersby. Suki's mother's effusive compliments reduced Marcelle to tears.

The rain clouds held off. All in all, the promenade had been a stunning success.

As she was bidding farewell to a divorcée who periodically took up residence at the Hotel Metropolis, Nobu and Asako came over. He introduced Asako, and they congratulated Marcelle on the promenade and complimented the dresses.

"I didn't realise you were *the* Marcelle Renaud who wrote for *Tokyo Women's Magazine*. I've read every page of every issue," Asako said with far more enthusiasm than had ever been voiced for Marcelle's time at the magazine.

"I'm an awful writer. They were glad to see me go."

"Nonsense. Your friend Suki Spenser said they all miss you terribly."

"Suki is a dear friend. She's also a liar." Marcelle shot a mock look of exasperation at Suki, who was chatting with a newspaper reporter. "So, that was what you all were discussing for so long?" It seemed like every time she'd turned around, Nobu and Asako had been deep in conversation with Suki and Griff.

Asako played with the hilt of her parasol. "We talked about the magazine. Then Spenser-*san*'s husband and my brother realised how many of the same people they knew from their Oxford days. After that revelation, that was all they wished to discuss." Asako rolled her eyes.

"You were right there, reminiscing along with us about England," Nobu said to his sister with the same feigned annoyance. "Mostly, we talked about what a fantastic promenade you put on."

"You deserve much of the credit. None of those newspapermen would've been here had you not asked them."

"They were easy to convince. You're designing the best dresses in Tokyo. There's nothing comparable." The admiration—nearly adoration—in his gaze contradicted everything Jiro had said. If all

Nobu wanted from her was a means of forcing a political enemy out of hiding, he didn't have to look at her with that much ardor.

"I'm going to observe the autumnal foliage, if you need me," Asako said breezily and left Marcelle and Nobu alone.

He stepped closer. The spice of his cologne made her head swirl. The last time they'd been this close, he'd left her boneless with deep, purposeful kisses. He hadn't just kissed her, he'd consumed her. "You look stunning. When I saw you walking the promenade, I wanted to whisk you away."

"To the mountains?"

"Wherever you'd like." Was he relenting on the grand romantic adventure in Karuizawa for a casual romp in the city? That was exactly what she'd wanted. Except, now that it was within her grasp, she felt…disappointed.

Escaping Tokyo with Nobu was the far more intriguing prospect. The boutique was guarded. Yumi-*chan* had all the protection she could ever need in the form of strapping Ryusuke.

"I envision us in the mountains." Even more so, she pictured their bodies entangled in positions that would leave her dizzy and eager for more. Exactly what she needed. "Before we go, I'll need to made headway on the orders we'll hopefully receive after the promenade."

Nobu pouted. "You're going to get hundreds of orders. It'll be the middle of winter before we get to Karuizawa."

Marcelle laughed at his desperate performance. "I have a new sewing machine, and I'm planning to hire a number of seamstresses depending on the promenade orders. We could leave in a week or two."

Nobu took her gloved hand and brushed his lips against her fingertips. Impeccably elegant and undeniably masculine. The combination threw her off-kilter. He was perfect.

Too perfect? Jiro's voice rang through her head.

"I'll wait as long as you need," Nobu replied.

Yes, he was too perfect. But that didn't mean he wanted anything more than a highly pleasurable love affair.

Which was exactly what she wanted from him.

CHAPTER ELEVEN

Marcelle

Marcelle turned onto a shopping street in Shimbashi and basked in the warmth of the sunny side of the street as she passed modest storefronts for rice brokers, metal works, tofu sellers, seamstresses, and a toy store with an assortment of spinning tops, wooden ball mallets, and playing cards. On a hook beside the door of Nomura-*san*'s one-room office, a wooden sign announced he provided legal and accounting services.

Jiro's agent was an expert on the intricate bureaucracies and ever-changing laws of the modern government. Yet, his neat kimonos, impeccable manners, and worn abacus always at hand belonged to the shogun's Japan.

She'd known him almost as long as she'd known Jiro. He'd assisted her in preparing the documents and obtaining the permissions she'd needed to open *La France Boutique*. He continued to advise her on keeping track of income and expenses. Of late, he'd become the liaison between her and Jiro, because, unlike her, Jiro trusted Nomura-*san* with knowledge of his whereabouts. She wasn't resentful. The two had known one another for decades. They had the sort of relationship where one knew what the other was thinking without a word being exchanged.

Nomura-*san* lowered his nearly bald head in a polite bow. "Welcome, Renaud-*san*." His weathered face was set in the serene expression he always wore. "Please sit. I'll bring tea."

Whenever she visited, they sipped tea in silence for a few minutes after she arrived, then proceeded to whatever business had brought her. Nomura-*san* broke today's silence by telling her about a nearby glass factory where the boutique's new window was being crafted.

Marcelle thanked him for making the arrangements and for the money for the sewing machine. Collecting it had been the reason for her trip to Shimbashi.

Nomura-*san* handed her a thick envelope. Knowing Jiro, he'd given her twice what she needed, and she was grateful. The promenade had generated dozens of orders. She'd use the extra money to purchase another sewing machine and hire a few more temporary seamstresses. She'd already hired two capable young women. Still, the work hadn't lessened by any noticeable degree.

"Hamada-*san* wants you to produce at the highest possible level," Nomura-*san* said, his voice full of the reverence he always showed for his employer.

"I hope to make him proud. He came to the promenade last week. He was in the disguise of a day laborer." She spoke without reservation. Jiro and Nomura-*san* didn't seem to keep anything from one another.

Nomura-*san* guffawed. "I wish I'd seen it. He had much to do in Tokyo. I hated him being here, but he insisted on coming. One of his most pressing concerns was the attacks at your boutique. He went there several times to check on the broken window, but, apparently, you're surrounded by guardsmen."

"I am, and I think they must be doing their job because we haven't had any more attacks on the boutique." Marcelle pondered the wisdom of bringing up Nobu with Nomura-*san*. He doubtless shared Jiro's wariness about Nobu and would be disappointed she hadn't distanced herself from the department store tycoon.

If anything, since the promenade, she and Nobu had grown closer. Knowing she was busy with dress orders, he visited the boutique every day to present her, Yumi-*chan*, and the new seamstresses with something from the department store, usually Japanese sweets and tins of tea. He even brought a set of gold embroidery needles. Not only were the needles gorgeous, but their sturdiness made detailed work much easier.

He never visited for long enough to become a nuisance. They shared tidbits of conversation. She learned little things about him like his fondness for leather satchels and his mother's aversion to pickled plums. She told him stories about her time as a lady's maid for the American envoy and of her relationship with Suki's mother.

None of his actions left any doubt about his intentions in wooing her. Jiro was wrong about Nobu and his family. Might Nomura-*san*, despite his loyalty, agree his boss was mistaken?

Marcelle took another sip of tea and returned the earthenware cup to the table. "I've recently become friends with Nobuyuki Koide. He opened a department store in Ginza. We're neighbors. But Hamada-*san* expressed misgivings about the friendship. He believes the Koide family are his enemies."

Nomura-*san* lifted his plentiful brows and exhaled between his teeth. "Hamada-*san* is concerned about you. He and the Koide family have been at odds over the years. He feels Koide-*san* is using you to gather information about his business dealings and personal liaisons."

"By attacking the boutique?"

"By seducing you. In doing so, Koide-*san* learned about the boutique and your relationship with Hamada-*san*. Then his family realized that by attacking the boutique, they could get Hamada-*san* back to Tokyo."

Marcelle had spent the past week telling herself Jiro was delusional in thinking the Koide family wanted to harm him. Hearing levelheaded Nomura-*san* say as much brought back the vexing questions she'd had when Jiro had cornered her in the park. "Why do they want him back in Tokyo? Would they harm him?"

"They want to shame him in front of his countrymen and the emperor. Once they get him back to Tokyo, they can prosecute him with made-up charges and watch him hang."

The image of Jiro in a hangman's noose was inconceivable. "I didn't realize he was in such danger."

"He has good reason to be scared of what will happen if they find him."

The fear in his eyes at the promenade haunted her every day when her thoughts drifted to his sage business advice, or she used the new sewing machine, or when she caught sight of the heirloom kimonos he'd lent her. His life was in danger, and she'd do anything in her power to protect him. Except for the only thing he'd asked of her. To stop seeing Nobu.

She trusted Jiro. She also couldn't fathom Nobu, or Asako, or their parents, who by Nobu's accounts seemed warm—if a bit demanding—having anything to do with a political stunt orchestrated to end a man's life.

Her heart told her Nobu wanted her for pleasure, for a fiery affair while he anticipated life with the perfect Japanese woman. That was the extent of it. He wouldn't have come to her promenade, introduced her to his newspaperman friends, and made efforts to converse with her best friends if he was simply manipulating her for information about Jiro.

"Is it possible there are others besides the Koide family who wish to harm Hamada-*san*?"

Nomura-*san* glanced out the front window of his store. Several young women chatted to one another as they as passed by with babies tied to their backs and food baskets in their arms. "He has many enemies. For Hamada-*san* it's too much of a coincidence that you became friends with Koide-*san* when the attacks on the boutique occurred."

"The events are close in time. Still, the way our friendship has unfolded makes me question him using me for politics."

"Beware, Renaud-*san*," Nomura-*san* said softly, his gaze full of concern.

Marcelle finished her tea, while concern filled her for the kind gentleman who'd only ever given her much-needed help and sound advice. He, too, was mistaken about the Koide family. "Please assure Hamada-*san* that I'm safe. No harm will come to me or the boutique."

***

In the rickshaw on the way back to Ginza, Marcelle realized she neither wished to sulk alone nor was she ready to return to the maelstrom of work at the boutique. The seamstresses and Yumi-*chan* would be fine without her for another few more hours. She could pay a visit to Suki. But that would mean telling her about seeing Jiro and the meeting with Nomura-*san*, and she wasn't in the mood to think about any of it. She needed a distraction, something beautiful, something detailed and artistic that she could lose herself in.

Her mind turned to the atrium of Koide Department Store. She pictured the assortment of luggage cases and the timepieces in their shiny displays that she never got to see, the furs they'd be selling for winter, the traditional Japanese umbrellas made from strips of bamboo and the ingeniously patterned *washi* paper.

Inspiring, airy, and anonymous, Koide's was the perfect place to while away a few hours. After she'd had her fill of the various departments, and her nerves had calmed, she'd inquire if Nobu was present.

She entered the store behind an older Japanese woman in an exquisite lime-green kimono, who proceeded to thrust her sandals at a store greeter.

"You don't need to remove your shoes." The greeter waved his hand at the customers strolling the atrium. "At Koide's, you can wear outdoor shoes inside."

The woman scowled at the fashionables befouling the store with what must have been all manner of outdoor dirt and the terrible luck it contained on the bottom of their stylish shoes. Her companion, a woman in Western dress who Marcelle took for a daughter, spoke a few words into the older woman's ear. The woman widened her eyes, put back on her sandals, and proceeded into the store's interior.

Marcelle exchanged knowing glances with the greeter, who looked as though he'd just endured his thousandth such exchange, then worked her way over to a glimmering display of pocket-watch cases. After turning several of the finely etched gold and silver cases in her palm, she moved on to the pearls and then the hat pins. All of it fed her soul.

On the second floor, a display of ormolu clocks had her intrigued for roughly seventeen minutes. The kimono *obi* sashes gave her an idea for the type of ribbon she might apply to the hem of a day dress. Reaching the third floor without tripping or straining a muscle was as sure a sign as any that her nerves had calmed. She wandered through the art gallery's paintings of Japanese farmhouses done in the style of Claude Monet. The lovely, blurred renderings coupled with the sentimental tune coming from the concert hall lulled her into a pleasant stupor that stayed with her as she made her way down the corridor to the store's offices.

A dozen or so secretaries crowded the room fronting Nobu's private office. Their jotting and scratching slowed to a halt when she appeared in the threshold. Within moments, every man in the room was staring at her.

She gave them a small bow. "I'd like to speak with Koide-*san*."

A secretary asked her to wait and entered Nobu's office. A moment later, Nobu emerged.

"Renaud-*san*," he intoned in clipped, businesslike Japanese, "thank you for coming by to discuss the silk bolts we'd been inquiring after."

"I've been meaning to come by all week. I have much to discuss," she replied in what she considered passable, businesslike Japanese.

"Then you must come this way at once." Nobu entered his office first, as he was the man and therefore of higher rank. After she entered, he shut the door with a light turn of the knob.

Marcelle gave him a playful smile. "Do your secretaries really believe I'm here to discuss silk bolts?"

"Not a single one. Nor are they impressed that I've thumbed my nose at propriety for the sake of bringing a woman into my office. They're very well-educated, but terribly unworldly." He studied her with a disbelieving gaze. "How did you get away?"

"I had a meeting about the new front window. Then I wandered around your store. I needed time away from the boutique."

Nobu appraised her as he would a wonderous discovery. She removed her hat, and his gaze rested on her hair. She removed her gloves and reticule and placed them on a table opposite his desk. His eyes flickered over her breasts and hips.

"I like the idea of your wandering the store, especially since you made it up to the third floor," he remarked as she crossed before him and took in his deliciously masculine scent of woodsy cologne and tobacco.

She moved over to the broad window overlooking the hub of Ginza Boulevard. A knot of bicycles, carts, and buses proceeded down the street. Pedestrians crowded the sidewalks. A building several stories high obstructed her view of *La France Boutique*. "You must feel very powerful up here."

Nobu came up behind her. "I'm powerful enough to have summoned you with my thoughts." His breath on her nape sent a tingling sensation down her back and around to her front. Her nipples hardened as though exposed to air.

"You did that?" she remarked as his arms encircled her waist. She leaned into his warmth. He was a salve for her senses, even more so than his dazzling display of goods.

"Every time I look at that sofa, I think about the last time you were here. I wonder if you'll ever come back again. And here you are."

"I've thought about your sofa, too." She exhaled heavily. Awareness of where she was standing, who was behind her, and what was about to happen made her tremble for his touch. She rested her hands atop of his and moved them up to her bodice, positioning his palms so her nipples were at their center. "I've thought about this…"

"It's almost all I think about." His soft words raised the fine hairs on her lobes.

After lacing her fingers through his, she pressed their hands against her pebbled nipples, and together, they kneaded, gripping and pressing, squeezing handfuls of silk and flesh from the sides of her bodice to the center. Delicious sensations gathered in her swelled quim. She let out a high, stringy whimper.

"This is the loveliest sound." Nobu's voice was rough, needy.

He was as wanton as she, and she wanted to drive him just as mad. His erection pressed into her backside, so she used the swells of her cheeks to caress the hard length.

His breath thickened, then he hissed a curse while he twisted her to face him. A brutal, crushing kiss—was it his? was it hers?—brought them together, its force like a punishment for weeks of unrelieved craving. He scraped his teeth on her lips, leaving a light sting. She scraped his tender flesh back.

They both moaned. The noise hovered between them.

Nobu eased away. "Not a dream, I don't think…" He probed her with his gaze. "This *is* really happening."

"It is, thank the gods," Marcelle said on her way to his mouth.

They joined in hot, breathy kisses with arms wrapped around one another, seeking purchase on bunches of silk and wool. He cupped the back of her neck and reached into her scalp, tilting her head and taking more of her mouth.

Restless, hard kisses grew slow, soft, and luscious. Their hips picked up the rhythm of their swirling tongues in a primal dance with neither beginning nor end, only a middle place where lovers coaxed one another to blissful heights.

Marcelle ran her touch along the sleeves of Nobu's fine wool jacket, up his arms and over his full shoulders. The impulse to nip him on that muscled flesh still pricked at her. Honoring the impulse, she dug her fingertips into his shoulders at the same moment he grabbed her buttocks and pushed his erection against her mound. His hardness sent a rush of liquid into her drawers. Her legs weakened. It occurred to her that they meant to spread for Nobu, to welcome him inside.

Her body, heart, and soul rushed to a desperate edge. She needed him inside her, filling her, wrecking her for any other man. She had no doubt he'd do exactly that.

She released her grip on his sleeve and bunched up her skirts. Let him ravish her against the window overlooking Ginza Boulevard.

Nobu placed his thigh between her legs. Pure instinct took over. She writhed against it, let it give her a taste of his strength and willingness to indulge her naughtiness.

"I want you on my sofa," he said against her parted lips.

"Have me here on your perch above the most famous boulevard in Tokyo." This must be an offer he couldn't refuse.

Nobu ran his lips down the column of her neck, then gave her collarbone a bite. Sparks flew behind her eyes. She grabbed him harder, willing him to nip her again. But he only kissed the place his teeth had been. "No. I want you on my sofa. I'm not finished with your ankle."

Of course. Unfinished business.

Marcelle released her bunched-up skirts. "Shall we return to the first floor and begin our trek up your stairs? If you start talking about lovers, I'll probably fall."

"Absolutely not. I can't afford another pair of boots." His voice was teasing but he took her mouth in a kiss that conveyed absolute seriousness about what he intended.

Marcelle slid from his embrace and walked over to the gray cushions where she'd sat weeks before. Like that time, she leaned back against the seat, then raised her leg.

Kneeling before her on his thick carpet, Nobu took her heel with the same reverence he'd used the day she'd twisted it. "May I?"

"Please."

Slowly, he undid her boot's laces and gently tugged the leather from her foot. After wrapping his hand around her ankle, he gave it a gentle squeeze. "Does this hurt?"

"Be careful." She kept her voice low and erotic. "It's very tender."

"I'll do my best." He moved his hand around the ankle, creating the most wonderful friction between her stockings and skin. "Please tell me if anything hurts, and I'll stop."

He sounded sincere, even in the middle of their game. His respect was astonishing. He never wanted to cause her pain. Not physically, not emotionally. Not her reputation or her business. And she believed him, not just because her body begged belief for the sake of an affair she craved, but because he'd been true to his word in everything he'd done. Men who hurt—the cheaters, philanderers, sneaks, robbers, confidence men—lied all the time. The big lies they doled out after the necessary time had passed for them to gain trust. The small lies abounded from the moment one met them, in the inconsistencies, the convenient forgetfulness, and awkward slips of the tongue.

Nobu didn't lie.

Jiro couldn't have been more wrong about him.

The truth buoyed Marcelle's spirits. "I'll tell you if there's pain."

"Good." He pressed his fingers into the pads of her foot, then moved over her arch and down to the back of her heel.

Marcelle purred in satisfaction. Her ankle loved him. Her foot loved him. Never had the bottom of her left leg been treated so well.

"Lean back," Nobu ordered.

She'd been gradually leaning forward so as not to miss a moment of his ministrations. Languid, she obeyed and rested against the plush cushion.

Nobu pushed into her calf muscle at exactly the place to force a painful unraveling. Unpleasant tingling shot into her ankle. She winced as she had done whenever she'd attempted to walk in the days after falling on his stairs, then the pain abated. The muscle relaxed.

She gaped at him. He presented such an elegant, refined façade that she hadn't thought him capable of knowing how to manipulate a leg.

"Better?" Nobu asked.

"Never better."

He massaged the loosened muscle up to the edge of her stocking garters. Running a finger along the inside, he relieved the pressure for a moment, then snapped the elastic. "That didn't hurt, did it?" He grinned like a mischievous boy.

"Not in the least." She'd rather he'd taken the garter off. She'd rather have all her clothes off and his touch over every needy inch of her body. His secretaries were simply too damn close for disrobing.

Nobu moved his massage to the back of her knee. Each press of his fingertips, each circle in the tender place behind the joint sent pain down to her heel and up to the swell of her buttocks. She sucked in a breath at the wondrous ache.

How could he bring her such pain and such pleasure? As soon as she thought the question, muscles she hadn't known were clenched finally relaxed.

"Keep going." She closed her eyes, anticipating the torment. He was heading for her thigh. It was going to lodge a fantastic protest.

Nobu ran his hand up the side of her thigh, at the same time lifting her skirts to her waist, exposing her skin to the air. Then he let out a low growl.

She imagined him glimpsing her white lacy drawers and the black silk ribbons cinching them at the bottom. He rested his touch on the outside of her thigh and with expert motions, released every coil in the heavy muscle.

Exhaling in relief, she let her jaw slacken and her knees open. She was in a very wanton position.

"Exactly what I'd hoped." His voice was barely audible.

He slipped his hand under her drawers and ran it up the delicate flesh of her inner thigh. She bucked her hips. Wild and unfettered, they aimed to lure his hand to her soaking, trembling quim, and somehow, they succeeded. He pressed his fingers against the seam of her wet drawers.

The subtle vibration of the silk against her swollen lips banished all needs, save one. His touch, hard or soft, cold or hot. It didn't matter, she needed his fingers inside her. "*Nobu*," she cried.

"Marcelle," he whispered. "You'll have to be quieter unless you want my secretaries to hear."

"Of course I don't want them—" Her words were swallowed in a gasp as he reached his fingers into the damp curls of her mound. At last. He twirled and circled, teased and played. At the very moment she was about to grab his fingers and direct them into her folds, he was there, dipping and caressing, making her squirm on his thick, gray cushions like a feral animal at the height of spring. Then he found her nub and swiped in time to her undulating hips.

Everything he did was so much better than she'd imagined, so much better than she'd ever had. She had the distinct impression he'd come into her life for the sole purpose of showing her exactly what a lover was supposed to do with her body.

Nobu shifted his touch under her buttocks, coaxing her forward on the sofa, closer to where he kneeled. Before it occurred to her how close she was to his mouth, he parted her swollen, trembling folds with his plush tongue. Biting her fisted hand, she kept herself from screaming in pure ecstasy.

He was everywhere between her legs, kissing, licking, murmuring or humming, she couldn't tell. Likely he was doing both. He seemed to be doing everything.

Then as sneakily as a thief in the night, her orgasm came. She couldn't have held it off had she tried, so she grabbed the back of his head, willing him to stay with her as she broke into a climax that bent her back and raised her chest and left her howling silently at his well-appointed office.

As the pulsing between her legs subsided, she released his head and sat up, expecting him to do the same. But he did nothing of the sort. Without even a glance upwards, he took her bud between his soft lips and pressed a finger deep inside her.

So focused he was on the task that she dared disobey his previous order to lean back on the sofa. Propped up on her elbows, she had no choice but to open her hips farther and jack her skirts higher so as not to suffocate him. The view made her jaw drop. She stared at him shoving two fingers in and out of her and feasting on her tortured nub until she broke into waves of frantic clenches.

The second orgasm left her in a heap. Nobu had unspooled her.

Recovering her breath, she reached down to his head where he rested against the sofa. Apparently, he, too, was exhausted.

"That was wonderful." She ran her fingers through his hair. "Now, how about the other leg?"

Nobu faced her. His incredulous expression made her shake with laughter. "At your service," he said, and he slowly ran his hand up her right leg.

Marcelle batted it away. "Don't you dare. I was only teasing. I'd perish on your sofa if you did that to me again."

"You mean I'm not allowed to do that again?"

"Oh, I insist you do that again. Perhaps when we're surrounded by all that fresh mountain air. Then I won't end up nearly losing consciousness."

Nobu rose from his place on the carpet and took a seat beside her. "When exactly are we going to the mountains?"

"We should be finished with the most pressing orders by the end of next week. Then Yumi-*chan* and the seamstress can start on the next set. When we return from Karuizawa, I'll correct all their mistakes." She doubted the mistakes would be many. Yumi-*chan* understood what their patrons wanted, and she'd become good at explaining their demands to the new seamstresses.

"Ryusuke and the other guardsmen will be there around the clock. You don't have to worry about their safety."

Marcelle also still paid Hidekazu and his gang to watch the boutique, even though there hadn't been a hint of trouble. "I'm worrying less and less these days. I hope that's not naïve." She placed her hand atop his. "I'd rather think about what to pack for a stay in the mountains. Will it be terribly cold this time of year?"

Nobu grazed her temple with his lips. "I wouldn't be too concerned about clothing. I don't anticipate we'll be dressed all that often."

A shiver of anticipation went through Marcelle. This trip to the mountains promised to be the start of a brilliant affair, although considering what just took place on the sofa, it was safe to say the affair had already started.

CHAPTER TWELVE

Marcelle

Marcelle gripped the rim of her train seat with all her strength. Women whose lives were a testament to beauty and refinement were meant to be on the flat plains of Eastern Japan, discovering new markets in Tokyo's wondrous neighborhoods, observing fashionables on Ginza Boulevard, and dining with friends in Tsukiji, not creaking up the side of a mountain in a train car that was probably one click away from teetering off its tracks and sending every one of its passengers careening toward their deaths in the spiky-rocked gorge below.

Nobu nodded at the window. "You're missing a spectacular view."

"No thank you," Marcelle said through clenched teeth. She stayed fixed on the train doors from which she might—just might—finally exit this journey of death. "How much longer?"

"It looks as though we'll complete the ascent in a few minutes."

"Fine," Marcelle hissed. The first five and a half hours of the train journey had been a delight. The countryside between Tokyo and Karuizawa presented views of rolling foothills and tangled valleys brimming with autumnal beauty. Farmers waved as the train passed their fields. Children ran alongside their carriage in a hearty competition. The boxed lunch of rice balls and sweet chestnuts had tasted like heaven. Then the train conductor entered their car and announced that travelers should prepare for a steep climb through the

Usui Pass. He should've instructed them to pen their final wishes. Prayers she hadn't recalled in years started running through her head at the first click of the train supposedly "locking" onto the absurdly narrow metal track.

"The Abt rack is the newest engineering method," Nobu pointed out as though she cared about engineering when her life was about to conclude in a pile of rubble. "You needn't worry about safety. When I was a boy, we used rickshaws and horse carriages to reach Karuizawa. The train is far safer, not to mention more comfortable, and fast."

The only thing going fast was the churning of her stomach. "How could this possibly be safe?"

"Abt racks have an excellent safety record."

"I'd rather they have a *perfect* safety record."

Nobu stroked her back. "In this case, excellent implies perfect."

"You *hesitated*. You truly don't know. We're about to be impaled on those awful rocks and you're talking about imaginary safety records."

Nobu increased the pace of his stroking. "We're going to make it to Karuizawa."

"Wonderful. I'm about to spend the rest of my life in Karuizawa, because I'm never getting on another train again."

"That would be Karuizawa's gain." He spoke in a smooth, confident tone that had no place on a train car suspended between life and death.

"Please sell *La France Boutique* on my behalf."

Nobu laughed at her. The man knew neither fear nor pity.

"I'll open a store in the countryside that no one will patronize. My talents will be forever squandered."

"You'd have plenty of customers. Foreigners adore Karuizawa. They own most of the villas around town. It's their way of avoiding Tokyo's summer heat."

Marcelle scowled. "I hadn't realized how truly insane Tokyo's foreigners were."

"If you were to glance out the window, you wouldn't think them insane," he said gently.

"You couldn't pay me to look out that window." Marcelle kept her gaze firmly on the train doors.

Once they'd reached the full height of the Usui Pass, the train shifted off the Abt rack and resumed a more natural, more horizontal angle. The view out the window caught the corner of her eye and she turned to it. There had never existed such breathtaking beauty. Tall, proud hillsides boasted miles of red, brown, and golden leaves illuminated by afternoon sunshine. Slowly, she released her death grip on the upholstered seat and took a breath of the clean, crisp air seeping into their car.

"Then you like it?" Nobu asked.

"Very much," she replied at the blinding radiance of Karuizawa.

They exited the train into a small, tidy station. A lad of about ten years took their baggage from the train conductor and greeted Marcelle with an English, "Hello." She'd made several excursions to the countryside over the years, mostly for a lovers' getaway, but never this far from Tokyo and never with as many signs in English. While Nobu summoned them a carriage, Marcelle waited at the station and took in the brick-paved, sloped streets running up to the edge of a small mountain. Lining them were shops and restaurants, every one of which she intended to explore.

"Was the train ride worth it?" Nobu asked upon returning.

She shifted her gaze from a quaint toy store to him. The wind tousled his hair, and his cheeks had a healthful ruddiness. The brightness about his eyes reminded her of when he talked about his store or the future of Ginza Boulevard. She never would've guessed he was equally at home in the countryside. Discovering this aspect of Nobu was like being gifted a small bauble. That alone was worth the trip. "Absolutely," she replied.

***

Marcelle and Nobu's small, uncovered carriage rambled over a tall bridge in the hills outside of town. Steam rose from the bridge's underside, bringing the sulfuric odor of mineral-rich hot springs. Several stories high, an inn of fine hewed wood, with large, beveled glass windows stood on the other side.

"Is that where we're staying?" Marcelle asked. She'd spent most of the carriage ride lost in thought. Tokyo was thoroughly Asian in its aesthetic even when it rubbed up against the West in Tsukiji and on Ginza Boulevard. Karuizawa was a surprising contrast. The town and the surrounding villas and farms reminded her of Bordeaux or Champagne. The farmhouses scattered along the hillside took her back to the bleak years she'd been handed off between her relatives, never knowing how she'd be treated or how long she'd be staying.

By the time she made it to Paris as a young woman, she'd lived in five different towns with five different sets of relations who'd needed her orphan's allowance. Always on the brink of being sent away and starting again, she used needlework to keep her hands and mind busy and still the aching in her heart. She was good at it. Others liked her work. As long as she could gift a cousin an embroidered pillow or a schoolfriend a lace handkerchief, she'd have their companionship for a time. She'd sewed her way to Japan and then into *La France Boutique*. Now she had a handsome department store owner sitting beside her on a carriage in the breathtaking countryside.

It'd been a long time since she'd felt as though fate was smiling upon her.

"The inn was built a decade ago for an imperial visit," Nobu replied. "Since then, the crown prince has spent several weeks here each summer."

The matron greeted them in the inn's foyer of polished wood and bronze sconces. She told them they were among three other patrons staying at the inn that evening, then led them down a startlingly quiet corridor.

Their rooms offered a view of rolling hills and the Usui Pass in the distance. Traditionally Japanese, the main room boasted woven tatami mats, low tables of lemon-scented hinoki wood, and thick, plush sitting pillows. Warmth from the fireplace soothed Marcelle's travel-weary body. While Nobu gave the matron instructions for their evening meal, she wandered from the bedroom to their private bathing quarters. The washing section was large enough to accommodate the crown prince and a dozen of his courtiers. Soaps, beauty oils, and the wood of the room's interior combined in a scent that was nature to perfection. Half of the bathing section was sheltered under a wooden canopy. The other half extended to the edge of the hillside, allowing them to soak above the valley brimming with autumn foliage.

The door to the main room shut and soft footfalls came across the tatami mats to the bathroom. Marcelle turned to Nobu as he came in and met him in the middle of the washing area.

Nobu brought his broad palm to her cheek. "Mademoiselle," he said, his voice heavy, "at long last, I've got you all to myself."

Marcelle leaned into his touch, then kissed his palm. Salty and masculine: an encounter with desire. She let out a blissful sigh. "I'm all yours."

He rumbled something about him "needing patience" and kissed the base of her neck, then trailed warm, wet kisses up to her jaw. A wave of sensual weakness traveled down her body, through her breasts, filling her middle and between her legs where she was already damp with longing. She tilted her head, giving him more room to explore.

"I love the way you smell," he murmured into her ear. "Like roses covered in morning dew." He nudged at the lobe of her ear with his tongue and gave it a gentle nibble.

Marcelle shivered at the light touch of his teeth over the tender skin of her ear and chin. Upon reaching her mouth, he enveloped her in a kiss that ignited every inch of her body. Unhurried, they stood in the bathroom, kissing in deep, languid turns of lips and tongues. So similar were their heights that their bodies joined in an erotic symmetry, their thighs, hips, and chests pressing together.

As he had in his office, Nobu moved his leg between hers, then lifted it against her swollen, wet quim. The light pressure lit sparks behind her eyes. She loosened her hips and rode his leg while he nibbled and pulled on her lower lip. A crack of pleasure stole through her.

Not yet.

She eased off his thigh and met his hungry gaze. "Shall we bathe together?"

"Bathe?" He looked around the room. "I suppose that's what we're supposed to do here." He kissed her mouth, hard and slow. "I'll need to unclothe you first."

Nobu wrapped his arm around her waist and led her through the bathing room door to the alcove on the other side. He undid the hooks of her traveling dress, a Western-style light wool garment she'd put together a year ago. As he peeled it from her body, he showered her with compliments on the evenness of her stitching and the straightness of her bodice tucks. Then he folded the dress carefully as only a man familiar with women's garments could and placed it in a basket for kimonos. Going down to his knees, he unfastened her stockings from her garters and removed the elastic pieces. He kissed the pinched skin from where they'd sat on her calves. His breath against her bare skin tickled and taunted as he rolled each of her stockings off her feet.

Neediness bloomed between her legs as he tugged at the black ribbons lining the hem of her drawers. Were he to touch her even once, she was going to come undone in the bathroom alcove. "Nobu, I need you so very much."

Kneeling before her, he pulled down her drawers, his gaze level with the pulsing core of her. He mustn't have been as desperate as she because he folded her lace and silk drawers neatly, even as he continued staring, seemingly mesmerized by her most intimate place. Finished with the task, he took hold of her rear and licked the wetness that had dribbled down the inside of her thigh. "I know. I can taste it."

She pressed her hands into his scalp to keep herself from keeling over. He licked the inside of her other leg, then rose and took her mouth in a penetrating kiss that drew a keening sound from her throat.

Nobu eased away. "That sound... I'll hear it again."

With remarkable efficiency, unsurprising from a man with knowledge of fashion, he took off her corset and chemise and placed them in the basket.

Naked, she looked down at herself. Taut nipples jutted toward him. A new trickle of wetness ran down the side of her thigh. Her body longed for him to make a claim, to mark her however he wished. She had a feeling he'd be marking her in many different ways over the next few days, and every one of them would ruin her for mountainside inns with any other lover.

One by one, Nobu removed her hairpins. Dark, curly locks fell down the length of her back and across her breasts. He stepped away, and his intense gaze roamed her body. She noticed tightness on the fall of his trousers where his erection pressed against the wool. "So fucking beautiful. I want a portrait of you just like this. Two portraits, one for my quarters at home and another for the office. Small enough to hide."

With those words, he sucked all the desire from her.

She'd vowed many years before never to sit for another boudoir portrait.

Boudoir photography had been the rage in Paris during her final year in the city, and Antoine, who'd prided himself on always being in vogue, had requested a naked photograph. She agreed to sit for the portrait to please him, also because she was curious about what it'd feel like to model nude and how her body would look on film. He accompanied her to the photographer's home to observe the process, which pleased her because she'd never exposed herself to a man she had no intention of sleeping with.

A few glasses of claret before the sitting made removing her dress and underclothes less difficult than she'd feared. The atelier was warm, and the bed strewn with fine linens that could have used an airing.

The photographer gave orders about how to arrange herself on the bed, then stood behind his camera. He narrowed his eyes in what seemed to be a master's gaze. How pleased she was to be in an expert's hands. "Could you open your mouth, *ma chérie*?" he asked.

She parted her lips.

"Farther," he ordered.

She let her jaw drop, although the pose seemed more obscene than fashionable.

The photographer shifted away from the camera and skulked to the bed, his movements determined, his eyes dark pools of unnerving lust. Upon reaching her, he pulled down the suspenders holding up his trousers.

Marcelle grabbed a piece of blanket and held it over her naked body. "*Stop this instant.*"

He paused with his hands on the top of his trousers. "I told your lover I'd give you the portrait for free if you sucked me off. Won't you be a good girl and behave?"

"Absolutely not."

Antoine barked out a laugh. "Get back here, mate. I never said you could."

The photographer pulled back up his suspenders. "You told me to go and ask, see if she'd mind."

Bile surged to Marcelle's throat. Antoine could be one of the most inconsiderate crusty, weeping scabs known to mankind. She was going to leave him for this. It was the final slight in a very long list of slights over the past few years. She should have already left. But then, what would she have?

Antoine raised his hands as though the whole fiasco had mysteriously gotten out of hand. "She does mind."

"Fine. You're paying full price, *mate*." The photographer gave a resigned shrug and resumed his place behind the camera. "Why don't you drop that blanket, and we can get this photograph over with?"

But Marcelle couldn't let go of the blanket. Her fist wasn't going to open.

"Let go of the blanket, Marcelle," Antoine called out. "We're paying for the photograph."

"I...can't."

Antoine was out of his chair and halfway to the bed when she realized what he intended: to tear the blanket from her hand and expose her. So, she dropped the blanket herself. She wouldn't submit to another humiliation.

She sat for the portrait. Neither Antoine nor the photographer objected to her steely gaze at the camera. She was so full of hate after leaving the atelier that she put the whole incident out of mind.

Antoine never showed her the final portrait.

By the time she thought to ask whether he'd sold it to one of his mates, as she suspected he must have, Antoine was married, and she was determined to avoid him at all costs.

Nobu furrowed his brow. "Does that make you uncomfortable?"

Marcelle wished she could take back whatever pain had appeared on her face. She'd loved the way Nobu had been looking at her. She'd love to give him that feeling from looking at her portrait. "I was wondering whether you'd demonstrate your boxing skills on the photographer if he looked at me with anything other than artistic detachment?"

Nobu bared his teeth. "I'd kill him with a single punch."

Of course he would. "Then I'll consider it." She gave him a provocative grin and twirled, knowing her long strands revealed and concealed her peaked nipples.

He wasted no time in removing his waistcoat, suspenders, trousers, and shirts. There was nothing lean about him. Everywhere, he was broad, full, and firm. His shoulders flared with layers of heavy muscle. She'd already decided to sink her teeth into that flesh at least once during this trip, preferably at the exact moment she came in his arms.

Unlike her garments, his got a meager fold. He finished and faced her. His chest tapered to a tight waist, and thighs, thick as tree trunks, must have kept him grounded in ways she couldn't fathom. And between those impressive thighs, his erection rose, dark, broad, and glistening.

"You're looking at me as though I were a dish of mutton chops," he said.

"I happen to love mutton chops." Marcelle closed the space between them and kissed him. They stood there kissing for what could have been hours. The only parts of them touching were his cock caressing the inside of her thigh with its jerky, silky hardness.

Then he turned her around. His erection caught between the seam of her buttocks, and his breath fell hot on the shell of her ear. "It's time to wash," he said and opened the door to the bathroom.

He went to the soaking bath already full of hot springs water and filled two buckets. He set those beside a stool, then took a seat with a bar of soap in hand. "Come here," he said with a nod at his lap.

Marcelle didn't know if he meant she should sit with her back or front facing him, but she wanted to face him, so she did, perched on his thighs.

"May I?" She placed her hand on the soap.

"As you wish."

Lavender and spice filled the air as she softened the bar in the water bucket. A luscious sound came from his lips when she soaped his nape and reached into his hair and scalp. Shutting her eyes, she imagined herself one of the blind men at the public baths who did the shampooing. Like those men, she probed into Nobu's slick hair to his scalp and circled the roots.

He bent back into her hands. "You're very good at this."

"I aim to please."

He pulled her wrist to his mouth and dragged a kiss across the inside. "As do I."

She let out a ragged breath at his lips' caresses. Reclaiming her hand, she moved the bar to his unusually wide neck. It was so wide, her joined hands failed to encompass the expanse. She washed the stubbly skin thoroughly, then ran suds through the dark hairs on his chest and around his dark-rouged nipples.

"That," he said and groaned. "Hold on, Marcelle." He widened his legs, taking hers along so that her feet no longer touched the wooden floor.

She looked down at the gap between them. The dark hairs of her mound and the tip of his erection were only inches apart. Nobu shifted his hips forward. The movement was a request for her touch.

Prepared to relish the first time she took hold of him, Marcelle reached for his shaft with her soap-slickened hand. This meeting between his most intimate flesh and her touch promised to be a moment of surrender for him, of power for her, of trust and erotic possibilities.

She moved forward, and tenderness, in a brush of whisper-thin silk, overwhelmed her anticipation of the formidable exchange. The feeling wasn't offensive or unfamiliar. She'd felt tender toward previous lovers. It was just too early for Nobu. It made her feel untethered and weak.

Setting aside the unexpected mix of emotions, Marcelle focused on the man before her and wrapped her hand around the thickness of him. He gritted his teeth and hissed as she moved up and down in slow, even strokes. Aching sounds filled the washing area, moved past the open-air bath, and disappeared somewhere in the woods beyond.

"Faster, my love," he growled between heavy breaths.

She gripped his shaft harder and increased the pace of her strokes. Nobu let out a curse. Cupping her face, he brought his lips to hers in a harsh kiss, then leaned away and studied her as though observing the spirit of temptation at work.

Giving a rough exhale, he took her hand and lifted it from his cock. With her still on his lap, her legs wrapped around his midsection, he rose to his feet.

"I'm impressed with your strength," she said as he turned around and placed her on the stool.

"You bring out the beast in me." He did sound guttural and beastly. After gripping the side of one of the water buckets by the stool, he lifted it above his head. The muscles of his chest and arms flexed as he poured it over himself, sending rivulets down his chest and over his hips and cock, so erect it almost reached his belly. "Close your eyes," he ordered, his tone playful.

She barely had them closed when he doused her over the head with the second bucket. The childish gesture made her giggle. "Are you trying to drown me?"

"That hardly serves my interests." He proceeded to fill another bucket from the hot springs bath. This time he added cold water from a barrel by the wall. Then he ladled the tepid mix into her hair.

"Not too hot?" he asked.

"Perfect."

He massaged her scalp and neck with soapy fingers. Truly, he was an expert masseuse. The kneading and releasing he'd done to the muscles on her left leg in his office had inspired her to do the same to her right leg that evening. Try as she might, she couldn't match his work. Now he found muscles that had likely been tense since she'd learned how to sew. Her gasps and cries of delight were more suited to a rollicking orgasm.

Nobu guffawed. "Don't you ever get a massage?"

"I ought to get massaged more often. But now that I have you..." The words stopped her. Did she really *have* Nobu? Was he hers?

"When you need a massage, you know where to find me," he finished, saving her from having to complete the thought. "There's a sofa in my office, you know."

Tenderness she'd felt when she'd taken him in hand chafed again, even rawer than before. Really, they needed to stop being so nice to one another and get to the business of fucking.

Nobu ladled more water over her hair, rinsing it of suds, then lowered himself behind her on the stool. His thick, hard cock bore into her lower back as he reached around for her breasts. Like the talented masseuse he'd proved himself to be, he lifted and kneaded, twiddled and pinched. She raised her chest to meet his touch while nestling her head in the curve of his neck, letting the seductive sensations pour through her.

From her chest, he moved down her abdomen. Marcelle watched him dip his fingers into her mound and settle between her legs. As he delved within her delicate folds, she shut her eyes.

Nobu was confident and precise, managing to slip a finger inside her and caress her swollen nub without the friction of his touch distracting her from the divine pleasure he so carefully, skillfully coaxed. She wanted to reward him, and sensing he wanted the reward, she writhed in his arms as the orgasm rolled through her and came from her in cawing noises that rivaled those of the nosy finches peeking into the bath.

Slumped against Nobu's chest, Marcelle lifted her head to find him grinning. "Beautiful. That's the portrait I want," he said.

"Of me coming in your arms? I think not," she said between rushed breaths.

He laughed heartily. "I promise no such portraits." He rose and filled another bucket. His muscles clenched under the weight as he eased it down next to the stool. "I'm not done with you yet."

He held out his hand. She took it and stood. In fact, he'd only washed her hair. There might have been suds on his hands when he cupped her breasts but that hardly constituted a proper washing after a long journey.

Nobu reseated himself, then wrapped his arms around the back of her legs, scooting her toward him. "Come here."

Once again, she straddled his plank-like thighs. The position would ensure her front was thoroughly clean. "What about my back?"

Nobu turned the soap in his hand and lifted his thighs, causing her to slide toward him. She slid until her midsection was flush against his chest. "I'll get your back."

He reached under her mantle of damp hair and soaped. Each circle of his hand over her slick back seemed to nudge them closer and his erection more fully into her folds.

Nobu let out a groan. "You have to stop moving like that, or I'm not going to finish your back."

Marcelle let her jaw drop. "You're the one moving me."

"Am I?" His dark eyes betrayed his innocent tone. Again, he moved the soap up and down her back.

This time she bucked against him. His hardness so close to her entrance made madness a very real possibility. "Are you ever going to stop?"

Nobu growled and set his wide, hot mouth on her breast. The brush of his teeth against her nipple brought an ecstasy she could no more control than the coming of night. With a lift of her hips, she positioned herself above his pulsing erection.

"Do it." His gaze was as demanding as the tension in his jaw.

Marcelle lowered herself with a whimper of neediness.

Nobu hissed some Japanese curse in her ear. "Don't move."

She didn't. Even so, the joining of their most intimate flesh created a storm of movement within her. She clenched the muscles surrounding his cock, willing the spasms to stop, but it was too late. The orgasm rode her, and she rode Nobu. "I'm sor—"

"Don't ever be sorry," Nobu said between clenched teeth.

The blissful sensations continued as he lifted her hips and pushed them back down on him again and again. The veins in his neck swelled. Not yet finished, he pulled her off, and she found herself on the wet floor, watching Nobu fist out his seed with a guttural moan.

When he finished, she collapsed on the floor beside him and rested her forehead on his trunk of a thigh. He threaded his fingers through her hair.

"I'm afraid I neglected my duty," he said once their breaths had settled.

Marcelle ran her hand along the slope of his knee and down the front of his calf. "You didn't neglect a thing." Light tremors still vibrated along her swollen quim.

"I didn't get you clean enough," he remarked.

Marcelle gazed up and found amusement dancing in his eyes as he pressed his lips tightly together. She laughed at his determination to keep a straight face. "You'll have to try harder next time."

"Gladly."

She sighed happily as he worked his fingers through her hair and into her scalp in one of his magnificent massages.

***

Marcelle woke to sunlight pouring through the white papered squares of the window's latticed shutters. She was full of sleep, of warmth, of Nobu. The previous evening they'd soaked in the bath until the moon rose over the mountainside. Afterward, they'd sat at the low table in the main room and dined on a meal of roasted birds and fried mountain vegetables along with a bottle of delicious *sake*. Satiated and blissfully happy, she dozed off on thick, downy pillows in front of the fire. When she awoke, Nobu lay reading a book under the lantern light. He set it aside and joined her on the pillows.

Slowly, he kissed her to awareness. Her body was pleasantly strained from the journey to Karuizawa when she'd grasped on to the train seats and from when she'd held on to Nobu on the stool in the bathing room. Her arms and legs throbbed with exhaustion, yet she craved more grasping, more holding. She unwrapped her sleeping kimono, not bothering to remove her arms from the sleeves. They left kisses on one another's mouths, necks, and chests; their only purpose seemed to be chasing the tastes left on their skin of soap and *sake*, of their meal and their sweat. He placed a pillow under her hips and knelt while he moved in and out of her wet, full sheath. Unhurried and steady in the meeting of their hips, they told one another about how perfectly their bodies joined, about how heavenly their lovemaking felt.

Covered in a fine sheen of sweat, the swells of muscles running down Nobu's chest and arms shone in the firelight. He eased back and pressed his thumb against her bud while he continued to thrust inside her. Their movements turned hard and erratic, unmooring them from the inn and the mountains, from the burning fire and the plush sleeping kimonos. Together, they reached their peaks in muted screams and gasps of pleasure that popped and crackled like embers releasing threads of steam.

Afterward, Marcelle had fallen asleep amazed at the enormity of the passion they created. Now, in the morning light, Nobu stirred and stretched on the futon beside her. Her back to him, he pulled her into the bend of his legs.

She hadn't realized how cold the room had gotten overnight, how cold she'd become, until his warmth enveloped her. Weaving her fingers through his, she brought their hands to the center of her chest, claiming him. Today, Nobu was hers.

He nestled even closer, his heat overcoming the lingering chill. "Good morning."

Marcelle turned her head. He peered down at her, his features soft. The lines around his eyes were yet relaxed. His gaze, in contrast, was fiery. "It looks to be a beautiful day," she replied.

"I've no doubt." He lifted the back of her kimono and moved a hand to her delicate skin wet with need for his touch, his cock, whatever he had to give. "You are a gift," he remarked, his erection twitching along the swell of her ass.

Rather than fight the damnable tenderness that seemed to accompany every moment with him, she fondled him with her hands, then guided him into her center. Whispering her name into her ear along with Japanese she didn't quite understand and English professions of his unending desire, he brought them both to a shuddering climax.

They breakfasted on roasted vegetables, tofu simmering in a dark broth, an earthy mushroom soup, and Nagano's newly harvested rice. After dressing, they boarded a carriage back to the town of Karuizawa. Marcelle led them through nearly every one of the shops on the main street until relenting for a cup of tea at a cafe owned by a German man whose Japanese wife made them fried maple leaves dipped in sweet miso.

Following tea, they visited a store selling luxurious kimono silks and accessories. Nobu introduced the shopkeeper as a friend of the Koide family.

When they left the store, he pulled a square wooden box from under his jacket. "I have something for you."

Marcelle beamed at the box and then at Nobu, who watched her with the eagerness of a child anticipating the exchange of presents on Three Kings Day. "Shall I open it here?" They stood on the main street before storefronts as pedestrians strolled by.

"I don't think I can carry it around the rest of the day."

Marcelle lifted the bronze latch and found a hair pin with precious stones scattered along a black lacquer surface. They looked like newly fallen autumn leaves. The pin weighed more than one would expect from the delicate design.

She held it up to the midafternoon sun. "Do you see the way the sunlight reflects off the facets?" she asked. "How could I have missed this piece? I looked at everything in that store."

"The owner was holding it for me. I sent a letter before we left about acquiring something that would be a reminder of our trip."

"What if I'd been awful and this trip had been an utter disappointment?"

"I would've given the pin to Asako," he said with a devilish grin. Then he held out his hand. She put the pin in his palm and watched him hold it up to the sunlight. The facets did their glittery dance for him. Placing it back in her hand, he met her gaze. "I never doubted we would enjoy one another and this place. I hope this is the first of many journeys together."

Usually, when a man presented her with jewelry and declarations about their future, Marcelle wanted to disappear out the rear entrance of whatever restaurant or hotel they happened to be in. Perhaps being out of doors made her feel less needy for escape. It could also be Nobu.

She removed her hat and placed the pin in her chignon. Among her dark curls, the stones must flare. She couldn't wait to get to a mirror. "I might be amenable to future journeys provided they don't involve train trips up mountain cliffs."

"Karuizawa will be disappointed to hear."

She looped her arm through his. "It's not terrible," she said with exaggerated weariness. "And the hairpins are lovely."

Nobu glanced down at her with undisguised adoration. "That pin looks perfect on you."

Sections of the village remained unexplored, but Nobu insisted they needed to see more of the area's autumnal glory. He seemed to be under the impression that their holiday would be lacking if they neglected to take in as much of the leaves as they could. She was coming to understand he was the sort of man who orchestrated the construction of department stores and mountain holidays to meet a very exacting set of standards.

It was easy to imagine his future wife. She'd be one of those serene beauties who strolled Ginza Boulevard with a bright greeting for every shopkeeper, her coiffure immaculate and her use of cosmetics flawless. Never would she be caught in a gown that borrowed from the styles of East and West. She'd wear one style or another and be the picture of perfection in whichever she chose.

Something melancholy pricked at Marcelle. It wasn't jealousy. Nobu's marriage was an inevitability she'd already accepted. It was more like grief. She wanted more time with him before he married, because once he decided to marry, their affair would have to end.

The day Antoine had announced his marriage and his intention to make Marcelle his mistress, she'd decided never to take that role. At first, resentment over Antoine choosing another woman had fueled her resolve. Then she thought about years spent being his diversion, their children a secondary family, until he tired of them altogether. Not only was the arrangement impractical for herself, but she also loathed the notion of being the woman who imposed herself on another family. Although it'd done so little for her, she yet respected the institution of family.

Cloaked in the moral superiority of a vow to never take the role of mistress, she refused Antoine, which had only made him more insistent and more generous with gifts of furs and jewelry and more insulting when she wouldn't sleep with him, then more threatening in telling her what he'd do if she didn't remain his lover. Plagued with images of Antoine using a knife to force her into his bed or to kill any man he suspected of taking his place in her bed—as he explicitly stated he would—she impulsively accepted the offer of employment from the American envoy's wife and left Paris for a new life in Tokyo.

She maintained her mistress vow in Tokyo despite offers from several men she would've gladly bedded were they unattached, then broke it for Jiro because the situation suited her.

Nobu was modern. It was one of the qualities she most liked about him. His bride would be a love match, or at least a match of mutual affection unlike a traditional Japanese union of expediency. Marcelle would never interfere.

As they wound their way through town and onto the pathways overlooking valleys of autumnal leaves, she wondered if she should tell him about her limits, so he didn't set his hopes on her becoming his mistress, if, in fact, he harbored that old-fashioned ambition for his marriage. Then they started passing foreigners likewise admiring Karuizawa's foliage. Marcelle exchanged pleasantries and conversation with them and set aside her wonderings.

Several British women near her age wished to know more about the kimono silk day dress she was wearing. Marcelle described the boutique's location on Ginza Boulevard and advised them on colors and prints she thought would best suit. They reciprocated with invitations to dinner and visits to their Karuizawa villas next summer.

"I'm impressed you made such quick friends," Nobu remarked after they'd parted from the two women.

They continued along a winding pathway edging the valley. "They wish to look beautiful, and I can help. I have the perfect dress in mind for the woman with the dark hair and green eyes. I'll cut it from a peach-colored silk I recently acquired. Her figure would look best in a higher waist, small bustle. I hope she comes to the store."

"Are we expected at dinner? I thought I heard them suggest it." His flat tone betrayed a lack of enthusiasm at the prospect.

"I declined the invitation. This day, this holiday, is for us."

Nobu leaned so close that his rough cheek grazed hers. "I feel likewise."

"Did you catch them saying they're missionaries?"

"I missed that. Does that mean they want you to attend their church?"

Marcelle huddled closer to Nobu. The temperature had decreased by multiple degrees. "I imagine so, although they didn't mention it. I let them believe we're married. They don't need to know we're lovers who cannot contain our sinful desires."

Nobu stiffened. "You told them we were married?"

He must have been embarrassed at anyone thinking him the sort of man who'd take a foreign wife. Among his circle of elites, a foreign wife was beyond the pale. "They assumed, and I didn't correct them. Didn't you hear the younger woman refer to you as my husband?"

"I missed that."

At the time, Nobu had drifted away from the conversation to watch a flock of birds heading south. Still, she hadn't thought him completely out of earshot. "I thought it wise to let the assumption stand since they are the religious sort."

"I see." Nobu took a breath as though to say something more. But nothing more was said.

They arrived at a clearing with an expansive view of the stunning valley. A half-dozen or so Japanese artists—men and women—stood before easels poised along the ridge. "I'd love to paint this scene," Marcelle said wistfully.

"Why don't I ask one of them to lend you some paper and brushes?"

She shook her head. "If you put a brush in my hand, I'll design dresses. Not a single tree would make it onto the paper."

"This is a sign, Mademoiselle Renaud," Nobu scolded. "You should take in beauty outside the world of dresses and gowns. It might enhance your designs."

Marcelle nudged him back to the pathway away from the artists. "I'm surprised to hear a devoted man of business speak of beauty, Koide-*san*."

"A man must expose himself to beauty daily or his soul withers."

Marcelle should have guessed at Nobu's artistic leanings. After all, he'd created a magnificent department store. "And what, pray tell, keeps your soul alive?"

"Gazing at you." He gave a tender look that made her legs so weak she stopped in her tracks.

"I can hardly suffice to feed a man's soul."

"Hmm." He ran his gaze up and down her body in a leering manner that made her giggle. "Actually," he said with an appraising sneer, "your nose is far too large."

Marcelle feigned outrage. "My nose adds definition to my face, enhancing what paltry beauty I possess. Your nose, I daresay, is hardly a thing of beauty."

Nobu tapped the high arch of his nose. "I take it you're familiar with the Japanese notion of *wabi-sabi*. Imperfection makes for beauty?"

"How convenient for your nose," she said with false haughtiness.

"And yours." He rolled his eyes, then peered around her head. "Then there's your ears. Well... we shall not speak of those."

She gave his ears a disgusted look. "Yours aren't exactly a shape I'd call appealing." Actually, his ears suited the size of his head as much as was possible, and the shell had a lovely slope. His lobes, which she knew from having nibbled several times over the past day and night, were the perfect size and thickness. But he had no way of knowing any of this.

"I've never had a complaint." Hurt crossed his face, and they both broke into laughter. "Beauty must be everywhere our customers turn, so they feel more inclined to purchase," he explained as they resumed their walk. "You see, I may understand what is lovely, but I'm still a shallow man of business."

"You'd make plenty of money by simply installing a moving staircase."

Nobu nodded. "I have every intention of seeing what that does for my bottom line." He gave her a suspicious look. "Would you still love me if I became an outrageously successful man of business?"

Marcelle glanced away to spare him the color of her burning cheeks. Naturally, he was teasing about her love. So why had she broken out in a rabid flush? She covered her embarrassment with an impish scowl. "Love? More like tolerate. And yes, I would still tolerate you."

He laughed and she joined along, hoping this was the last they'd speak of love. Their affair was going to be necessarily brief. Why ruin it by sulking over feelings?

***

As the sun set, they soaked in the bath together, gazing off into the trees and hillsides silhouetted against a twilight-blue sky. Afterward, she left the soft wool lounging kimono from the inn in its basket and affixed the jeweled pin to her hair.

Nobu read at the low table in the main room, and he swallowed hard when she walked toward him, her hair up, bare breasts and hips swaying with her footfalls. He complimented her lack of attire and choice of accessory, then held out his arms for her to come into his embrace.

She knelt before him on the pillow next to the table and held his gaze as she teased her already hard nipples. Sharp pressure shot into her wet quim. She gasped from the quaking it left in its place.

Nobu's breath quickened. "What can I do for you?"

"Untie your kimono."

Nobu obeyed, his jaw flexing with a desirous bite she'd noticed when their coupling was imminent. Sure enough, when he opened his kimono, his cock was at the ready.

Marcelle placed a jar of rosewater-scented balm she'd brought with her on the table and dipped her fingers inside. Spreading the cool cream onto her breasts, she kneaded the soft flesh, reveling in the contrast between the heat of her skin and the coolness of the cream. She added more of the balm and lowered herself onto Nobu's erection until it was enveloped between her cream-covered breasts.

He let out a string of guttural Japanese and jerked his hips upward, so she met the glistening tip of his erection with her tongue. Salty musk and a hint of rose water.

"Just like that," he hissed between clenched teeth.

"Lean back." He did, and she lapped at his swollen head while moving up and down with her breasts snug around him.

Nobu dug his fingers into her shoulders and released the fullness of his seed onto her neck. It trickled to the top of her chest in a warm cascade while he uttered her name over and over. Never had she felt so appreciated for simply doing what she'd wished.

Nobu brought her to his chest, and Marcelle wrapped her arms around him and listened to his breath settle as the musky rose scent of their bare skin washed over her. When a maid knocked on the door with a request to tend the fire, Marcelle realized she'd drifted off to sleep.

The maid returned later with dinner and bottles of *sake*. Once they'd eaten, they poured one another cup after cup of sweet wine. Wits sharpened, they shared stories of eccentric and demanding patrons that left them gasping for breath. Under heavy eiderdown blankets, their naked bodies pressed together, Marcelle sighed with utter contentment. "I could stay here forever."

He stroked her arm, lulling her to sleep. "Marcelle in the mountains. Who would've thought?"

"It's not only the mountains. It also has to do with the company. As long as you were here with me, I could stay forever."

Nobu pulled her tight against him. "I know exactly what you mean."

CHAPTER THIRTEEN

Nobu

Nobu stretched his arms outside the blanket. The morning air stung his exposed skin as his sleeping kimono worked its way up his arms. Enough of that nonsense. He dipped back under the blanket and drew up to Marcelle who slept on her side, facing away from him. He could've sworn he hadn't awakened her, but she took his arm and pulled it around her waist. Her breathing remained constant and deep. Perhaps she hadn't awakened. She'd done that before: pulled him to her in her sleep. May the gods help him, he loved that about her. He couldn't think of anything he didn't love about her.

What in the name of gods East and West had he done to earn the good fortune of waking in a luxurious room in one of his favourite places in the world alongside the most compelling, beautiful, assured, talented, and unashamedly seductive woman in Japan?

This was no ordinary affair. They were kindred spirits. Their attitudes toward business and pleasure couldn't be more similar. They'd bring one another exceptional joy during their time together. And if his string of good fortune continued, she'd hold off on marrying for a good long while.

He assumed she planned to marry. She'd never said otherwise. As curious as he was about the sort of man Marcelle fancied for a husband—foreign or Japanese, young buck or thoughtful older gentleman, charismatic or retiring, she could have her pick—he preferred ignorance. Her chosen was a luckier man than Nobu.

Until the day she told him she'd found a husband, or wished to end their affair in any case, Nobu would be by her side. As much as it was going to hurt *Okasan* for him to put off marriage, he wasn't going to marry until Marcelle was through with him. Then he'd accept his fate.

As they sat for breakfast, Marcelle set out her plans for the day's shopping. "I also want to revisit the store with that gorgeous piece of lace. We were in such a rush to see everything yesterday, I didn't have a chance to inspect the lace more closely. I can't shake the feeling that it'd be perfect for the new front window at the boutique."

Nobu raised his brow. "I was in a rush to see everything?"

"We both wanted to see what the other stores had to offer before deciding on our purchases. At least that's how I remember it." She carried a glimmer in her eye that he found incredibly charming.

"After the lace?"

"Then we'll return to the store where you bought me this pin." With a knowing look, she tapped the pin in her hair. To his dying day, he'd recall the sight of that pin glimmering in the firelight while he made love to her breasts. "They have the most exquisite cameo broaches," Marcelle continued. "Yumi-*chan* would be thrilled to get one."

"Might I take you somewhere afterward?" he asked.

"You may." She gave him a shy smile. "Can I inquire where that might be?"

"It's a surprise."

"I adore your surprises." She sighed blissfully, a sound that stirred him, even after they'd made love an hour before and more times over the past two days than he'd imagined when he'd first thought of taking Marcelle to Karuizawa. Would he ever get enough of her?

***

Nobu sat in the carriage beside Marcelle, listening to her musings on the discovery of an even more perfect cameo for Yumi-*chan* at a different store when they stopped in front of the gated pathway to the Koide family villa. Much of the two-story Western-style wooden home was visible from the road, unlike the summer months when the trees in the front garden were so full of leaves, nothing could be glimpsed behind them.

Nobu helped Marcelle down from the carriage and asked the driver to return in an hour.

She glanced around and gave him a quizzical look. "Being abandoned in the middle of the forest is the *surprise*."

"It's hardly the middle of the forest." He pointed at their nearest neighbour's villa a few minutes' walk down the road. "We're surrounded by neighbours. This is my family's villa." He pushed open the iron gate. "My parents and sister were here in August. I was too busy with the store to join them this year."

Marcelle craned toward the gabled roof and its long eaves, then winced and brought a hand to her nape. "My neck. Sometimes it cramps up."

Nobu placed a hand around her slender nape and gave a few massaging squeezes. "I'll have to watch you on the steps to make sure you don't turn on your ankle."

Marcelle slowly shook her head, and he let go. "I'm fine. Really, it happens all the time." Even so, her jaw clenched with a stiff smile that left him unconvinced she was entirely well. "This *is* a wonderful surprise bringing me here. How fortunate to have a country home in such a lovely location."

Nobu put her arm through his and led them up the woodsy pathway to the villa. "*Otosan* built this house the year we returned from London. Before, when I was a child, we had a more traditional Japanese home, but after we got back, *Otosan* wanted something like the homes he'd admired in the Alps of Switzerland and France. Then he removed most of the trees at the back of the house so they wouldn't interfere with his view of the night sky."

"The clear mountain air makes for good stargazing," Marcelle remarked.

An urge came upon him to tell Marcelle all about *Otosan's* hobbies and *Okasan's* parties and Asako's longing for her life in London. He didn't want to make her uncomfortable, though. She hadn't been raised in as close a family as his. Yet he felt compelled to open himself to her, and he wanted her to do the same. That was the kind of affair he envisioned them having.

"My *otosan* draws the night sky," he began tentatively. Marcelle wore a curious expression, so he told her about their rooftop balcony in Tokyo and *Otosan's* study where he painted his sketches. When they reached the front door, Nobu opened his jacket and removed the house key from a chain he'd clipped to his trousers.

He'd taken the key before leaving Tokyo. At the time, he'd wondered whether they might happen to pass through the hillside where the villa was located and pay a casual visit. Now he felt as though he was revealing a precious piece of himself.

The scents of wood, wax, and fireplace soot greeted them. They crossed the foyer inlaid with mosaic and covered in a film of dust. He took her through the parlours and dining room of the first floor. Smaller than the ones in his family's Tokyo home, they were nevertheless similar in décor. *Okasan's* fondness for English country homes was apparent in the heavy, wood furnishings, upholstered seating, and Persian carpets. He told her all of it.

"The house is quite charming," Marcelle said while they walked through the second-floor room he always used when he stayed at the house.

Nobu joined her near the window overlooking the woods fronting the house. "I was thinking if you managed to find the courage to brave another Abt rack through the mountains, we might come to Karuizawa in the summer. We could stay here, at the family villa."

Marcelle crossed her arms over her chest. "Would your family approve of you bringing a lover to their home?"

"I probably wouldn't tell them as much, at least I wouldn't say anything to *Okasan*. I told *Otosan* about you. I asked him to look into the incidents at your boutique. He knows people who keep an eye on delinquent citizens who'd likely attack foreigners."

Marcelle turned on her heel and walked to the window on the opposite side of the room. "Then your father isn't opposed to foreigners?"

"Absolutely not." Nobu followed her. "*Otosan* approves of progress. He wants us to be on equal footing with foreign nations. My family is very Western. You can see from the way *Okasan* decorated the villa. You've met Asako. She'd far prefer a life abroad than one in Japan."

Marcelle let her shoulders fall. Nobu took heart in seeing her relief. "Plainly, your family has embraced Western values. But even Western families don't allow their children to bring lovers to their country homes. Your future wife might not like knowing your neighbors and shopkeeper friends became acquainted with your former lover."

Marcelle was being gracious to worry about his future wife. But neither of them should waste their time together thinking about marriages that were hopefully years to come. Nobu settled his hands on the oxblood wool cape resting on her firm shoulders, then ran them down the length of her lightly muscled arms to her elbows and rested them there. "No one will shame my future wife. In fact, I don't plan to get married for a while. I want to be with you for as long as you'll have me… that is, until you decide to marry."

She wriggled in his grasp. He took the hint and let go. "What if I decide not to marry? I might take a husband if the right circumstances present themselves. I'm also satisfied to remain unwed. You, however, must marry. You're the only son in an aristocratic family. I'm surprised you're not already married."

"I'll marry when the time is right. I want more of you, Marcelle. I'm not ready to give you up."

She met his gaze and hers softened. "I'm not ready to give you up, either." Her tender tone steadied his racing heart.

Nobu pulled her toward him. She unfolded her arms and wrapped them around his midsection, enveloping him in the spicy lavender soap from the bath and her distinctive honey sweetness.

Easing back, she looked up at him. "When you *do* marry, please don't ask me to be your mistress. I won't be that woman for you."

He bit back a confession that he wasn't planning on taking a mistress. He wanted to desire his wife as much as he desired the woman in his arms, although that was unlikely. Hell, he'd be happy to feel for his wife a fraction of what he felt for Marcelle. "I'd never ask you to be my mistress."

In the shadow of large trees filtering most of the waning light, he studied the curve of her forehead, the sea of dark blue in her eyes, the tense twitch at the corner of her lips. Even women with the strength of Marcelle had moments of vulnerability. She deserved more security in their affair. In her life. He could give that to her. "Let me be your benefactor. This Hamada-*san* has left you in danger. Where was he when *La France Boutique* was attacked? How has he helped you these past weeks? Break all ties with him. I'll give you all the assistance you need."

"I can't." Marcelle shook her head. "I don't need... You've helped so much with the guardsmen and with speaking to your father on my behalf. But my arrangement with Jiro is as it should be."

"Hamada-*san*'s given name is Jiro?"

Marcelle again crossed her arms. "It is."

"I've never heard of a Jiro Hamada. You said he was a prominent man of business, an important investor in Tokyo companies. Isn't that right?"

She leaned against the window frame. "He's quite wealthy. It seems he's also involved in politics. That's why he travels abroad so often."

"If Jiro Hamada is traveling on political matters, my family would know him." Nobu couldn't imagine to whom Marcelle was referring. Perhaps Jiro Hamada was based out of Kagoshima or Ehime and represented those men of business in foreign political matters. But even then *Otosan* would know the name Hamada. Marcelle ought to break all ties with the suspicious character. Her loyalty was making her vulnerable in ways she need not be.

He took a step nearer Marcelle. "What prompts you to continue your relationship with him? You said the affair was over. Why not leave him in the past?"

Marcelle crossed the room to the bed and gripped a floral decoration on the ornate cast-iron frame. "He understands *La France Boutique*. He's always helped me with the store. He's never given me any reason to question his loyalty or his dedication to my work." Letting go of the bed frame, she met Nobu's gaze. "I cannot sever ties with him simply because the man I'm conducting an affair with wishes me to do so."

Nobu glanced out the window. The carriage hadn't arrived, yet there was nothing more to be said. Marcelle was loyal to Jiro Hamada. Her connection to him surpassed any feelings for Nobu.

A bitter taste filled his mouth. "We should go outside and wait for the carriage." He walked past her and out of the room.

***

As the sky lightened, Nobu woke from a fitful sleep. Neither of them had said a significant word since leaving his family's villa. After the inn's maid had cleared dinner and prepared their futons, Marcelle had lain down, and he'd stayed in the main room by the fireplace, pondering who this Jiro Hamada was and what kind of hold he had on Marcelle. When he finally took his place on the futon next to Marcelle's, he laid still, listening to her even breaths. She might have been sleeping. He wasn't going to get close enough to make certain. He turned from her and rested his eyes. Sleep came eventually.

Every bird in Karuizawa must have gathered on their room's veranda to herald the first rays of sunshine. Nobu wasn't surprised when Marcelle stirred.

She faced him, and a tear spilled from her eye. "No man has ever made me feel the way I do when we're together."

The knot in his chest loosened. He ran his hand down her round, strong shoulders that moved bolts of fabric and executed the most precise stitches. Emotion swelled his throat. He was falling in love with Marcelle. He'd been falling in love with her since his grand opening when she'd called him a cutthroat capitalist to his back.

Whatever Jiro Hamada felt for her was nothing compared to what Nobu felt. He'd never have stopped sleeping with Marcelle. He'd never leave her to fend for herself when her store was being attacked. "You're the most important person in my life. This means I want to protect you and care for you. I won't have any peace as long as Jiro Hamada is your benefactor. I can't do it."

Marcelle rose to her elbow. "I know that. But what about when you marry, what will you do with *La France Boutique*? Will your wife allow you to continue giving assistance to the woman with whom you had an affair?"

"I'll place *La France Boutique* under the care of a trusted associate…my secretary Ishida-*san*. He's going to manage the next department store I build and become a powerful man in his own right. I'll make certain he does well by you. We can draw up an agreement between the three of us. Can you trust me to do that for you?"

Her luminous blue gaze held his. "I'll tell Jiro I no longer need him to be my benefactor. The time has come for us to part ways."

Nobu's limbs pulsed with victory. Marcelle was truly his. He ran a finger down the side of her downy cheek, and her plush lips parted. She sucked down on the finger, igniting his body. "Marcelle, I need to be inside you."

Heavy-lidded and breathing in light gasps, she moved to her back and untied her kimono *obi*. He savoured the sight of her long hair spread across the pillow and her dusky nipples nubbed to points. After straddling the sides of her legs, Nobu undid his *obi* and poised at her entrance.

"Take me inside," Marcelle rasped. She tilted her hips upward. A small mewing from her lips completed the demand.

With a mammalian grunt, he plunged past her silky folds into her warm, wet sheath. "Oh, the gods, this is where I need to be."

"Then stay," Marcelle hissed between breaths.

"Always," he ground out.

If he had his way, he'd never leave.

CHAPTER FOURTEEN

Marcelle

Glowing with pregnancy, Suki gave Marcelle's hand a squeeze as their carriage turned into the outer gates of the Oshima residence. "I don't know what's going to be more entertaining," she said with a tease in her voice, "the moving pictures or witnessing your meeting Nobu's family."

"You think it's going to be entertaining to watch me trip over the carpet, break the leg off a side table, and cut my hand on whatever precious vase I happen to destroy?" Even though she'd barely had a nibble all day, Marcelle's midsection felt constricted. She had a hard time catching her breath. This all-too-familiar illness was a case of the nerves, and it reduced her to a birdbrain. If history was any indication, before the night was out, she'd likely be cut, burned, bruised, sprained, or mildly poisoned.

This night seemed altogether too fated. Suki's husband, Griff, had received an invitation to view the moving picture, *Voyage to the Moon*, through a friend at his lawn tennis club. Since it was a French production, Suki had suggested Marcelle and her new beau join them. As fate would have it, Nobu and his family had also been invited to the showing as his father was keen on astrology.

Since he and Marcelle would view the showing together, as they'd planned, and he was determined to make his parents realize he was off the marriage market, he'd thought it best to introduce her to his parents. She'd be introduced as a friend and fellow Ginza Boulevard proprietor. Even so, his parents had already caught wind of their son's flirtation. They knew Marcelle and Nobu were more than friends and Marcelle knew they knew as much, which meant everyone knew they knew they were being introduced to their son's lover, even if no one was going to call it that.

Nobu's enthusiasm for making the introductions convinced her to agree, which she now regretted because her hands shook and perspiration slickened every crevice of her body. Fortunately, Asako would be attending as well, and Marcelle looked forward to seeing the very British young woman again.

There was also a small degree of comfort to be had in that when Marcelle fell face-first into an esteemed guest's fruity custard while greeting Nobu's mother, she'd look gorgeous doing so. She'd chosen a dress cut from golden kimono silk printed with clusters of autumn-hued leaves. A narrow sash of the same pattern cinched her waist. Bright and elegant, the outfit was meant to catch the eye without overwhelming it, to intrigue the viewer enough that she might consider paying a visit to *La France Boutique* and ordering one for herself.

But the ribboned edging on the dress and intricate kimono pattern might be lost on Nobu when he realized she'd fastened her chestnut curls with the pin he'd given her in Karuizawa. The thought of seeing the now-familiar hunger in his eyes when he recognized the bauble sent a thrumming rush of desire through her. More perspiration sprang to her decolletage. She wiped it with a gold-threaded handkerchief as she'd probably be wiping it all evening. Nobu's presence would doubtlessly keep her glowing. Guests at the moving pictures display were going to be impressed by her vibrant appearance. Truly love's flush was the most generous accessory.

The Oshimas' magnificent home occupied the grounds of a feudal lord's estate from the shogunate era. The family was Japan's foremost steel manufacturers, and, apparently, friends of Nobu's mother's family for many generations. Their families had been on the winning side in the Boshin War, which had defeated the shogunate and restored the emperor to the capital. Their reward had been grand estates that had once belonged to families on the losing side.

The white stone façade of the Oshimas' house called to mind manor homes in the north of France. The bottom two stories were broken up by windows framed in dark green shutters. Dormer windows jutted out from a sloped roof where four tall chimneys let smoke into the night sky. Dozens of guests, mostly in Western attire, chatted in groups within the brightly lit rooms of the bottom floor.

Marcelle swallowed against her dry throat. "I'm going to forget all my Japanese."

"How could you?" Griff asked from the opposite end of the carriage bench. "You speak like a native. You've been here almost a decade."

"Eight years. And French is the only language I can recall when I'm nervous."

Suki patted Marcelle's knee. "You'll be fine. If you need a Japanese word, just ask. I'm sure Monsieur Koide will be at hand."

And his mother, and his father, and, hopefully, his sister.

The Oshimas' front parlor was the size of a small ballroom. Like a ballroom, chandeliers hung overhead and gilt-edged mirrors bookended walls covered in gold and scarlet paper. Velvet drapes of the same colors framed the windows. Griff introduced Suki and Marcelle to their host Monsieur Oshima, who told them he'd hired the most popular *benshi* moving pictures narrator in Tokyo to give a short lecture before the showing and provide ongoing commentary while they watched. Suki dragged Griff away to thank a family friend who'd purchased advertising space in *Tokyo Women's Magazine*. Madame Oshima complimented Marcelle's dress. "I'm too old to wear such a stunning piece, but my granddaughters would adore it. Perhaps I could visit your boutique?"

Her boutique. Since she'd decided to end her business relationship with Jiro, the boutique had felt more like hers. He'd always gloried in her successes, as the store was a means for him to prove to the world what a woman could accomplish. Likewise, she'd come to regard her accomplishments as a means to impress him. With Nobu as her guarantor, she wouldn't be distracted by the imperative to impress someone with her successes. And they'd belong to her.

Marcelle described *La France Boutique*'s location to Madame Oshima, then stepped away for the matron to continue greeting her guests. Bursting with pride at having received exactly the sort of compliment she'd hoped on her dress, Marcelle glanced around the parlor, wondering if Nobu's mother might have been within earshot.

Someone tapped her shoulder. Turning, she came face-to-face with the most desirable man in Tokyo, who also happened to be her lover. Nobu's black three-piece suit with a burgundy necktie complemented her dress to a tee. She hadn't told him what she'd be wearing. Seeing their tastes align made her break into a silly schoolgirl smile.

"Good evening, Mademoiselle Renaud." He bowed.

She nodded in turn. "Good evening, Monsieur Koide. It's a pleasure to make your acquaintance once again." How she wished he would take her in his arms and set her nerves to rights with one of his bone-melting kisses. Since they'd returned from Karuizawa almost two weeks ago, he'd come by the boutique every day to make certain his guards were on duty and the women working inside were safe. They stole kisses in her backroom and spent two nights at a lover's inn with an underground passageway where luminaries could enter without being seen. Next week, after she finally finished all the orders from the Ueno promenade, Nobu was going to take her to one of Tokyo's new hotels. Not that she minded their discreet inns, as they were ideal for a quick nighttime romp, but hotels were better suited for daylong lovemaking, exquisite cuisine, and sleeping side by side.

Scarlet sprang to Nobu's cheeks. "Is that...?" He nodded at the hairpin.

"I received it from a most discerning gentleman on the occasion of a trip to Karuizawa."

He leaned closer. "I think you're wearing far too much clothing to do it justice." Her chest speckled with heat at the memory of his hard length between her breasts. "There are a few people I'd like to introduce you to, if you're ready," he said with a shy smile.

The parlor's rich, tobacco- and perfume-scented air made her slightly dizzy. Or was it her nerves making her dizzy? "I'd love to meet your family."

Nobu looked around the hall. Halfway through the perusal, he came to an abrupt stop. His posture tensed. "I cannot believe..."

Marcelle followed his gaze to his sister, Asako, his mother, who Marcelle had recalled from Koide Department Store's grand opening, and a beaming young woman. Nobu's mother didn't even spare a glance in Marcelle's direction when she came to stand beside her son. His mother spoke to Nobu in rapid Japanese, which Marcelle gathered referred to his mother's pleasure at having encountered the young woman by her side.

Asako stretched out her hand to Marcelle, who clasped it. "I was thrilled to hear you were coming to the showing this evening. I've been meaning to come by your boutique, but my dear brother won't allow me until you're finished with all the promenade orders."

Marcelle swelled with gratitude for Asako's warm greeting. "We're almost finished with the orders. I hope you stop by soon."

Nobu's mother whispered into Asako's ear. She mumbled a response, then turned to Marcelle. "*Okasan* would prefer I speak Japanese out of respect for our friend," she said in English with a nod to the young woman whose beaming was directed right at Nobu.

"I speak Japanese," Marcelle replied in Japanese with a tentative smile at Nobu's mother, who'd yet to acknowledge Marcelle's presence.

"*Okasan*," Nobu intoned in a soothing voice. "I'd like to introduce you to my friend, Renaud-*san*. She's from France and owns a boutique on Ginza Boulevard."

Marcelle fell into a low bow that brought her face-to-face with the skillful stitching at the waist of Madame Koide's taupe gown. As she attempted to rise with utmost elegance, her neck twinged with spiking pain.

Reflexively, her head tilted to the side with the spasm.

Asako gasped. "Are you hurt?" she asked in English.

Stifling a pained gasp, Marcelle pressed her fingers between her spasmed neck and shoulder. "Just a little muscle pain," she replied also in English because she couldn't find the right Japanese. But at least she hadn't spoken French.

Nobu gripped her nape with firm but gentle pressure and kneaded.

His mother widened her eyes at the sight, then pivoted the equally wide-eyed young woman by her side away from Marcelle and her son. Asako let her jaw drop and stared at Nobu with his hands on Marcelle's neck in the middle of a moving picture's party.

Humiliation burned her cheeks to what must be the darkest hue of scarlet in the hall. Hardly a color to match her autumn-hued gown and hardly the best manners in meeting the woman who'd birthed and raised her paramour. Not that she needed his mother's approval or admiration. She just wanted the woman who Nobu claimed was a foremost fashionable of the upper social echelon to appreciate her style and, perhaps, recommend *La France Boutique* to her friends. She'd simply wanted to impress Madame Koide, and the woman couldn't be less impressed.

Within moments her muscles obeyed and loosened. Even his briefest massages were unreasonably good.

"How is that?" he asked.

Marcelle tested out her neck. "Better." She turned to Nobu's mother and the young woman, even though they weren't looking in her direction. "I apologize for the muscle strain. It's a pleasure to meet you," she added in highly polite Japanese.

Nobu's mother looked her way and nodded her perfectly coiffed head at Marcelle. "It is always a pleasure to welcome foreigners to the country even though our weather is terrible and our food offensive to the foreign stomach. I imagine your heart longs for your family back home."

The greeting was *de rigueur*. Polite society demanded self-deprecation and expressions of empathy at every turn. "I find Japanese food quite delicious." Marcelle said in perfect Japanese.

Nobu's mother's *de rigueur* reply should've been mock surprise at Marcelle's appreciation for Japanese food followed by the supposition that Marcelle might indeed be Japanese at heart. Instead, she tilted her head to the side as though Marcelle was an unfathomable curiosity. "How odd that our food meets your standards."

Marcelle was speechless. This was a cut like she'd never experienced in Japan.

Nobu cleared his throat and nodded toward the young woman standing next to his mother. "I'd like to introduce Nagahara-*san*," he said in Japanese.

Marcelle went through the expected sequence of greetings with the young woman, who managed a polite smile despite halting speech that attested to her barely veiled discomfort.

Nobu's mother nodded toward the hall where *Voyage to the Moon* was going to be shown. "You'll escort the Nagaharas' daughter to our seats," she said to Nobu. "We'll be sitting with Viscount Nagahara and the rest of the Nagahara family this evening." She spoke in clear, simple Japanese. Her message was equally clear. Marcelle would not be sitting with the Koide family, and this young lady would take the seat by Nobu's side.

Nobu clenched his jaw. "*Okasan*, I'd been planning to assist Renaud-*san* in understanding the narration."

His mother reared back. "You must help the Nagaharas' daughter better appreciate the European style and manners presented in the pictures."

Mother's and son's gazes locked. Beads of sweat accumulated on Nagahara daughter's brow.

Marcelle couldn't bear the tension. "Koide-*san*, it sounds like you need to explain the European ways to Mademoiselle Nagahara," she said in clear, simple Japanese, just like Madame Koide.

"I'd intended to share the moving pictures with you," he said to her softly in English.

Marcelle forced a smile. "I insist."

Nobu looked between his mother and Marcelle. He must know she was doing everything in her power not to offend his mother, even though it seemed her very existence was an unforgivable offense. "If you insist," he said, his voice full of misgiving. "I'll see you after the showing."

Before disappearing into the hall alongside Nagaharas' daughter, he turned back and gazed at Marcelle with more concern than necessary. She was plenty fine attending the showing without him. That was the point of an affair—dallying about for enjoyment, not taking one another as seriously as they would a paramour they were courting for a walk down the aisle. When it was time for either of them to marry, they'd part. Nobu seemed to think that day would come when she found a husband. Now that Marcelle had met the juggernaut of Madame Koide, she had no doubt Nobu would be marrying well before she found a husband. Probably to a woman quite like the Nagahara girl, if not her.

Marcelle sat with Suki and Griff in the back row of chairs facing the ivory-clothed wall where the moving pictures would be projected. Nobu sat a few rows ahead, towering over everyone around him. The hall went silent for the *benshi* narrator's introductory remarks on the theme of space travel and the moving picture's director and actors. Once the pictures began, members of the audience gasped and exclaimed. Marcelle saw Nobu turn several times to the Nagahara girl with a remark. The trifle-of-a-thing nodded. Twice she seemed to offer commentary of her own, to which Nobu nodded in turn.

"He's enjoying his lovely company," Marcelle whispered to Suki.

Suki patted Marcelle's arm. "He's being kind."

"She's darling."

Marcelle willed herself to focus on the images twirling along the cloth. The story of several curious astronomers' trip to the moon and the rather sinister—albeit easily disposed of—aliens they encountered proved intriguing. The movie lasted no more than a quarter of an hour and was followed by closing remarks from the *benshi* narrator. Marcelle hadn't realized she was staring at Nobu until his broad grin came suddenly into focus. She bristled with embarrassment. She shouldn't have been staring at him alongside the Nagahara girl, and he shouldn't be so pleased at having commandeered her attention.

The Oshimas' guests retired to the large front parlor where round tables had been placed for guests to take refreshments. Marcelle sat with Suki and Griff, and an older gentleman who eagerly questioned Griff about England's generous overtures toward Russia. Were these meant to garner support for their position in the Boxer Rebellion taking place in China?

Suki was telling Marcelle about her son Henry's dramatic games of battleship with his American playmates when Nobu and an older gentleman came to the table.

Noting that he'd left the Nagahara girl elsewhere and feeling much relief because of it, Marcelle chided herself for harboring jealousy toward a young woman who'd make a lovely bride for Nobu.

Jealousy was a frivolous, unbecoming emotion.

She'd learned all about frivolous emotions from her time with Antoine. Namely, she'd learned that she shouldn't fall in love with a man just because he treated her to visits to the theatre and fine clothes with jewelry to match. She shouldn't feel offended when he flirted with her so-called friends and bedded one of them. Probably more. She shouldn't feel resentful when he insisted she care for his unstable, alcoholic aunt so he could bed her friends. She shouldn't break down when he returned from a stay at his parents' chateau with a new bride in tow. All those useless emotions had amounted to a state of despair.

Granted, they'd resulted in her impulsively and naïvely accepting the offer from the American envoy's wife to join her family in Japan, a choice which had made her happy.

Nobu, too, made her happy. Still, she had to keep in mind two undeniable fates: their affair would end, and Nobu needed to court for marriage. If she wished to spare herself the heartache of frivolous emotions like jealousy, she'd have to excuse herself from events where he ought to be courting pretty young women.

The older gentleman interrupted the man speaking to Griff. "Come now, Mitsui-*san*. No one wants to hear about international discord. We've just enjoyed a fascinating story set in moving pictures. You should be discussing the fine points of celluloid or the proposition that cannons can be used for space travel. I, for one, believe that one day, we'll have a cannon powerful enough to send man to space."

Had Marcelle's eyes been closed, she would've thought Nobu had been speaking, his voice was so similar to the older gentleman's in tenor and manner of British pronunciation. Eyes open, she never would've matched them as father and son. The elder Koide stood several inches shorter than his son, which was common between their generations. His eyes were narrower, his chin longer, and the lines on his face belonged to a man who'd spent a lifetime observing and scrutinizing, a contrast to the lines around Nobu's eyes that came from his natural affability and the generous smiles he gave Koide's customers.

The gentleman next to Griff laughed. "Right you are, Koide-*san*, which is why we rely on you to give us a vision for the future."

Nobu presented his father to Griff, Suki, and finally to Marcelle. The touch of warmth in Nobu's father's tone, his patient pause after they'd gone through the formalities as though he was willing to stand there all evening listening to whatever opinions she wished to offer, all reminded her of the mayor of Bordeaux campaigning for his position. Both men listened with an aim to please.

Marcelle wished to oblige. "I found the moving pictures quite intriguing."

"Did you? Would you agree the moon's surface resembled Roquefort cheese?"

"I believe it did," Marcelle replied, and Nobu's father continued with his observations. While he was questioning the perplexed looks on the spacemen's faces—"Weren't they scared out of their wits?" he asked those seated around the table—Nobu's mother and Asako came to stand beside him. Asako gave Marcelle a friendly smile. Once again, Madame Koide succeeded in making Marcelle feel invisible.

"This is what man dreams of," Nobu's father continued. "Taking flight into the great expanse of space and stepping foot on the moon. How else can we know what it means to be human? In all truth, we won't know until we encounter the alien. Then we'll know who we are as a species." Monsieur Koide turned to his wife. "I'd like to host a showing for anyone who was unable to attend this evening. *Voyage to the Moon* should be shared with as many people in our nation's capital as possible."

Madame Koide nodded heartily. "What a brilliant idea. You'll have to speak with Oshima-*san* about acquiring the services of the *benshi* narrator. He was outstanding. Now, let's allow Nobu's friends to enjoy their evening. It was an honor meeting you all." She bowed in the direction of the table, which spared her the necessity of directly acknowledging any of them. "Please inform our driver that we're ready to leave," she said in Japanese to Nobu.

His father and Asako bid them good evening and followed Madame Koide toward the table where the Oshima family sat with their guests. Nobu remained behind Marcelle's chair.

She shifted in her seat to face him.

"I'm sorry we weren't seated together for the showing," he said in a low voice. "*Okasan* had ideas of her own this evening. She should've been more welcoming toward you."

"She was civil," Marcelle replied with an equanimity she didn't feel. Nobu's mother couldn't have been more obvious in her regard for the foreign *modiste*, or more insulting in conveying this regard.

"She behaved like an ill-mannered brat. She needs a slap upside the head," Nobu said with a teasing glimmer in his eye.

Marcelle feigned a horrified gasp. "Don't you dare. Her coiffure is magnificent. I'd hate to see it ruined."

Nobu tilted his head back with laughter. "I'll share your compliments." He gave her shoulder a discreet squeeze. Marcelle longed to lean against him and direct his thick muscular fingers to the troublesome places in her neck and shoulders. "I'm going to have a word with *Okasan* tomorrow. She shouldn't be encouraging Viscount Nagahara's daughter."

A knot of greater proportions than the one lingering in her neck tightened in her chest. Nobu must marry well. The viscount's girl was certainly an appealing prospect. Charming, pretty, and an able conversationalist. What more did he want? "Don't dismiss the Nagahara daughter outright. She seems to have charm."

Nobu's gaze darkened. "I'm not going to entertain any marriage prospects as long as I can be with you. I thought I made that clear." His voice was edgy.

Mon Dieu, how she loved his insistence. Reaching up, she covered his hand with hers. "You made that perfectly clear."

Their gazes locked. The night had been as much of a disaster as Marcelle had feared, but the molten look in Nobu's eye made it all worth it.

After Nobu bid the table good night, Suki turned to Marcelle. "He adores you," she whispered in French.

"So he says," Marcelle whispered in return. She might as well have confessed her agreement and replied *As do I*. Her best friend wasn't a fool.

In truth, their mutual adoration was making for a blistering, passionate affair. An affair she was going to resist corrupting with useless emotions.

CHAPTER FIFTEEN

Nobu

Otosan rose from his seat at the head of the dining room table. "Duties at the Foundation Party headquarters will keep me there all day, if anyone inquires."

"We'll direct any inquiring parties to the headquarters," *Okasan* replied from her seat to Nobu's right.

As *Otosan* turned toward the dining room door, the maid rushed to his place and set about clearing tableware that had held rice, soft-boiled eggs, pickles, and salted mackerel.

"One moment," Nobu called to *Otosan*'s back. "I have something I'd like to say about last night." Asako, seated across from him, raised a questioning brow. *Okasan* was impassive. "I want you all to hear it."

Otosan murmured his assent and returned to his seat at the head of the table.

Last night, Marcelle had to endure him sitting beside another woman and conversing with her when he should've been sitting and conversing with Marcelle. Each time he'd glanced in her direction, she'd been smiling and speaking amiably with Suki and Griff Spenser. He'd had to suppress the impulse to leap from his seat and barrel his way to the last row and take his rightful place. Hell, he'd wanted to declare in front of everyone that this beautiful, talented marvel of a woman was his. They were lovers and would continue to be for quite some time, so everyone should accept their affair and leave them to it. It would've been the social spectacle of the year. And it would've sent a much-needed message to *Okasan* and the aristocratic daughters.

Okasan lifted her chin upward. "I thought last night was splendid. The moving pictures pleased *Otosan*. I had a chance to speak with my dear friend Oshima-*san*. Let's not forget how lovely the Nagahara daughter looked. I think she's quite taken with you, Nobu."

"She's lovely. Her future husband is a fortunate man," Nobu replied, his voice hard.

Okasan schooled her features into an expression of pleasant surprise. "I take it this means you'd like to propose?"

"I have no intention of making her my wife."

"She's everything you want in a bride." *Okasan*'s tone reminded him of a caress on his boyhood cheek. "Did you notice how the pink lace of her dress favoured her porcelain skin?"

Nobu turned away from *Okasan* and addressed *Otosan*. "Do you recall Renaud-*san*, the French woman I introduced you to last evening?"

Otosan nodded. "Is she the woman whose store was attacked?"

"She is. Fortunately, she and her store have been free of incidents in recent weeks."

"*Ha*," Asako declared. "That would explain why you haven't been around."

Nobu shot her a glare for the annoying, if rather insightful, observation. "I took Renaud-*san* to Karuizawa a few weeks ago."

Okasan drew a hand to her chest. "I thought you went with Haneda-*san* and Abe-*san*."

Nobu shook his head. He'd been purposefully vague with *Okasan*, telling her he would be in Karuizawa with friends. "I took Renaud-*san*. We had a delightful holiday. My feelings for her make it impossible for me to entertain the idea of marrying the Nagahara girl or any other woman at this time. Perhaps when Renaud-*san* decides to wed, I'll return to seeking a wife."

Okasan gripped her teacup with both hands.

Otosan sucked breath through his teeth. "You need a wife to care for you and spoil your children. You're nearly thirty years old. Why deprive yourself any longer?"

"He's in love," Asako said matter-of-factly.

Nobu doubled the venom in his glare. Why must she fan the flames? "Right now, I only wish to be with Marcelle."

Okasan's clicking sounds of disapproval filled the room.

"Marry and make her your mistress." *Otosan* shrugged. "Have what you want and do right by your family."

"She's not interested in becoming my mistress. Besides, when I marry, I want a love match." Or at least an easy marriage with mutual goodwill. Marcelle might have made it impossible for him to achieve anything close to love with his future bride. That was his fate, and every second by her side was worth losing the opportunity to find a nobleman's daughter who might give him a marriage of affection. "It takes time to make a love match. I'm too busy to devote myself to the task."

Okasan huffed. "My dear son, if you're running around Tokyo with this foreign woman, no woman of high birth is going to marry you. You'll never get a title."

Nobu suppressed the urge to tell *Okasan* he couldn't care less about becoming a member of the nobility. Saying so would disparage the prize she held most dear. He bowed his head. "Whatever becomes of my quest for a title, I'll have to accept."

"There are other issues to consider, such as your future service in government," *Otosan* said. His tone was light, but Nobu knew from experience that his politically gifted *Otosan* always kept the tone light when issuing a warning. "Men far less cosmopolitan than you gain political momentum every day. You need every possible advantage to position yourself for a place in the Diet. A public affair with Renaud-*san* might alienate those who'd give you their vote otherwise."

Nobu nodded rather than tell his family once and for all he had no interest in titles or political office. "I'll keep that in mind."

Okasan stood. "My weak heart cannot take any more of this conversation. I'm appalled, Nobu. Absolutely appalled."

Likewise, *Otosan* stood. "We'll speak of this later." He followed *Okasan* from the room.

Nobu listened to their footfalls down the hallway and up the stairs, then turned to find Asako shaking her head at him.

"I'm not sure if I should thank you for distracting them from the never-ending drama of my letter to London. Or throw daggers at you for freeing *Okasan* to focus on finding me a husband."

"My obstinance concerning the aristocrats' daughters should give *Okasan* plenty to occupy herself for quite some time."

"*Forever* wouldn't be long enough." Asako sat back in her chair and gave him a suspicious glare. "You're really trying for a love match with an insipid, kowtowing detriment to women's progress?"

"I'd prefer a happy marriage." His gut ached as he said the words, but what else could he say? That he'd rather marry a woman at the vanguard of women's progress? That he'd rather marry Marcelle? "I want that for you, too. I'm still looking for someone who'd make a good match." He'd meant to make inquiries about the proclivities of a few men he suspected had a similar disposition as Asako. But after the holiday in Karuizawa, his plate had been full of obligations at the department store and making sure Marcelle was safe and sated with plenty of lovemaking.

"Take your time. Perhaps you have bought me a little with your love declaration for Renaud-*san*."

He wouldn't call what he'd said a love declaration. But what he felt for Marcelle was tender and passionate, as much like love as he'd ever known. He'd wished for a love match, and now he had it. He wasn't giving it up anytime soon, and he was glad to have informed his family of as much.

CHAPTER SIXTEEN

Marcelle

Marcelle woke in a rush of anticipation. This afternoon, maids and delivery boys would come to *La France Boutique* to collect dresses their employers had ordered after the Ueno promenade. Uniting dresses with their owners made Marcelle feel like a matchmaker joining two souls whose fates had been written in the stars. It also freed her from reviewing every neckline, hem, seam, and decoration to make infinitesimal, and mostly unnecessary, corrections.

Sunlight streaming into her boardinghouse room promised a crisp fall day of blue skies and abundant sunshine. Contented, Marcelle sat up in bed. Everything about the past few days had exceeded her expectations. Not only had they finished the promenade orders, but she'd also had a magnificent celebration of the event with Nobu at the Imperial Palace Hotel. Two nights ago, they'd dined on velvety Matsutake mushroom soup, pâte terrine, seared wild Japanese boar, a salad of endive and goat's cheese, and apple soufflé at the hotel's popular French haute cuisine restaurant. The Japanese ingredients and alterations in preparation, notably in the chef using less cheese and more soy sauce, had given the dinner a familiar appearance and slightly exotic flavor.

Later that night, they sat naked facing one another on the hotel room's canopied bed. Nobu cupped her breast while he licked her nipples and glided the pad of his thumb over the raised nubs. Her brazen squeals filled the bedroom. Every part of her yearned for the fullness of him driving into her without a shred of mercy.

"Would you like something hard tonight?" he asked in a rough whisper.

Nobu always seemed to be reading her mind. She ran her hand between his legs and squeezed his full erection. "That's exactly what I want."

He dipped his tongue inside her mouth and swirled in the way she loved, then released her with a resigned sigh and she released him—they had such difficulty releasing one another. He walked across the bedroom, his muscled buttocks flexing silver in the moonlight. From his satchel, he pulled out a white silk bag suited for a pair of slippers and brought it to the bed.

"May I?" she asked, her fingers already around the rope ties.

"It's all yours."

Marcelle unwound the ties and tugged the bag's sides to reveal a glass dildo the length and girth of which surpassed any erection she'd ever laid eyes on. She found her mouth watering. The muscles around her entrance clenched. The cock was angled to connect with the special place at the front of her sheath that made every muscle in her body go limp. Most conveniently, inside the bag hid a jar of oil. "Is this for me?"

"It's all yours. Take it home and pleasure yourself there. You could also pleasure yourself here." Nobu gestured to the bed. "Or you can let me do the honours."

Marcelle ran a finger along the cool, smooth column and flared head. "My very first glass dildo. I've wanted one since I heard about the glass blowers in Edogawa, but I'd never seen one for myself." Nobu's gaze followed her hand. The muscles in his neck bulged from restraint or perhaps anticipation. The sight caused liquid to leak from her quim onto the sheets. "Since you've been so kind to gift this precious piece, why don't you do the honors?"

No man had ever looked at her with such gratitude. "I was hoping you'd say that." He crushed her mouth in a penetrating kiss.

Marcelle turned over and presented him with her rear. "Will you do it from behind?"

"Fuck, yes," Nobu said through gritted teeth.

The pop of the oil stopper came, and she took in a waft of honeysuckle.

"Do you want me to heat the dildo or keep it cool?" Considerate and needing everything to be perfect had made Nobu successful in so many ways.

"Cold," she replied. "I'm so hot already."

Nobu must have been fast in his application of the oil because she was caught unaware when he nudged the slick glass piece against her mound.

Marcelle gasped at the intimidating hardness, at the shock of the coldness.

Nobu continued rolling the instrument over her mound and into her folds, teasing her pearly nub. "Is it cold enough?"

Mercilessly so, much to her delight. "Plenty."

She opened herself at the same time Nobu slid the broad rounded tip inside. The stretch burned just as the cold glass soothed. Shivers coursed through her.

Nobu held the dildo steady. "Tell me what you need, Marcelle."

Arching her back, she wriggled her hips, bringing the glass to the place that sent ripples of weakness over every inch of her. She moaned and bucked and rolled it inside her until she needed him. "Nobu, in and out."

He obeyed, moving the dildo in and out, finding the special place, making it spring forward each time he retreated. Neither quickening nor slowing, his constant motion sent a vicious burn twisting and curling through her.

Perspiration covered her skin in a thin sheen. She swayed and rocked, but he never faltered. He reached around and thumbed her precious bud. His touch made her see stars. The orgasm that followed tore through her in inescapable spasms that left her clutching possessively against the unrelenting glass.

Nobu removed the dildo, then pressed a thumb inside her as though to feel her spasms for himself. "Can I do that for you again?" he asked, bent over her back, his abrasive cheek scraping hers.

"This time, I want you."

Nobu responded with a deep plunge inside her and a groan that was more of a yell. After the glass, he was more firm than hard but just as relentless, crashing into her until they came in a symphony of gasps and screams that must have offended the esteemed ears of more than a few Imperial Hotel guests.

Blissful memories from their stay at the Imperial Hotel married with the blissful approach of the lovely fall day, and Marcelle rose from bed. She allowed herself a leisurely toilette and breakfast, then bid the boardinghouse matron farewell while making a mental note to ask Nobu to send more sweet bean cakes from the department store. The matron had been making her irritation at Marcelle's nighttime absences apparent with ever-increasing tsking and comments about a woman's virtue. Bean cakes from Koide's had yet to fail in putting an end to the fuss.

On her way to *La France Boutique*, she stopped at the patisserie just outside Tsukiji's gates. A Japanese *patisseriere* who'd trained in France had conveniently opened his own patisserie between the boardinghouse and her store. This morning seemed like the perfect day to indulge in her favorite *brasillé* pastries. She caught up with the baker whose Parisian brogue was so accurate, she often had to remind herself they were in Tokyo while they chatted over *brasillé* and *le chocolat chaud*.

Before leaving, she bought croissants for Nobu, as croissants were his favorite, Ryusuke, and the other guardsmen who patrolled her part of Ginza Boulevard. Over the past month, there hadn't been a hint of trouble at the boutique. Nobu's father hadn't heard anything alarming about anti-foreigner sentiment in Ginza, so Nobu was content the lunatic was no longer targeting the boutique. Recently, his guardsmen hadn't been patrolling as often.

The veil of threat hanging over the boutique had lifted, and questions about Nobu and his family that had played in her mind since seeing Jiro at the promenade had quieted. He'd been wrong about Nobu and his family using her. She wished he knew how wrong he'd been, that he wasn't somewhere in the world worrying needlessly.

This week, she was planning to tell Nomura-*san* of her decision to cease having Jiro as her benefactor. While she dreaded severing ties with Jiro and Nomura-*san*, it felt inevitable.

Marcelle turned the key in *La France Boutique*'s lock without any resistance. Had she neglected to properly lock the door the previous evening? She had a distinct memory of Ryusuke checking the lock to make certain it was in place before she boarded a rickshaw to Tsukiji and he escorted Yumi-*chan* to her boardinghouse. Yet…it turned.

Tentatively, she swung the boutique door open. The fetid odor of animal rot assaulted her nostrils. Bile surged to her throat. Without a glance inside, she slammed the door shut.

What had the anti-foreigner fanatic done now? Had he killed an animal and spread its blood? What kind of man committed such a vile, repulsive act?

Marcelle turned up Ginza Boulevard in the direction of Koide Department Store. Nobu would know what to do with a dead animal in the store. He'd have a guardsman remove it and assist her in cleaning up the mess. Thank the gods she had him.

Halfway between her boutique and the department store, Ryusuke headed toward her. At her frantic wave, he increased his pace.

He furrowed his brow as he neared. "What's happened?"

"There's something in the store. I think someone must've entered last night. The door was unlocked when I arrived." The metallic, putrid scent lingering in her nostrils piqued at the memory. "When I opened the door, I smelled blood."

Ryusuke's facial muscles twitched. "Yumi-*chan* didn't come in, did she?" He shouted behind him as he sprinted to the store.

She'd given Yumi-*chan* and the seamstresses a holiday for their work these past weeks. Marcelle hurried behind him as fast as she could. "I told her not to since we'd finished those orders." Panic gripped her. Had Yumi-*chan* come in anyway to help hand over the dresses and encountered the madman? Marcelle swallowed against sharp dryness. "Didn't you escort her to her boardinghouse last night?" she called at Ryusuke's back.

"We went to a lover's inn last night," he said between short gasps for air. "She told me she was going to the baths today."

Marcelle said a quick prayer to gods East and West that Yumi-*chan* and the other seamstresses had stayed away from the store.

Ryusuke reached the entrance and flung open the door, sending the foul odor into the street. "Stay here. Let me do this."

Marcelle cupped her nose and mouth and listened as Ryusuke stepped through the shop. Neither did he cry out nor sob despairingly.

It wasn't Yumi-*chan*.

Marcelle peered into the front window. Nothing was amiss. Ryusuke must have gone into the backroom. A long curtain separated the backroom from the front of the store. Placing a dead animal in the backroom wouldn't attract the attention of passersby. Only she would know, and it would make her sick. Whoever had done this was horrible, perverse scum.

Ryusuke emerged from the backroom his face pale and nostrils flared. As he approached the front door, Marcelle stepped back.

"*Do not go inside.*" Ryusuke stepped onto the street. "I'm going to get help."

"Then it's not Yumi-*chan*?" She knew it wasn't. Ryusuke would be torn to pieces if it was. But she didn't know what else to ask the man who looked as though he'd just seen a ghost.

"There's a dead body inside. No, it's not Yumi-*chan*." He paused and considered her as though he had a hundred questions, then turned on his heel down Ginza Boulevard toward Koide's.

The sight of this body must have sent Ryusuke into shock. Had the madman killed himself inside? An act of self-immolation to demonstrate against foreigners living in Japan? Even worse, had he committed violence against a foreigner and brought the body to her store? Ryusuke hadn't said if the body was foreign or Japanese.

Marcelle pressed closer to the glass of the boutique's new front window, then pulled away at the wretched smell seeping through. To generate such an odor, the body must've been in the backroom for hours.

"Marcelle," Nobu called. He and Ryusuke weaved between a scurrying servant and an old man with a walking stick as they raced down the block. "Please tell me you haven't been inside," he said upon arriving at her side.

"I haven't."

Nobu hunched over and placed his hands on his knees for several heaving breaths. Then he rose and pulled her to his chest. "Thank the gods you're safe."

She pressed her face between his neck and shoulder. His sweat dampened her chin. He wasn't wearing a jacket. Had he torn it off to get to her faster? For that, she was grateful. Never had she needed someone as much as she needed him now. "Thank the gods nothing happened to Yumi-*chan*."

Nobu stroked her back. "Or to you."

Ryusuke, who'd slipped inside the boutique without her realizing, opened the front door from the inside. "It's only his body."

Marcelle stepped from Nobu's embrace. "Whose body?" she asked Ryusuke. "The madman's body?"

Ryusuke remained impassive.

Nobu ran his hands down Marcelle's arms. "I'm going inside. I want you to stay here."

He was being quite valiant, but he needn't expose himself to a dead body as a way of protecting her. "Are you certain you want to see this?"

"I have to." He entered the store, followed by Ryusuke.

Marcelle glanced down at the box of croissants in her hand. She had to get rid of them. No one at Koide's would want croissants tainted with the scent of death. She couldn't leave them on the street either. Watching some poor animal tear at them felt obscene. Nor could she give them to Hidekazu and his gang. And where were those ruffians? Like the department store guardsmen, they'd been coming by less often. Even so, they were supposed to be walking by. Not that there was anything obviously wrong about the boutique that would've caught their attention.

Nobu and Ryusuke emerged from the store. They exchanged words Marcelle didn't catch, and Ryusuke took off in the direction of Koide Department Store.

Nobu faced her with a look of confusion. "Ryusuke is going to locate a friend of mine in the police department." Placing his hands on his hips, he exhaled. "Marcelle, do you know Hitoshi Inada?"

"Hitoshi Inada? Is that the man inside?"

Nobu nodded. "It seems he met his end in your store."

"Is he one of those anti-foreigner fanatics?"

"On the contrary." Puzzlement etched itself deeper into his features. "He welcomes foreigners. He's one of the fiercest advocates of modernization."

Nobu's confusion infected her. "What was he doing here?"

"I haven't a clue." He gave her a queer look, almost suspicious. "Did you recently purchase a clock from Koide's?"

"No."

"There's a parcel next to Inada-*san*'s body. It's from the department store. Inside was one of our ormolu clocks." He tilted his head to the side as though expecting her to respond.

"How odd," she said, not knowing how else to respond.

"I agree. Hitoshi Inada isn't an ally of the Koide family. He and my *otosan* are opposed in many ways having to do with the Foundation Party. Inada is known as the political maverick of Japan."

At that moment, she knew in the way she'd known as a child that the time had come to leave one uncle's home for another, that once again, her world had come untethered. "Jiro," she whispered.

"Your benefactor? Does he have something to do with Inada?"

He'd talked about the Foundation Party and politicians with different ambitions for Japan when he'd warned her about Nobu. "I need to see the body." She lunged for the door.

Nobu intercepted her with a solid grip of her shoulders. "You shouldn't see what's inside."

"I have to know who died in my store." She was desperate to know whether she was experiencing a flight of fancy. Was Jiro Hamada in fact Hitoshi Inada?

She struggled against Nobu's grip to no avail.

"What's going on, Marcelle? Why do you need to see a dead man's body?"

She gave up trying to break his hold. "To make sure it's not Jiro."

Nobu's features softened as though he'd solved the riddle. He released her. "You think Jiro Hamada is Hitoshi Inada?"

"I don't know."

He looked back at the boutique and let out a harsh breath.

She sensed his relenting. "I need to know."

He grunted something about the police not letting her in once they'd arrived. "Inada-*san* died from a knife wound to his throat. It's gruesome. Let me cover him. You can see his face."

She shuddered at the image that came to mind. "Please show me his face."

Nobu went inside and returned to the front door a few minutes later. She already had a handkerchief over her nose and mouth.

As it appeared from the outside, the front room was undisturbed. Boxes of dresses were lined up for the afternoon pick-up. The sewing machines and her small trunk with needles, thread, and scissors were in their usual places on the worktable. She placed the box of croissants beside the trunk.

He went to the curtain at the backroom's threshold. "I've covered the body with a length of fabric. You'll be able to see his face."

She nodded calmly even as she dug her nails into the palms of her clenched hands.

He opened the door, and on the floor of her backroom lay the body of her dear friend, protector, mentor, lover, stalwart partner, and man whose passing was cutting through her like a freshly sharpened sword.

Marcelle's legs buckled. Nobu caught her in a solid embrace before she collapsed onto the floor. "It's Jiro," she said.

Nobu steadied her out of the boutique and into fresh air and bright sunshine that seemed to mock the sadness settling into her. She buried her face in the handkerchief, and her tears fell.

He continued holding her tightly. "I'm going to take care of matters with the police," he said. "Why don't you go to Suki and Griff's house? I'll meet you there."

She nodded, keeping the handkerchief before her eyes, not wanting to see anything but Jiro, alive.

***

Marcelle took refuge in the Spensers' study, on the chair by the fireplace where she'd spent evenings swapping stories, gossip, fears, ambitions, and longings with her best friend. She shed tears at memories of Jiro Hamada, or Hitoshi Inada. She'd never had a sense that she'd truly known him. Yet, he'd known her. He'd known her in a way that no one had ever known her. He'd taken stock of her soul and seen what she needed for a good life: a lover, a shop, a devoted assistant, loyal patrons, independence, and the assurance of knowing he'd help when her front window broke. He'd given her the first real sense of security she'd ever known, and she loved him for it.

No matter who he was. His agent Nomura-*san* had only ever referred to him as Hamada-*san*. The people he introduced her to had never used the name Inada. He must have had two—at least—

distinct identities. Whatever name he went by, Jiro had been good to her. He'd never done wrong by her. Nor had he ever done anything to make her question his trustworthiness.

But he'd been convinced Nobu was using her.

She knew why he'd gone to *La France Boutique*. He'd somehow seen her with Nobu, having ignored his warning, and wished to warn her anew. Once again, he'd been acting on her behalf. Then he'd been killed. Someone—perhaps the man who'd attacked Yumi-*chan*—had followed him into *La France Boutique* and ended his life with a knife to his neck.

How could she not bear some of the blame? If only she'd been more considerate of Jiro's warning, perhaps written him a letter telling him all the reasons Nobu wasn't using her, he might not have come to the store. If only she'd begun to sever ties with him sooner, Jiro might have cared for her less.

Suki brought fresh tea to the study. She took a seat opposite Marcelle and poured them cups. They sipped while Marcelle confided more fears to her best friend. What would become of her store? What about Yumi-*chan* and the seamstresses she'd just hired? The dresses ordered after the promenade? The croissants she'd left on the worktable? Her boutique had been tainted with a hideous death. Would her customers ever step inside again? Had *La France Boutique* died with Jiro?

Suki told her not to overthink the unknowable future. Give herself time to mourn Jiro, or Inada.

Hours after Marcelle had sat down in the study, Nobu's voice carried through from the entrance. Moments later he knelt beside her, his hands on hers. Warmth from his touch eased her frayed edges.

"Suki says you need to eat."

Marcelle observed his pallor and crumpled suit. "You look as though you could use a good meal as well."

He gently thumbed the back of her hand. "I'll eat once I know you're well."

Jiro's accusations against Nobu seemed even frailer with his passing. That day at the promenade when he'd asserted Nobu knew his identity, Jiro had been correct. Yes, Nobu knew him. He knew him as Inada. But he hadn't known Inada was her benefactor until he'd seen his body in her boutique. "What happened with the police?"

"Would you like me to tell you alone, or do you want the Spensers to hear as well?"

"It'd be best for you to tell all of us," she said. The news probably wasn't something she'd wish to repeat.

They gathered in the Spensers' dining room and ate a meal of steaming rice topped with runny egg, a dish of boiled onions and eggplant in a sweet sauce, miso soup with chrysanthemum greens, and plates of sharp pickles. Marcelle sipped at the soup until she could bear the rice. Dutifully, she finished every bite, although it made no impression. But it restored her energy. When the maid brought them cups of green tea, she felt strong enough to hear what Nobu had learned.

From his seat beside her, Nobu told them about how his friend on the police force, a former detective who'd risen to a prominent role in the bureaucracy, thoroughly inspected the store. "The crime was rather straightforward. Hitoshi Inada was attacked from behind and the killer..." He rested his gaze on Marcelle. "Do you want me to continue?"

"I want them to know," she replied. Nobu talking about Jiro's death wasn't going to bring back the horrifying sight of her benefactor's dead body. It'd never left her mind.

"The killer cut his throat," Nobu continued. "He was the victim of an awful death."

The maid brought them small bowls filled with cut persimmons and pomegranate seeds. Marcelle took a spoonful of a few seeds but got no pleasure from the burst of juice.

"Does the detective have any ideas about the culprit?" Griff asked from his place next to Suki as he sat opposite Marcelle and Nobu.

"He hopes to learn more when they inquire at the neighbouring stores. Based upon the state of the body, Inada-*san* died around seven o'clock this morning, which means they can eliminate Yumi-*chan* and Marcelle as suspects since there will be many witnesses to their whereabouts."

Nobu's matter-of-fact recounting contrasted his striking words. "They suspect I'd hurt Jiro, I mean Inada-*san*?" Marcelle asked.

"He died in the store," Nobu said. "He was also your benefactor, which I explained to the detective. I hope you don't mind my sharing that information."

"Not in the least. The detective can speak with the agent, Nomura-*san*, if he has any questions. Our arrangement followed the letter of the law. Inada-*san* was quite strict about legal matters."

"That sounds like him," Nobu replied with a wry smile.

She couldn't tell if he was recalling a man whose respect for the law was worthy of admiration or someone who'd been unnecessarily legalistic. That he had opinions on Jiro, or Inada-*san*, left her with a queer feeling of having discovered a new connection to her lover, one she was yet wary to explore.

"They have to eliminate you as suspects," Nobu continued, "but I don't think they believe either you or Yumi-*chan* have the physical strength to carry out such a crime. It'd be helpful if someone in one of the neighbouring shops or your street ruffians saw something that marks the criminal."

Marcelle took a sip of tea and wondered what had become of Hidekazu and the ruffians. They hadn't been as attentive lately since they knew she was relying on Ryusuke and the other department store guardsmen to make rounds. "If the ruffians saw anything, they'll be sure to tell me. Their greatest joy is sharing gossip of any kind. As for the neighbors, most of their shops don't open that early. Those who live above their stores might have heard something though." Like her neighbors, Marcelle was rarely in the store at seven o'clock. Jiro knew as much, which meant in going there, he hadn't planned to see her. "Did Inada-*san* leave a letter or note of any kind?"

Nobu shook his head. "But he brought a package from the department store with an ormolu clock inside. My friend, the detective, showed my clerks the clock. One of them recalled selling it to a man just yesterday. The man matched Inada-*san*'s description."

Why would Jiro bring her a clock? Was it a message? Was Jiro's time running out? Was he running out of time to warn her about Nobu?

"He was carrying a hefty sum of American gold," Nobu continued, "which the killer left on his body. It's possible the killer didn't know the money was on him. Based on the condition of footprints in the room, the detective suspects the killer committed the crime and left the boutique in haste. With all that American money, and knowing Inada-*san*'s politics, it seems likely he was on his way to the Philippines to aid in their conflict against the United States. He was famously anti-colonial.

"The detective's first theory was that someone was following him with an eye at stopping him. But if that was the case, then the killer would've known about the gold. So, why didn't he take it? There are also the anti-foreigner attacks on the boutique, which I told the detective about. The detective thinks Inada-*san*'s killer could've been a fanatic trying to vandalize the boutique once again. Inada-*san* was already inside, so the fanatic took advantage of an opportunity to punish a Japanese man for his affiliation with the foreign boutique. There was no sign of a fight. Nor was the front door harmed. I presume he had a key."

Marcelle nodded. "He had a key."

Suki set aside her empty bowl of persimmons. "Is Marcelle in danger?"

"I believe not," Nobu replied. "For whatever it's worth, if this anti-foreigner fanatic had wished to attack Marcelle, it's safe to assume he already would've done so. His target seems to have been the store." Nobu had been addressing his remarks in equal measure to Suki, Griff, and Marcelle. Now, he faced Marcelle. "Did you have any notion he was the maverick politician?" he asked gently. The question nevertheless felt accusatory.

Suki reached across the table and placed a hand firmly on Marcelle's arm. "I had no idea," she said firmly, taking strength from her friend's gesture. "He never gave me the impression he was anything other than a man of business, a successful one, for certain. I knew he had strong beliefs, particularly about political matters. His opinions about the *eta* outcasts set him at odds with much of Japanese society. He thought people were foolish to think the *eta* were different from anyone else in Japan."

Nobu nodded. "His views were refreshing and much needed in this country. Most Japanese are stuck in a feudal way of thinking. There were rumours of him having fathered several children with *eta* women," he said in that same gentle tone that seemed to mock the rage of grief welling up inside her and compelled her to defend Jiro. "I have no idea whether he had *eta* children. He told stories of his children growing up. I always assumed those were children he'd fathered with his wife." Marcelle's throat swelled at the thought of Jiro's children. Hopefully, they were old enough to have known him well.

Suki poured tea into the empty cups in front of Griff and Nobu. "This must be a difficult situation for his family...but what about that clock?" she asked Nobu. "Do they think it was a gift he'd meant to give Marcelle? Was it something he was taking with him to the Philippines?"

Nobu finished his bowl of persimmons and placed his fork on the tea saucer. "My clerk said Inada-*san* made the purchase quickly. He didn't ask any questions about the piece. The clock is rather ornate with cherubs playing on the pedestal. There are vines and garlands and other foliage."

Marcelle knew that clock. "It was a gift." Nobu examined her with that same look of curiosity he'd given her when he'd first asked if she knew Hitoshi Inada. "He wanted to buy a clock like that when we were considering items for *La France Boutique*. I told him it would compete with my designs."

The clock had also been a message. She was sure of it. She looked down at her folded hands resting on the table. The truth needed to come out. Jiro had been killed in her store. The last time she'd seen him, he'd warned her about the Koide family. She couldn't keep this knowledge to herself. While she believed Nobu and his family were innocent in Jiro's death, what if Jiro's mistake in thinking Nobu was using her was something the detectives needed to know?

Her best friends in the world were seated around her. What did she have to fear in telling them? That Nobu would think she should've told him about Jiro having said he was using her. This was an omission for which she'd have to take responsibility.

She met Nobu's curious gaze. "The day of the promenade, Jiro, I mean Inada-*san*, was in Ueno Park. He waited for me near the turnaround. I hadn't expected him. I was shocked to see him. He was dressed in disguise, like a day laborer. He found me because he wanted to tell me he thought Nobu was using me to help his family draw him out of hiding. The clock was his way of giving me something I didn't necessarily want. This time it was a warning about Nobu. I'm sure of it."

Nobu's jaw tensed. "You met Inada-*san* in the park the day of the promenade?"

"He found *me*," she said softly. "He seemed out of sorts, and frightened. I found his accusation against you to be utterly baseless. I assumed he was having delusions from the strain of hiding."

Nobu furrowed his brow and fiddled with the dessert fork on his saucer.

Suki squeezed Marcelle's arm. "It's time to bid Henry a good night," she said with a nod at Griff. "We'll leave you alone." Her gaze held a questioning look as though asking if Marcelle preferred she stay.

Marcelle rested her hand on Suki's. "Tell Henry I said good night. I'll be upstairs shortly." She'd already sent a message to the boardinghouse that she'd be spending the night at the Spenser residence. Suki and Griff had said she could stay at their home for as long as she wished. It seemed a better choice than grieving alone in her rooms.

Suki and Griff bid Nobu good evening and left them alone.

"I never believed a word he said against you." Her voice cracked on the swell of emotion. The guilt of hurting Nobu coupled with her grief over Jiro was going to crush her.

Nobu moved his chair closer until Marcelle's legs were between his. "I wish you'd told me about having seen him. Inada-*san* was an idealist, a ruthless one. You never know what a man like that is going to do."

He'd never hurt me, she almost said, but that would be argumentative, and she had no will to argue with Nobu. Besides, Jiro had been caught with gold to fund a rebellion against the United States, which seemed a whole lot like evidence of ruthlessness and far-flung ideals. "I seem to be learning new things about him every minute." She braced for his reply to a question she couldn't bear hearing him answer in the negative, but one she had to ask. "Can you forgive me?"

Nobu took her hands in his. "Yes, I forgive you. I just wish you'd told me. Then I would've known you were in danger. I could've done more to protect you."

She loved his impulse to protect her, and she loved how his hands fully enveloped hers. "I'm grateful."

Nobu stood and pulled her up against him. "You should rest. I'll return tomorrow as soon as I can."

She sighed into his embrace. "Will you be able to rest?" After what Nobu had been through today, Marcelle doubted his sleep would be peaceful.

"I'll be fine." He eased back and gazed into her eyes, then traced a line with a gentle finger along her cheek and jaw. "Since the day we met, you've been the last thought before sleep and the first thought I have upon waking. I want you beside me, so I don't have to imagine you there."

"I will be soon," she said, hoping it was the truth.

Nobu kissed her in a light caress. The feel of their skin joining gave her faith in their connection. She hoped Nobu felt it, too.

CHAPTER SEVENTEEN

Nobu

The sensation of being suspended in the clouds before plummeting earthward wrested Nobu from sleep. He lay awake, letting thoughts rake the terrain of his mind. One chafed the most. Hitoshi Inada had been Marcelle's lover. No wonder Nobu hadn't been able to obtain information on *La France Boutique*'s ownership. Inada had allies deep in government. He was the maverick politician, a man who'd never held office, but whose money and influence could be felt in every corner of power.

Tired of staring at the shadows falling across his walls, Nobu went downstairs to *Otosan*'s study and poured himself a whiskey. Seated in *Otosan*'s favourite chair by the banked fire, he considered the man *Otosan* hated.

Inada had amassed a fortune in textiles—leather and silk—before moving into the sugar business. His plantation in Taiwan was a model for enterprising Japanese looking to venture overseas. Because of his success and the successes of those he inspired, the Japanese government tightened its hold on the Taiwanese colony despite Inada's objections. He believed capitalists, not governments, should be at the helm of international expansion. Through private investment in their country, the Taiwanese themselves could establish their own democratic legal and economic institutions. Japan's administration of the colony interfered with the good works of Japanese citizens pursuing ventures abroad and the aims of the Taiwanese people whose sovereignty deserved preservation.

Presented with his well-known charisma, Inada's views won over supporters within the Foundation Party. With his money in their pockets, Inada-*san* established a forceful minority dedicated to his internationalism. The largest clique in the Party, *Otosan*'s clique, hated Inada for threatening Japan's aspirations in Asia. Even more so, they hated him for threatening the future of their Party.

Were the maverick politician to set his sights on creating a schism in the Party, there was a good chance of his success. *Otosan* often fretted that if the conservative Foundation Party split, far-right extremists would seize power in the Diet, and Japan would become a military state.

After finishing his whiskey, Nobu stood before the map of the world *Otosan* had mounted on the wall. The pictures surrounding it were either gifts from *Otosan*'s fellow night sky painters or night views painted by *Otosan* himself. Constellations Nobu could identify and clusters of stars whose meaning eluded him hung next to paintings of planets, comets, and the sun. The map was the only nod to Earth. At the map's centre was Japan. Surrounded by oceans and continents, she was small, vulnerable. *Otosan* probably liked to reflect on her geographic insignificance. It must have spurred his desire to protect her, to make her more powerful than her size suggested.

Nobu understood Japan's need for defence against the colonial beasts of Europe, but on matters of Japan's colonial ambitions, he leaned toward Inada's vision of Japan's role in the world. Indeed, he and Inada would likely have found themselves in agreement on many issues surrounding Japan's modernization. Inada was a vocal advocate of human equality and practiced what he preached. Rejecting Japan's feudal ways of thinking about so-called lesser persons, Inada had made his fortune by accepting former outcast, *eta*, laborers who were elsewhere rejected on the grounds of their being unclean and inferior.

He was the kind of man to foresee Marcelle's success as a woman of business.

Nobu placed a finger on Paris. He'd love to go there with Marcelle. Had Inada thought the same? Had he imagined himself with Marcelle on the Mediterranean shores because her eyes were the colour of the sea? Did Inada want to stroll with her through the towns of the Côte d'Azur, where they'd bathe in the warm waters and sip rosé?

Where had Inada taken Marcelle?

Nobu had been satisfied with Marcelle having had an affair with Jiro Hamada, the older man of business who'd indulged a Frenchwoman's dreams of becoming a *modiste*. Next to such a man, Nobu could regard himself as the better choice. Next to Inada, Nobu felt slighter. Inada was barely fifty years old, if that, physically vigorous, and known for his uncanny intelligence, wit, and that damn charm. Nobu had no doubt he was a consummate lover.

How could Marcelle not compare him and Nobu and find Nobu lacking? Yes, he was twenty years younger, wealthy, cosmopolitan, and a decent enough lover—he'd never had any complaints—but stacked up against Inada, he couldn't claim absolute superiority.

To her credit, Marcelle had never made him feel inferior. Nor had she made it seem like she was pining after the older man. If anything, between Inada's appearance at the promenade and her boutique, it seemed like he was the one pining after Marcelle.

Nobu picked up his glass off the table and walked over to the tray of decanters. He poured a whiskey and downed it in a long sip.

Inada had deceived Marcelle. The moment she'd realised Jiro Hamada was Hitoshi Inada, she looked as though she'd faced a tsunami. That was why Nobu had forgiven her for not telling him about Inada having been at the promenade. Rather, he'd *understood* about her not telling him. She said she hadn't believed Inada's accusations against his family, that she'd thought him delusional for the strain of having been in hiding. Still, she should've told him. He could've eased her worries. There was no way *Otosan* or *Okasan* or anyone in his family had attacked her to draw Inada out of hiding. True, *Otosan* and Inada didn't share the same views about Japan's future, but *Otosan* didn't resort to violence. He was a diplomat, not a criminal. Inada's accusations were pure folly.

When the promenade had taken place, her allegiance had been split. Inada had been her benefactor, and she'd been satisfied with the arrangement. Then she and Nobu had grown closer. She'd been on the brink of breaking ties with Inada altogether. Nobu was going to become her benefactor in Inada's stead. She'd planned to take measures to dissolve their relationship after she'd completed the promenade orders. That would've happened in days.

Had she been free of Inada, would he never have come to the boutique? Would the maverick politician still be alive?

Nobu placed his glass on *Otosan*'s desk where the maid would see it when she came in to start the morning fire and left the study for his room. He was relieved Inada's hold on Marcelle had been severed. In truth, he was relieved Inada had been decidedly severed from Marcelle's life. For that, he felt uncomfortably guilty.

***

The following morning, Nobu decided to visit *Otosan* at the Foundation Party headquarters before going to Marcelle at the Spenser home. If anyone knew how the police investigation was proceeding, he would.

A sign written in formal calligraphy announcing Inada's death had been posted on the tall wrought-iron gates at the end of the pathway leading to the Party's headquarters. Nobu nodded at the clerks in the marble foyer, all of them in black mourning suits. They bowed back and uttered expressions of sympathy. The curved staircase with its acorn-topped newel post and thick carpeting resembled those in the gentleman's club he'd frequented in London. The mingling of scents, of tobacco, floor wax, rich fabrics, and tea was nearly the same. But the club he'd attended in London was a place for men of power to pursue leisure. The Party headquarters was for men seeking power whose collective objective was to build an upstart nation into an untouchable one. The walls practically thrummed with this grandiose aim.

A clerk led him to the third floor and down a wood-panelled hallway lined with paintings of the Foundation Party's esteemed members who'd devised Japan's modern government. The clerk rapped softly on a door before opening it slowly. Nobu peered over his shoulder to the room's interior. Leaders of the Foundation Party, all of whom Nobu knew personally, some of whom had invested in his department store, sat around a long table. Watanabe-*san*, *Otosan*'s best friend, was speaking about a funeral. Nobu assumed it was Inada's.

Crouching down, the clerk scampered to *Otosan*'s seat and whispered into his ear. *Otosan* met Nobu's gaze. He muttered something to Shimizu-*san* seated beside him and rose from his chair.

Otosan led Nobu to a private office several doors away from the meeting room. Moments later, a clerk arrived to tend the fire and another placed green tea and rice crackers on a table near the hearth. Nobu and *Otosan* sat in upholstered armchairs with the table between them. The clerk poured them tea from the earthenware ewer. Black tea had never appealed to *Otosan*. Even so, anyone who'd served it to him would swear it was his favourite. *Otosan* was that good at dissembling.

He thanked the clerks and requested the door be shut on their way out. "The murderer has confessed," *Otosan* announced after the clerks had excused themselves. "The newspapermen have their story and this whole debacle will be behind us shortly."

Nobu jerked his head toward *Otosan* at the unexpected news. "Who was it?"

"A man by the name of Masao Nagai. I don't know his particulars. We were told the police received a message about a suspicious-looking man boarding a ship. When they went to investigate, they found Nagai and the knife he used to cut Inada-*san*'s throat."

Nobu winced at the memory of Inada's body.

Otosan took a long sip of tea and placed the cup firmly on the table. "Rest assured, it's over now. The police said Nagai confessed a desire to kill Inada-*san* because he'd been too friendly with the Frenchwoman, Renaud-*san*."

The killer had blamed Marcelle.

Unsurprising after the previous attacks on *La France Boutique*. But if Inada's killer had been observing the boutique these past few weeks, he would've noticed the Japanese man paying the most attention to the foreign women was Nobuyuki Koide. "Did the man confess to throwing a rock through her window and attacking her assistant?"

"As far as I know, he hasn't been questioned on that matter."

Nobu finished his cup of tea and refilled his and *Otosan*'s cups. "Will you request the police question him about the attacks?"

Otosan grunted his approval. "I'll request it. But this incident is going to be put to rest very soon. The newspapers will report Inada-*san* was killed by an unstable man attempting to rob Renaud-*san*'s store. There was an altercation and Inada-*san* succumbed. Everyone will agree the killer has no place in proper society. He'll hang. That will be the end of it."

Nobu returned the teapot to the table. The murderer would hang. Justice would be done. An expedient, efficient, conclusion. Too expedient to conclude the killer bore the entirety of the responsibility for Inada's death. Plenty of Japan's politicians, bureaucrats, and businessmen disagreed with the maverick politician. It could be the killer was one such man. He might have used Marcelle's foreignness as an excuse to end Inada's life. Or the killer could've been operating on someone else's behalf. A colonial supporter? Someone who hated Inada for giving the *eta* a place in modern society?

Inada had worried about the Koide family. Who else had the maverick politician worried about?

For now, Nobu had to brush those suspicions aside, because it was most important to know without a shred of doubt whether it was the killer Nagai who'd attacked the boutique. Marcelle's safety depended on it. While there was no fathomable way *Otosan* or anyone in the Koide family had been behind the attacks, as Inada had tried to convince Marcelle, someone else besides the killer could be responsible.

"Is the Inada faction satisfied with this turn of events?"

Otosan's relaxed posture made the question almost unnecessary. Inada's death was doubtless the most critical juncture in the Party's history. Were the Party to schism in its wake, those remaining, namely *Otosan*'s faction, would have negligible influence in the Diet. "They're quite satisfied with the outcome of the police investigation. The Party leadership is going to advocate that Inada-*san* be given a state funeral. Prime Minister Ito will agree. Inada-*san* will be honoured as a true patriot, which will make his clique very happy."

"That sits well with your faction?"

"Anything to maintain Party harmony," *Otosan* said with a knowing grin. "And Party harmony is good for the nation." *Otosan* raised his brow at Nobu. "So, what will become of your Renaud-*san*?"

"Inada-*san*'s death will be the end of her boutique." Nobu wondered if Marcelle realized that a murder in her boutique had doomed the property. No patron would enter a store where a murder had occurred. The place would have to be burned down. Whether patrons felt Marcelle herself had also been tainted by Inada's death was yet to be seen.

"You ought to set her up elsewhere," *Otosan* suggested in the manner of offering an innocent piece of advice despite there being nothing innocent about it. *Otosan* and *Okasan* had said nothing to him about Marcelle since the breakfast when Nobu had announced his intention to continue the affair until she married, but their silence had spoken volumes. *Okasan*'s suggestions he court her friends' daughters hadn't ceased. They were pretending Nobu had never said a word about the affair. That was their way of telling him they simply didn't accept it. They were never going to accept it.

"I have contacts in Osaka, the Terashimaya family," *Otosan* continued. "They're planning to open a department store similar to yours. I'm certain they'd feel themselves fortunate were *La France Boutique* of Tokyo's Ginza Boulevard to take residence in their store."

Nobu made sounds as though he was mulling over what was *Otosan*'s very well-considered gambit. "Osaka is quite far from Tokyo. Such distance would make our relationship difficult."

"You can't possibly be thinking of continuing the affair after this." *Otosan* regarded Nobu with practiced incredulity. "You know she and Inada-*san* were lovers and he presented her with the boutique?"

"Inada-*san* was a man of business. He could tell Marcelle was a good investment and invested."

Otosan bit into a rice cracker and chewed a tad longer than necessary. "Doesn't it bother you to have Inada-*san*'s castoffs?"

Anger licked at Nobu. *Stay calm*, he ordered himself. *Don't let it flare.* He was going head-to-head with *Otosan*. Emotion would only throw him off his game. *Otosan* knew as much, hence the provocation. "I should be flattered Renaud-*san* finds me more appealing."

"Are you certain of that?"

"As certain as I am of anything." Nobu bit into a rice cracker to staunch the roiling ire in his gut.

"You're thinking with your prick," *Otosan* said matter-of-factly. "What do you think Inada-*san* was doing in her store when he got killed? Did they have a planned assignation?"

"He was warning her to stay away from me." Nobu had already decided to share Inada's warning about the Koide family. *Otosan* should know Marcelle had been going against Inada's wishes in continuing her affair with Nobu. *Otosan* prized loyalty. "Last month,

Renaud-*san* had a promenade in Ueno. Inada-*san* found her and told her I was using her to draw him out of hiding on behalf of my family."

Otosan's face remained in the calm expression he'd adopted.

Nobu let the silence build between them, as *Otosan* would've done had he been the one to present Marcelle's accusation. *"Wait long enough and you'll get your answer,"* Otosan liked to say. *"It might take days, weeks, even years, but eventually you'll get the truth."*

"It's *bollocks*, you know." *Otosan* used English for the profanity.

Nobu had expected *Otosan* to reply as such. But there was something unsettling about the response. Was it the shift to English? Did that weaken his denial? Was he guilty of something? Of protecting someone? "I thought so as well. But it seems Inada-*san* was insistent. A few days ago, he purchased a clock from Koide's. It was with him when he died. Renaud-*san* believes it was a signal for her to end our affair."

Otosan folded his hands in his lap. "You give much credit to her word."

"I believe her."

"Have you considered that the clock could have another meaning? A reminder that time was of the essence. Renaud-*san* was supposed to carry out his orders related to, say, a trip to the Philippines to fight injustice. If indeed fighting injustice was his aim. Inada-*san* always found ways to make a ton of gold. Societies falling apart present exactly those sorts of opportunities. Before departing, perhaps he was telling her what to do in his absence, how to gather information."

"Then you believe Renaud-*san* and Inada-*san* were foreign agents?"

"Inada-*san* most certainly had dealings with foreign governments. But he's passed his time on our dear Earth." *Otosan* unfolded his hands and rested his arms on the chair's sides. "The Party leadership is presently concerned about Renaud-*san*'s reasons for being in our country." The warning in *Otosan*'s voice was loud and clear even if he spoke in quiet, even tones.

Marcelle was being treated as a foreign agent.

"Are they concerned because you told them what I told you about the man who attacked Renaud-*san*'s boutique and her assistant? That he'd accused Marcelle of being a spy?"

"I had no choice but to tell them. These accusations concern our country's survival. Japan has become a barrier to Europe's colonial dreams in the east of Asia. There are plenty of nations fretting over that fact."

Nobu had never asked *Otosan* to keep the rock-thrower's spying accusations a secret. On the contrary, he'd explicitly asked *Otosan* to inquire about anti-foreigner sentiment because of the accusations. But *Otosan* had somehow raised alarm about Marcelle when he was supposed to be inquiring about any dangers against her. "Then they're taking the word of a rock-throwing, anti-foreigner fanatic?"

"Even a broken clock is right twice a day."

"Renaud-*san* is not working on behalf of France or any other nation. If she were, she never would've shared those accusations made against her. She told me because she found them absurd."

"Indeed," said *Otosan*, rapping his hand on the table. "That's quite advantageous. Makes it easier to deny culpability."

"Renaud-*san* is no spy."

"How can you be certain? Think about it. Do you remember five years ago after we acquired Taiwan from China there was a resolution in the Diet to sell the island to France?"

Nobu remembered thinking it'd be better to let France take control of the opium-infested island. "As I recall, it was barely taken up for debate."

"Kawamura-*san* from the Inada faction was the one to propose it." *Otosan* sounded like he'd put Nobu in checkmate.

"That's because Inada-*san* was an anti-colonialist. Renaud-*san* had nothing to do with it. At the time, she was working as a lady's maid for the American envoy's family. She met Inada-*san* after she left that post."

Otosan gazed at him pityingly. "The Frenchwoman has worked for the Americans, too. This looks very bad, son." *Otosan* tapped his fingers on the armrest. "She needs to leave Tokyo, perhaps even Japan. You cannot continue this affair. What will happen when your lover is accused of being an enemy of the state? Think of your store, of your family."

"Renaud-*san* is a clothing designer, not a spy. She wants nothing do with France. She was appalled that Inada-san accused our family of being behind the attacks on her boutique. She's our ally in this, and I'm not going to end the affair."

"You ought to stay away from her. Tell her to leave Japan. She should return to her country. Her store will never have another customer after what happened there. Let me arrange compensation for her. You could give it to her as a parting gift. As her lover, that would be the most appropriate means of turning it over."

Nobu would sooner throw *Otosan*'s compensation into Tokyo Bay. "I'll do no such thing."

"Think about it, son." He rose from his chair. "I have to get back to the meeting."

Otosan left Nobu to stew, but Nobu had no intention of being the obedient son. Before the door shut behind *Otosan*, he got up to leave.

***

In the rickshaw to the Spensers' home, Nobu indulged his anger at *Otosan*. If the man had any respect for his son's wishes, he would've dismissed rumours about Marcelle being a spy as falsehoods. In fact, he'd done the opposite. He'd seen an opportunity to rid the Koide family of his son's paramour and had ushered those allegations along. It would be just like *Otosan* to promote a little character misalignment here, plant a few suspicions about subterfuge there, until everyone in the Foundation Party leadership believed Renaud-*san*, Inada's lover, was a spy.

Otosan had left Nobu no choice but to come up with a plan for refuting the allegations, even if these never became more than casual rumour. The barest hint of association between a Party member's son and a spy was unthinkable for the Party. If they felt the rumours had any chance of becoming legitimate accusations, they'd put Marcelle on the next ship back to France. The best way to refute the rumours as they presently stood would be to question the person who'd first accused Marcelle of being a spy. This would be the man who threw a rock through her window and attacked Yumi-*chan*.

Likely, Nagai, the man who'd murdered Inada, was the vandal. Questioning him about his basis for making the accusation against Marcelle would dispel any rumour that she'd colluded with Inada to undermine Japan's colonial agenda, notably by working to sell Taiwan to France, because his accusation was in fact baseless.

Then again, Nagai might not be the vandal. Without the vandal to question about the possibility of Marcelle being a spy, she'd only have her word in her defence. And a foreigner's word wasn't going to carry weight against the Foundation Party.

In any case, he wasn't going to burden her with this news today.

Suki led Nobu to the back parlour. The sounds of playful French and laughter came from within the room. "Marianne and Lucian, my husband's niece and nephew, are teaching our son Henry how to speak French. Apparently, he makes the most delightful mistakes."

"It sounds like Marcelle is doing better today."

Suki turned the knob on the back parlour door. "Children are a good distraction from one's troubles."

Inside the parlour, Marcelle sat on the sofa next to Henry, holding one of his wooden trains. She broke into a smile as Nobu walked towards her.

"I was wondering where you were," she said after Suki had escorted everyone from the room to give him and Marcelle time alone.

Nobu took a seat next to her on the sofa and drew her up against his body. She relaxed into him. Theirs wasn't a relationship of withholding, of deception. No matter that *Otosan* couldn't see it. "I went to the Foundation Party headquarters this morning."

"Did you learn anything about yesterday?"

He told her about what *Otosan* had said about Inada's killer being caught with the knife and the likelihood he'd soon be put to death.

"But why did he kill Inada-*san*?" she asked.

Nobu stroked the length of her finely muscled arm. "The newspapers will report Inada-*san* died while trying to prevent a robbery at your boutique. What they won't report is the killer's confession that he attacked Inada-*san* because he didn't approve of him being friendly with a foreign woman." Nobu infused delicacy into the last part of what he said. She deserved to know the truth of the confession, but it wasn't an easy truth to hear.

She gazed at him with red-rimmed eyes. "But when would he have seen Inada-*san* and me together?"

The words summoned an image of Marcelle in Inada's arms. He was ashamed of where his mind had gone and ashamed of how irritated those images made him feel. Inada was dead. "Perhaps when he was at the store?"

"That would've been over half a year ago." Marcelle furrowed her brow into a deep pleat. "He held a grudge all that time? Then just last month decided to attack the store and Yumi-*chan*? And then...Inada-*san*?"

"It seems that way. They've yet to question him about the boutique attacks, but the killer was a lunatic." Nobu's feeling that the killer's timely confession was too convenient and his fears there could be another man or men involved in the attacks and Inada's death might be just that—feelings and suspicions. He wouldn't burden Marcelle with them. She was safe at the Spensers' home. For now, he'd let her grieve in peace.

Marcelle quivered against his chest. "What will the Inada family think? Will the police tell his wife and children he was killed because of me?" Her voice wobbled with the question.

"I don't know what they'll tell the family. The family might not ask to know the details of his death. Some think it's better to let these matters go with those who pass." Nobu pressed her closer to his chest. It wasn't enough to stop her trembling. "You needn't worry about the family becoming impoverished because of their *otosan*'s passing. Inada-*san* was very wealthy. His wife is the daughter of an important banker. They won't suffer."

Marcelle accepted his handkerchief and wiped tears from her cheeks. "I have no doubt he has made provisions for his family. He was a generous man. But they have to live without his guidance. He was a good teacher."

Also a shrewd opportunist whose political manoeuvring was going to wreak havoc on the country. "Some people thought he was determined to split the Foundation Party, the consequence of which would be radicals seizing the reins of government. Then there's the gold he was taking to the Philippines. He courted danger, and didn't hesitate to speak out on matters that angered people. Most people still don't think the *eta* outcasts and women are worthy of the same opportunities as ordinary citizens. They think it's an affront to the natural order. Inada-*san* didn't give a fig, and people thought he deserved to be ruined for it."

Marcelle clenched the handkerchief. "He was brave."

He also pushed his country toward unforgivable militarism. "He might have gone too far in trying to change the world." Nobu's tone was snappish. He oughtn't give in to weakness when Marcelle needed his calm and strength. "Since the newspapers are going to name *La France Boutique* as the place where Inada's death occurred—"

"No one will ever step foot in the boutique again," she finished.

Now was the ideal time for him to offer her a department at Koide's. He'd dreamed about it more times than he could count.

What better way for them to see one another whenever they wished? But what would become of her department when she married? What if she was deported to France for being a foreign agent after he set her up in the store? How would the merchants in other departments feel when their sales declined for their association with an enemy of Japan's?

"And the dresses," she said. Tears pooled in her eyes. "There were so many dresses ready to be picked up. No one will claim them. Everyone will say the dresses carry the stench of Inada-*san*'s death. They'll think the same of me, that I have that stench, that my luck is bad."

Marcelle sounded panicked. He took her hand and massaged the backside with his thumbs. She seemed to love his massages, and he loved giving her relief. "Your patrons probably won't claim those dresses, but they'll still want your designs. You make good clothes. For that, they'll forgive your bad luck. 'Everyone has bad luck,' they'll say."

She gave him a wan smile. "I'm afraid mine is worse than others."

The smile opened a space inside him. He pressed his lips against her forehead. When he pulled away, she gazed up at him with her sea-blue eyes. She was warmth and joy, sex and laughter, the same *modiste* he adored. "You and I found one another. Your luck can't be too bad, Mademoiselle Renaud."

She gripped his hand tightly, giving him the impression of being her lifeline. "I don't know what I'd do without you."

"You have me, and this will pass," he said with a squeeze of her hand. It would pass. It had to because he wasn't going to lose Marcelle.

CHAPTER EIGHTEEN

Marcelle

Marcelle spent two nights at the Spenser home, letting sadness over Inada's death come and go until it settled into a light ache. The name Jiro Hamada died with the man in her boutique. He'd become Hitoshi Inada to her. She didn't begrudge him for having kept his real name a secret—she was merely his lover, after all. How much he'd concealed now enhanced him. His other life made him fuller, more heroic. He'd taken responsibility for so many people. The ideals he'd embodied were so many, he'd needed more than one name.

Nobu had been shocked and obviously unpleased at the revelation Inada was her benefactor. Yet his affection hadn't faltered. He'd visited her every day at the Spenser home. Although the visits had been short—he had obligations at the department store and to his father in preparing for a state funeral—his reassurances had relieved an impending sense of doom about the future. She trusted his conviction that she'd once again sell dresses to a long list of patrons.

Three days after Inada's death, she met Yumi-*chan* at *La France Boutique*. They took inventory of the sewing machines, bolts of silk and lace, needles, thread, and decorative pieces. They unpacked the boxes of dresses that would never be picked up. Later, they'd take the dresses to a shrine where the priests would burn them. Neither she nor Yumi-*chan* melted into a puddle of tears in readying to leave Ginza Boulevard. There were other Tokyo neighborhoods where they might find space to open a boutique. The west of Tokyo, particularly the Azabu district, was becoming popular with foreigners and cosmopolitan Japanese alike. Whether they could afford to open a new boutique depended on the arrangements Inada had made for her in the event of his death.

The day before Inada's funeral, which she wouldn't be attending, Marcelle visited Nomura-*san*'s office in Shimbashi. The older gentleman bowed low and offered sympathies for her loss. She responded in kind. As far as she knew, Nomura-*san* revered his boss as much as any man could revere another. He brought a pot of pungent green tea to the low table by the front window of his narrow office. Marcelle took her usual place on the silk pillow and accepted a full cup.

"Hamada-*san* was on his way to the Philippines," Nomura-*san* said after they'd taken several sips in silence. "He was going to help the people resist the imperial ambitions of the United States."

Marcelle recalled Inada's commitment to government in the hands of the governed. "He felt strongly about democracy."

"He believed every man deserved leaders of his choosing. The United States, of all places, should know this and allow others to elect their governments as they see fit. But like other imperial powers, the United States decided the governed were incapable of ruling themselves. Hamada-*san* was going to prove them wrong."

"I'm sure he would have." Nomura-*san* referring to Inada as Hamada gave her a sense of familiarity that felt like a salve on her scalded heart. "You still call him Hamada-*san*."

"He'll always be Hamada-*san* to me. It was the name he chose. Those who call him Inada-*san* knew the man who operated within the world, not the man who'd risen above it."

"Did you ever suspect his true identity?"

A faraway look cast a shadow over the older man's face. "I always knew he was Hitoshi Inada, but he told me to call him Hamada. It was an honor."

There was so much more she wanted to know about the man with whom she'd shared a bed and business: Who was he close to? What had his wife been like? Nobu had said she was from a wealthy family. Was she caring? Cold? Where had he been hiding over the past year? And why? Nomura-*san* seemed open to speaking about Jiro. She couldn't let this chance pass. She settled on the question about which she had the most curiosity. "Did Hamada-*san* have a family among the *eta* outcasts?"

Nomura-*san* refilled their teacups and took a long sip. "Hamada-*san* wasn't ashamed of his dealings with the *eta*. He employed us and demonstrated our worth to those who'd rather ignore our existence."

"You are *eta*?" She never would've guessed. Then again, there was no way to know by simply looking at a person or hearing him speak.

"I was born in an *eta* village outside Osaka. Hamada-*san* opened a factory there when I was just over thirty years old. I labored for him from the time it opened. He noted my facility with numbers and brought me to Tokyo. He erased my *eta* past, gave me a new name. Eventually, I caught sight of a darling young woman of peasant ancestry who worked as a housemaid in Bunkyo. Because Hamada-*san* had concealed my *eta* background, I could register our marriage as a normal Japanese. My wife doesn't know she married an *eta*. Our children don't know they bear tainted blood. I trust you'll keep my secret."

He gazed gently at Marcelle. He must wonder whether she was about to contort her face in revulsion at his being a descendant of men who handled corpses and butchered animals, who tanned hides for leather. Or maybe he waited for her to press a handkerchief to her mouth and politely excuse herself from the office.

He'd be waiting a long time. Hearing how he'd outrun his background only made her feel kinship with the man she deeply respected. She, too, had left a world behind. "I'll never tell a soul."

"Yes, Hamada-*san* had a lover among the *eta* and fathered three boys with her. They're no longer children, really, but they haven't reached twenty years either. They've been raised in the same *eta* village where I was born in Osaka. Hamada-*san* offered to arrange a marriage between their mother and a regular Japanese. We're quite adept at concealing *eta* identities. But she was too foolishly in love with Hamada-*san* to accept his offer. One day, their sons will leave the village and their *eta* status as I did mine. Now that Hamada-*san* has passed, this is my responsibility alone." The edges of Nomura-*san*'s mouth trembled.

Sadness tightened her throat. Jiro had been lost to so many people all because an anti-foreigner lunatic had spied her and Jiro being close months ago. She'd brought death upon him. She'd deprived children of their father. "Were there other families?"

"None among the *eta* as far as I know. I believe he would've told me. His Tokyo wife was from a merchant background, a fine woman I've met on several occasions when Hamada-*san* called me to his home. They have eight children still living. I believe that is the extent of his progeny. In Japan at least." Nomura-*san* gave a little chuckle at the last part.

Marcelle gripped her skirts to dry her damp palms. She had to ask. As Jiro's mistress, the foreigner who'd been the reason for that lunatic to end Jiro's life, she wanted to know the depth of the blame against her. "Does his family know Hamada-*san* was killed because the murderer didn't like that we were lovers?"

Nomura-*san* eyed her as though she'd gone mad. "I have no idea what information has been passed along to the family. Nor have I heard anything about him being killed because you were lovers. I only know what the newspapers reported. That Hamada-*san* died in the course of a robbery at *La France Boutique*."

With a woosh of an exhale, Marcelle summoned all the fortitude she could muster. Nomura-*san* had been loyal to Jiro and loyal to her. He deserved to know the truth of Jiro's passing even if it meant him blaming and despising her. She'd live with his hatred. She cared for him too much to let him labor under a falsehood. "The killer confessed that he killed Hamada-*san* because he'd seen us together."

Nomura-*san* shook his head back and forth. "Renaud-*san*, I promise you, the killer gave a false confession."

She swallowed hard. Nomura-*san*'s certitude was unnerving. "How can you promise such a thing?"

"Hamada-*san* knew who was after him and why. It had to do with the world of politics beyond my comprehension. That was the reason for his absence most of this past year. His enemies had decided he must die. He was trying to escape them. He took shelter with allies across Japan from Hakata to Sendai. Then his enemies cornered him at your store. Whoever killed Hamada-*san* was part of a larger plan devised by people who had been plotting against him for a very long time. Let me assure you that Hamada-*san*'s spirit is not pleased at his having passed at your store. Nor is it pleased that you've been dragged into this false confession."

The weight she'd shouldered for the past days receded with such force that it left her dizzy. Nomura-*san* was absolutely convinced she wasn't to blame. Someone else was to blame. Jiro's enemies.

As far as Jiro was concerned, these enemies included—and were perhaps led by—the Koide family. Yet, she'd seen nothing of Nobu or his family to make her suspect they were plotting against Jiro.

The only plotting that interested his mother was making marriage matches for her children. Nobu's father was a bureaucrat whose hobby was astronomical paintings. Jiro had enemies, but she had no reason to believe they were among the Koide family. "Did you know Hamada-*san* bought a clock at Koide Department Store the day before his death?"

Nomura-*san* widened his eyes. "I didn't."

"The clock was with him when he came to *La France Boutique* that morning. I thought it was meant to warn me against an affair with Koide-*san*."

Nomura-*san* gave her a wistful smile. "That was something he would do. He didn't like that you were having an affair with Koide-*san*. Are you still?"

"I am. The funeral is tomorrow. Koide-*san*'s father will speak at the funeral. Needless to say, I won't attend." Nobu had offered to arrange for her to attend discreetly, but there was no reason for her to go. Her grief wouldn't benefit from hiding in a corner to witness a ceremony beyond her understanding. "Will you be there?"

Nomura-*san* lifted his hand in dismissal of the suggestion. "I hadn't planned on attending. Knowing Koide-*san* will be speaking makes me want to attend even less."

"Do you think he's responsible for Hamada-*san*'s death?" She steeled herself for his response.

Nomura-*san* picked up his earthenware cup and examined what might have been a tiny chip in the rim. "I cannot say. Many men wished for Hamada-*san*'s death. Koide-*san* might have been among them."

He also might *not* have been among them.

Nomura-*san* set the earthenware cup back on the table and met her gaze. "I want you to know Hamada-*san* cared for you. The day before his death, he told me he was going to check on the boutique to see that the new window had been properly installed. He also wanted to see if you needed any other supplies. He was planning to be in the Philippines for a long time."

Grief for Jiro welled up in a breath-depriving ache. He'd always been attentive to her needs. Nomura-*san* was right. Jiro's spirit was upset to have died in her store. "*La France Boutique* must be shuttered. No one will enter the store after what took place there. I'm thinking of opening a new boutique in Azabu or Shinjuku."

Nomura-*san* folded his hands on the table. "I'm afraid there aren't any provisions for *La France Boutique* in the event of Hamada-*san*'s death."

Marcelle suppressed a gasp of surprise. She hadn't expected to receive a great deal of money from Jiro, but she'd thought there'd be a modest sum. Then again, he'd always encouraged her to exercise independence. "Will I get to keep the sewing machines?"

Nomura-*san* nodded. "Those are yours and everything else in the store. There's a small amount reserved for emergencies and expenses such as broken windows and promenades in Ueno. I'll turn that over to you. I'm afraid you'll need far more capital to open a store in Shinjuku."

Capital and Jiro's sage advice. She needed both. "I miss him," she said.

Nomura-*san* nodded. "There will never be another like him. Our country is worse for his passing."

After bidding him farewell, Marcelle boarded a rickshaw to the boardinghouse. Once under way, she considered asking the runner to change course and take her to Koide Department Store. Seeing Nobu would brighten her mood. But she didn't want to burden him with her troubles. The usual dealings at the department store and preparations for Inada's funeral had drained him.

The previous evening when he'd visited her at the boardinghouse, his fatigue had been obvious. After the matron excused herself from the front parlor to respond to loud banging on the second floor—doubtless one of the boarders drawing the matron away from the parlor to give Marcelle a moment with her beau— Nobu reached out his hand between the sturdy, wooden chairs where the matron had encouraged them to sit. Marcelle entwined their fingers, and he let his shoulders fall. Weariness had become his constant companion the past few days.

"I'll miss seeing you tomorrow and probably the next day, and even the day after. The funeral and business at the store are commanding all my time."

"I'll be fine. Yumi-*chan* and I are going to explore the west side of Tokyo to see where we might open a new boutique."

"I wish I could join you." The distress in his gaze left her with no doubt he'd prefer a day of searching for places to open a new business over what was in store for him.

Were she to request the rickshaw runner take her to Koide's now, her mood would sap what little energy Nobu had. But he'd offer to help her, she was certain of it. As though observing a melodrama, she envisioned their interaction unfolding. She, the female in distress, throwing herself into the hero's arms because she couldn't afford a new store. He, the wealthy, powerful hero, pulling her close and giving her money and property and offers to help in any way he could. Overjoyed, she'd press a kiss to his mouth and bask in the hero's desire to please her. Then they'd take their bows for a splendid performance of the needy female using her wiles to prevail upon her lover.

Not this time. She'd become more capable than that needy woman. She was a talented woman of business. What she faced was a business obstacle. The greatest tribute she could make to Jiro was to secure funds for a new boutique through her initiative and give the world a demonstration of what a capable woman could do.

CHAPTER NINETEEN

Nobu

Nobu stepped up to the altar in front of Hitoshi Inada's body. He bowed, brought a pinch of incense to his forehead, returned it to the bronze bowl, and bowed again. Then he prayed for Inada's generous rebirth, as was the mourner's duty.

He glanced at *Otosan* standing beside him in the same sort of black mourning kimono Nobu wore. He likewise had his palms together in front of his chest and head bowed forward. Nobu imagined him requesting Inada's spirit keep its distance from the Foundation Party's headquarters and refrain from destroying the Party and Japan. *Otosan* released his hands from prayer and issued a sigh that resounded of man's inevitable submission to the wiles of fate's decree that one pass before another. The sigh was pitched perfectly for the occasion.

They returned to their seats in the front row, which they'd been given by virtue of *Otosan* having been chosen by the Foundation Party leadership to give a speech on their behalf. Members of Inada's faction couldn't be trusted to give the speech, and *Otosan* had emerged as the one rival factions agreed could deliver words that extolled Inada-*san*'s modern views and his dedication to the nation while praising the Foundation Party's enduring commitment to moulding Japan into a modern world power.

Naturally, *Otosan*'s speech went off without a hitch. The funeral reception left Nobu nauseous from having consumed too little food and too many cups of *sake* while under a cloud of tobacco smoke. Afterwards, he joined *Otosan* at the Foundation Party's headquarters for whiskey. A dozen or so members of *Otosan*'s faction settled into the grand drawing room, its walls covered in tapestries of glorious samurai battles and imperial picnics under canopies of pink cherry blossoms. Secretaries brought tumblers of whiskey, along with dried fish and crispy rice cakes.

Otosan accepted congratulations on his speech and refills of his tumbler. Whiskey sloshed onto his shirt as he gestured with his glass to a Party member across the room who'd just posed a question. "Baron," *Otosan* slurred. "The title will be baron, if anything. One cannot advance to prince without patronizing the right sleeping quarters."

Otosan was drunk. He never got drunk. Except when it fit his aims.

The esteemed members of the Foundation Party, all of them scarlet-faced, bleary-eyed, and covered in perspiration, fell into spasms of raucous laughter. Nobu leaned toward *Otosan*. "It's been a long day..." he began in an overture to their departure when a colleague seated on *Otosan*'s opposite side slapped him on the shoulder.

"Isn't Koide-*san*'s wife the daughter of a marquis?" the shoulder-slapper asked the assembled. "I should think his sleeping quarters would be worthy of at least as high a title," he concluded to peals of laughter.

Otosan ran a hand down his face, which had become suddenly sombre. "My wife thinks a title is no longer possible. Not after what happened to Inada-*san*."

Silence descended. Nobu's *sake*-compromised mind sifted through what *Otosan* had said.

They weren't going to get a title because of Inada? What the devil was Otosan *getting at?*

"But Inada-*san*'s death has nothing to do with your family," one of the members seated on a sofa next to them called out. Deep concern etched lines on his ruddy face. Nobu had assumed the same. Had he been mistaken?

Otosan burped, then used his kimono sleeve to wipe his mouth. If only he'd lose the contents of his stomach, then Nobu could drag him from the room and keep him from speaking, because he had a feeling that he wasn't going to like what *Otosan* was about to say.

Otosan's stomach held, even as his head lolled. "The Frenchwoman who owns the shop where Inada-*san* was found," *Otosan* began with everyone's attention on him, all of them nodding as they followed along. "My son won't marry because of her."

Alarm sobered Nobu by degrees. What was *Otosan* doing?

A light chuckle passed through the group as though they were awaiting the final line of a joke. *Otosan* responded by reaching for his whiskey glass, missing the target, and knocking it and its contents onto the thick Persian carpet.

"But the Frenchwoman was Inada-*san*'s lover," one of the younger Party members blurted out.

Nobu's jaw clenched. A rumble went through the room as the men reassured one another they'd heard correctly. Nobu was putting off marriage because of Inada's former lover.

"My son...my son..." *Otosan* hung his head without finishing the thought.

All eyes fixed on Nobu. He downed the rest of his whiskey. Someone refilled it. He took a long sip. "Renaud-*san*, the Frenchwoman, and I are friends," he finally said to the faction members' curious gazes.

Otosan coughed into his cup. Nobu prayed this was the moment *Otosan*'s stomach rebelled. But he only looked warily at the empty vessel. "How could you be sleeping with a spy?" He clenched his face as though on the verge of tears.

Nobu pressed himself into the chair to keep from rising and knocking his father unconscious. This cruel, indecent ploy to get him to abandon the affair with Marcelle was going to destroy her. Ambitious, cold-hearted men had heard *Otosan* identify a spy in a rather public manner, and they had much to gain for demonstrating to the world how spies were treated in modern Japan.

Marcelle was doomed.

The grand sitting room buzzed with Party members speculating to one another. Nobu had to stop the madness. "The Frenchwoman was Inada-*san*'s lover. Of course she was a spy," one of the Foundation Party members seated near the fireplace shouted above the din.

"Inada-*san* was always fond of the French," one of the young members called out, as though this was some kind of brilliant observation.

Otosan raised his finger like the feudal lord leading his samurai into battle pictured on the tapestry behind his seat. "Inada-*san* told us to sell Taiwan to the French. Don't you all remember?" Party members murmured assent. "I fear this woman was involved." His sudden clarity in speech was accompanied by sharpness in his gaze.

Otosan wasn't drunk. He was getting rid of his son's lover to please his wife.

Nobu could already hear his excuses. He'd say he had no other choice but to hang Marcelle out to dry. Nobu's stubbornness in continuing the affair had left him no option but to expose Marcelle to public scrutiny.

"How else could I make you see reason, son? You disregarded your parents' wishes. This is all your fault."

Nobu would deal with *Otosan* another day. The immediate problem was saving Marcelle from getting deported from Japan or, even worse, exposing her to the wrath of a drunken, angry Foundation Party mob. Anything less than a resounding defence was going to leave them feeling as though they had little choice but to go after Marcelle. "Renaud-*san* is not a spy. I promise you. She is a *modiste*. She makes dresses. Yes, Inada-*san* was her lover, but she had nothing to do with his interest in selling Taiwan. The negotiations with France took place long before they ever met. In fact, Renaud-*san* had no idea Inada-*san* was the maverick politician. He used another name with her. He called himself Jiro Hamada."

"Why bed a Frenchwoman if not to use her connections?" asked a pudgy man leaning against the wall.

Another faction member slammed his whiskey glass on the table. "To train her on how to seduce Koide-*san* and get information on our faction, of course." The man pointed at Nobu. "She became your lover to get information on us."

"Fetch a carriage," Shimizu-*san* said, pointing at one of the secretaries who brought the whiskey. He was one of the more sober members of the Party in attendance, but he was notorious for being one of the meanest among them. "We're going to settle this once and for all."

The room erupted in a buzz of comments encouraging Shimizu to "go on and settle."

Nobu rose so fast the blood drained from his head. "Does this mean you're going to Renaud-*san*?" he shouted at Shimizu.

"That's exactly what it means." Shimizu stood, and a half-dozen faction members seated around him rose in tandem. "We're going to Tsukiji. That's where the newspapers said she lives, right?"

"She lives in Tsukiji for certain," the shoulder-slapper said. "The papers say she lives in a boardinghouse. It's a house full of women."

"We'll find it," Shimizu called out as he headed to the door with his cronies in tow.

The shoulder-slapper gave Nobu a conspiratorial smile. "You know what that means, a bunch of women living together?"

Nobu would've slapped the man for implying Marcelle was a whore, but Shimizu's cronies were following him out the door and there was no way he was letting them anywhere near Marcelle. He scrambled around the sofa towards the drawing room door.

Otosan sprang from his chair. "*Wait*. The French Legation will have your heads if you cause an incident."

Shimizu stopped at the threshold and turned back to *Otosan*. "We're only going to deliver a message. Tell her she needs to get out of Japan before we have her thrown out."

The faction erupted in rallying cries.

"Don't make us Ito's enemy," *Otosan* shouted over the din. Nobu had to give *Otosan* credit. This was a clever move when it came to Shimizu, who prided himself on having a close relationship with the Prime Minister.

"My apologies, son," *Otosan* said with a shrug at Nobu as though to say *he'd tried*.

Nobu only saw the shrug out of the corner of his eye as he left the drawing room, behind Shimizu and his drunken cronies.

Nobu pushed his way through the posse as they hastened down the hallway. "Don't go to Tsukiji," he said as he reached Shimizu. "You're making a terrible mistake."

"I'm only doing what needs to be done for the Party." Shimizu scowled at Nobu. "What possessed you to have an affair with Inada-*san*'s mistress?"

"I had no idea..." he began as they rushed down the carpeted front stairs of the Party Headquarters. Nobu's chest constricted for need of breath, and his stomach was about to upend itself. He swallowed hard. "She has nothing to do with spying. She's not a foreign agent."

Shimizu didn't even look in his direction. "Is the carriage ready?" he shouted at the lobby attendants.

"Very nearly, Shimizu-*san*," one of the attendants replied.

"Good." He headed to the doors at such speed it was a miracle an attendant managed to open it before he walked straight into the dense wood.

Outside, several attendants checked the leather ropes on the horses' buckles. Shimizu boarded the carriage.

"Only three of you are coming with me. The rest go back to the gathering and sober up for the love of your mother. I need to know everything that happens inside." He gave Nobu an imperious look. "Join them. Your *otosan* needs you. Don't be an ungrateful cunt."

The carriage conductor took off down the pathway to the main gates. Shimizu's cronies headed back into the Headquarters, and Nobu turned back to the attendants. "Fetch me a rickshaw."

They stared at him as though they'd never heard of a rickshaw.

"Now," he said. The word spurred them to action.

Nobu could've sprinted the entire way to Tsukiji, but a sweaty Japanese man in a black mourning kimono entering the foreign quarter was going to earn him the wrong kind of attention. Like Shimizu, he had to enter politely, as though he was merely going to the Hotel Metropolis for a night of carousing.

But neither running nor a rickshaw would beat Shimizu's carriage to Tsukiji. Fortunately, Shimizu didn't seem to have a clue as to the whereabouts of Marcelle's boardinghouse, and Nobu knew well its location.

***

The boardinghouse matron, a petite Japanese woman who had the aspect of one plagued by constant, considerable irritation, greeted Nobu's question with a look of disdain.

"Then no one has been here asking for Marcelle?" He repeated the question.

The matron puffed out her chest and glared at him as though he had two horns, bright red eyes, and reeked of alcohol and tobacco, which he couldn't deny, save for the horns. "No one—" Her gaze drifted to the road behind him.

The clop of horseshoes and the stunned expression on the matron's face told Nobu that, yes, in fact, no one had yet come asking for Marcelle. But they would be. Soon.

"Shut the door and don't let anyone inside or outside," Nobu hollered at the matron as he took off through the garden.

He arrived at the boardinghouse's front gate at the same time as Shimizu's carriage. The cronies stepped out, followed by Shimizu.

Nobu stood between them and the front gate. He decided to give his elder by about a dozen years the respect he deserved for his loyalty to the Party and offer him a chance to leave before his presence caused an incident. "I suggest you leave, Shimizu-*san*. I cannot allow you anywhere near Renaud-*san*. It'd be best if you left now."

"Get out of my way, Koide-*san*." Shimizu headed straight for Nobu the way he'd headed straight for the Foundation Party Headquarters door when the attendant managed to get it open right as he passed.

He stood his ground, and Shimizu, the slighter man, bounced right off Nobu's chest.

The hit sent vomit up the back of Nobu's throat. He sucked it down with a low growl. "I told you I'm not allowing you near the boardinghouse."

Shimizu pushed at Nobu's chest. "This is Foundation Party business. I'm going to talk to that woman."

Nobu hadn't boxed since he'd started devoting his life to Koide's construction. He couldn't expect to hit with the same force he once had, but he knew *how* to hit. "Shimizu-*san*, I apologise," Nobu said because the man was his elder and had never treated Nobu poorly. But he wasn't actually sorry for what he was about to do. Shimizu had threatened to confront Marcelle. That was intolerable.

Shimizu scowled and levelled his shoulder at Nobu's chest like a bull ready to gore the matador. He shifted his weight to his back foot, and Nobu connected his fist with his jaw.

It wasn't the most powerful blow Nobu had ever landed, not by a long shot, but Shimizu fell hard on the ground. While Nobu stared at the heap before him, one of the cronies took up Shimizu's previous stance and rammed Nobu in the gut.

He landed on the hard-packed earth, then sprang to his feet in time to avoid being kicked in the ribs.

The kicking motion left Shimizu's man off-balance. Nobu took advantage of the weakness and delivered several blows to the man's gut that left him doubled over.

"Stop this," shouted one of the cronies helping Shimizu to his feet.

"That's exactly what we should do," Nobu fired back. "Get out of here and we'll call a truce. The last thing you want is to make Ito your enemy. If you keep this up, the French Legation is going to march right into his office with a complaint against you."

Nobu silently thanked *Otosan* for giving him the ammunition to use against Shimizu.

Shimizu snarled under his breath and hissed something to the crony beside him.

Thinking the matter close to being settled, Nobu glanced back at the boardinghouse, and Shimizu landed a jab to Nobu's chest, depriving him of air. While he struggled for breath, Shimizu dealt him a fist in the jaw exactly like the one he'd just received.

Immediately, Nobu tasted blood. For a man Shimizu's size, he could pack a wallop.

"Now we're even," Shimizu said, rubbing his jaw where Nobu had hit him. "I'll even be in your debt were you to deliver our message to the Frenchwoman. Tell her to leave Japan. We won't have any of her spying in our country."

Still stunned from the blow to his chest, Nobu gasped for air. "Just leave her alone."

"Believe me," Shimizu hissed, "I want nothing to do with the likes of a foreign whore."

Nobu clenched his fist. He was going to kill him. The man ought to die for being here in the first place. And then he'd called Marcelle a whore. While Nobu considered the wisdom and manner of delivering a fatal blow, his insides twisted and churned. He couldn't stop it. Vomit poured out of him onto the ground outside the boardinghouse gate.

Shimizu and his cronies let out peals of laughter.

"Get out of here." Nobu spat out what he could of the vile taste of blood and vomit coating the inside of his mouth.

"Shall I send the carriage back for you?" Shimizu asked once he and his cronies had boarded.

Nobu spat again in response, and the carriage took off down the wide street, dark under the shadows of the tall trees and shrubbery from Tsukiji's well-maintained gardens.

Slowly, he turned to the boardinghouse and was greeted by the sight of boarders crowding every window. Marcelle threw open the door and bounded down the front steps.

Straightening, Nobu spat out more blood from the gash on his tongue where he'd bitten down during the hit. Then he moved his jaw from side to side. The bones were all in the right places.

Marcelle drew up to his side. "Are you hurt?" Panic clung to her words.

"I'll be fine...." In a day or two he'd be fine, except that he'd still be dealing with the ramifications of the Foundation Party believing Marcelle was a spy.

She crinkled her nose and touched his upper arm, then pulled her hand away. Between the alcohol, tobacco, vomit, and blood splattered over his kimono, he must have smelt like something out of a sewer. "Why don't you come inside the boardinghouse? I'll get some towels to wipe you down."

"That's not necessary. I'm not going to stay." He pressed his fingers into the muscles around his jaw while he glanced at the street where his rickshaw runner had left the vehicle. The young fellow was nowhere to be seen, likely off somewhere relieving himself. Nobu had told him the errand would take a while.

"What...what are you doing here? And who were those men?"

Nobu considered the array of half-truths and omissions he could offer to make the situation less alarming. But she had to know the truth, eventually. "I came here to make sure those men didn't get to you."

Marcelle dropped her jaw. "Those men were trying to get to me?"

"They're not going to get to you. I won't allow it. *Otosan* and the Party won't allow it either." No one wanted an international incident, and after the way *Otosan* had provoked the Party against Marcelle, he had plenty to make up for.

"Why do they want to get to me?" Her voice quivered. "Am I in danger?"

"You're not in danger. I told you, I'm going to protect you."

"But what do they want from me? Is it because of Inada-*san*?"

Nobu nodded towards the wide avenues of the foreign quarter. "I'll explain everything. Can we take a walk?"

Marcelle looked back at the boardinghouse where her fellow residents stared agape at the sight outside their gate. "Let me get a cloak."

She returned with a dark blue velvet cloak over one of her brilliant designs cut from a silk dyed in shades of burgundy and mint. In a far more profound way than Shimizu's blow, she took his breath away.

He wanted to draw her into his arms and tuck her into his side, but he couldn't even offer his arm to walk, since his kimono sleeve, like the rest of him, was covered in filth.

They started down the road towards Tsukiji's inlet.

"Nobu," Marcelle said, interrupting his trying to formulate how he'd tell her there was a good chance she was going to be accused of espionage. "I'm very upset."

The fragility in her voice made his hairs stand on end. He'd never heard her scared. Even when the rock had been thrown through the boutique window and Yumi-*chan* attacked, she'd shown only courage and resolve.

"You've been in a fight with men who were coming after me. I have to know. Who were those men and why were they coming for me?"

He cleared his throat against ugly bile heaving upwards from his stomach. He didn't want to increase her fears, but he needed information that would help him defend her, which meant he couldn't afford to diminish the gravity of what she faced. "I'm afraid everyone in *Otosan*'s faction knows about the affair. It's become a bit of a scandal, including rumours that you and Inada-*san* were working for France. Were *spies*, really. People think you played a role in his proposal to sell Taiwan to France. The men who came after you wanted to tell you to leave Japan."

Marcelle halted. They'd reached the end of the road where it turned into a pathway that ran along the inlet. "I cannot leave. I refuse to return to France. This is my home. At least I thought it was." Her gaze shone with a desperate emotion Nobu hated. Turning from him, she hastened down the pathway as though escaping a demon.

He hurried to her side. "As long as you tell me the truth, I can put a stop to the rumours."

"What truth? This is utterly ridiculous. I'm no more a spy than you are. I had absolutely nothing to do with Inada-*san*'s foreign dealings."

"Slow down, Marcelle," he said gently. He referred to her pace, which his stomach, on the brink of upending again, couldn't handle. He also wanted her to stop panicking. It wasn't like her, and he had to know everything about her relationship with Inada that Shimizu and his ilk could use against her.

She slowed her pace and wrapped her arms around her sides. "Will they make me leave Japan?"

"I'm not going to let that happen. But I need to know if they have any reason to think you're a spy."

"Like what?"

"Have you ever passed messages… maybe to a Frenchman… on Inada-*san*'s behalf? Have you ever accepted messages from a Frenchman, and given them to Inada-*san*?"

"Nobu, this is absurd. I'm a dressmaker, not a spy. I've never done anything like that in my life." Tears pooled in her eyes.

He had a handkerchief in his pocket but there was no way she'd accept anything from his disgusting kimono. Fortunately, she didn't let the tears spill down her cheeks. "Did Inada-*san* ever ask you for information about *Otosan* or the Foundation Party?"

"Never," Marcelle said between clenched teeth. "If you recall, he thought you were using me to get information about him."

Nobu recalled as much. Inada had tracked her down in Ueno Park to tell her. Because he cared about her and wanted to protect her from him. "Did you love him?" The question slipped out before he could stop it.

But maybe he hadn't wanted to stop it. He'd been needing its answer since the moment he learned Inada was her benefactor.

He wasn't ordinarily an insecure man. He knew his worth. In London, he'd never catered to women who begged entry into his bed to explore their worldliness with an Oriental. He deserved better than to be treated as an object. He was intelligent, well-born, charming, and ambitious. A catch. But since learning Marcelle's Jiro Hamada was really Hitoshi Inada, a demon had been rearing its ugly head. He had to slay it once and for all.

Marcelle pleated her brow. "Is it really important that we discuss this now?"

He'd defend her to the Foundation Party even if she'd loved Inada, even if she was still in love with him. But if that was the case, he'd have to retreat from their affair. He couldn't be with her if her heart was with Inada. "It's important that I know more about your affair in case anyone...." He clenched his hand, ignoring the protest of the swollen knuckles from where he'd hit Shimizu's jaw. It wasn't just anyone who needed to know about the affair. It was him, and the pity in Marcelle's gaze made him suspect she knew as much. Even so, he wasn't ready to admit his insecurity. "In case anyone raises questions about the extent of your loyalties."

She slowed her pace and turned her gaze to the fishing boats bobbing on the water. "I owe a great deal of my success to him, not only for the money he provided, but for the business advice he gave."

Her response sounded a lot like the remembrances of Inada he'd listened to all day. "You had an affair with him. Doesn't that mean there were feelings of love between you?"

She stopped and exhaled sharply. Meeting his gaze, she seemed to have gathered strength that had eluded her since she'd come upon him at her front gate. "Yes, we had an affair, and yes, I cared deeply for him, but he was a difficult man to care for."

"Because he was away from the city?"

"In part. He was distant in many ways."

Even so, she'd cared deeply for him. How deeply? How close had she been to falling in love? "Had Inada-*san* stayed in Tokyo, would you have grown to love him? What about children? Did you want to have his?"

She threw up her arms then let them fall to her sides. "I never wanted his children. That would've ruined me. I'd have had to give up the boutique and be a kept woman. Not that he ever spoke of wishing for me to have his children. From what I've come to understand, Inada-*san* had plenty of children. There was no room for me in his heart. Nor was there room in mine for him. We appreciated one another. That was the extent of it. The affair had been over long before he disappeared. He even said so in Ueno when he found me at the promenade."

This was yet another revelation about that day in Ueno. Nobu gritted his teeth against the irritation it provoked. "You and Inada-*san* discussed your affair?"

"I thought he was jealous of my feelings for you."

Inada had been jealous of him. Nobu liked the notion. He was also feeling increasingly foolish for having pressed Marcelle. But he was about to defend her to the Foundation Party and likely many other powerful men. "I'm sorry I had to ask. But I needed to know more about your time with Inada-*san*."

Marcelle resumed walking along the inlet pathway toward the recently reopened Hotel Metropolis. "Your father is in the Foundation Party. Does he believe I'm a spy?"

Nobu wanted to throttle *Otosan*, and after what *Otosan* heard about the fight with Shimizu, he'd know his son could indeed throttle. But he needed *Otosan* to quash these rumours and keep Shimizu and his cronies on a short leash. Neither he nor Marcelle could afford to make an enemy of the man.

"It's hard to tell... *Otosan* always does the politically right thing." Nobu found his stomach roiling, and swallowed hard. "He might...for example...for the sake of elevating his faction over Inada-*san*'s faction, he might entertain the notion you and Inada-*san* were in cahoots with France. But I know *Otosan*, so I know this, in the end he'll pull back. He won't let anyone hurt you. He's not that kind of brutal."

Moonlight sharpened Marcelle's features. "What about the rest of the Party? What are they going to do to me? Will they come after Yumi-*chan*, too?"

She increased her pace, and he matched it. "They won't come after you or Yumi-*chan* because they don't want to draw ire from the French Legation. They know there isn't going to be any evidence against you aside from rumour. The worst that could happen is they try to push you out of Tokyo, even out of Japan."

Marcelle gasped and came to a stop before the university grounds at the inlet's end. "That sounds an awful lot like what *someone* did to Inada-*san*. Is that what the Foundation Party does? Force people into hiding? Lure them to Tokyo by attacking their boutiques? Then kill them?"

Nobu raised his hand to stop her barrage of accusations. "I don't know what happened to Inada-*san*. Maybe... they might have threatened him. But, Nagai, the killer... the killer said he went after Inada-*san* because he was your lover." The last word stuck to the top of his dry mouth. He let his hand fall to his sides. Even he thought the confession was likely disingenuous.

Marcelle gathered her cloak snugly around her. "He could very well have lied. Nomura-*san*, Inada-*san*'s accountant, the one who helped me set up *La France Boutique*, believes the killer's confession is a lie. He said it was Inada-*san*'s enemies in politics who killed him."

"There are men in government who have no scruples. Men in the Party are that way, too. They get ideas in their head, and they want so badly for Japan to be the biggest country in Asia. In the world. And they think men like Inada-*san* are getting in the way."

"Like your father?"

Never Otosan.

"You have to understand, Inada-*san* was wrong about *Otosan*. He, and his friends, like Watanabe-*san*, they wouldn't hurt anyone. Start rumours, perhaps. But that's as far as they'll go."

"But those rumours could get me driven out of Japan."

"You won't have to leave Japan. I promise. My *otosan* will ensure nothing happens to you."

"How?"

Threatening *Otosan* with a beating would be his preferred method of bending the man to his will. He deserved a good beating. But that was not an option for a son who needed his *otosan*'s influence. "I'll give him what he wants. I'll tell him I've ended our affair...tell him I'm going to marry a nobleman's daughter, someone important. Then after some time—"

Marcelle speared him with a look that cut off his words, then turned on her heel just as Nobu grabbed her wrist. With a strong twist, she freed herself from his grip.

"Marcelle...you have to, to trust me."

"Leave me alone," she hissed. "I know I'm not someone important. I'm not worthy of you. I'm not worthy of this country. Tell your family whatever you want. Tell them you were delusional to ever spend a single moment with me. Tell them how fortunate you are to be rid of me."

This time she rushed down the pathway before he could grab her again.

"*Marcelle*." Breaking into a run, he almost halved the distance between them when he tripped over tree roots and fell flat on his stomach. Whiskey and *sake* rushed his throat and poured out in a hot liquid that made its way down the inside of his kimono. He had no choice but to let her go.

CHAPTER TWENTY

Marcelle

Yumi-*chan* braced herself against the stone railing. "I must rest." She gave a heaving breath.

Several places ahead on the steep stairs, Marcelle followed suit. Despite the late October breezes, perspiration seeped into the fabric of her simple day dress. At least hauling the promenade dresses up the eighty-six steps to Atago Shrine gave her something to combat the sense of futility that seemed to increase each day since Inada's death. "Will the priests give us tea when we make it to the top?" she asked between short breaths.

"We'll get water to cleanse our mouths. Atago priests must allow supplicants a few extra sips."

The shrine claimed to occupy the highest point in Tokyo. Marcelle believed it. Mt. Fuji and her attendant foothills rose against the stark blue sky to their south. Tokyo Bay glimmered in the sunlight to their east. Past Shimbashi station to their north were the redbrick buildings of Ginza Boulevard, the stone façade of Koide Department Store commanding space at their center.

"Shall we continue?" Marcelle asked.

Yumi-*chan* boosted her basket of dresses onto her hip. "If a samurai on horseback can do this, so can we."

"I believe it was the horse who suffered," Marcelle replied. The shrine had been constructed by the first Edo shogun as a site for identifying fires in the city. A young samurai wishing to fulfill the shogun's request for a plum branch from the shrine rode his horse up the steep set of stairs. The horse swiftly braved the ascent. The descent nearly killed him. Even so, the shogun got his plum branch and the samurai's legend lived on.

Marcelle looked up at the tall red gates of the shrine's entrance, balanced her basket on her hip, and ascended the next stone, making certain to stay to the side. Gods walked up and down the middle. She had no desire to test the spirits' wrath. It already felt like fate was conspiring against her. Or maybe it was just the Koide clan.

Almost a week had passed since she'd left Nobu on the pathway along Tsukiji's inlet. Each day, for three days afterward, he'd come by the boardinghouse. Twice she'd been at Suki's house or the *Tokyo Women's Magazine* offices where she felt safest. The one time she'd been at home, she'd refused to see him.

Their affair was over. They needn't see each other ever again.

She was grateful he defended her against those violent politicians, something she'd come to appreciate more each day when she recalled how his cheek had swelled as they'd walked along the inlet. She was grateful, too, that he sent Ryusuke to the boardinghouse each day to ask after her. Ryusuke assured her that Nobu's jaw had healed from the punch he received from a man called Shimizu, and Koide-*san*, Nobu's father, had made certain no member of the Foundation Party would come after her again. She assumed this meant Nobu had told his father he'd ceased the affair with Marcelle.

This was the way it should be. She wasn't going to pursue an affair that could ruin her life. And she wasn't going to spend time with a man who didn't respect her.

The other night Nobu had the gall to call her unimportant, at least compared to the woman he'd eventually marry. Even in the haze of anger that had followed, she could acknowledge he hadn't said she was unimportant to him. She was his lover. But in his mind, she was unimportant *in general*. Not important to his dreadful, deceitful father and calculating, inconsiderate mother. In the Koides' world, she had no social standing. She was nothing.

While this bothered her, it didn't bother her as much as Nobu, in all seriousness, entertaining the possibility she'd been working with Inada to spy for France. *That* was perfectly outrageous. Even more outrageous was his unwillingness to consider that his father could be responsible for Inada's murder. Nomura-*san* believed the killer had made a false confession and Inada-*san*'s enemies were to blame. That included the Koide family, Nobu's father in particular.

When she'd been in Nomura-*san*'s office, she'd been unconvinced of Nobu's father's guilt. His vindictiveness in spreading rumors about her being a spy had made her reconsider.

More than any lover, she needed the precious Tokyo life for which she'd labored. Her affair with the cutthroat capitalist department store owner had come to an end. She wasn't going to bemoan the loss. She was going to burn dresses and pray for another chance in the city she loved.

The Atago priests had water drawn for refreshment at the shrine's entrance. She and Yumi-*chan* drank from the wooden cups, then used them to wash their hands. Purified, they waited in a small line beneath the flaring eaves of a gilt-edged timber roof beyond which stood the fire god's sanctuary.

When they reached the front of the line, Marcelle glanced into a room no larger than the size of *La France Boutique*. Ceremonial objects painted gold and vermillion had been placed around the elaborately carved golden box containing the fire god. Yumi-*chan* pulled the bell to alert the god of their arrival. Marcelle joined her in throwing coins into the collection box. They bowed twice to the fire god, then clapped their hands twice to celebrate him and ward off any evil spirits lingering nearby. Then they prayed in silence.

Marcelle introduced herself as a French *modiste* living in Tsukiji. Gods liked this kind of information. In the event of a fire in Tsukiji, the fire god would know to save Marcelle Renaud, who'd worshipped at his shrine. Finally, she made a request for safety from fires, literal and figurative, particularly those started by rumormongering—possibly murderous—fathers who wanted to burn their sons' lovers.

Following their prayers, they bowed again. For the first time in weeks, hope flickered in Marcelle's heart. She'd done everything she could to save her Tokyo life. She'd leave the rest to the gods.

The priests accepted the baskets of dresses and a small monetary gift of appreciation for burning the impure garments.

Their descent was easier than that of the samurai's horse. After leaving Atago, they walked through Ginza to Tsukiji, where Yumi-*chan* bid Marcelle farewell at the gates. Marcelle promised to tell Yumi-*chan* as soon as she had the funds to take on an assistant. Yumi-*chan*, in turn, promised to drop whatever employment she managed to secure once she could resume her place alongside Marcelle. By that time, she added, she might be a married woman. Her relationship with Ryusuke might be the best thing to come from *La France Boutique*.

Over the past week, Marcelle sent letters to patrons who'd ordered the doomed garments, informing them of her intention to have the dresses ritually burned. She also told them she'd be taking commissions for alterations and new dresses. A few patrons replied with thanks for disposing of their dresses and assurances they no longer needed her services. Had Marcelle been wondering why they wouldn't be using her services, she had letters from other patrons who replied they wouldn't have anything to do with a foreign country's spy.

Marcelle could still rely on a few patrons among the geishas and the foreign community, but they wouldn't be enough to sustain a business.

Yumi-*chan* was going to seek new employment, and Marcelle was going to ask Suki's mother if she might assist in her store while she waited to find out if she was going to be sent back to France. Provided Nobu's father made the spy rumors disappear, she would start over in a less fashionable part of Tokyo where she could afford a room once she'd sold her two sewing machines and gold needles. Or she could go to Yokohama where the foreign community was larger. There, she'd have plenty of patrons. But that would mean parting from Suki, Griff, Henry, and Yumi-*chan*. Even so, Yokohama was better than Paris.

Marcelle took a circuitous route through Tsukiji on the way to her boardinghouse, meandering past Suki and Griff's home and the Garricks' home where Suki and her mother had resided after her father had abandoned his family for a return to France. This cruel act nevertheless gave Suki and her mother a satisfying, loving, joyful life with the Garricks. From adversity, joy was possible, Marcelle reminded herself as she walked through the front door of the boardinghouse.

Annie, one of the young boarders, met her at the entrance with a broad grin. "He was here," she reported in a conspiratorial whisper. Last year, her parents and siblings had left Tsukiji for Sendai on their medical mission. Annie stayed behind to continue her work at the missionary school. A spirited young woman, she had a romantic imagination that had infected most of the young women at the boardinghouse with dreams of beaux like Nobu.

Marcelle's capricious heart leapt. "Did he provide a reason for his visit?"

"He asked after you," she whispered, "then left a letter." She motioned to the mail tray on the round table by the entrance.

Marcelle adopted an expression of indifference. "How did he appear?"

"Disappointed to have missed you." Annie pursed her lips. "When are you going to take him back?"

Much to her fellow boarders' disappointment, Marcelle had informed them she and Nobu had ended their flirtation. But with Nobu coming by nearly every day to declare his undying love—as they saw it—he'd turned them into advocates for their blissful reconciliation.

They didn't know how he'd insulted her and how his dangerous, evil father hated her and sought to drive her from Japan, because she hadn't wanted to crush their hopes and dreams. So, she'd defended her decision to end the affair as a matter of incompatibility. "We're not meant to be together. He'll realize it soon enough."

Marcelle carried the letter up to her room and placed it on her writing table. She considered the wisdom of burning it in the fire. But doing so had a high possibility of resulting in regret, an emotion she strenuously avoided. Taking a seat on her solid wooden chair, she opened the missive.

Dear Marcelle,

I came to the boardinghouse today to speak with you. Given your avoidance this week, I thought it best to pen this letter beforehand.

I understand why you've been reluctant to let me apologise for my behaviour last week. It was unacceptable. I was well into my cups, but that is no excuse for doubting your integrity. I'd do anything to take back my hurtful words.

I've been thinking there's another way we can get Otosan *to correct the spy rumours and still be together. I've been thinking we could marry. Were we to marry,* Otosan *would have to protect you from unfounded rumours for the sake of our family's reputation. When I proposed this to* Otosan, *I believe he recognised the truth of the matter. Our marriage would make you untouchable.*

Marcelle's hands shook as she placed the unfinished letter on the table. Nobu's father would never allow them to marry. He'd have her deported to France or India, or the Dutch East Indies before letting them marry. Nobu's precipitous action would be the end of her Tokyo life. Didn't he realize his father wanted to get rid of her? How could he do something so foolish?

Hoping for something reassuring but despairing the possibility, she returned to the letter.

Nothing would please me more than having you as a wife. I'd cherish you and our children. I wish to have you by my side, and I believe I'd be a good man for you to have by yours.

A good man for her? He was putting her in danger. This affair between them, the affection, the connection—maybe it was love— had made him selfish. How could he not see the predicament he was putting her in? He was making her his father's enemy.

She'd seen what happened to his father's enemies.

Marcelle put down the letter and walked to the sink. Splashing water on her face, she hovered by the basin, letting the droplets fall where they may. It did nothing to cool her panic.

She was going to have to reject him. Soundly. She returned to her chair and the letter.

I'm leaving tomorrow for Osaka city in Western Japan. The Terashimaya family is planning to open a department store, and they've asked for my advice. I'll be there for several weeks. I understand you may need time to consider the proposal. Perhaps, when I return, you can share your feelings.

Ever your devoted,

Nobu

Marcelle pulled a plain, ivory sheet of paper from the drawer of her writing table and dipped her pen in ink.

Nobu,

I hope this letter reaches you prior to your departure. I don't wish for you to think there's a chance for marriage between us. There is no chance. Please inform your father that I've rejected your proposal in no uncertain terms. He can be assured we're no longer engaging in an affair. Please ask that he cease spreading rumours about my being a spy.

Marcelle

CHAPTER TWENTY-ONE

Nobu

Nobu finished Marcelle's letter and wandered down to the first floor in search of Asako. He found her seated on the sofa in *Otosan*'s study, reading an English-language newspaper while tapping at her lip as she did when concentrating.

"Textile workers have gathered over ten thousand signatures for their suffrage petition. I wish I was back in London to celebrate." As she scrutinised him, her pensive look transformed into something like horror. "Has a demon possessed you, dear brother? Because you look awful."

Nobu collapsed on the wingback chair opposite her. "My affair with Renaud-*san* seems to have come to an end."

Asako let her jaw drop. "But you love her."

Of course, Asako knew exactly how he felt about Marcelle. "I do, and I intend to marry her."

Asako set the newspaper on the cushion beside her. "How do you possibly think you're going to get away with marrying a foreigner? Much less one who's ended an affair with you?"

Nobu crossed his legs. "I'm working on it. I shared my intentions with *Otosan* yesterday. He wasn't encouraging."

Otosan had called him a fool, told him he was a disappointment to his parents, and thrown him out of his study. Prior to being tossed from the study, Nobu had pointed out that not only should *Otosan* put an end to the spy rumours for the sake of his future daughter-in-law and the family name, but also because they were baseless allegations that could only exacerbate tensions between Japan and the West. Since Marcelle was in fact not a spy, the French were likely to cause a diplomatic furore over an accusation against their citizen. *Otosan* had grumbled about Nobu's ingratitude, escorted Nobu to the door and slammed it behind him.

Nobu took this as a sign that while he continued to object to Nobu marrying Marcelle, he was in full agreement with his son's reasoning. It was the same logic *Otosan* had used the night of Inada's funeral when Shimizu and his cronies left to confront Marcelle. In the following days, *Otosan* had delivered warnings to the Foundation Party that any member's attack on Marcelle would lead to dire consequences for those individuals and the Party. So far, his threats seemed to be working.

Equally unsurprising was Marcelle's rejection of his proposal. Nevertheless, he was going to make Marcelle his bride, not just to ensure her safety from rumours and Foundation Party members, but because he wanted to spend his life with the sophisticated, cosmopolitan woman who shared his appreciation for beauty, business, and nights of feisty bedsport. Like him, she was a mix of cultures, traditions, and languages. Individually, they were adept at navigating the modern world. Together, there was no ambition too bold.

When he'd sent the letter, he'd been fairly certain she'd reject his proposal, but he'd done it anyway because he'd wanted her to know how serious he was about making her his wife. Getting her to agree was going to require patience and a clever approach. He needed Asako for the latter.

"*Otosan* recommended I stifle any urges to tell you or *Okasan* about my ill-advised plan to marry a common *modiste*."

"You're telling me anyway," Asako observed.

"I need a favour. Well, I'm actually going to be doing you a favour. In return, I need your help with Marcelle."

"No more calling her Renaud-*san*?"

"She's going to be your sister. You might as well get used to her Christian name."

Asako let out an amused snort. "How are you so certain she's going to be my sister?"

"We had a misunderstanding that I intend to make up for when I return from Osaka. While I'm away, I need you to keep an eye on her."

Asako cocked her head to the side. "Intriguing. But how do you propose I keep your ladylove in my sights?"

"Ever since the promenade, you've been talking nonstop about *Tokyo Women's Magazine* and the wonderful Suki Spenser. I think you should write for them."

Asako practically leapt off the sofa. "How could I possibly?"

"Go to their offices tomorrow and speak directly to Suki. When I visited Marcelle at the Spensers' home, Suki mentioned that a woman like you would be the perfect contributor to the magazine. Something about your proficiency in languages and nonsense about you being young and spirited and a fighter for women's rights. I told her I'd pass her unreasonably generous remarks along."

Asako aimed her empty teacup at his head. "It took you this long to tell me Suki Spenser called me a *fighter* for women's rights."

Asako brimmed with uncharacteristic exuberance. He chastised himself for not telling her sooner. "I should've mentioned this earlier. I'd been meaning to." But he'd been an ass to Marcelle and dangerous, life-threatening rumours about her were spreading. He'd heard from several department store patrons, who were also family friends, that the recently departed patriot Inada-*san* had been seduced by a spy trying to manipulate Japanese politics on behalf of France.

"You're forgiven," she said with a pitying gaze, then sighed. "*Okasan* will never allow it."

"You needn't worry about *Okasan*. She's going to be very busy while I'm in Osaka. I've tasked her with visiting the department store each day and making a full report of anything out of order. I told her there isn't to be a fur cape or silk cravat out of place."

Asako's head tilted back with laughter. "That'll keep her plenty occupied. I'll tell her I'm taking *koto* lessons. She's always whining about me picking up one of the feminine arts. The *koto* has a nice sound."

Nobu had difficulty imagining Asako plucking the wooden instrument's strings. "Are you really going to learn the *koto*?"

"To work at *Tokyo Women's Magazine*, I'll learn any silly instrument. Do you think Suki Spenser was just being polite when she called me a perfect contributor?"

"She meant it. All the articles appear in English and Japanese."

"I know. It's perfect." Asako beamed as though lit from within.

He really should've encouraged Asako to approach *Tokyo Women's Magazine* years ago when the magazine first launched. Then he would've met Marcelle through Asako, and she never would've gotten involved with Inada because she would've been involved with Nobu.

"I need you to use your place at the magazine to find out how Marcelle is faring. I know she often visits the magazine offices. Suki is her best friend. You could even inquire with Suki on my behalf. Tell her I'm using you to keep an eye on my future wife. She'll understand."

Asako lifted her gaze upwards. "Would you like me to request an announcement in *Tokyo Women's Magazine* of your upcoming nuptials?"

Nobu tilted his head to the side, giving the proposition due consideration. "I should get Marcelle's permission first."

"That's more like it, dear brother. Never act without the woman's permission."

Nobu bid Asako good night, content that in his absence Marcelle would have Ryusuke checking on her whereabouts, and Asako would be getting information on her through Suki. He was also pleased to have given Asako a much-needed new lease on life. Next, he had to find her a husband.

CHAPTER TWENTY-TWO

Marcelle

Yumi-*chan* peered into the window of the small hardware store on the block before Nomura-*san*'s office. "Is this the hardware store where you found those brass buttons with the green dragons?"

Marcelle placed a hand on her hat to keep it from going askew in the wind. "It is. We can stop there on our way back."

Yumi-*chan*, who'd yet to find a new position, had joined Marcelle in Shimbashi to help fetch the Inada family's heirloom kimonos. After Inada's death, Ryusuke had taken the kimonos to Nomura-*san*'s office for safekeeping. On Marcelle's behalf, Nomura-*san* had exchanged messages with Inada's wife about her wishes concerning the kimonos. She didn't think they needed to be ritually burned, as they belonged to the family of the man who'd died in the boutique. She then suggested that Marcelle keep the garments, which had provided inspiration for her designs.

That was unthinkable. The priceless garments belonged to Inada-*san*'s wife and her family.

Nomura-*san* welcomed them into his narrow office. Marcelle and Yumi-*chan* took places on one side of the low table, and he brought them tea. After several sips in silence, he put down his cup. "Hamada-*san*'s wife is willing to gift you the heirloom kimonos, as there were no provisions for *La France Boutique* in the event of her husband's death." Nomura-*san* leaned across the table. "I showed the kimonos to my wife. She thinks they're worth enough to start a new boutique on Ginza Boulevard."

Yumi-*chan* widened her eyes. Marcelle felt a stab of guilt for the disappointment she was causing but she simply couldn't treat Inada's kimonos like currency. "I'm returning them. They're part of her family history." She paused as an alternative explanation for the generosity came to mind. "Do you suppose she's making this offer to avoid meeting me?" An even more troubling explanation, one she often considered, followed. "Does she blame me for her husband's death?"

Nomura-*san* shook his head. "Absolutely not. She knows more about Hamada-*san*'s enemies than anyone. The killer's so-called confession about having seen you with Hamada-*san* holds no water with her. I have every reason to believe she's looking forward to meeting you. Hamada-*san* told her about your store. She's a traditional Japanese woman. Your affair is of no matter to her."

"In that case, I'll pay her a visit and return the kimonos myself." Japanese women's support, emotionally and monetarily, of their husbands' dalliances and the children that resulted would forever be a mystery to Marcelle.

"It speaks to the goodness of your spirit that you won't consider keeping them for yourself." Nomura-*san* handed her two envelopes. She'd also come to his office to collect the catastrophe money Inada had set aside for the boutique. She'd assumed one envelope would suffice. "As you are a capable woman of business, Renaud-*san*, I'd like to make an investment in your new boutique wherever it may be and whenever it may open." He tapped one of the ivory-colored envelopes. "I've matched the modest amount you'll receive from the catastrophe funds. I expect repayment whenever you're in a position to make it. No interest will be necessary."

Tears pricked the back of Marcelle's eyes. Nomura-*san*'s faith in her was like a firm embrace she hadn't known she'd needed. To think she'd been on the verge of severing ties with Nomura-*san* to make Nobu her benefactor. "I'm grateful to you, Nomura-*san*. We'll use it to further our business."

"I'll also assist in preparing the necessary legal documents for leasing space, although I won't be able to act as your guarantor. Perhaps Koide-*san* could take that role?"

Mention of his name tore through her. "That wouldn't be appropriate," she said, keeping her tone light. "Our affair has come to an end. I'll find another guarantor."

Nomura-*san* murmured approving words. "Hamada-*san* would be pleased to know you're no longer seeing Koide-*san*." He took the final sip from his teacup. "Be persistent. Never give up, Renaud-*san*. That's what Hamada-*san* would have wanted."

Each clutching a bulky box of kimonos, Marcelle and Yumi-*chan* left Nomura-*san*'s office and made their way through shop after shop in the downtown neighborhood. Craftsmen beckoned them inside small factories to watch their creations come to life on wooden pegs, small-scale spindles, and metal blocks. Marcelle purchased spools of vivid red, white, and silver thread and an ivory hair clip for Yumi-*chan* as thanks for her help. Yumi-*chan* balked at the gift. Marcelle insisted.

As they moved beyond Shimbashi's main streets, thriving businesses gave way to broken-down homes and occasional stalls, several of which served spicy noodle bowls with roasted pork. Others offered rice bowls with meats grilled over open flames. The scent took Marcelle back to the brief sojourn she'd had in Macao on the way from France to Tokyo.

By that point in her journey, she'd reconciled herself to a new life in Tokyo. When she'd first boarded the ship, she'd been thinking only of escaping her Parisian life. Newly married, Antoine had insisted Marcelle become his mistress, just as he'd insisted she care for his alcoholic aunt and insisted she forgive him for bedding an acquaintance of hers, since everyone knew the woman was a seductress. Each of those times she acquiesced, knowing he was using her and hating him for it.

Then the American envoy's wife presented her with a way to leave Antoine. People called her courageous for boarding that ship to a mysterious destination with a family she didn't know. In her mind, she was simply trading one kind of misery for another, a familiar misery with Antoine for a foreign one with an American family. What was courageous about that?

Aboard ship, the envoy's family treated her with the respect owed a lady's maid. Even so, the familiar misery began to have more appeal. Many days she spent on the upper deck considering whether she ought to throw herself in the sea or return to Paris and beg Antoine's forgiveness. Then a lively, cosmopolitan woman, also approaching twenty years of age, befriended Marcelle. The young woman was traveling with her parents to Macao for their third Asian exploration and regaled Marcelle with tales of Tokyo life. As the ship pushed through the equatorial heat and into pirate's seas, a new life in Tokyo seemed to promise less misery than she'd feared.

The city had given her opportunities to take control of her life, to make decisions for herself, to create a beautiful store, to foster loyal patrons, splendid lovers, and dear friends. Much was lost to her because of Inada's death and Nobu's father. Still, she had her fertile imagination and friends like Yumi-*chan*, Suki, and Nomura-*san*. What would it take to get her back to where she'd been before she'd met Nobuyuki?

She and Yumi-*chan* had a meal of savory Chinese noodles, then resumed their strolling in a neighborhood along the bay where every dwelling seemed to be a family factory. "Do you suppose those factories are producing textiles?"

Yumi-*chan*'s gaze darted around the bayside neighborhood. "They might be. It's an *eta* neighborhood."

"How do you know?"

Yumi-*chan* pointed to a one-story building with a thick plume of smoke rising from the top. "Over there is a tanning factory." She craned her neck. "The sign says they tan hides for leather goods. It looks like that's a butchery on the other side of the road."

A tanning factory for leather goods meant there were likely leather goods being produced nearby. "Shall we walk through the neighborhood and see what's of interest?"

Yumi-*chan* crinkled her nose. "You really shouldn't. *Eta* contamination will attach itself to you."

Marcelle adjusted the kimono box in her arms. "I doubt that very much."

"Why? Most people think the *eta* are disgusting and you'll turn out the same if you go there."

"I fail to see what makes *eta* abhorrent to anyone. They're doing jobs for all of society. If they passed their contamination along, wouldn't we all be contaminated by now? Does entering the *eta* neighborhood bother you?"

Yumi-*chan* shrugged. "My *okasan* is *heinin*. An outcast as much as the *eta* for having been a prostitute. I grew up in an *eta* neighborhood in Utsunomiya."

Like Nomura-*san*, there was no telltale sign Yumi-*chan* was different from an ordinary Japanese citizen. "Is that why you came to Tokyo? To escape the stigma of being raised among *eta*?"

"Partly. People from Tokyo don't associate my home with the *eta*. Although I believe Inada-*san* knew. When I first started working at *La France Boutique*, he asked whether I'd grown up along the Tamada River. I had no choice but to answer yes. That much was clear from my registered address. I suppose he never told you."

Yumi-*chan*'s recollection brought a wave of affection for Inada. "He supported many *eta*, at least that's what I've learned since his death. I believe he'd want us to take a look around the neighborhood. Shall we?"

A mildly acrid smell from the tanning factories tinged the air. Otherwise, the streets felt familiar. People went about the daily tasks of work, shopping, schooling, and visiting temples as would occur in any other neighborhood. Marcelle imagined Inada's objective lens looking over the thriving neighborhood and resolving to reward the *eta*'s ingenuity and industriousness by offering fair wages and means of advancement in Japanese society.

They walked toward Shimbashi's shopping district on their return to the train station, where they could catch a rickshaw to Tsukiji. Several blocks before the district's main streets, Marcelle caught sight of a two-story structure with a sign whose characters seemed to indicate it was a factory for the manufacture of police uniforms.

She stopped and rested the kimono box against her hip. "Are they making Western-style uniforms in there?" she asked with a nod at the building.

Yumi-*chan* walked up to the sturdy wooden door where a notice had been posted. "They were until last month. The factory owners abandoned it for financial reasons. Not a fire or a pox or anything like that."

Destruction by fire or the spread of disease within its walls would have condemned the building just as Inada's death in *La France Boutique* had condemned the store. They looked inside the front windows. The small manufacturing enterprise had workspace for about a dozen sewing machines and the laborers to run them.

A vision took shape in Marcelle's mind. Women workers pressing fabric through sewing machines to produce her designs on a scale that would allow women of lesser means to wear her dresses. This had always been a dream of hers for the very distant future, one she'd thought unlikely to ever materialize. It seemed too ambitious to imagine Japanese women who couldn't afford to shop on Ginza Boulevard wearing beautiful, well-made dresses that brought together the traditions of East and West.

"What could we do with this space?" she asked Yumi-*chan*.

"Make many more dresses than we do now."

"More women could afford our designs if they came from a factory like this."

"We could make dresses that suit the lives of everyday women," Yumi-*chan* said excitedly and fumbled the box of kimonos.

"With silks from the local vendors." Marcelle nodded toward a nearby warehouse with a sign indicating it produced bolts of silk.

Yumi-*chan* shook her head. "Ordinary women would prefer Western-style dresses of wool and cotton. They might also want the shape of their dresses to bear resemblance to kimonos. At *La France Boutique,* we made dresses from Japanese fabrics and gave them a Western shape, which was fine for our patrons who had a more Western-style everyday life. Ordinary Japanese women might like a simple, Western-style dress that nevertheless draped around the body like the kimono."

Marcelle envisioned sturdy cottons with billowy sleeves, wrapped tops belted at the waist, lengths that extended to just above the ankle, or higher, which would make for ease of movement in getting up from the floor. "You're absolutely correct. Do you suppose we could afford this space?"

Yumi-*chan* returned to the sign. "You can contact the owner. They're eager to lease."

Marcelle considered the possibility of using the money from Nomura-*san* to secure the lease now, then wait to invest more in the business as she brought in revenue from working at Suki's mother's shop. But how could she ever work enough hours to afford the labor costs? "What about seamstresses? Were we to produce on a large scale, we'd need many more women working with us."

Yumi-*chan* bounced the kimono box against her hip. "*Eta* women would command less in wages."

Of course she'd employ *eta* women. "As soon as we have buyers for the clothes, I'll increase their wages."

A chill of recognition danced along her skin. Inada, her Jiro, had led her to the factory. He was taking care of her in death as he had in life. Tears welled in her eyes. She turned from Yumi-*chan* and meandered around the factory.

On the backside, a small garden separated the uniform factory from a confectionary factory. Although rather loud, it filled the space with the scent of sugared azuki beans. The factory probably presented neighboring businesses with a mountain of sweets during the July and December gifting seasons. She could see her workers sipping tea, eating bean cakes, and chatting in the garden during their breaks.

Inada would love that. *This* was where he wanted her to be. He'd led her on a path to a new livelihood and a new reputation. No longer a *modiste* for the wealthy, she'd design for women who worked, for women who served, for women who oversaw households of their own, for ordinary women strolling parks with their beaux, their families, their friends.

Marcelle returned to the factory. Yumi-*chan* gazed into the front window, scrutinizing the interior in the same manner she used when devising new ornamentation for a gown. *Together*, they'd make this enterprise a success.

They'd need help. Perhaps Suki's husband, Griff, could assist her in identifying foreign investors. Maybe one of her neighbors on Ginza Boulevard who'd been sympathetic to her boutique closing would act as guarantor in exchange for a stake in the factory. She'd have to be careful who she'd allow to invest, since she didn't want to let anyone down. Nor did she want any investor imposing his vision. But something told her this was going to be a success, her and Yumi-*chan*'s success.

Nobu would be thrilled at seeing her design dresses for everyday life. He'd invest, become her guarantor, and the dress factory would manifest as quickly as she could put designs to paper. She envisioned them together, his mind working in tandem with hers to think through the allocation of factory space and the acquisition of materials. Her perfect partner in business. And everywhere else.

The loss of him gathered around her like an impending storm. Marcelle steeled herself against the maelstrom of emotions. She'd allow them to thrash at her when she was alone in her room, as she did each night.

She drew to Yumi-*chan*'s side with the most radiant smile she could muster. "We're going to bring this factory to life. It's going to be magnificent."

Yumi-*chan* memorized the name and address of the leasing company, and they left the factory for Shimbashi station. Down the narrow side streets toward the shopping district, they discussed hip-to-waist lengths of the *yukata* cotton kimonos. Marcelle suggested they consider a longer length for a day dress, one that would function to minimize the waist, when raised voices behind them made her turn.

Coming toward them apace were three men dressed in dark blue laborer kimonos. As they approached, Marcelle saw tattooing on their chests and sleeves. If she wasn't mistaken, they were members of a gang, and they were walking toward Marcelle and Yumi-*chan* as though they'd already decided to plow right through them.

One of the men pointed at Yumi-*chan* and said something to her that Marcelle didn't understand.

Her face turned stark white. "Run," she hissed at Marcelle and thrust the kimono box at her chest.

Even if she could carry two boxes of kimonos and run, she wasn't leaving Yumi-*chan*. "What's going on?"

Two of the men grabbed Yumi-*chan* by the arms and lifted her off the ground while she kicked and wriggled.

Marcelle dropped the kimono boxes without a care for the precious heirlooms and rushed forward to help Yumi-*chan*. A third man grabbed her shoulders in his painful grip. "Stop," she shouted as loudly as she could, hoping to draw attention from the stores and residences along the narrow street.

"Tell Ryusuke the gang found me," Yumi-*chan* called out in a mixture of French and English as the men dragged her down the street. "They're taking me back to the brothel, or somewhere. I don't know."

The men must have been part of the gang that had forced Yumi-*chan* into the brothel and tattooed her. But she'd run away from them years ago. The monastery where she'd fled was supposed to have paid the gang for Yumi-*chan*'s freedom. Had they not paid enough?

Marcelle twisted her shoulders in the man's grip. "We have kimonos. Priceless kimonos. Take them. Tell those men to get their hands off Yumi-*chan*. Please."

A middle-aged woman emerged from one of the dwellings along the street. With a finger pointed at the gang members holding Yumi-*chan*, she shouted in rather imperious Japanese.

Yumi-*chan* called back to the woman in a pleading tone. The men yelled at the woman in such a threatening manner that every muscle in Marcelle's body tensed.

Not backing down, the older woman shouted back. The men said something to one another, then the one holding Marcelle released her. She headed straight for Yumi-*chan* but one of the men holding her used his arm to stop Marcelle from coming nearer.

The older woman stomped down the street toward the stores.

Marcelle's body went cold at the words "fight" and "kimonos" being traded between the men until finally, they let Yumi-*chan* go. Marcelle embraced her, the toughest woman she knew, who now shook in her arms.

The gang members grabbed the boxes of kimonos and ran. Several men emerged from a pub down the street. The middle-aged woman who'd come to their rescue guided them in the direction of the attackers. The pubgoers ran full speed in their hemp sandals down the dirt-packed road.

Yumi-*chan* gripped Marcelle's sleeve. "The kimonos," she said between chattering teeth, "What are we going to do about the kimonos?"

"Forget about them. They're not important. What's important is that you're safe." With those words, Yumi-*chan*'s trembling abated. "Are you injured? Did they hurt you?"

She stepped from Marcelle's embrace and shook out her arms. "It's going to take more than that to injure me."

"Don't tempt fate," Marcelle warned, relieved Yumi-*chan* appeared unharmed.

"I'm fine, but you have to give those kimonos to Inada-*san*'s widow. What will you do?"

"I'll tell her what happened." When she visited Inada's widow, she'd explain the circumstances. While the widow had been willing to present them as a gift that would inspire artistic creations, she might be upset to learn they'd been stolen and likely sold. In that case, Marcelle would offer her the catastrophe funds, not that these would begin to compensate for the kimonos.

The middle-aged matron came to Yumi-*chan*'s side. As she questioned her about injuries she might have suffered, a rickshaw drew up behind them.

Marcelle and Yumi-*chan* thanked her and gratefully boarded it. "To Tsukiji," Marcelle told the runner.

Half an hour later, they were at the offices of *Tokyo Women's Magazine*. Suki sent one of her writers to summon a doctor to examine Yumi-*chan*'s arms and ribs, which she admitted were tender. Suki's assistant went to summon Ryusuke from Koide Department Store.

Marcelle and Yumi-*chan* sat at the round wooden conference table in the writer's room. Suki brought them a pot of green tea and a plate of bite-size sweet potato cakes that she explained were part of her daily pregnancy regime. Taking a bite, she murmured about the cakes' perfect texture while wiping crumbs from the top of her swollen belly.

Marcelle sipped the tea, and the soothing brew eased the soreness in her shoulders where the gang member had grabbed her. "For years, I worried about something happening to those kimonos. Now, just before I'm set to return them, they're stolen."

Suki finished chewing her cake. "I'm going to send someone from the conservative faction to speak with the gang. The Jinzai nunnery paid for Yumi-*chan*'s freedom." Suki had started a charitable organization at the Jinzai nunnery to aid women who wished to leave brothels and other such places of nighttime entertainment. She also had questionable friends among a faction of conservative supporters.

"They said something about interest on my debt having accumulated recently." The pleat between Yumi-*chan's* eyes deepened. Marcelle was certain she was in more pain than she let on.

"That would be a violation of our agreement with—" Suki stopped at a howling sound from the doorway.

Ryusuke rushed to Yumi-*chan's* side, and Suki encouraged them to speak with one another in her private office. Ryusuke mumbled thanks while he picked up Yumi-*chan* and carried her into Suki's office. He shut the door behind him.

"They're a darling couple of lovebirds." Suki grinned.

"They'll marry soon. She's going to visit his parents—"

"Renaud-*san?*" a woman called from the threshold.

Marcelle's heart did a small jig at the distinctive British accent.

Asako fell into a bow. "I'm sorry for disturbing you."

"You're not disturbing us at all." Suki motioned for Asako to take a seat at the table. "Asako Koide is the newest writer for *Tokyo Women's Magazine.*" She gave a beatific smile. "I can't imagine a better fit for the position."

Asako's cheeks reddened at the compliment as she took the seat Suki had indicated.

"She knows English and Japanese with far greater fluency than anyone on staff, and she's a staunch advocate for women's rights," Suki said as she walked over to a table on the far side of the room where goods for serving tea had been placed.

Marcelle grinned at Asako. She'd liked her from the moment she'd seen her standing with such confidence beside her mother at Koide's grand opening. Nobu had mentioned his sister's frustration with her life in Japan and how she clashed with their mother. Perhaps this was a sign his mother was giving Asako the freedom she desired.

Suki poured out a cup of tea and handed it to Asako. "Last week Asako came to our offices and proposed to be a writer for the magazine. Her initiative reminded me of how I became a columnist at the *Tokyo Daily News*. But she's far more talented a writer than I'll ever be. She's already produced a thousand words in English and as many characters in Japanese on the differing strategies of British and Japanese women seeking the vote. She's hoping it will be instructive for the latter, although we all know this is the last place on Earth where women will be given the vote."

Asako lifted her cup of tea, which did little to conceal the bloom on her cheeks.

"Suki is very fortunate to have you," Marcelle said.

Asako produced a sheepish smile. "My brother encouraged me to approach Spenser-*san* about writing for the magazine."

Suki let out a small laugh and stood from the table. "Asako, for the hundredth time, you must call me Suki. I'll let you two speak. I'm going to see what's taking Hina so long to fetch the doctor."

Asako furrowed her brow. "Is Spense—I mean Suki, well?"

"She's fine. The doctor is for my assistant, Yumi-*chan*." Marcelle related the events of the afternoon from when they left the factory to arriving at *Tokyo Women's Magazine*. "Her ribs seem injured to me, but she's too tough to admit it," Marcelle concluded.

Asako had listened to every word with nods, murmurs, and deep concern etched into her bold features. "Would you mind my telling Nobu what happened? He would want to know."

The sound of his name made every nerve in Marcelle's body tingle. She worked to steady her features. "I suppose he'll learn about it from Ryusuke shortly. Has he returned from Osaka?"

"He'll be there until the end of next week, at least that was his plan. Once he hears what's happened, he'll be on the next train out of Osaka."

Marcelle imagined Nobu bursting through the boardinghouse door. The other boarders would love that. "He's a considerate friend."

"He wants to marry you." Asako relaxed into an adoring smile that gave Marcelle a light brush of contentment. That was how it'd feel to have Asako as a sister-in-law.

She couldn't allow herself to entertain the idea. "We aren't going to marry. Our affair has come to an end."

"I feel obliged to warn you that my dear brother intends to woo you when he returns from Osaka, which is currently looking likely to happen very soon."

Marcelle restrained herself from pointing out that, in fact, this was a sign that he did *not* give a whit about her well-being. If he did, he'd let her live her life without fearing she was about to be sent back to France. "I wish he wouldn't."

Asako cocked her head. "I'm sorry to hear that. I'd been hoping you'd make him a love match. For Nobu, such a match is possible. In our family, in most Japanese families, it's a child's obligation to marry and produce grandchildren regardless of whether there's love between the couple. In large families, a girl can get away with spinsterhood, but in small families that's impossible. Nobu and I must marry. Since I can never have a love match of my own, I'd hoped he would find one." Asako spoke so unequivocally that Marcelle's heart ached for her.

"I hope Nobu makes his love match." She managed not to let sadness make its way into her words. Truly, she did want him to have a love match and she didn't want to hear a word about it when it happened.

"I wish it could be you," Asako said with a shy smile. "He loves you. He's never wanted to be with any other woman the way he wants to be with you."

That storm of emotion over the loss of Nobu inched closer. His love was going to destroy her. His father would punish her if Nobu continued like this. She couldn't allow herself to be swayed by his love or this irritating, unrelenting need she had for him. Yet she *was* swayed. Nobu's doggedness was overwhelming. "I'm trying to wish he'd find another woman. I just can't." Her voice wobbled on the waves of emotion.

Asako handed her a white handkerchief stamped with purple lilacs.

Marcelle dabbed at her eyes. She might as well have declared her love for Nobu. She felt entirely exposed but not embarrassed, because Asako was looking at her as though she'd witnessed a miracle. "Are you going to tell him that you made me cry?"

"Should I?" Asako asked with the eagerness of a woman being offered a trip up a moving staircase.

"As you wish." Marcelle surrendered. Nothing today had gone as expected. There had been Nomura-*san*'s generosity and the loss of the kimonos. There had been the gang's attack and the embrace of friendship. Since she'd begun her Tokyo life, control over her decisions, her welfare, and her relationships had kept her out of trouble. That control had been key to her success in every way. Surrendering it to Asako and Nobu might ruin her life.

She should have nothing to do with the Koide family. She should fear them, loathe them. But she couldn't. Not Asako. And never Nobu.

"He's going to take this as a sign you love him."

"Let him," Marcelle said pleasantly. "In the meantime, I'd love to hear more about the article you're writing for the magazine."

While Asako described suffrage aims among the women she'd known in London, Suki arrived with her writer and the doctor in tow.

"Perhaps we could continue talking another time?" Marcelle asked.

"It'd be my pleasure," Asako said with a delightful smile.

CHAPTER TWENTY-THREE

Nobu

The boardinghouse bell's shrill cadence cut through the night air.

A young woman opened the door, and she narrowed her eyes at Nobu with what seemed utmost suspicion. "How may I help you?"

"Is Renaud-*san* available to receive a caller?" His words came out in cloudy puffs of breath.

The young woman wrapped her arms around her middle as a rush of wind blew past her into the house's interior. "Let me see," she said and retreated inside.

Nobu flexed his fingers. Sweat had chilled his hands despite his thick leather gloves. He'd come straight to the boardinghouse after changing from his traveling clothes, freshening up, and getting more information from his astonishingly wonderful, terrifically clever sister who'd sent him the telegram about another attack on Marcelle and Yumi-*chan*.

When he'd arrived home, he'd found her in the back parlour, handling the *koto* as though it was a misbehaving child.

"She cried over you," Asako said before Nobu even announced his presence.

"An angry cry?"

Asako regarded him as though *he* was the misbehaving *koto*. "I believe she misses you."

"That's incredible." Hope stirred his gut until he recalled the reason for his rushing across Japan. "How is she faring? What about Yumi-*chan*?"

"They were both shaken up, but the doctor says they're uninjured. You should go to her."

"I shall." He calculated that it should take him no more than thirty minutes by rickshaw to reach her boardinghouse. It was nearing dusk, which meant she might be home for the evening meal.

Asako scowled at one of the finest renderings of the stringed instrument, then gave its smooth wooden exterior a few gentle pats. "It's not the *koto*'s fault I'm so terrible. I should've come up with another excuse for how I've been spending my time. *Okasan* is going to be quite disappointed when I give her that performance she's been requesting."

Nobu gave the parlour door a furtive glance. "Never mind *Okasan*, I'll give her another task at the store."

"You *must*. She's taken such delight in monitoring the store on your behalf. She says your clerks treat her like a queen from the moment she enters. Really, it'd be best for everyone in the family if you kept her there."

Whatever Asako wanted, he'd give her. "How about tomorrow you tell me about your work on the magazine?"

"Depends on my souvenir from Osaka," she said with a greedy smile.

He had a few special gifts for her. Not only had he purchased her a pewterware vase with rose stencilling, but he'd also met a gentleman who might prove a good candidate for brother-in-law.

They made plans to speak the following day, and Nobu left for the boardinghouse.

After what seemed like hours, the door finally opened. Breath caught in Nobu's chest at the sight of Marcelle. Not only was she safe and well, but her grace, beauty, and elegance electrified the night. A mass of curls topped her head. Her generous mouth was set in a calm smile. But what made him feel as though he was stirring to life after a long, restless sleep were her cerulean eyes glowing with welcome.

"I'm back," he heard himself say. His mind was blank from being close enough to wrap his arms around her waist and draw her to him. Oh the gods, he wanted the scent of her nape filling him.

"How was your trip?" She joined him on the portico.

"Successful." Could he come up with something better than a one-word answer? "I was troubled to hear what happened to you and Yumi-*chan*. How are you faring?"

"I'm fine, so is Yumi-*chan*." Marcelle examined him as though he was an intricate detail on a rare silk. "Shall we go somewhere?"

Nobu had barely eaten since he'd gotten the telegram from Asako. "Would you like to get a bowl of soba?"

She stepped toward him. "The matron served grated yam for dinner," she whispered. "So, the answer would be yes, I'd love a bowl of noodles."

Marcelle returned inside for her cloak while he stood dumbfounded on the portico. She hadn't turned him away. Granted, Asako had said she'd cried over him, but he hadn't expected her to greet him with such warmth. Was it possible she was considering accepting his proposal?

Taking his arm without a word, she walked as near to his side as she had during those blissful days in Karuizawa. Taken aback by the intimacy, he went speechless, and since Marcelle didn't engage him in any kind of conversation, they walked in silence to Tsukiji's most popular soba restaurant, which also happened to be one of the finest in all of Tokyo.

They ate the piping hot bowls quickly, blowing off the steam rising from chopstick-fuls of noodles, then slurping the buckwheat strands covered in a rich, savoury broth. After thanking the proprietor and taking their leave, Nobu suggested they stroll at the park near the lawn tennis club.

"Certainly." She took his arm. "The broth was superb. I had more of an appetite than I'd thought."

"Were you busy today?" he asked as they made their way through the university district, still alive with students and their tutors at the pubs.

"An errand took me to Shimbashi. Recently, I discovered a factory that had been making Western-style police uniforms. The arrangement of the space is perfect for manufacturing any kind of clothing. Today, I inquired about a lease. I think I'll be able to afford it. The owner is anxious for a tenant."

"Would you be making uniforms?"

"Uniforms for girls would be fascinating," she replied slowly, and her gaze drifted to the side. Then she turned back. "Not yet. I'd like to manufacture dresses for everyday wear. Yumi-*chan* suggested we create dresses nearer to the design of the kimono, using ordinary fabrics. It was a brilliant idea. If we're going to design for Japanese women who aren't shopping on Ginza Boulevard, we have to design for their preferences and customs. No one can comfortably sit down on and rise from on a tatami mat with a corset and a mass of skirts billowing about."

As always, Marcelle's thinking was impressive, but she might be erring in her understanding of modern Japan. "Japanese women no longer sit on the ground. We now have chairs in our houses."

"Only the wealthy eat their meals at dining room tables with chairs. Most Japanese continue to use the floor."

He had to concede the point once he thought about it. Ordinary Japanese still lived in two rooms and ate, slept, and lounged on the floor. "Then you'll be designing for the working classes?"

Her face seemed to glow in the moonlight. "I envision working women in Western-style dresses that mimic the more relaxed kimono style of the *yukata*."

"You'll be doing many women a favour," Nobu said as they reached the dirt pathway at the park's entrance. "Then you're planning to give up the designs you were doing at *La France Boutique*."

"Right now, I'm inspired to design differently. I feel like fate led me to a new kind of work."

"That's going to be an expensive undertaking." He felt compelled to point this out even though she must have already realised it herself.

"The lease and labor expenses are turning out to be less than I'd thought. I have supplier friends who are willing to give us fabrics and other materials in the form of a loan. Griff has started asking his investor friends if they're interested in women's garments. It may be a while before I have a profitable enterprise, but every day I feel more confident that Yumi-*chan* and I are going to be making clothes for more women than we'd ever dreamed possible."

"I'd be happy to invest." As soon as he'd spoken the words, he realised that she must know as his future wife he'd build the factory for her.

Yet she made plans to build the factory herself.

Marcelle wasn't going to be his wife.

They headed down the circular pathway through the trees. Several older couples were taking a nightly stroll, their capes and coats billowing in the cool breezes.

"I'm not certain I need to pursue additional investment at this point," she remarked.

The words stung. New businesses craved capital. She wouldn't take his money, even as an investor.

Her chest rose against his arm with a large inhale. "Have you heard anything from the detective about Inada-*san*'s death?"

The police had done an excellent job of applying expeditious justice in the case of Inada's murder. The killer had confessed. He'd be hanged for his crimes, if they hadn't hanged him already. Nobu ended up asking his detective friend directly to question Inada's killer about the attacks on *La France Boutique*. According to his friend, the killer confessed to the attacks there. The police concluded the anti-foreigner fanatic had been vandalizing the boutique and finally killed Inada for his involvement with Marcelle.

It was a convenient conclusion for the police and the Foundation Party. It might very well be the truth. Nobu had been around politicians for too long to believe anything was that clear-cut, but he also had no grounds to question it. "It seems the killer will be hanged for his crime. He confessed to vandalizing the boutique and attacking Yumi-*chan*."

"Then it's settled?"

"It appears so. Aside from the brothel gang's attack on you and Yumi-*chan*, have you been bothered by anyone from the Foundation Party or anyone harbouring anti-foreigner sentiment?"

"None."

"If you sense any kind of threat, I'll put guardsmen on your boardinghouse and the new factory. I don't want anything to happen to you."

"That's very generous of you."

She held on to his arm, yet her words were stiff. She was being politely affectionate—reserved really—which wasn't like her. "You may find that as you begin supplying the factory, you might need additional investment or advisors for the interior or sales space if you're going to sell from the factory as well. I'm willing to help in any way I can."

Marcelle let out a small sigh. "I'm not certain about our becoming involved in business matters."

Her words lingered in the air. The truth was she didn't need him at all. Even so, she was still by his side. He'd prepared an apology for this evening. Giving it before she slipped away became suddenly imperative. "I understand why you might hesitate. I acted horribly after Inada-*san*'s funeral. I had no business questioning your feelings for him or whether you'd colluded with him to spy on behalf of France. For these things, I apologise from the bottom of my heart."

"You know how ridiculous it is to think I'd spy for anyone, especially France."

"I agree. It's ridiculous. I believe I've convinced *Otosan* as much."

"Have you?" she asked pointedly.

"Before I left, I explained how accusing a Western nation of spying on Japanese soil based on nothing but rumour could create an international dispute that would lower Japan in the eyes of the world."

A chill swept across the green space. He recalled how she pressed herself up against him on the trip to Karuizawa. She wasn't doing that now.

"Perhaps he's put an end to the rumors. They spread widely enough that my patrons, I should say *former* patrons, have distanced themselves from me." Marcelle pulled her arm from his and came to a stop. "Suki's friends in the conservative faction spoke with the gang that attacked us. They run the brothel where Yumi-*chan* had been laboring. Someone they wouldn't name told them Yumi-*chan* had a wealthy employer who'd pay to ensure her safety. The conservative faction has made certain that the gang understands the nunnery already purchased Yumi-*chan*'s freedom and they're not to extort any more funds. Do you think it could be a member of the Foundation Party who told the gang?"

Nobu wouldn't put it past *Otosan* or his cronies to tell the gang about Yumi-*chan* as a way of bullying Marcelle out of Tokyo. *Otosan* could be relentless in his aims, and he aimed to keep Nobu and Marcelle apart. Indeed, Inada's accountant and Inada himself had testified to Marcelle about *Otosan*'s relentlessness. But they'd overestimated his cruelty. In truth, *Otosan* was a reasonable man. "I'll speak with *Otosan*. If it was someone from the Foundation Party who told the gang, he'll know, or at least could find out. I'll make him understand you're not to be bullied again."

They'd stopped halfway around the pathway. The night's cold seeped into Nobu's bones. He wanted to hold Marcelle to him, but she'd angled away. He folded his hands across his chest. He wasn't giving up on the love he was certain existed between them. "I meant what I said when I asked you to marry me."

Marcelle let out a sharp laugh. "Marriage is out of the question. Your family has made that clear."

"They'll accept my choice of wife. They have to. I'm an only son."

Marcelle met his gaze. "I'm not going to force myself into a family that's trying to force me out of the city." The muscles of her throat clenched as though she was refraining from unleashing a series of verbal blows. How he wished she would hit him, yell at him, cry as she'd cried to Asako.

Instead, she placed her arm back in the crook of his elbow. "Please take me home."

They walked in silence from the park toward the boardinghouse. When it came into view, Nobu placed his hand over her forearm. "I'll never stop loving you, Marcelle. I'll continue to fight for you until I have no fight left in me." Her grip on him loosened. His tightened. He wasn't going to let her go. "I'm not going to presume you love me the same way I love you, but I know you care."

"I do care for you, Nobu." She turned to him, but her face was caught in the shadows, making it impossible to read. "There may be circumstances where I can imagine us continuing our affair. But I cannot be with you, not until I know being with you won't get me thrown out of Japan."

Relief eased the tightness in his jaw and shoulders. An affair was a start. First, he had to get *Otosan* to make certain the rumours were no longer spreading. *Otosan* also had to take measures to restore Marcelle's reputation and vow not to retaliate against her in the future. Then they could return to lovemaking and French meals and discussions about fashion and the future of commerce in Tokyo.

He'd never been more content than when she was simply in the same room. He sensed she felt similarly. If she hadn't, she wouldn't have given him a path back to the way things had been.

Nobu opened the gate to the boardinghouse garden. "Our affair isn't going to get you thrown out of Japan. I promise."

Marcelle smiled warily. "I hope so."

Her gaze reached for him the way it did before they fell into a spell of unrestrained kisses. His body sprang to life, readying to pull her into his embrace and show her the depths of his love. He shifted to take her in, and she turned away.

Still, the glimpse of passion gave him hope.

They bid one another good night at the boardinghouse's front door, then Nobu shut the gate behind him and headed toward the gates of the foreign quarter, thinking of all the ways he could outmanoeuvre the vindictive politician, unrepentant rumourmonger, and spiteful man that was *Otosan*.

CHAPTER TWENTY-FOUR

Marcelle

A maid from the Inada home led Marcelle across a front garden of gracefully pruned pine trees and azalea bushes to the front door where Inada-*san*, the widow, stood waiting.

Marcelle bowed to the matronly figure, then rose and took in an ordinary face with a flat nose and broad mouth. Even so, she was attractive, thanks to skin like flawless alabaster and elegant, assured movements, both attributes of a wealthy upbringing. Afternoon light played on the facets of a jeweled clip holding her hair in a fashionably low chignon. Naturally, her mourning kimono had been cut from the most radiant black silk money could buy.

The previous day Marcelle had reviewed her visiting etiquette with Suki. Even so, she was a bundle of quivering nerves. As Suki had instructed, Marcelle bowed low from the waist. "I must offer my deepest apologies," she began.

"You needn't apologize," Inada-*san* said in gentle, refined tones. "Please come inside."

Marcelle remained in the bow. "I came today to return the kimonos your husband lent me. They gave me much inspiration, and I'm grateful for having had them in my possession. But the other day, my assistant, who used to labor in a brothel, and I were accosted by men from the brothel. I gave them the kimonos to ensure our safety. Your kimonos are gone." The rehearsed apology came out without a hitch.

"Please, rise," Inada-*san* said with unruffled elegance. "I don't care about those kimonos. If they saved you and your assistant from harm, they've done more for you than they've ever done for my family."

Marcelle rose and sniffled from the swelling of relief and gratitude. Inada-*san* gestured toward her home's interior. "Come in and have a sip of tea. I want to know more about you. You must be anxious to pay your respects."

Suki had explained that Marcelle would likely be given the chance to visit with Inada's spirit. She followed his widow down a corridor that smelled of green tea, polished wood, and incense from a Buddhist altar. Their stockinged feet swished over the unblemished flooring. At the end of the corridor, Inada-*san* slid open a door and bowed. Then she turned back to Marcelle. "When you've finished paying your respects, come join me." She gestured toward an adjacent door.

Marcelle stepped inside the parlor. Persian carpeting and heavy, Western-style furniture had been pushed to the walls, and the Inada family altar had been set up along the length of the opposite wall. Its open golden doors revealed a statue of the Buddha with gold serving vessels and ornate floral arrangements before him. A tablet with the names of the Inada ancestors had been placed next to the Buddha. Marcelle could make out a recently carved entry in flowing calligraphy. Propped on an easel before the altar was a painting of Inada. He'd been a slight man, but the painting made him seem large and imposing. Yet, the artist had captured the depth of intelligence in Inada's gaze and the light set of his mouth, which seemed a testament to his openness.

Marcelle greeted the portrait with the tentativeness of encountering a friend after many years of their paths not crossing. This friend had a different name, a different history, and ambitions she'd never glimpsed during their time together. But he was a dear friend all the same. She lit a stick of incense and placed it in front of the altar. Joining her hands at her chest, she asked Inada's spirit to find rest and renewal in the afterlife. She then complimented him on having a beautiful home and charming wife and requested his protection for her and Yumi-*chan* and the factory she felt certain he'd led her to. Finally, she asked for a good visit with his widow.

Lightness infused Marcelle's step as she backed away from the altar and bowed once more at the door before taking leave.

In the corridor, she slid open the door Inada-*san* had indicated. Beyond it was a traditional Japanese receiving room with tatami flooring and an alcove decorated with a hanging scroll of snow-covered mountains rendered in gray watercolor paints. A door covered in squares of translucent paper had been opened to a garden of maple trees with leaves on the verge of their yearly red splendor.

Inada-*san* directed Marcelle to take one of the generous silk cushions beside a low table set up before the garden. The maid followed with a tray that included black tea and a cake stand piled with lemon chiffon cakes, rum cakes, and almond tarts that looked as though they'd come straight from Paris's most upper-crust patisseries. On a separate plate was an assortment of mochi, golden in the afternoon light streaming through the window.

Inada-*san* indicated the plate. "My idle son, well, the idlest of my sons, brought a mochi souvenir from his recent travel to the Izu peninsula. It's rather bland, but perhaps you might be able to stomach a bite."

After that kind of introduction, Marcelle had no doubt the mochi was going to be the most delicious morsel she'd ever consumed. "I adore mochi." In truth, it was one of her favorite sweets.

Inada-*san* filled Marcelle's plate with each kind of cake and a piece of mochi. After a sip of black tea, Marcelle chose the mochi to start. The smooth pounded rice gave way to airy sweet potato that melted on her tongue.

"The mochi is exquisite," Marcelle said.

"Then I shall try one myself." Inada-*san* gave her a broad smile. "Delightful," she declared after consuming the pillowy rice confection. Such a frank, short response was intended to do away with the formality of their conversation. The visit was becoming one between two women of mutual regard, albeit from different and unequal social spheres.

"It's a pleasure to finally meet you," Inada-*san* continued in light tones. "My husband often praised your talents. I understand you design clothes with elements from your home country and mine."

Marcelle spoke about discovering the world of fashion in Paris and then Tokyo, and how she wanted to bring the aesthetics of these places together in her designs. She told Inada-*san* about collecting discarded cuts of kimono silk to make her first dresses, which turned the logic of the kimono on its head by drawing attention to the waist rather than away from it. Then she described her journey in opening *La France Boutique* and finding her first patrons among the foreign community and how she'd had more Japanese patrons than foreign when she'd been forced to shutter the store. She concluded with praise for Inada-*san*'s husband. "All that I was able to achieve with *La France Boutique* was thanks to his support."

"You deserve the credit. My husband merely had a knack for identifying competent people. He never would've made his fortune in leather goods had he not been willing to employ people whose place in society is less valued than ours."

"I understand he provided much for the former outcasts."

Inada-*san* shook her head. "They provided much for him. He became rich from their leather-working skills. I often imagine what would have happened had my husband been able to fulfill his dreams for Taiwan."

"For him, death came too soon."

"For us, too." Grief made a fleeting appearance in her downcast gaze.

"I cannot tell you how upset I've been over the circumstances of your husband's death at my store." Marcelle wanted to give the matron a chance to express any resentment about Marcelle's involvement in her husband's death.

Inada-*san* refilled their teacups. "The men who wanted my husband dead were determined to kill him one way or another. That it occurred in your store was an unfortunate coincidence."

Marcelle took a sip of tea and wondered whether the widow was still holding back her opinions. Mostly, she'd come to the Inada home to give Inada-*san* an opportunity to dispel her anger, frustration, remorse, or whatever negative feelings needed airing. It was the least she could do for the family of the man who'd given her so much, and perhaps something only she could do for them. So, she pressed ahead. "Did the police tell you about the murderer's motive for the killing?"

"The police told my eldest son that it was because of my late husband's affections for you. No one in our family believes a word of it. We'll never know which of my husband's enemies ordered that poor man to kill my husband."

"And the Koide family are among your husband's enemies?" Marcelle asked because she'd regret not asking.

Inada-*san* raised her brow. "Indeed, they are."

"I believe your husband came to the boutique that morning to warn me about the Koide family. I was in an affectionate relationship with Nobuyuki Koide. Your husband was convinced that Koide-*san* was using me to gather information for his family's political gain."

The matron folded her hands on her lap, then looked back up at Marcelle. "My husband went to the boutique that morning to assure himself it was in good condition after those unfortunate attacks. We believe his enemies had been tracking him and took advantage of him being at your store. As for the Koide family, the elder Koide sought to eliminate my husband's influence in Foundation Party affairs. Even so, my husband was successful. Ultimately, that was why he had to die."

Marcelle's stomach clenched on the mochi. "Do you mean Koide-*san* had your husband killed?"

"I know Koide-*san* wanted my husband gone, as did many members of the Foundation Party, and nothing happens in the Foundation Party without Koide-*san*'s approval."

Marcelle felt the color drain from her face. Nobu had said the same about his father. "I didn't realize Koide-*san* was such a dangerous man."

Inada-*san* broke into a small laugh. "The most dangerous men are most adept at disguise. Koide-*san* is proficient in concealing his intentions. He went to great lengths to draw my husband out of hiding this past year. He regarded my husband as a constant threat to the Foundation Party's existence. And he was right to be wary. Even in hiding, my husband managed to keep his faction of the Foundation Party intact. They were united in protest against Koide-*san* and his faction's permissive attitude toward colonization. My husband believed the Foundation Party either had to align with an anti-colonial stance or split if there was to be a strong voice against our country's colonial ambitions."

Political squabbles had never been among Marcelle's interests, but she knew they were of great—if not deadly—importance to others. "I didn't realize how great the political disagreements between your husband and Koide-*san* were. It makes sense your husband would think Koide-*san*'s son was using me for information. But I assure you he was not."

"My husband believed he was," Inada-*san* said with finality that marked an aristocrat speaking to someone who was not. "Koide-*san*, the father, learned of my husband's role as your partner in *La France Boutique* because your Koide-*san* was making inquiries. He wanted to know your partner's identity. His personal secretary is a spy for the elder Koide. He informed Koide of his son's interest in a lovely French lady."

Marcelle wrapped her mind around the implications. Nobu's personal secretary was a spy for his father.

Nobu wasn't safe in the place he felt most at home.

"The elder Koide used bureaucrat friends to learn your partner was my husband," Inada-*san* continued. "Bureaucrats talk. That's how my husband, even while he was in hiding, learned of Koide-*san*'s quest for information about the boutique's ownership. This alarmed my husband because he'd meant to distance himself from the boutique to keep it, and you, safe. He'd feared Koide-*san* would use the boutique to draw him out of hiding. Then that was exactly what he did."

Marcelle's heart strained her chest. "Are you saying that Koide-*san* is the one who threw the rock through the window and attacked Yumi-*chan*?"

"He'd never stoop so low. He'd hire someone else to do it." Inada-*san* spoke as though this was common knowledge.

Marcelle swallowed against the dryness in her throat. "Then you think he hired someone to kill your husband, too?"

"My husband thought it inevitable he'd die at the hands of Koide-*san*'s faction. His only wish was to spare those around him. You are among those for whom he cared deeply." Inada-*san*'s gaze embraced her with such concern that Marcelle felt she was tucked in the woman's arms. "The police said you saw my husband's body in death. He never would've wanted you to see him like that."

"Koide-*san*, the son, identified your husband for the police." Marcelle let out a deep breath. She had to ask the question she wished didn't need asking. "Do you believe the younger Koide was in any way responsible for your husband's death?"

"My husband believed it possible. Koide-*san*'s father wields great power. A son wants to preserve his family's influence." Inada-*san* gave her a pitying look. "Are you fond of him?"

Yes, terribly so.

It'd taken every ounce of restraint in her possession not to kiss him good night after he declared his intention to fight for their affair. The kiss would've been passionate with longing. It would've been the best kiss of her life. It also would've undermined her ultimatum that he find a way to cease the rumors against her before they resumed their affair. "He wants to marry me," she blurted out without reason.

"Perhaps he's a better man than my husband thought of him. Perhaps a better man than his father."

"He often bemoans the pressure on him to leave the world of business for politics. He'd prefer to own department stores across Japan." When had she become Nobu's defender?

"I've heard Koide Department Store offers everything a lady could want." Inada-*san* gave a short laugh. She must have been the only woman of means who hadn't set foot in the store. She gestured to the rum cake on Marcelle's plate. "How does it compare to the cakes in your country?"

Marcelle set aside thoughts about Nobu's secretary and his father being responsible for the attacks on *La France Boutique*. She'd tend to those after she'd concluded her visit with Inada-*san*. Taking a bite of the cake, she gave the matron a gracious smile. "Actually, it's much better."

"I admire you, Renaud-*san*. You're a talented dress designer and successful woman of business. What are your plans for the store?"

"I'm afraid *La France Boutique* is finished."

Inada-*san* murmured that she'd thought as much. Marcelle told her about the factory in Shimbashi and how she'd like to design everyday dresses for women of the working classes. She refrained from mentioning that she'd felt Inada-*san*'s husband had led her there. Today's visit had made plain the tenuousness of Marcelle's claim on Hitoshi Inada. He hadn't meant for her to have a claim on him. He'd never revealed his real name. Still, he'd cared for her, and she for him. In this way, their relations had been simple and beautiful.

"That sounds like a wonderful plan," Inada-*san* said when Marcelle had finished. "I'd like to assist in opening your factory. I have funds. Just tell me how much you need."

Marcelle's mind reeled with possibilities. Inada-*san*'s investment would mean she could open the factory and have a storefront as well. "I'll have to examine our needs. I very much appreciate your interest."

"My husband was right about you, Renaud-*san*. One day you'll be dressing every woman in Tokyo."

Inada-*san* finished her tea and Marcelle followed suit. When they exchanged farewells in the home's wooden, traditional entryway, Marcelle promised to visit again. As she left through the front gate, she carried with her the distinct impression that Inada-*san* was going to become important to her, perhaps even more so than her husband had been.

***

The large Roman numbers on the clock in the Koide Department Store atrium indicated it was almost five o'clock when Marcelle arrived. Customers crowded around display cases filled with a stunning variety of merchandise that seemed to multiply every time she visited the store.

She'd come straight from the Inada residence. What she had to say to Nobu couldn't wait. Inada-*san* was convinced Nobu's father had played a role in vandalizing *La France Boutique*, attacking Yumi-*chan*, and killing her husband. Nobu didn't seem capable of entertaining the notion that his father was this sort of evil monster. He'd accepted that his father had been spreading rumors about her being a spy in order to sabotage their affair. But that was a minor sin compared to the crimes Inada-*san* had accused him of. He must be the most deceitful, conniving man in Tokyo. Yet, when she pictured him, he was still the charming, cordial gentleman she'd met at the moving pictures. If the accusations against him were true, he was indeed a master of disguise.

Marcelle entered the third-floor offices to welcoming smiles from the secretaries, including the one she knew as Nobu's personal secretary and spy for his father. He bowed, then invited her to wait while he informed his boss of her arrival. Marcelle bowed in turn as a matter of course while she seethed inside. Had this secretary not reported to the elder Koide on his son's inquiries concerning *La France Boutique,* the elder Koide might never have discovered Inada's connection to the boutique. Her benefactor might have reached the Philippines alive.

Nobu flung open his office door. "You're here."

To avoid giving his secretary a hint of the true nature of her visit, Marcelle presented Nobu with an outrageously flirtatious smile. "I had hours to spare and decided to visit my favorite department store in Tokyo."

His gaze transformed from perplexed to confused, then he finally seemed to take her hint and gave her a playful smile. "I'm so pleased you chose ours. Might you spare a few minutes for a cup of tea in my office?"

"I'm afraid there's no time for tea, but I'd very much enjoy a few minutes in your office," she replied with a bat of her eyelashes and private smile that must have looked to all the assembled secretaries like she planned to fling herself on his sofa and spread her legs.

Nobu widened his eyes. Did he think the same?

Marcelle entered the office first, and he closed the door behind them. Before he could wrap his arms around her from behind and make her feel whole and desired and forget about his father's cruelty, she faced him.

Nobu stepped back. "What happened?"

The question was loud enough for his traitorous secretary to hear. Marcelle placed a finger to her lips. "Shush."

He looked at her quizzically as she walked backward to the window overlooking Ginza Boulevard. Then he followed.

This put them opposite from where his secretary was probably listening in some discreet fashion behind the door. He'd probably perfected the skill. Marcelle's stomach churned at the thought of him having overheard her orgasms on Nobu's sofa.

Nobu gazed at her expectantly, with all the loving concern she expected from the man who claimed to love her and wished to marry her.

"I have to tell you something," she said in a whisper.

He took a step closer. Their knees brushed, but he made no move to embrace her even though his body seemed to jerk with sudden restraint.

"I met with Inada-*san*'s widow today. She told me many things about what occurred before her husband's death. Inada-*san* has it on good authority your secretary is a spy for your father."

Nobu's gaze darted to his door, then back to Marcelle. He shook his head. "She must be mistaken. Ishida-*san* would never betray my confidence."

"He told your father you'd been inquiring about *La France Boutique* to learn the identity of my partner in the store."

Nobu let out a sigh. "I wanted to know more about you and your status. I was already very interested in you even before your tour of the department store."

Of course, the inquiry had to have been made before her tour of the department store since the rock had gone through the window that morning. "It seems your father used his connections to learn my partner was Inada-*san*. Then he sent a man to the boutique to break the window and assault Yumi-*chan* and eventually kill Inada-*san*."

Nobu stepped away from the window and ran a hand through his perfectly set hair, then paced around the office, seeming to keep his footfalls light so as not to alert his spy of a secretary. Finally, he returned to her side. "Why?" he whispered. "Why would he do those things?

"He attacked the boutique to draw Inada-*san* out of hiding. It worked. His widow believes he was being followed by someone when he went to the boutique on the morning of his death. Whoever was following him took advantage of an opportunity to kill him."

Nobu shook his head, his gaze fixed on Ginza Boulevard. "*Otosan* is a man of nature. He draws pictures of the night sky. Did Inada-*san*'s widow offer you any proof of these accusations?"

"Only her word."

"Do you believe her?"

"I do. What she said about your secretary inquiring about the ownership of *La France Boutique* and how everything followed from that point makes sense to me."

Nobu clenched his jaw. "There might be truth to Ishida-*san* being a spy. On several occasions, *Okasan* has talked about our patrons' spending habits and locations we're considering for another store, when I hadn't told her anything of the sort. I suspected she was sneaking through my correspondence or even department store records. It makes far more sense that *Otosan* was telling her what he'd learned from Ishida-*san*."

Nobu walked over to the rack by the door and gathered his overcoat and hat. She followed. Placing the coat over his arm, he leaned down, and his damp temple brushed against her forehead as he placed his lips near her ear. "You've done me a favour in telling me this. Just as you've been doing me favours in telling me everything you learned since Inada-*san*'s death. I couldn't believe *Otosan* had anything to do with Inada-*san*'s murder. It's still unclear to me how it could be possible. But if that's the case, then he hurt you and Yumi-*chan*. He terrorised you. Then he had a man killed." Nobu shook his head as though he couldn't believe the words he'd just uttered. "I'm going to speak with a friend of *Otosan*'s. He'll know what *Otosan* is guilty of. Not that he'll tell me anything directly, but he'll tell me something."

Nobu's heart beat a fury against her shoulder. She ached for him. "Is there anything I can do?"

Easing back, he ran a hand down her arm and cupped her elbow. Heat spread across her skin. "Leave the office with a contented smile on your face as though I've just committed yet another indecent act with you on my sofa."

Ordinarily, this absurdity would've made her laugh. He might've even intended to make her laugh. But the tension between his brows stifled the urge. "I'll do my best."

His gaze intensified as though he needed more from her. "I trust you, Marcelle. You may be the only person I can trust."

He could trust her. She was faithful and sincere, and may the gods help her, she adored him. She rested a touch to his shoulders and kissed him with a drag of her lips across his.

Nobu groaned. He took her nape in hand with a gentle, yet firm grip, then possessed her mouth with a hungry kiss that scraped abrasions against her lips and left her wanting for more.

"Please, never stop kissing me," he said in short breaths.

Marcelle swept her tongue through his mouth. His lusciousness never failed to summon desire that cut straight into her soul. It gripped her, and she pulled away. How could they piece together the remnants of their affair after what his father had done and what he might do once Nobu learned the full truth? "That's not a promise I can make."

Nobu ran a thumb down her cheek. "One day you will." He opened the door before she could explain why that was impossible.

His secretaries stared unashamedly at the door. Nobu lifted his brow and gave her a naughty grin. She took his arm and returned the look tenfold. It must have been a delicious performance because his secretaries shifted in their seats as though they'd become suddenly uncomfortable.

She and Nobu walked down the stairs, across the atrium while engaged in conversation about upcoming department store events and winter goods until they reached the line of waiting rickshaws.

"Our kiss reassured me in a way I needed," he said after helping her into the rickshaw.

She didn't regret their kiss. It'd been impulsive and perhaps wrongheaded given the scant chance they had for any kind of future together. But it'd also been lovely. "I'm glad for having done it."

He rapped the side of the rickshaw as though testing its sturdiness. Did he fear for her? Did he need to keep her safe that badly? "Go directly to your boardinghouse and send a message to Ryusuke at the department store if you sense any danger."

"I'll be fine. Ryusuke can keep his eyes on Yumi-*chan*."

"I have no doubt Yumi-*chan* is protected, wherever she is."

"I think they'll marry soon."

"They're not the only ones." Nobu brought the back of her hand to his lips. "Stay safe, *mon amour*."

Before she could enumerate all the reasons why they'd never marry and banish, once and for all, his foolish hope, he stepped back from the rickshaw and urged the runner to make haste.

CHAPTER TWENTY-FIVE
Nobu

Nobu ducked under the short *noren* curtain hanging above the pub door where he'd arranged to meet Watanabe, *Otosan*'s longtime friend and closest confidante. After sending Marcelle back to her boardinghouse, Nobu had gone to Watanabe's home and asked Watanabe's wife to tell her husband Nobu wanted to meet at a nearby pub for advice on a potential marriage partner. Watanabe's wife had assured Nobu she'd send her husband to the pub as soon as he walked through the door.

Speaking firstly with Watanabe seemed the best approach for learning if there was any truth to Inada's widow's claims. Confronting *Otosan* with only what Marcelle had learned would leave *Otosan* chortling at the idea of him having hired Nobu's secretary to spy on his behalf. He'd outright deny he had anything to do with the attacks on *La France Boutique* or Inada's death. Nobu could hear him in his consoling, patronizing tone dismissing all claims as speculations of a distressed widow and an unhinged *modiste*.

Yet, Marcelle had told a compelling story about *Otosan*'s involvement in Inada's death. If there was any truth to it, the Koide family wouldn't survive. Nobu might forgive *Otosan* for using Ishida to spy on him. But not for the attacks *on La France Boutique* or for ordering Inada's death. His guilt would mean the end of the family.

Watanabe knew whether *Otosan* was guilty. Provided Nobu could get Watanabe's tongue wagging, he might leave the pub with a better idea about the truthfulness of the Inada widow's accusations. Watanabe probably wouldn't even realise he was imparting as much to Nobu, because for *Otosan*'s most trusted confidante, several bottles of *sake* left him oblivious.

The pub matron led Nobu to one of the tables between tall wooden screens that afforded patrons a degree of quiet. He sank onto the cushion and crossed his legs before the low table. An hour later, the gas lamp on the wall illuminated Watanabe's bald head as he greeted Nobu with his usual carefree smile. Nobu responded likewise. There was no need for formalities between Nobu and the man he'd referred to as uncle.

Nobu rang a bell, and the pub's matron brought them a bottle of *sake*, plates with roasted fowl and dried fish, and skewers of grilled shiitake mushrooms.

Over the first bottle of warm, sweet wine, Watanabe told Nobu about Prime Minister Ito's disputes with the House of Peers over funds for a new railway in Northwestern Japan. Over the second bottle, Watanabe told him about the prime minister's praise for the Foundation Party's efforts toward unity in the aftermath of Inada-*san*'s passing. Along with the third bottle, the matron brought a plate of lightly grilled oysters topped with yuzu citrus juice and soy sauce.

Watanabe used a finger to nudge the oyster's flesh from the shell and slid it into his mouth. "So, you're finally ready to marry?" he said after swallowing.

"I'm going to marry Renaud-*san*, the Frenchwoman."

Watanabe let out a stream of air between his teeth. "I thought you realized the difficulties of such a union."

"She'll make a supportive wife and excellent mother. She descends from a prominent, although impoverished, French family."

"Lineage in the aristocracy should make your *okasan* happy." Watanabe guffawed.

"*Okasan* loves titles," Nobu replied dryly.

"Her aspirations know no bounds." Watanabe broke into laughter as though the comment had been a comedic accomplishment.

"Eventually she'll be won over by Renaud-*san*, and she won't make a lot of noise about the union, at least not publicly. I'm more concerned about *Otosan*."

Watanabe used the rolled-up pub towel to wipe sweat from his brow, then took another gulp of *sake*. "Your *otosan* is rightfully concerned about her past with Inada-*san*."

"His concerns are unwarranted. Inada-*san* supported her store. They had a brief affair. Afterwards, their relations were mostly confined to her business. She had nothing to do with his crusades in Taiwan or the Philippines or wherever he saw government getting in the way of capitalism's free rein."

Watanabe leaned against the wooden partition and exhaled smoke from his pipe. "You're a fine young man, Nobu. I hope you'll be happy."

"I'm certain we will. But *Otosan* remains opposed to our marrying. He hasn't been himself recently, especially since Inada-*san*'s passing. I'm concerned about him."

Watanabe pointed at Nobu with his pipe. "Your *otosan* is loyal, too loyal. He'll do anything for the Foundation Party. It's costing him now. But it's not as bad as when you left for Europe. That was the worst I've ever seen him."

Nobu couldn't recall *Otosan* being distraught when they'd left for Europe. He'd seemed eager to explore the continent. On the other hand, *Okasan* had been inconsolable. "I thought he was content to take a position overseas."

"What choice did he have after the spring debacle? Leaving Japan was the only way to survive it."

Nobu had never heard of a "spring debacle," but he wasn't about to admit as much. "Yes, the spring debacle," he said and rang the bell. When the matron arrived, he asked for another bottle of *sake*. "I think he tried very hard to keep us from knowing about all that had happened. He wanted to protect us."

"Your *otosan* would do anything for you. Taking care of his household is what he does best."

Nearly all his life, Nobu had felt the same. He wasn't certain any longer.

The matron arrived with their fourth bottle of *sake*. Pouring the clear liquid into Watanabe's *sake* box, Nobu nodded and murmured his agreement. "*Otosan* has done well for his family."

Except when he set out to slander and banish the woman Nobu loved.

Watanabe licked the side of the box where his *sake* had dribbled, then finished it off with a hearty swig. "The problem with your *otosan* is..." He smacked his lips as though to claim the final droplets of the sweet wine. "His problem is... he wanted too much, too fast, which is why he got caught." Watanabe burped heartily. "He was the heart and soul of the Foundation Party. He was going to elevate us above all the others. But he was hasty, impatient."

"I take it you're referring to his dealings with China?" Nobu knew *Otosan* used to negotiate with northern Asian countries before they left for Europe. He assumed that meant China.

"China? No, your *otosan* never negotiated with the Chinese. He dealt with Russia."

"Oil." Realisation forged its way through his confusion. He recalled heated discussions between his parents when they first moved to Europe. *Okasan* usually ended these discussions with something like. "If it weren't for oil..."

Watanabe tapped the table with his forefinger. "Your *otosan* should have let one of the experienced fellows take over the negotiations for the oil rights. But your *otosan* wanted to reap the rewards. The Russians paid him unreasonably well." Watanabe gave him a fat-cat smile. "A great sum of money. The influence he bought was tremendous."

Usually, the distribution of Russian bribes for arranging a sale of oil to the Japanese government would've meant *Otosan*'s promotion up the ranks, not his exile to Europe. "Then *Otosan* secured many allies," he observed.

"And enemies." Watanabe swirled an inch of *sake* around his box before draining it. "Inada-*san* hated the bribes. Thought they were the reason bureaucrats should stay out of foreign trade." Watanabe glanced to the side as though summoning an important thought. "Inada-*san* was a purist, a purist of capitalism. He wanted the men of business to bring in the oil. The government could buy it from them, not the other way around. But your *otosan* knew what had to be done."

Nobu had always known *Otosan* and Inada had a history of disagreement. He'd assumed it was ideological, not that it involved his *otosan* taking Russian bribes.

Watanabe banged the bowl of his pipe against the table, scattering flecks of ash. "Not only did your *otosan* get the oil, but he also got designs for navy ships. He was a true hero, your *otosan*." He gave the table another bang. "With plans for Russia's navy vessels, the Foundation Party gained an edge in military support. It wasn't only the money. Your *otosan* did it for the Party, for the nation." Watanabe sat back and pressed tobacco into his pipe. Most of the leaves fell to his lap. "The Party ought to have stood by him, kept him in Japan where he belonged. But the Inada faction made him go."

Inada had exiled *Otosan*. He was the reason the family had ended up in Europe. He was why Nobu could hold conversations in five languages and recite the fundamental tenets of the Magna Carta. Nobu had stepped into Harrods and known exactly what he'd do upon his return to Japan because of Inada. If it weren't for Inada, Nobu never would've crossed paths with Marcelle.

Watanabe's head lolled, then shot upright. "Your *otosan* is a hero to his country. All those years in Europe he learned about foreign economies and foreign militaries."

Nobu cradled the *sake* box. *Otosan* had never talked about gathering information on European militaries. As far as he'd known, his *otosan* was a diplomat, not a spy. What else about *Otosan* wasn't he aware of? Did he commit murder in Europe? More recently in Japan? Was he seeking revenge on Inada for his faction ensuring *Otosan* was banished to Europe?

Watanabe's head lolled forward again. He was on the brink of losing consciousness. Nobu had to move fast. "*Otosan* has always been my hero, you see. I hate that he's troubled over my marriage decision, but I wonder, is that all that has him in such straits?" He let out a sigh. "Uncle Watanabe, is my marriage truly causing him this much pain?"

Watanabe looked down at his pipe as though wondering whether it might be possible for the pipe to fill itself. "Troubling your *otosan*? Nothing troubles your *otosan*. He's the one who takes care of the troubles." Watanabe's tongue tripped over his words. "Your *okasan*, she gives him troubles. But look. He's going to get the title she wants. He always gets what he wants. All he has to do is impress the others. He's good at that." Watanabe stretched his jaw in a yawn so loud Nobu swore he saw the partition walls shake. "Your *otosan* was never one to regret. But maybe he's older. Maybe he regrets Inada-*san*. He didn't have to go after him like that. I never thought he had to go after him like that."

Otosan had gone after Inada-*san*. In what fashion? "What do you mean go after him? Uncle Watanabe... did *Otosan* have Inada-san killed?"

Watanabe settled his head against the partition and shut his eyes. "He didn't have to, you know that."

Nobu knew no such thing. "Why didn't he have to?"

"Because...he was already dead. Obviously." Watanabe's breathing deepened.

Nobu jostled the man's knee. "Uncle Watanabe," he called. But he was already asleep.

Nobu rang for the matron and requested a rickshaw runner to assist in escorting his companion home.

***

At the first rays of sunlight, Nobu snapped awake to wait for the sound of Asako's footsteps as she left her room. Petulant, cynical, and defiant, his sister nevertheless possessed the most capable mind of any person Nobu knew, and he needed her insight. Watanabe had said outright *Otosan* had gone after Inada.

Not that he'd killed him, but that he hadn't needed to because Inada was already dead. As *Otosan* had wished. Fortunately for *Otosan*, someone had spared him the trouble of carrying out a murder. Still, he'd gone after Inada. What had he done to him? Forced him into hiding the way Inada had forced him into exile? Drawn him out of hiding by attacking *La France Boutique*? That would make him partly responsible for Inada's death.

His *otosan* was conniving and manipulative. He used deceit, trickery, smoke, and mirrors to achieve his aims. But Nobu couldn't fathom *Otosan* was so ruthless and cruel to cause a man's death.

Watanabe could fathom it. Inada's widow believed as much. She told Marcelle the attacks at *La France Boutique* had been *Otosan*'s doing. Even the thought of *Otosan* having anything to do with attacking Marcelle and Yumi-*chan* drove Nobu to anger he wasn't able to comprehend, much less allow himself to feel.

It couldn't be.

Yet *Otosan* had been a spy. Nobu was being naïve in his thinking. Filial obligation clouded his judgment.

It wouldn't cloud Asako's.

As soon as Nobu heard the light tap of her feet down the hallway, he rose. She was nearing the dining room when he grabbed her by the elbow.

She gasped. "What in the name of gods East and West are you doing to me, dear brother?"

"I must speak with you," he whispered in rapid English no one in the house could decipher save Asako. "Tell *Okasan* you have an early *koto* lesson, then meet me at the Tsukiji gates in an hour's time."

"I don't want to talk about the *koto* with her. She knows I can't play. Yesterday, I gave her a demonstration of my progress. It must've been excruciating to sit through."

"Did you have one of your fights?" Nobu ground his teeth. He didn't have time to act as mediator.

"It's far stranger than that. *Okasan* simply complimented my progress and walked out of the room."

"I wonder if *Okasan* has noticed you're happier since you started the *koto*, and she doesn't care if it's the instrument or however else you've been spending your time, as long as you're not squabbling with everything she says."

Asako furrowed her brow like she did when considering her next chess move. "She's seemed different of late. You've given her plenty to do at the department store, which means she only has time to focus on improving one of us. Recently, *Otosan* has been her target."

Okasan's interest in *Otosan* must mean she had concerns about his dealings. "Can you at least tell her you're exploring new avenues for improving in *koto* and leave the house soon?"

"She probably won't care what I say. She's been acting so strangely."

It was nearing nine o'clock. "Tell her something and meet me at the gates in an hour."

***

Nobu had been waiting almost half an hour when he caught sight of Asako walking toward Tsukiji's gates. Her gait and the way she tilted her head were thoroughly British. In her dark brown overcoat and broad hat, his sister could easily pass for one of Tsukiji's foreigners slipping inside the quarter after an early morning errand in Ginza.

He led them from the Tsukiji gates back into the Ginza district to the patisserie Marcelle loved.

The *patisseriere* greeted Nobu like an old friend, which was probably how he greeted everyone Marcelle introduced him to, and gave him a table at the far end of the café. When his wife brought their *pain au chocolat* and tea, the *patisseriere* stood behind her with a plate of freshly baked madeleines.

"So what troubles you, dear brother, that we cannot discuss at home?" Asako said after a bite of the warm, buttery cake.

Nobu finished one of the madeleines and gave an approving raise of his brow to the *patisseriere*. "It has to do with something I've learned about *Otosan*."

Asako frowned. "*Otosan*? What a bore. I was hoping you and Marcelle had set a wedding date, to hell with *Otosan* and *Okasan*."

"I'm going to marry Marcelle: to hell with *Otosan* and *Okasan*."

"I doubt he'll notice if you brought Marcelle home as your wife tomorrow with all the hours he's been spending on the rooftop."

Nobu's mind journeyed back to *Otosan*'s sojourns into the woods when they'd lived in Europe. At the time, he'd thought *Otosan* was cleverly escaping *Okasan*'s ceaseless ire at having to leave Japan. Now he wondered if *Otosan* had been using those excursions to meet contacts from whom he obtained secrets to pass on to Japan.

And he'd accused *Marcelle* of being a spy.

"I have reason to believe *Otosan* went after Inada in some fashion. The attacks on Marcelle's boutique might be his doing. He might have contributed to Inada-*san*'s death," he said in a low voice.

Asako set her teacup on the table. "*Otosan*... attacking boutiques? Killing a man? Never."

He told Asako what Marcelle had learned from Inada's widow and the conversation he'd had with Watanabe.

"*Otosan* accepts Russian bribes and plans for ships, then gets sloppy in handing out the bribe money. This I can believe," Asako said with a roll of her gaze. "He loves impressing people. The way he talks about your store to everyone he meets is atrocious. But if that's how we ended up in Europe, I don't care. I'm just glad we did. I simply can't see him as a killer. *Otosan* would never stoop to something as dreadful as murder. It's too obvious. *Otosan* is sneaky. He'd destroy someone by souring his reputation or ruining his businesses."

"I agree. Yet Watanabe thought *Otosan* had regrets over what he'd done to Inada-*san*. If he was the one who sent a man to *La France Boutique*..." Nobu fisted his hand on the table. The thought was too painful to finish.

Asako's gaze settled on a group of women walking along Ginza Boulevard. They were dressed as though heading to Koide Department Store. Then she looked back up at him and curled her mouth into a mischievous smile. "Maybe it's time we finally did something. We'll leave *Okasan* and *Otosan* a note explaining our lack of trust in them and disinterest in residing in Japan. They're so busy that, by the time they bother to read it, we'll be on a ship back to Europe. I'll live in London. You and Marcelle can reside in Paris. We'll never have to worry about *Okasan* or *Otosan* again."

He heard the lilt of fantasy in her voice and knew she was only being half-serious. He also knew the serious half was *very* serious. "Marcelle has no desire to reside in Paris. She loves Tokyo, and I have a store to run. Besides, we have to think about our dearest *Okasan*. If *Otosan* has committed a crime of some sort, and I'm increasingly sure he has, *Okasan* may not be fully aware of what he's done."

"I doubt that. She's letting me get away with lying about the *koto*. That's very unlike her."

Nobu took the last bite of his *pain au chocolat*. "I'm going to speak with *Otosan* tonight. Unless he can convince me that he had nothing to do with the attacks on Marcelle's store and Inada-*san*'s death, I'll be moving to a hotel."

"You'll leave me with *Okasan* and *Otosan*?"

"You can stay with Aunt Tomoko if you like." He finished his tea in a large gulp. "I actually might have a way for you to rid yourself of the Koide family, at least in name."

"Are you speaking of marriage?"

"I met a promising gentleman while in Osaka. His firm is overseeing the interior design of the Terashimaya department store. We happened to share a meal, and he isn't married. During our conversation he expressed interest in exploring areas of Tokyo well-known for evening entertainments of a certain kind." Such areas were notorious for homosexual encounters. Sato-*san*, the gentleman in question, had seemed to be obliquely asking about Nobu's interests in such encounters. Nobu had obliquely shared his disinterest and questioned Sato-*san* as to his tolerance for bluestockings.

Asako pinched her mouth into a firm line. "I'll never move to Osaka. I have my work at the magazine. Like Suki Spenser, I intend to continue working even after being forced into the burdensome institution."

"Suki Spenser went quite willingly. But that's beside the point. The gentleman in question mentioned having interest in moving his firm's headquarters to Tokyo, as it is the hub of Japan's growth in retail. I told him about having a sister who had reservations about marriage, and I believe he understood the implication. Needless to say, any man from a peasant background would be thrilled at the prospect of marrying into a samurai family."

"*Okasan* would never allow it. She has nothing to gain from a peasant marriage." Asako picked up the last madeleine and turned the golden cake in her hand. "Seeing as you have knowledge of *Otosan*'s connection to some very unsavoury activities, why don't you use it to settle our marriage partners? You get Marcelle, and I get to remain a spinster, or at least marry the peasant man of my choosing."

Nobu appreciated her pragmatism. But she was suggesting that he was willing to remain quiet about *Otosan*'s crimes, if that's what they were. That was impossible. "He should pay if he's guilty."

Asako laughed that dry laugh that made him feel like a fool even before she began explaining why he was the biggest fool she knew. "Dear brother, you're not that daft, are you? You'll lose all standing in society if you betray your family in such a manner. No one will shop in Koide Department Store again, much less invest in all those new stores you have planned. You'd hate that."

Nobu glanced out the window. Gusts of wind threatened to upend hats and parcels. "There are other ways for men to take responsibility for their sins."

Asako blinked rapidly. "Are you suggesting suicide?"

The word was like a dagger through Nobu's heart. He had no wish to see *Otosan* dead. "I was thinking he should retreat to the countryside with *Okasan*. Quit the Foreign Ministry and the Foundation Party, and all his cronies. He and *Okasan* can claim illness."

"*Okasan* will no sooner leave Tokyo than return to London. Even if *Otosan* accepts exile to the countryside, before he goes, *Okasan* is going to make certain he gets his title. It's her life's dream to be the toast of Tokyo." Asako gave him a bitter smile. "Can you live with that, brother?"

He levelled his gaze with hers. "We're all going to have to live with the truth."

She fiddled with the edge of the madeleine plate. "Society is unfair. Denial is sometimes the only way to peace. Exposing *Otosan* or having him exiled will damn us all. If he's committed a crime, we can use his guilt to obtain his blessing for our marriages. Then you and Marcelle can set up your own household. You'll never have to see him again, but you'll preserve appearances for all our sakes."

"That's not punishment enough."

"Accepting an unjust world is our fate."

"Dear sister, you're sounding more Japanese every day." He appreciated her impulse to pragmatism. But he was an idealist. If *Otosan* had done anything to put Marcelle in harm's way, there should be no leniency on him. And if he participated in Inada-*san*'s murder, he must answer for it.

CHAPTER TWENTY-SIX

Nobu

Otosan looked up from his telescope when Nobu stepped onto the rooftop terrace. "I've got another view of Jupiter. Come and see for yourself."

Ignoring the offer, Nobu walked to the opposite side of the terrace where the gas lamps of Ginza and Tsukiji twinkled in the distance and Marcelle was safely inside her boardinghouse. All was well with her. All was well with the store. Nobu had spent the day there as usual, consulting with his deceitful bastard of a secretary and receiving *Okasan*'s daily report on her impressions of the store's merchandise and how the clerks were serving the customers. All the while, he'd been thinking of how to get the upper hand with *Otosan*, the seasoned diplomat and consummate politician, and learn the truth. Admittedly, Nobu was incapable of outfoxing the fox, but if he asked the right questions and took *Otosan*'s answers with full knowledge of the man's capacity for obfuscation, he'd get the truth.

"Did you know I met with Watanabe-*san* last night?" Nobu asked, his gaze fixed on Tsukiji.

Otosan pulled a glass from the box containing his drawing utensils and filled it with whiskey. "Watanabe-*san* missed the morning address from Nishikawa-*san*. Our efforts to convince the tsar it's in his best interests to leave northern China are a waste of diplomatic effort. I'm afraid there will be a decisive confrontation sooner than we hope." *Otosan* handed Nobu the glass.

Nobu took it with his fingertips and placed it on the terrace railing. "Watanabe-*san* told me why we had to leave Japan for Europe."

Otosan stood next to Nobu while sipping his drink. "He mentioned as much this afternoon. He worried that due to a half dozen bottles of *sake*, he'd spoken out of turn. I told him you were old enough to hear the truth."

"I told Asako this afternoon. I thought she deserved to know about her past."

"You shouldn't have done that." *Otosan* finished his glass. "Women don't understand these things. Your *okasan* still resents us having to leave Tokyo." He nodded at Nobu's glass. "Aren't you going to drink that?"

The amber liquid appealed, but not now. "Did you do it for the money?"

Otosan left Nobu's side and sat on the terrace bench. "Not for the money, for the nation. The tsar's representatives approached us when I was on the committee overseeing our northern Asian interests. They requested the rights to sell oil in Japan. In exchange, we received a large sum of money for our personal use and plans for a naval vessel that have since made our navy into one of the most powerful in the world. Indeed, in the not-too-distant future, the Russians may end up perishing against their extraordinary vessels in our well-disciplined hands."

Nobu leaned against the railing. *Otosan* sat with his thighs wide, his empty glass in hand. He was at ease. He'd already taken measure of how much Nobu knew and how much more he'd reveal. "How did this turn into a debacle?"

"We failed to distribute the bribe from Russia in the most equitable manner," *Otosan* said as he refilled his glass. "The Inada faction didn't receive a share. Frankly, our faction thought they didn't deserve it after dressing us down for interfering with the flow of capital. In retaliation, they leaked details of the deal to a newspaper reporter. For good reason, they didn't mention we'd obtained the naval vessel plans. That would've been treasonous.

"In any case, Prime Minister Ito ordered the paper to keep it quiet and gave them a story on Education Ministry bureaucrats' plans for using ancestral lands to build schools. The bureaucrats in possession of these lands got five times their worth when they sold them to the government. It was the least Ito-*san* could do after we'd delivered those plans. But by then, the story had spread around government circles. Since I was the one present at every one of the meetings with Russia, my name became associated with the deal, and I ended up taking the blame."

Nobu bristled at *Otosan* painting himself the martyr. Watanabe-*san*, in his drunken haze, had said *Otosan* had taken the lead in making a deal with the tsar's representatives. *Otosan*'s ambition had gotten him into trouble. "Watanabe-*san* said you worked on behalf of the government while in Europe."

"I provided our government with intelligence on the industries and armies of the European Continent. I was invaluable to our national defence. After nearly two decades abroad, I was finally able to please your *okasan* with a return to Tokyo. The Party, the whole of government, welcomed me back with open arms."

"What did Inada-*san* think of your return?"

"Inada-*san*..." *Otosan* said with the irritation of a man slapping at mosquito. "I daresay he was quite pleased to have me back in Tokyo. I'd been a divisive figure in the Party. My return presented a chance to split the Party in his favour. But try as he might over the past five years, it didn't happen. We stayed together."

Otosan's responses had the panache of many rehearsals. He'd been well-prepared to parry with his son. Nobu was tired of parrying. It was time to go for the jugular to see just how right Watanabe and Inada's widow had been about *Otosan*'s role in the maverick politician's death. "Then why did you hire a man to kill him?"

Otosan lifted his face to the sky and let out a hearty laugh. "Who told you this? Inada-*san*'s lover? The one you took to our home in Karuizawa?"

Nobu never mentioned that he'd taken Marcelle to the villa. "Who told you we visited the villa?"

"I know everything, son." Otosan placed his empty glass on the bench next to him and pulled a pipe from his supply box. Running a finger through the chamber, he cleared it. "So, you believe a woman over your *otosan*, your family?"

"She doesn't lie to me."

"All women are liars." *Otosan* packed tobacco into the pipe's chamber. "They have to be. Deceit is their foremost weapon." He lit the pipe, inhaled deeply, and exhaled slowly. "I had nothing to do with Inada-*san*'s death. Yes, he was my enemy, but his death did nothing for me. I've borne his ire for decades. Why would I decide to kill him now?"

"Watanabe said you would've killed him yourself, but someone beat you to it."

Otosan took another drag from the pipe. "Watanabe believes my hatred for Inada runs far deeper than it does. I might have given him that impression, and that impression might have coaxed ire from Watanabe toward Inada. One doesn't allow those in one's circle to become too chummy. They might start plotting against you."

"Divide and conquer?"

"Keep the peace."

Even *Otosan*'s closest allies were the target of his manipulations. Where did that leave his family? Nobu felt as though a brick had been dislodged from his wall of filial piety. It might very well crumble. "Tomorrow I'll kick Ishida out of the department store for passing information to you. You've been using him to keep tabs on me. I know he told you about the afternoon Renaud-*san* injured her ankle. Then I recently learned he told you about my interest in the identity of Renaud-*san*'s business partner."

Otosan pointed to his chest with the pipe's mouthpiece. "Like me, Ishida-*san* has your best interests in mind. He passed along that information because he hoped I could assist you. You were the one who wanted to learn more about your lover's store."

Nobu nearly applauded *Otosan*'s talent in making himself the hero. He was as slick as the substance that had gotten him in trouble. "Then you learned her partner was Inada-*san*. Had you been assisting me, you'd have told me. Instead, you used that information to draw Inada-*san* out of hiding."

"He was inciting rebellions in Taiwan and the Philippines. No man is allowed to conduct foreign policy on his own. It was madness. Using violence to interfere with our government's policies or the policies of foreign governments is not acceptable in the modern world."

"So, you had him killed."

"No." *Otosan* slammed his fist against the bench seat. "I got him back to Tokyo."

"By attacking Renaud-*san*'s store."

"No one was hurt."

Nobu's breath caught in his throat. He should hurl *Otosan* off the terrace, make him pay here and now for what he'd done to Marcelle and Yumi-*chan*. But doing so would make Nobu just as guilty. There were other ways to make *Otosan* pay. "Her assistant was tied, gagged, and left on the floor. Then this violent assassin killed Inada-*san* in cold blood."

Winter gusts tousled the thin hairs atop *Otosan*'s head. "I never sent an assassin. The man I sent to the boutique was the childhood associate of a young Foundation Party member. He's *not* the man who killed Inada-*san*."

"Inada-*san*'s killer confessed to having vandalized the boutique."

"That's because he was bribed." *Otosan* rapped the pipe bowl against the bench, scattering orange flecks of lit tobacco. "My task was to draw Inada-*san* out of hiding so we could reason with him. When he returned to Tokyo, my part was finished. I didn't know there were plans for his assassination. Had I known I was leading a mouse into a nest of vipers, I never would've played my part. Son, I had nothing to gain from Inada-*san*'s death."

Nobu wanted to believe in *Otosan*'s innocence. Asako didn't believe *Otosan* was a murderer. But even if that much was true, had he known about an assassination plot? Had he known that someone in the Party intended to have Inada-*san* killed? "So, if you didn't arrange for Inada-*san*'s killing, who did? Who in the Foundation Party stood to gain from Inada-*san*'s death?"

Otosan rose from the bench and paced the terrace. "You wouldn't believe me if I told you."

"I'm listening."

Otosan stopped and leaned back against the terrace railing. "Since his death, the Inada faction has capitulated to our platform with haste, surprising those of us who've negotiated with them for years. It's as though they'd been set free from an unwanted master."

"Then they're behind the killing?"

Otosan let out a deep breath that could be resignation or frustration, perhaps confusion at the dismaying turn of events. Or simply satisfaction at a well-played game. "Rumours are one thing. Proof is another. I have no proof the Inada faction was involved in his death."

Nobu was getting nowhere because there was nowhere to go. "At the very least, you're protecting the Party. You're as guilty as any of them."

Otosan met Nobu's gaze with equal tenacity. "I'm not responsible for Inada-*san*'s death. I was shocked someone dared carry out such an act. Why do you think they asked me to speak at his funeral? I'm innocent."

Nobu couldn't listen to another word. *Otosan* had admitted to attacking Marcelle's store and Yumi-*chan*. For that, Nobu would never forgive him. Were Ryusuke to learn of the admission, he'd kill *Otosan* on the spot.

Without a backward glance, he left *Otosan* on the terrace. Then he left the house without a farewell to *Okasan* or Asako, neither of whom he believed in danger from *Otosan*'s ruthlessness because *Otosan* thought he'd won. He thought he had Nobu beat.

CHAPTER TWENTY-SEVEN

Marcelle

"You have a visitor," the boardinghouse matron called outside Marcelle's door. She was loud enough to wake the whole floor and perhaps the one above, and that was the point. It neared midnight, and Marcelle's late-night visitor—probably Nobu—had awakened the matron, so she was waking them all.

Marcelle left her writing desk where she'd been sketching displays of the sales space she'd like to put in the factory.

"Koide-*san* is here," the matron said when Marcelle opened the door. Her voice was so full of contempt, Marcelle, or Nobu, was going to have to hasten several dozen sweet bean cakes to the boardinghouse.

"I'm terribly sorry for the late hour. This must be a dire situation." Marcelle gave the matron an empathetic smile. "Let me change and I'll be downstairs shortly.

The matron harrumphed her way down the hallway. Marcelle shut the door. Had Nobu learned something dire about his father and the Foundation Party? Were they going to come after her? Was she in danger?

Hands shaking, she changed into a simple, midnight blue dress with black lace trim and headed down the staircase.

Nobu stood in the front parlor. Relief poured through her at seeing his eyes widen as he always did when he saw her.

The matron sat on one of the wingback chairs and speared Nobu with an annoyed glare.

"A dire situation?" Marcelle greeted Nobu with a reserved handshake for the matron's benefit.

"Your betrothed needs you," he said too low for the matron to catch. His cheeks were flushed, and his eyes bright. He exuded a bold energy that seemed to be the very essence of his spirit.

"My betrothed?"

"I am. But the matron shouldn't be the first to know. Why don't you tell her my sister is in crisis over a loose thread or a missing ribbon, and only you can help?"

Marcelle let out a small giggle at the absurdity of the excuse, which seemed to make Nobu glow with pride. He knew her. He knew she'd giggle like a schoolgirl just as he knew she'd leave with him in the middle of the night. He was so certain of their love, certain that he could convince her to marry him.

At least there was a possibility they could return to their affair. Perhaps his "dire situation" was going to give them a path back to a place where she'd been so happy.

Marcelle bowed at the matron. The older woman appreciated the humility of others. "Koide-*san*'s sister needs my assistance with a French translation she must complete by tomorrow morning. It's for a professor at the Imperial University. I must go forthwith."

The matron looked entirely unconvinced, but the owner of Tokyo's department store and son of one of Tokyo's most influential families was standing in her parlor. Her deferral to his status was a foregone conclusion. "Should I expect you home before the morning?"

"I'll probably rest at the Koide home through the morning. I'll send word if my plans change."

Marcelle gathered her reticule and cape and stepped into the chilly night. A rickshaw runner waited in front of the boardinghouse gate. Nobu helped her inside and took the seat beside her. "To the Waterfall Inn," he called to the runner.

"A lover's inn?" she asked.

Nobu brought her hand to his thigh and laced his fingers through hers. "Betrothed couples should spend the night together."

"Then we're betrothed?"

"I'm not going to spend another night without you." He thumbed the top of her palm. "I left home and I'm not going back. Not until *Otosan* confesses his crimes and pays for what he's done."

Marcelle's heart pounded. "Inada-*san*'s widow was right about your father?"

Nobu squeezed her hand in his. "I'm not certain if she's entirely correct about *Otosan* orchestrating Inada-*san*'s death. But he did hire the man who attacked your boutique."

Nobu's father had attacked her.

To hear it confirmed made her heart break. It was grief. Not only was she grieving for herself for having been made a target of a powerful man, and for Yumi-*chan,* who'd borne the brunt of the attack, she grieved, too, for Nobu. For him, the cut was new.

He let his shoulders slump against the rickshaw's backrest. "Ishida, my secretary, told him I was investigating the owner of your boutique. *Otosan* used his connections to learn it was Inada-*san*. He sent that man to break your window and later to attack Yumi-*chan*."

"To draw Inada-*san* out of hiding."

Nobu murmured an affirmative.

Marcelle stiffened. "Then this man killed Inada-*san*."

"*Otosan* says no, but how can I believe him? Asako doesn't think he would stoop to murder. I tend to agree, but I base that on the man I thought I knew, when the truth is, I've never known him. He's always been a step beyond my reach."

Nobu's grip on her hand tightened. "I'm going to learn the truth and make sure he's held accountable. Then I want us to marry. I'd thought we could resume our affair, and when my parents realised I wasn't going to marry anyone but you, they'd accept you and forgive me for going against their wishes. But none of that is important any longer. Learning of *Otosan*'s crimes has changed everything. I no longer care what he believes about me, and *Okasan*'s forgiveness is of no consequence.

"All that matters is having you by my side. You're my family. Please, Marcelle, marry me."

Breath caught in Marcelle's throat. She looked over at Tsukiji's gates illuminated in the gas lamps' faint glow. She'd known his family would never let her marry him. But what if *she* was his family?

"I don't know if I'm very good at being family," she speculated aloud.

"I'll show you how it's done."

"*Your* family," she mused, smiling so hard it hurt, so hard it brought stinging tears to the front of her eyes. "I'd like that."

"Good," Nobu said softly.

They rode in silence toward the Waterfall Inn, hands joined, swaying with the ruts and rocks scattered along the road, breaths slow and steady.

CHAPTER TWENTY-EIGHT

Nobu

Nobu awoke at the Waterfall Inn with a profound sense of lightness. He didn't have to give up Koide Department Store for a career in politics. He didn't have to marry a nobleman's daughter. He didn't have to fret about being the cause of his parents not receiving a place among the nobility.

The best part of all. Marcelle was going to be his wife.

Last night, they'd made love tenderly, mouths open, tongues swirling, the whole of him buried deep inside her. Slowly, steadily, they'd joined until she'd throbbed against him, and he'd released inside her, their moans ricocheting across the moonlit room. Limbs entangled with his future bride's, he'd fallen into a deep, contented sleep.

Along with a sense of lightness, he'd awakened with an answer as clear as the autumn day. He knew how to verify *Otosan*'s claim that the man he'd hired to draw Inada out of hiding wasn't the same man who'd killed Inada. The police had said the killer had confessed to the attacks on *La France Boutique*. But men heading to the noose could afford to own a multitude of sins, especially if confession meant a monetary gift for their bereaved families. Nobu would find out soon enough whether the killer had told the truth and *Otosan* had committed a heinous act of revenge.

Perhaps because of all the lightness the morning had brought, what he wanted most was Marcelle's weight upon him. He ran a lazy touch down her bare arm. Her delicate lashes fluttered as she opened her eyes. The arresting blue of a midday sky settled on him.

He kissed her forehead and the sides of her face and her downy cheeks.

"This is how you wake up your betrothed?" she asked between breaths that caressed his ears and hair and sent shivers through him.

"My betrothed, my wife, the mother of my children. This is how I plan to wake her."

"Lucky woman."

"I'll be the lucky one, if you'll ride me, Marcelle. Can you ride me this morning?"

Marcelle grinned in the adventurous way he loved, especially when they were naked. She eased her knee up between his thighs, not stopping until she brushed his engorged cock. The contact sent spikes of pained anticipation through the core of him.

How he loved it when she was in control.

She stroked up and down, and he moved his hips along with each tantalizing press against his thick erection. He'd take any body part of hers on him. Even a knee.

"You need to be ridden, Nobu."

He groaned. "You don't know how badly."

Marcelle sat up and pulled away the sheets and blankets, then straddled his legs. No, it hadn't been her weight he'd needed. It'd been her nakedness above him, her long locks skimming her taut nipples, the unreasonably lovely curve of her hip, her thighs soft and inviting.

The dark centres of her eyes had grown to twice their size. With one hand, she trailed a pathway from her navel to the curly hairs between her legs. Dipping fingers between her folds, she gasped and wriggled at her touch, her lips parting with a rush of air.

"Then you want to ride me?" Nobu ground out the question between clenched teeth.

"Fuck yes."

Dirty language from her perfect raspberry lips was going to be the death of him, provided he survived the next few minutes because he was going to perish if she didn't take him inside her.

He raised his hands above his head. Marcelle wanted to ride. Let her ride.

She poised with his tip at her entrance, her petal lips silky around his erection. Inch by inch she eased onto him, his mind breaking at the slow pace, the muscles in his hips begging to thrust.

Once he was fully inside, she paused. Their gazes locked, and his existence collapsed into a single point.

"I love you, Marcelle," he whispered. He couldn't say it any louder, his throat wouldn't give.

"I love you, Nobu," she replied, her voice like his, soft and rough.

And that was how she rode him, ground into him, softly, then roughly without a moment of reprieve. Every movement unadulterated ecstasy. He held himself at bay until her quim tremored with the beginning of her climax. Her lower lip trembled. Her eyes unfocused. He took over the ride, lifting and lowering the fleshy pads of her ass as she cried his name and showered him with her orgasm. Then he buried himself deep inside and let go.

***

Yumi-*chan* met Nobu and Marcelle outside the Police Affairs Bureau in Kasumigaseki. The imposing European-style building was a few blocks from the Foundation Party headquarters. Nobu had averted his eyes when they'd passed. The Party deserved a fatal blow for what *Otosan* had done to Marcelle alone. If any of them were involved in Inada's death, as *Otosan* claimed, those men must pay with their lives.

Portraits of the emperor, the crown prince, and the Meiji-era police superintendents hung on the walls of the bureau's grand lobby. A clerk greeted Nobu as though he was a visiting dignitary and escorted him, Marcelle, and Yumi-*chan* to a receiving room that probably wouldn't have looked out of place at Buckingham Palace.

The clerk brought tea and rice crackers. A few minutes later, Nobu's childhood friend, a longtime detective, entered. After greeting them and exchanging pleasantries with Nobu, he placed a set of sketches on the table next to their tea service. "This is Masao Nagai, the man who confessed to ending Hitoshi Inada's life. His confession matched the course of Inada-*san*'s death as we understood it from evidence at *La France Boutique*." He looked between the two women. "Nagai was put to death last week," he said gently.

Nobu turned to Yumi-*chan*. "Is this the man who attacked you?"

She picked up each sketch and gazed at it. Then she wiped her hands on her kimono and shook her head. "The man who attacked me had large eyes and his chin was less pronounced. He was fuller in the body. This is not him."

The knot in Nobu's gut eased. This wasn't the man *Otosan* had ordered to draw Inada-*san* out of hiding. That man, whoever he was, had attacked Yumi-*chan*, but he hadn't ended Inada's life.

Nobu glanced over at Marcelle. She looked as relieved as he felt. Then he turned to his friend. "What do you know of Nagai?"

"His family is registered in Iwate prefecture. He was a day-labourer there. A petty criminal. He has no political principles, as far as we could tell. Nor are we sure what brought him to Tokyo or how long he'd been here. There doesn't seem to be any connection between him and Inada-*san*. Most likely he was hired to kill him."

Iwate prefecture was a Foundation Party stronghold. *Otosan* often bemoaned the several members of the Inada faction from Iwate who served in the Lower House of the Diet. "We caught up with him the night of Inada's killing after he boarded a ship to Hokkaido. Someone sent a message to the police that Inada-*san*'s murderer had purchased passage on the ship. We suspect whoever hired him set him up to take the fall."

"I take it you have no idea who that might be."

"Even if we did—"

"You couldn't tell me," Nobu finished for his friend. "He was put to death rather quickly."

His friend gave a firm nod. "Swift justice is justice nevertheless."

***

Nobu handed *Okasan* his overcoat and stepped into the slippers she'd placed in front of him. "Where's Asako?" he asked.

Okasan folded his coat neatly and hung it over her arm. He could practically hear her considering the merits of holding it hostage until he agreed to return home. "In her room. Writing. She's always writing."

"*Otosan* is on the roof?" At the department store that afternoon, *Okasan* had begged him to reason with *Otosan*, as he seemed to have abandoned his wife and daughter for his paintings of the night sky, except that he hadn't produced a single painting in a week.

Nobu wanted nothing to do with *Otosan*, but if he was going mad, he shouldn't be living under the same roof as *Okasan* and Asako.

Okasan stepped aside and looked over to the broad staircase. "He's been up there since the end of the evening meal. Tonight, he requested *sake* instead of whiskey. The maid has already taken two bottles up there." *Okasan*'s eyes pooled with tears. "Please come back home and live with us. Your *otosan* isn't the wicked man you believe he is. He only wishes to serve his nation."

"He sent a man to Renaud-*san*'s store. The miscreant destroyed her property and assaulted her assistant."

Okasan hung her head. "It's a terrible thing. But you must forgive him. You're his son. You owe him your life."

Filial piety had been the foundation of his moral world. *Otosan* had shattered that. "How can I forgive?"

Okasan fisted her kimono skirt. "Accept him for the flawed man he is, as I have done."

"I won't accept someone hurting my family."

Okasan gasped. News of her son's new family practically knocked the wind out of her.

Nobu gave no heed to her reaction and headed toward the staircase.

Expecting to find *Otosan* with face pressed to the telescope or sitting on the bench with sketchpad in hand, it took Nobu a moment to register *Otosan*'s figure silhouetted against the night sky, his face tilted upward.

"Go away," *Otosan* slurred, his body swaying precariously. "I need to find the stars."

Ignoring the order, Nobu took several steps towards where *Otosan* stood on the terrace railing. *"Get down from there,"* he shouted.

Otosan's legs wobbled and his chest jerked forward as though to compensate for the imbalance in his feet.

Nobu sprinted across the terrace as *Otosan* leaned into the darkness, his arms flailing wildly. Nobu grabbed hold of his waist and pulled him back from the edge. Together, they slammed into the terrace floor.

"Ow," *Otosan* cried and rubbed the side of his head. "You nearly knocked me out."

Nobu's breath came out in short bursts. "What were you doing up there?"

Otosan rolled up to a sitting position. Blood spilled from a gash to his temple. "One more time, I wanted to see the stars," he murmured, his head lolling forward. Then he straightened up. "Don't tell *Okasan*. She'll never let me up here again."

Nobu handed *Otosan* a handkerchief. "Why should she when you're on a mission to kill yourself?"

"I won't be such a fool again." *Otosan* spit blood onto the terrace floor. "You're here, which means I won't have to."

Nobu pulled *Otosan* to standing and supported his weight. *Otosan* winced.

"Did you break any bones?" For some reason, Nobu couldn't infuse anger into his voice. Only pity.

"Doubt it," *Otosan* said with a grunt.

Nobu brought them over to the bench. After seating *Otosan*, he took the space beside him. Other than the wound on the side of his head, *Otosan* had cuts and scratches from the rough wood of the terrace floor planks. He'd be bruised for days to come. "You'll have to tell the Ministry you're too ill for work."

"I should quit. Isn't that what you came here to tell me?"

"It is."

Otosan pulled the bloody handkerchief off his temple. He was going to need stitches. Nobu walked over to *Otosan*'s supply box and fished out a clean towel.

"Thank you, son." He threw the dirty handkerchief to the floor, then pressed the towel to his head. "When I was up on that ledge, I thought to myself, if my son tells me to quit, I will. For your forgiveness, I'll leave the madness of Tokyo politics."

Nobu walked to the terrace railing a few feet from the bench. *Otosan* didn't appear to be on the verge of keeling over, and Nobu couldn't bear to spend another second next to the man. "I'll never forgive you for what you did to Renaud-*san*'s store," he said with no uncertainty. "I learned more about the man who killed Inada-*san*. He was from Iwate Prefecture, which everyone knows is an Inada-faction stronghold. Did you know that? Is that why you're so certain of their guilt?"

Otosan spit blood on the wooden planks and wiped his mouth. "Any of them, or all of them for that matter, could've ordered Inada-*san*'s death."

Cold winds whipped against Nobu's back. He should've kept his overcoat. "Is the Party going to investigate Inada-*san*'s death?"

"The Party," *Otosan* said, clutching the side of his rib cage, "is more united than ever. There won't be any investigation. They killed Inada-*san* because they didn't want to be associated with his radical, violent anti-colonialism." Less than slurred from drink, his words seemed to be dragged by pain.

"Do you agree with what they did? Do you think killing Inada-*san* was for the best?"

Otosan let out a stream of breath between his teeth. "Killing Inada-*san* was wrong. We could've reasoned with him. He wasn't entirely unreasonable."

Nobu gazed up at the cloudy night sky. The stars were barely visible. Had *Otosan* truly planned to end his life on a night when his great abyss was so unclear? Or had the trickster heard Nobu coming and jumped up on the terrace railing in a bid for his son's sympathies? He'd sobered up rather quickly after his fall. "What will you do?"

"Since you ruined my plans to leap from the terrace, I suppose I'll go back to Europe. Far less backstabbing, revenge, and assassinations, at least for the foreigner looking in." Beads of sweat shimmered on *Otosan*'s brow. "Do you think *Okasan* will join me?"

"Never. She and Asako can live with Renaud-*san* and me when we marry."

"Of course you'll marry her. You should set up your household here." He looked around the rooftop terrace. "This is a beautiful home."

"Renaud-*san* and I will set up our own household. Perhaps *Okasan* and Asako will remain here in the family home, tell everyone they're awaiting your imminent return from foreign lands." Nobu walked over to *Otosan* and reached down to help him stand. "But before Europe, even before the night is out, we're going to summon the doctor to fix your face."

Otosan took his hand. "You're good to me, son," he said with a glimmer in his eye.

Nobu had a feeling he'd just played right into the master politician's hand.

CHAPTER TWENTY-NINE

Marcelle

Asako stood in the entrance of the Koide home when Marcelle came through.

"My sister, Asako Koide, whom you've met," Nobu announced from behind Marcelle.

Asako greeted her in her usual flawless English, but this time added a deep formal bow, appropriate for the woman who someday soon was going to become her older brother's wife, and thereby rank higher in the family.

It was far from the easy familiarity Marcelle had come to enjoy with Nobu's sister, and she hoped it wouldn't become common. "Thank you so much for having me at your lovely home," she replied with a bow that might have been at the right depth. Today was her first visit to the Koide home and her first "real" introduction to his mother and sister.

Asako led Marcelle and Nobu into a parlor that could have been an eighteenth-century Parisian salon. Persian rugs covered the floor. Ornate ivory moldings lined the upper walls, and above them, bars crisscrossed the ceiling. A golden chandelier hovered above several small statues of children at play near the center of the room. On the opposite side was a large glass display case, which looked like something from Koide's. It was filled with numerous woodland creature figurines.

Asako sighed. "*Okasan* has been dreaming of the day she'd sit down in this room with the poor lass Nobu was going to marry and inform her of exactly how to keep the house in pristine condition." Asako's casual comment broke with the formality of their greeting at the entrance.

Marcelle sighed for the reprieve. Once Nobu's mother joined them, it'd doubtless resume.

Nobu tsked at his sister. "*Okasan*'s dreams need a bit of reworking. Speaking of our honourable matron, I'm going to inquire about her plans for joining us."

Nobu left, and Marcelle walked through the statues and around a plush sofa upholstered with golden threaded flowers. "Everything in this room is gorgeous." She wandered over to the display case. A swan figurine caught her eye, and she opened the glass door and lifted the piece. The marble cooled her sweating palm. She moved it to the other hand for similar relief, but before it could ease her nerves, the figurine slipped from her grip and bumped along the carpeted floor.

"It fell under the sofa," Asako called out from the other side of the sofa.

Desperate to rescue the swan before Nobu's mother joined them, Marcelle dropped to the carpet. Sure enough, the piece of marble had tumbled under the sofa.

She stretched every muscle in her arm to reach it. It was almost in her grasp when a sharp pain shot straight through her shoulder to the back of her neck. "*Zut*," she cursed without thinking. What if Nobu's mother had walked in at that moment? Like her son, she probably knew a bit of French.

"Have you injured yourself?" Asako fell to the carpet, which happened to be the best vantage point to witness Marcelle at her clumsiest.

"I'm fine," she called out gaily. Grabbing the sneaky swan at last, she wriggled from below the sofa, rear-end first.

"What has happened here?" an older female voice called out in well-articulated English.

Heat tore through Marcelle. Her future mother-in-law's first impression of her son's betrothed—they weren't counting the horrible moving pictures showing—was of Marcelle's rear end straight up in the air.

She bolted upright, which did no favors for her spasmed shoulder muscle, which responded by jerking her neck so far to the side that her ear practically stuck to her shoulder. Even so, Marcelle fell into a low bow before Madame Koide. Upon straightening, a movement that provoked a wave of spikes in her neck, Marcelle opened her hand with the swan figurine. "I'm sorry to greet you in such a fashion. I dropped the swan," she said in English, since Madame Koide had started the conversation in English.

"Are you hurt?" Nobu asked from somewhere beside her, although exactly where he stood was a mystery because the muscles of her neck were too rigid for her to find him.

"The muscle froze," she said through gritted teeth.

"You need to sit." He ushered her to sit on the gold-threaded sofa under which her humiliation had begun. He took the place beside her and massaged the muscle.

"You shouldn't..." She started to discourage the intimate touch in case it offended his mother, although she desperately needed one of his massages. Fortunately for her shoulder, she couldn't finish telling him to cease due to the searing pain.

"Asako, get a poultice and bandaging," Madame Koide ordered and sat on a matching chair next to the sofa.

"So, you were playing with *Okasan*'s toys?" Nobu asked with a twinkle in his eye.

Marcelle forgave the insolent question because as he spoke, his expert hands coaxed a rush of blood to her neck and the muscle unclenched. Managing to hold her head upright, she no longer had to look at Madame Koide askance. "The swan is gorgeous," she said to the woman whose samurai nose and firm jawline were an exact match for Nobu's.

"I agree," Madame Koide replied, her neat brows rising with her words. Her skin was like whipped cream with drops of strawberry juice that were her lightly stained her cheekbones. The woman defied all laws of cosmetics and appearance. Marcelle should have expected it. Nobu had said his mother was a marvel.

"I must apologize for my husband's absence." She spoke with pure equanimity. "He had an urgent trip to Europe."

"I was sorry to hear he had to depart prior to our meeting." Apparently, this so-called urgent trip was going to last her husband's lifetime.

When Nobu's father had informed the foreign minister of his intention to quit, the minister had suggested Koide-*san* spend the remainder of his career in Europe. Thus, Nobu's mother could tell everyone her husband was sacrificing the comfort of his home country for another sojourn among the Europeans. According to Nobu, his mother hadn't spoken to his father—not even a word of farewell—once Nobu told her about the attacks on the boutique and Yumi-*chan*. To keep his mother busy and distracted from gossip about the Koide family's loss of a title and their obvious familial strife, Nobu had given her additional tasks at the department store. At this point, she was practically in charge of the store's daily operations.

Two days prior, Nobu had insisted his mother leave Koide's after she'd completed her usual morning rounds on the first floor. Several hours later, at the time Marcelle had specified for a tour of the department, Inada-*san*, the widow, walked through the gilded doors.

They perused every piece of jewelry in the display cases, every fur-clad mannequin, every hat, parasol, and piece of luggage on the first floor, then those on the second floor. Inada-*san* didn't express any interest in making a purchase. When Marcelle had invited her on the tour, she'd promised her there wouldn't be a Koide in sight. In accepting the invitation, Inada-*san* had confirmed she wouldn't have to interact with anyone in the family.

As they reached the third floor, the orchestra's rendition of a Haydn sonata grew louder.

"I'm curious about what you wanted to tell me," Inada-*san* said on their way toward the art museum. "You mentioned in the invitation that you had something important to share about my husband's death."

While they strolled the exhibit of Kuroda paintings, Marcelle told her about Nobu's father admitting responsibility for the attacks at *La France Boutique* and about him claiming the Inada faction had hired the killer.

Inada-san stopped before the painting of a woman beside Lake Ashi. "He drew my husband out of hiding. He made it possible for his murderers to do their work."

"Nobu wishes to make amends any way he can."

Inada-san squeezed the silk ties of the bag hanging around her wrist. "He can force my husband's killers to suffer for what they did."

Marcelle rested a hand on Inada-*san*'s arm. "I cared a great deal for your husband. I want to punish whoever killed him. So does Koide-*san*."

Marcelle escorted Inada-*san* down the stairs and out to the waiting rickshaws.

Before boarding the rickshaw, Inada-*san* stood before Marcelle, her posture erect and her gaze resolute. "Your eye for fashion is everything my husband said it was. I couldn't have had a better *modiste* giving me a tour of Tokyo's illustrious department store. Even more so than before, I'd like to invest in your factory."

Marcelle couldn't have been more flattered, and they made arrangements to meet the following week to discuss how Inada-*san* might best assist the factory.

"In going to Europe, my husband is proving himself a devoted servant of our nation," Madame Koide replied.

Asako returned to the parlor with an assortment of ointments and bandages. Thankfully, Nobu convinced her that Marcelle was healed before she set about practicing her admittedly lacking bandaging skills. On the table in front of the sofa, a maid placed a tea set and an assortment of finger sandwiches and scones alongside tiny pots of jam and bowls of clotted cream.

Nobu, his mother, and sister waited for Marcelle to take a shrimp sandwich and scone with cream and jam onto her plate. They continued to observe as she gave the traditional Japanese words of thanks and took a bite of the sandwich. After she'd declared it delicious, they finally took plates of their own.

"My son tells me you wish to set up your own household," Madame Koide said.

Nobu's mother had begged him to reconsider his plans for a separate home, even offering to demolish the present Koide home and let them build whatever they wished. "We wanted this house to remain as lovely as you've made it." Marcelle gave the room an admiring gaze.

"I've purchased a property in Tsukiji," Nobu said. "We're going to raze the house and start anew."

Madame Koide dabbed the sides of her mouth with a handkerchief. "I had no idea your plans had advanced."

"I finalised the purchase yesterday," Nobu continued. "We're using an architect who studied with a rather well-known American, a fellow named Frank Lloyd Wright. His prairie style suits the Japanese aesthetic surprisingly well. Renaud-*san* and I wish to bring together the worlds of the East and West."

"That's possible here in our neighbourhood," Madame Koide replied stiffly. "I know of several properties that ought to be demolished. You could move down the street. Are you able to break the deal?"

"We prefer the foreign quarters. It's near Ginza as well as Marcelle's factory."

Mention of the factory always gave Marcelle a surge of delighted anticipation. She and Yumi-*chan* had finalized designs for their first line. Since they were planning a spring promenade for the debut collection, they were using light wools and heavy cottons. The dresses were straight in form to emphasize the elegant Japanese female shape. Most of them had a low neckline and a high, yet loose, waist that drew attention to the smooth slope of the shoulders when bowing. The sleeves ended a few inches above the wrist for ease of movement and an aesthetically pleasing reveal of the wrist's underside.

Madame Koide pulled a fan from her kimono's *obi* sash and waved it in front of her face. "I understand Renaud-*san* takes much joy in her work."

Before Marcelle could assure Madame Koide that she took even more joy in planning a future with her son, Asako let out a hearty laugh. "Mother, many women enjoy activities outside the domestic sphere."

Madame Koide's lips formed a hard line, giving the impression of enormous effort being exerted in keeping them shut. "I understand," she finally said between clenched teeth. "Taking residence in Tsukiji will benefit my son and his bride."

"Thank you—" Marcelle began.

"Such a circumstance," Madame Koide interrupted with a devious smile directed at Asako, "will make it easier for my devoted daughter and her future husband to set up their residence with me in this house."

Asako responded with the sort of smirk daughters reserved for mothers. "Mother, you know my work at the magazine is critical to our nation. I'm assisting foreigners in better understanding Japanese culture. It may be a while before I could possibly even consider marriage." His parents' assent to Asako's choice of spouse had been one of Nobu's conditions for his cooperating with the fiction of his father's peaceful departure from Japan.

Madame Koide responded with the type of smirk mothers reserved for their daughters. "I'm so proud of your service to our nation. But in a few years, you'll be faced with far fewer prospects for marriage than you are now."

"Your advice, as always, is duly noted, dearest mother."

Marcelle beamed at Madame Koide. "Your kimono is spectacular," she remarked in an obvious attempt to change the topic of conversation.

"This thing?" Madame Koide gave her kimono cut from burgundy floral silk a disgusted look. Marcelle had seen the piece displayed at Tokyo's most revered store. "If only I could've worn something more appropriate to meet my son's future wife, but this weary covering was all I had available."

Marcelle reiterated her praise of the kimono, adding that it belonged at the empress's garden party. Madame Koide issued another denial before conceding its negligible worth, then regaled Marcelle with tales of the kimonos she'd worn over the years. Marcelle relished the matron's stories of treasured silks, mismatched *obis*, and rogue stitches. The way she infused humor into her tales reminded Marcelle of listening to her son.

"I can see where Nobu gets his appreciation for fashion," Marcelle remarked after a story about the kimono Madame Koide had worn to meet the British prime minister.

Madame Koide dismissed the comment with a shake of her hand. "My son has a far better eye for fashion. At first, I thought the department store was going to be an embarrassing failure. He's proved me wrong." The warmth in her eyes made Marcelle feel proud for Nobu. "You and my son must have plenty to discuss when it comes to fashion."

"We're fond of dress."

Madame Koide rested her gaze on Asako. "I'm pleased to finally have a daughter who loves wearing beautiful things."

Asako grunted. "Well, thank you, Renaud-*san*, for making up for my shortcomings."

Marcelle barely heard Asako's response. The word "daughter" echoed in her head. She was going to be a daughter. By law, this would be fact. If their conversation was any indication, she might also be a daughter in affection.

"Are you well?" Nobu whispered into her ear and handed her a handkerchief.

Marcelle hadn't noticed the tears spilling down her cheeks. She dabbed the sides of her eyes, but the tears kept falling. "I'm fine, really. It's just that I never had a mother, and to hear your mother call me 'daughter' was a surprise."

Wide-eyed, they all stared at her.

"A pleasant surprise," Marcelle added in case there was any misunderstanding. She was crying, after all. "I never considered the possibility of anyone calling me 'daughter.'"

Madame Koide pulled a handkerchief from her *obi* and dabbed at her eyes. "I always wanted another child but was unable to bear any after Asako." She cleared her throat. "While I'm thrilled to become an *okasan* again, I'm especially looking forward to being a grandmother."

"*Okasan*," Nobu scolded.

Marcelle laughed at her mother's audacity. "For you, *Okasan*, I'll do my best," she said with a small nod of deference and a ridiculous grin that wouldn't be going anywhere anytime soon.

CHAPTER THIRTY

Nobu

In the rickshaw they'd hired to take them from Nobu's home to her boardinghouse in Tsukiji, Nobu took Marcelle's hand.

The afternoon tea had been perfect.

How different this visit—the first official introduction between his family and his future bride—would have gone had *Otosan* been there. The man Nobu had known whose sense of adventure had seen his family living on the other side of the world, the man of grand hobbies and artistic talent, the man who'd been so proud of Nobu that he'd thoughtlessly bragged about his accomplishments at the risk of stirring envy in his peers. An unforgivable offense, but *Otosan* got away with it because of his charm, his poise, and his ease with others.

That man would've been the pivot around which the afternoon tea had spun. He would've ensured the Koide family experienced the tea as a moment of familial warmth—despite what would've been *Okasan*'s fierce objections to Nobu marrying Marcelle. He would've left them with shared hope for the future of the Koide name. He was a true diplomat.

Nobu grieved the loss of that man, his *otosan*. The other man, the one Nobu had come to know in the past months, provoked raw anger Nobu had yet to calm. That was the man who'd wrapped personal ambitions in ambitions for his nation, the one who'd traded in secrets, who twisted words, who bullied and manipulated, who thought it convenient to use the woman his son loved to draw his enemy out of hiding. And he didn't know what to do about this stranger. He only wanted to punish him as he deserved.

A week before, Nobu had treated his friend from the police bureau to dinner at the Imperial Hotel. He shared what *Otosan* had told him about Inada-*san*'s death being orchestrated from within the Inada faction.

His friend swirled brandy in his glass. The play of browns and golds seemed to mesmerise him. "Then another man deserves to hang for the crime."

Nobu fiddled with the stem of the brandy snifter. "Or men. Might you be able to investigate the Inada faction?"

"How likely are they to turn on one another?"

The faction had been united in stalwart opposition to *Otosan*'s faction for years, then organized Inada's death. "Not likely, I'm afraid."

"I'll see what I can turn up in the way of evidence."

Nobu hadn't heard from his friend since their dinner.

Having Marcelle by his side calmed the anger and grief thoughts of *Otosan* provoked. Having his *okasan* and Asako ignore the gossip circulating through the upper classes about the Koide family's bad luck and embrace Marcelle made him feel whole. Each of them was elegant, graceful, and made of hard matter Nobu envied.

He wrapped his hand around Marcelle's. "Might we stop by the property on the way?" He sounded like an overeager child. "Obsessed" was how Marcelle described his enthusiasm for their future home. Apparently, all he talked about was Frank Lloyd Wright and land prices.

She sighed as though woefully resigned. But Nobu knew she was equally enamoured with the construction of their married home. "I'll stop by the property of your dreams," she said with an exaggerated roll of the eyes.

The afternoon had unfolded in the clumsy, charming way Marcelle carried out every interaction that brought her nerves to the fore. He chuckled at the memory of her backside in the air as she rose from under the sofa. She had a fantastic backside. It served well for a nibble now and then.

"What's making you laugh?" she asked.

"I was recalling how you lost and found *Okasan*'s swan."

"That was humiliating. You shouldn't laugh."

"I was merely surprised you wished to greet *Okasan* rear-end first."

She gave him a light slap on the thigh, then rested her hand there. With that devilish smile he loved, she moved her hand nearer his groin. "Damn you," he growled playfully.

With a giggle, she moved it a touch farther.

She knew she could get her revenge by presenting temptations beyond his grasp. They couldn't spend *every* night at a lover's inn. They'd spent the previous night at one, which meant it'd be a few more nights before he could get away again. Leaving *Okasan* and Asako for more than a night or two at a time resulted in awkwardness. Even though he never told them outright where he was spending the night, they were aware, and he was aware of their awareness, which made everything awkward.

Okasan had requested he resume living in the family home when *Otosan* left for Europe. Nobu moving out had raised a few eyebrows already. With *Otosan* leaving on his heels, tongues were wagging about strife in the Koide clan. So, Nobu agreed to return home until the Tsukiji house was finished. Then he'd marry Marcelle.

The rickshaw left them in front of the property next to the Garricks' residence where Suki and her *okasan* had moved after her father abandoned them for France. They walked through the gardens he was going to completely redesign. As they passed a copse of peach trees, Suki's *okasan*'s studio came into view.

Nobu was going to surprise Marcelle with a studio of her own. Although she had plenty of space for designing in the factory, artists such as his future wife needed solitude to do their best work.

"Does Suki's *okasan* still use the studio?" Nobu asked.

"I get the impression she works exclusively from her store in Ginza."

"She's a formidable woman."

"I hope to be as active at her age."

Nobu looped an arm around Marcelle's waist. "I've no doubt you'll be opening your tenth factory, at least, by the time you reach fifty."

Marcelle leaned against his shoulder. "I worry about our *okasan*. I'm afraid she's lonely in that big house with only Asako and the servants."

Nobu let out a sigh. It was one of *Okasan*'s favourite refrains. "That's why I have to stay there until our home is ready."

"That might take as long as a year."

"I'm hoping Asako will agree to marry before then. I've invited Sato-*san*, the man from Osaka, to visit. They'd be a perfect fit. I can only hope she accepts."

"We both know she doesn't wish to marry."

"But she must." This was an argument they'd had multiple times. The easiest way for Asako to have the freedom she desired and the type of companionship that suited her was to marry. She was a healthy young woman and the only daughter. *Okasan* wanted her to marry. There was no way Asako would be an exception to the rules. After she wed and produced a few grandchildren to keep *Okasan* occupied, she could pursue whatever kind of relationship pleased her. "Besides, if Asako marries sometime soon, then I can leave the family home. We'll move into a hotel for the remaining months until the house is finished."

"That's a good point," she conceded with a brush of her lips against his cheek.

Nobu turned her toward him and brought her flush against his body. This was what he loved, the way they connected, the way their bodies fit together, the way she was open to him with her mind and heart.

Marcelle fingered the sleeve of his jacket. "What if we married sooner?"

"How is that possible?"

She met his gaze. "I could move into your family home while ours is being built."

He hadn't even considered asking Marcelle to make that kind of sacrifice. A daughter-in-law would be expected to assume responsibilities in the household that Marcelle couldn't fulfil as long as she wished to complete plans for the new line of clothing. "What about the factory?"

"Would *Okasan* allow me to work outside the home?"

He hadn't considered that, either. "I think she understands you're used to working outside the home. But you're at a critical time for starting the new fashion line."

Nobu had always envisioned them beginning married life in their new home. Living with *Okasan* and Asako would mean basking in their newly married bliss with two insufferably nosy women. But extending his stay at *Okasan*'s home and having Marcelle with him would lessen the pressure to finish the house as soon as possible. He wouldn't mind additional time to ensure every beam had been correctly placed and every window was straighter than straight.

But what of the inevitable disagreements that arose between daughters-in-law and their *okasan*s? Did Marcelle have any idea of what she was getting herself into? "Living with *Okasan* and Asako would mean being with them every day. Is that something you want?"

Marcelle smiled like a girl hesitant to reveal a secret wish. "I've always wanted to know what it'd be like to be part of a family. Now I have a chance. *Okasan* keeps saying we can live with them once we're married. She and Asako are welcoming me, not because I'm an orphan child with a much-needed allowance, but because they're extending their love for you to me."

"After seeing you with *Okasan* and Asako this afternoon, I'm beginning to suspect they're going to end up preferring you over me."

The last rays of sunlight illuminated Marcelle's face. "Would that make you jealous?"

A vision flashed through his mind of him sipping whiskey on the rooftop terrace. "If I'm going to put up with a houseful of women, I want sons. Many sons."

Marcelle sighed. "Then we ought to marry soon."

"I'd marry you tomorrow were it possible." He pressed her to him, burying his face in her voluminous curls, breathing in the delicious scent of her. "Will you marry me tomorrow, Mademoiselle Renaud?"

"Any time you wish, *mon amour*. Any time."

CHAPTER THIRTY-ONE

February 1901

Marcelle

A surprise from Nobu had never failed to overwhelm. Two days ago, he'd ordered Marcelle to stay away from the factory while he prepared the surprise. She was happy to accommodate since she was planning the spring promenade, which could easily be done from their quarters in the Koide home. Gods East and West must be smiling on her because Tokyo Station had agreed to let her put on a promenade in the station's atrium at the beginning of April. It would be the formal introduction of *Marcelle*, a fashion line designed and manufactured by women for women's comfort and style.

The past months had sped by like the emperor's carriage along Ginza Boulevard. The *Marcelle* clothing line had thrust her into a whirlwind of decisions about costs, efficiency, machinery, wages, and myriad considerations that had left her thrilling about what each new day would bring. While she purchased equipment and hired workers for the factory, Nobu made and remade plans for the new house and a new department store in Shinjuku. One day she'd have a moment to reflect on the tender moments of Nobu's seemingly boundless affection, on the warmth of *Okasan* and Asako's care, on the generosity of stalwart friends, patient architects, enthusiastic investors, loyal patrons, and dedicated employees. Until then, she was spending her days in awe of how her and Nobu's life together were unfolding.

Their rickshaw pulled in front of the factory. Everything appeared as it had several days before when she'd last visited. Then a glimpse of movement inside gave her a start. Was the surprise in the factory's interior? "Have you enlisted your army of architects to surprise me with a new partition wall?"

"I hadn't thought of a new partition wall but now that you mention it, I suppose I'll have to go back to the architect." Nobu gave her a private smile that reminded her of his expression earlier that morning when he'd whispered lusty words into her ear before reaching between her thighs and commenting, rather naughtily, at her readiness for him.

Marriage to a man who could send her reeling toward the height of passion with a single look was a life's pleasure of which she'd never tire. "I suppose we should go inside and see what surprises are in store."

Nobu helped her down from the rickshaw and told her to wait in front of the two-story factory where the dresses of *Marcelle* would be produced in the months to come. "The surprise is best viewed from the exterior. Allow me to summon our guests." He walked toward the front door.

They had guests?

He flung open the door and out came familiar friends, beloved friends, friends who were new to her, and friends she'd treasured almost since the day she'd arrived in Japan. *Okasan* and Asako were there, too.

Suki, heavy with the final stages of pregnancy, wrapped her arm through Marcelle's. "Your husband is a gem. You are truly fortunate, *mon amie.*"

Suki's *okasan*, along with her American brother and sister-in-law, Roger and Rosie, offered words of congratulations. Asako and *Okasan* echoed the sentiment. Sato-*san*, Asako's suitor visiting from

Osaka, gave Marcelle a deep bow and formal words of congratulations on her achievement.

At Nobu's invitation, he'd been visiting Tokyo for the past week. Ostensibly, he'd come to advise on the interior design of Nobu's new store in Shinjuku, and just happened to be spending each evening dining with Nobu's *okasan*, sister, and wife. Standoffish at first, Asako quickly warmed up to the gentleman whose ease with formality seemed to set comfortable limits on their interactions. *Okasan* praised his manners and listened with rapt attention to Sato-*san*'s stories of his studies in the United States and discovery of a sport called baseball.

After completing university in Japan, Sato-*san* matriculated in courses at Georgetown University, where he became an enthusiastic fan of the Georgetown baseball team. Asako's interest piqued noticeably when he told them about how women in the United States attended games alongside male fans, drinking as much beer as the men and jeering just as loudly at the opposing team. She grew even more intrigued when he reported that women had established their own teams such as the Bloomer Base Ball Club of Boston. They played in scandalous trousers and beat the men's teams.

Marcelle advised Asako to marry him. He was a lovely man, and Nobu had assured them Sato-*san* would allow Asako the freedoms she desired.

Yumi-*chan* tapped Marcelle on the shoulder. No longer an assistant, Yumi-*chan* was partner in the new business. "Take a look at the roof."

Scaffolding had been erected in her absence. Before she had time to wonder what was attached to the crisscrossed metal beams, Nobu whisked away a swath of fabric to reveal a sign as tall as he. In bright crimson script, it read *Marcelle, Fashion for Women by Women*.

She'd thought they'd only be able to afford something simple and certainly at ground-level. This eye-catching monument announced to everyone in Tokyo of the arrival of her workers, her customers, her investors, of Yumi-*chan* and herself. From start to finish, the factory had been a labor of love fueled by their combined energy and creativity. Now the world knew. And her husband, rather than hiding the scandal of having a wife who was also a woman of business, had commissioned a sign that boasted her success. She sent a kiss up to the rooftop where Nobu stared at her as though he couldn't bear to miss a moment of her reaction.

The factory's foyer made for an elegant party venue. Rows of flowers courtesy of her investors had been lined up to partially obscure the workspaces and sewing machines. Tables covered in crisp white linen were weighed down with platters of winter crab, roasted venison, rich pâtés, cheeses, and fruits carved to resemble shells and flowers.

Nobu handed her a glass of champagne. "Congratulations, Madame Renaud Koide."

Had they been alone, she would've wrapped her arms around him and kissed him silly. "I love the sign. It's perfect."

"Like you." He made her feel as though she might be.

Griff, whose group of investors had ensured she'd be opening a Ginza boutique that autumn, said a few words of praise for Marcelle's venture and raised his glass in a toast to the new factory.

"*Kampai*," the guests responded and drank down their champagne.

She had several bites of crab and pâté while sharing news of the upcoming promenade with investors who'd been seated with her and Yumi-*chan* at the head table. Yumi-*chan* wore the first dress Marcelle had given her, a fusion design cut from an ice-blue kimono silk printed with lavender hibiscus. The color made Yumi-*chan*'s skin glow, and the low bodice and bustle accentuated her waist. The style reminded Marcelle of how much their approach had changed, thanks to her partner.

"I still love that dress on you," Marcelle said once the conversation had drifted from factory business.

"It'll always be my favorite. Were you surprised by the sign?"

"Absolutely. Did you help Nobu with the design?"

"I figured that since Koide-*san* owned a successful department store, I should defer to his judgment. Had I designed it, there would have been roses and lilies around the name. His vision was far more professional."

The week before, Yumi-*chan* had added rosebuds along the cuffs and hem of a dress meant for the factory's first run. The detail made the dress extraordinary. "Your roses are perfection."

"I wouldn't go that far," Yumi-*chan* said modestly, but Marcelle heard pride in her voice.

Ryusuke came to their table and placed a hand on Yumi-*chan*'s shoulder while offering his congratulations on the factory. Yumi-*chan* gave her husband a look of adoration that made Marcelle feel as though she might melt in her seat.

Guests were finishing the meal when she realized that an investor whose contribution ought to have earned her a seat at the head table was nowhere in sight. She glanced over at Nomura-*san* seated at the other table. He'd become her accountant, legal adviser, and the factory's general manager. Their gazes met and she tilted her head toward the row of congratulatory flowers. Nomura-*san* would know she needed a moment of his time. He always knew exactly what she needed.

Several minutes later, she and Nomura-*san* stood in front of an ornate arrangement of irises from *Tokyo Women's Magazine*.

"Koide-*san* has given you a memorable fête," Nomura remarked.

"It was a complete surprise."

He murmured something about it being a surprise to him as well. "Koide-*san* contacted Yumi-*chan* and me a week ago with the idea. Then he somehow managed to assemble the guests and the food in a few days' time. Does a French chef work in your home?"

"No, but Nobu has become acquainted with Tokyo's finest French restaurants over the past few months. Does the cuisine suit you?"

Nomura-*san*'s hesitation effectively communicated his incompatibility with the cuisine. "I'm impressed with the beauty of the food's presentation. Japanese have much to learn from the West."

"The West has much to learn from the Japanese about how to arrange flowers." Marcelle nodded at the rich purple blooms in front of them. "I wanted to ask you about Inada-*san*. I assume she was invited to join us today."

"She sent her regrets. The civility necessary to attend this afternoon's event would've been too much for her."

"Did she accept the committee's findings?" Several weeks after Nobu's father left for Europe, an unsigned letter arrived at the Tokyo Metropolitan Police detailing how members of the Foundation Party had commissioned gangsters to intimidate members of an opposition Party. The accusations were directed at the lawmakers from Iwate prefecture who Nobu's *otosan* had said were responsible for Inada-*san*'s death. Evidence of their responsibility for Inada-*san*'s murder had yet to manifest. But evidence did exist for their other crimes, and the letter, presumably from Nobu's *otosan*, gave the police means to bring those men to justice.

"Hamada-*san* had no tolerance for men who ignore the rule of law. Law and kindness toward others give modern people a basis upon which to engage with one another. Laws can always be better, and politicians are responsible for making them so. When they ignore the law, they're worthless."

"You should go into politics, Nomura-*san*."

His hearty guffaw drew the attention of several party guests. Reddening at the uncharacteristic outburst, he straightened and brushed the sleeves of his suit jacket. "Not me, but I hope one day my people will have a place in the Diet. Thank you, again, Renaud-*san*, I mean Koide-*san*, for employing *eta* in your factory. You make it possible to hope the sons of the women you employ will hold the highest posts in our nation."

"I'll do everything I can for them," Marcelle said.

Nomura-*san* nodded. "I know you will."

***

Later that evening, after they'd retired to their quarters, Nobu ordered Marcelle into a chair by the fireplace. Kneeling before her, he took her ankle into his lap and kneaded the bottom of her foot.

She let go of a deep breath and surrendered to his masterful touch. "Your talent with massage has been one of the best surprises of my life."

"I'll always credit that ankle massage for luring you into my bed."

Recalling his hand on her calf that day in his office still brought a blush to her cheeks. "I was impressed by your knowledge of pressure points as well as your audacity in removing my boot."

A knowing smile crossed his face. "No man in his right mind would pass up the opportunity to get inside your stockings." He took care of her other ankle. "I wanted you from the moment I laid eyes on you at the department store opening."

"The first time I laid eyes on you I strained my neck so badly that I yelped in pain. I was terrified you'd see what a fool I was."

"I saw you."

"No, you didn't. You looked around, but I hid behind Yumi-*chan*."

"Do you really think you could hide behind Yumi-*chan*?"

Of course not. There was no hiding behind a woman almost half her size. "You wanted me then?"

"I did."

Marcelle gave him an arched brow. "You wanted a clumsy Frenchwoman who couldn't maintain her composure around the new Ginza proprietor."

"No." He pulled her to stand in his arms. Brushing a strand of hair from her face, he met her gaze. "I wanted, and still want, the

Frenchwoman strong in spirit, sensitive in heart, with a good head and a luscious body."

"You're too generous," she teased, while emotion welled within her. "You do so much for me. I feel like I owe you a debt that can never be repaid."

"*Mon cherie*, we're family. Calculations aren't part of the equation. You give and you take."

"So that's how family works?" She softened her voice into the amorous tone she knew would heighten his already obvious arousal. "You'll have to teach me more."

His lips caressed the shell of her ear, sending shivers through her body. "How about I take you to bed, and we teach one another?"

She gave a long, slow grin. "Shared control? That happens to be a language I've mastered."

ABOUT THE AUTHOR

Heather lives in Tokyo with her professor husband and two young daughters. Once upon a time, she earned a doctoral degree in cultural anthropology for her thesis on adolescent friendship in Japan. Presently, she writes witty, sensual, contest-winning romances set in Meiji-era Japan (1868-1912).

Heather spends her free time translating ancient Japanese poetry and observing the passing of seasons while sipping green tea. Just kidding, she has no free time. But she does watch something that makes her laugh while she does the dishes.

Perennial obsessions include the weather forecast (she checks three different apps at least three times a day, as no single app can be trusted), Baltimore Ravens football (hometown obsession), and making smoothies that taste like candy bars.

Feel free to chat her up about any of her obsessions, or even better, about historical Japan—any era is fine, she loves them all.

She also enjoys exchanging book recommendations, discussions about the craft of romance writing, and stories about life in present-day Tokyo. You can reach out through Instagram, TikTok, Facebook, Twitter, or her website.

Connect with Heather:

website: heatherhallman.com

FB: /hallmanheather

IG: @heatherhallman_author

TikTok: @writing_romance_in_japan

www.BOROUGHSPUBLISHINGGROUP.com

If you enjoyed this book, please write a review. Our authors appreciate the feedback, and it helps future readers find books they love. We welcome your comments and invite you to send them to info@boroughspublishinggroup.com.

Follow us on Facebook, Twitter and Instagram, and be sure to sign up for our newsletter for surprises and new releases from your favorite authors.

Are you an aspiring writer? Check out:
www.boroughspublishinggroup.com/submit and see if we can help you make your dreams come true.

Love podcasts? Enjoy ours at:
www.boroughspublishinggroup.com/podcast

Made in United States
Orlando, FL
04 February 2023

29463398R00214